Praise for *USA *****
Jennifer Sn *****

"Heartwarming, romantic, and utterly enjoyable.
—*New York Times* bestselling author Melissa Foster
on *An Alaskan Christmas*

"This first title in the Wild River series is passionate, sensual, and very sexy. The freezing, winter-cold portrayal of the Alaskan ski slopes is not the only thing sending chills through one's body."
—*New York Journal of Books*

"Set in the wilds of Alaska, the beauty of winter and the cold shine through."
—*Fresh Fiction* on *An Alaskan Christmas*

"Jennifer Snow's Alaska setting and search-and-rescue element are interesting twists, and the romance is smart and sexy... An exciting contemporary series debut with a wildly unique Alaskan setting."
—*Kirkus Reviews*

"Readers will enjoy the mix of sexy love scenes, tense missions, and amiable banter. This entertaining introduction to Wild River will encourage fans of small-town contemporaries to follow the series."
—*Publishers Weekly*

"*An Alaskan Christmas* drew me in from the first page to the last. I tried to read slower so that I could savor the story and feel every emotion. I reveled in every nuance, felt the cold, the wind and snow, and loved the small town and the mountains... I can't wait to return to Wild River."
—*Romance Junkies*

Look for Jennifer Snow's next Wild River novel,
available soon from HQN.

For additional books by Jennifer Snow,
visit her website, www.jennifersnowauthor.com.

JENNIFER SNOW

Alaska Reunion

HQN

ISBN-13: 978-1-335-46301-2

Alaska Reunion
Copyright © 2021 by Jennifer Snow

Wild Alaskan Hearts
First published in August 2021.
This edition published in September 2021.
Copyright © 2021 by Jennifer Snow

For questions and comments about the quality of this book,
please contact us at CustomerService@Harlequin.com.

HQN
22 Adelaide St. West, 40th Floor
Toronto, Ontario M5H 4E3, Canada
www.Harlequin.com

Printed in U.S.A.

CONTENTS

Alaska Reunion

To the Beaconsfield High School graduation class of '99!
Fun times and great memories!

CHAPTER ONE

Alisha Miller has invited you to join the group Wild River High Class of 2011 Reunion.

FOR TWO DAYS, Ellie Mitchell had stared at the notification. She'd hovered over the accept button and then chickened out at least eighty-six times. High school felt like a million years ago. Did she really want to revisit that time in her life for one nostalgia-filled evening?

Now an emergency room nurse at Wild River Community Hospital, it made sense that Alisha wanted to have this reunion. She'd been captain of the cheerleading squad, senior class vice president (only because she'd opted not to run for president) and head of the debate team. Everyone loved her because she was that rare mix of popular, pretty *and* nice. She was always front and center at school events—not in a boastful, look-at-me way but in an uplifting, school spirit way.

Ellie had been more of a behind-the-scenes participant in school activities. She was a worker bee on student council and the school's event planning committee. She was the setup and takedown crew, never center stage. And she'd preferred it that way. Half of her classmates might even have forgotten she was in their graduating class. She hadn't exactly stood out.

At least not until senior year, when she'd stepped out

and been noticed. But it had less to do with her and more to do with her dating Brent Lanigan, class president and star quarterback with big dreams for himself after graduation. Ellie still wasn't sure how it had even happened. One day she was tutoring him to ensure that his grades were high enough to keep playing football, the next he'd gone in for an unexpected kiss, and then the rest of the school year they were seeing one another.

She sighed. The reunion was tentatively scheduled for three weeks from now, and she could see that over half the class had RSVP'd already.

Brent hadn't yet. Would he attend? Would that affect her own decision? Probably. She was just that pathetic.

She tucked her cell phone into the back pocket of her jeans as the clock hit 9:00 a.m.

Time to open Flippin' Pages bookstore, the place where she'd worked since graduation. Having started as a clerk ten years ago, she was now the store manager, taking care of everything from ordering inventory, doing the bookkeeping and scheduling to running store events. Despite being a small town indie bookstore, it was actually one of the local hotspots thanks to their weekly book club meetings, author appearances and read-aloud story time for kids. Every week the place hosted something for locals, and things picked up even more during the tourist seasons.

Going to the front door, she flipped the closed sign to Open and unlocked it. She flicked on the interior lights and a cozy, inviting feeling washed over her. Flippin' Pages was located in one of the older buildings along Main Street in Wild River, Alaska, and its historic charm was one of the things that drew people to the store. It was three stories high, with a magnificent spiral staircase leading to the upper floors, deep mahogany wood accents throughout, original hardwood flooring and patterned tin ceilings, and patrons admired the building's historic vibe as well as the impressive selection of books it housed.

Like the incredible delivery that had arrived the day before. Ellie couldn't wait to dig into the box of donated classics that had come in courtesy of the estate of an older man who'd died the previous weekend. Hyped books from fresh new authors were always exciting, but old, second-hand donations were Ellie's favorite.

Blame it on her old, romantic soul, maybe, but there was something magical about antiques and collectibles. Old items passed down through generations, that had a history…that had existed long before she had, held a mysterious quality that she was drawn to.

Grabbing a box cutter from behind the counter, she carefully sliced through the cardboard and opened the box of books. Reaching inside was like opening a present on Christmas morning. Joy and anticipation wrapped around her as she took one of the books out and turned it over in her hands.

A well-loved first edition of *The Scarlet Letter* by Nathaniel Hawthorne.

She ran a finger over the cover—octavo, original brown cloth, 1850 dated on the spine. There were only twenty-five hundred of these in the world, and it would sell for quite a nice price, but that wasn't what appealed to her most. She took a deep breath and carefully opened the flap to the inside page.

Yes! There was an inscription. That was always the best part. Almost as though she were eavesdropping on the past.

To My Dear Michael,
May this book take you on a fantastical journey.
All my love,
Rose

Ellie sighed. Michael and Rose. What had their lives been like back then? Who were they? What had they meant to one another? Relatives or secret lovers? She brought the book to her nose and inhaled deeply.

"Were you just smelling that book?" a male voice asked over the chime of the door opening.

Ellie quickly put the book on the New Antique Arrival shelf and turned as her coworker Callum McKendrick entered the bookstore. "I smell all the books," she said. "And you're late." He was always late. It was almost endearing how predictable his lateness was. Like if he ever arrived on time, she'd know something was wrong. He breezed through life without a care to societal conventions like being on time for work. And got away with it.

"Only four minutes," he said, checking an imaginary watch. "Better than yesterday."

She laughed and shook her head. "Better than yesterday."

"What have we got?" he asked, rolling up the sleeves of his light blue shirt and bending at the knees to peer inside the box. His thick, dark hair fell into his face and he pushed it back. Everyone in town called him Clark Kent because he looked exactly like the fictional superhero at six foot three, with a muscular build, wide shoulders and a broad chest. His jet-black hair was always slightly too long, and his dark-rimmed glasses did nothing to tame the sex appeal he radiated.

Ellie liked to believe that their regular customers came in for the literary experience and wide selection of art the bookstore provided, but it probably had more to do with the sexy bookseller.

"This is that estate donation from the lady who called yesterday," she said, making room on the shelf for the rest of the books. She couldn't believe the condition they were in. Someone must have cherished them enough to preserve them and take care of them. A lot of the old books that came into the store needed restoring, but not these.

"I can't believe none of his children or grandchildren wanted these," Callum said, taking out a copy of *Moby Dick*. "These look like they could be first editions."

"They are," she said, pointing to the date on the spine. "That's why we will be selling them for a small fortune."

"Also because you don't want anyone to actually buy them," he said with a wink.

No doubt that little flicker of an eyelid had women fainting in old 1800s fashion, but Ellie was immune to Callum's charm. He was at least several years younger than her and he flirted as often as he exhaled.

"I don't do that," she said.

"Yes you do."

"Fine. You know me too well," she said with a laugh, but her smile faded as her cell phone chimed in her pocket. Taking it out, she saw a new post in the reunion Facebook group, from Cheryl Kingsly—one of Alisha's longtime best friends. Cheryl was a personal trainer now, and Ellie often saw the two leaving the gym together.

Can't wait to be reunited with my Wild Cougar Family! Do we have a venue yet?

Immediately little dots appeared that showed someone was typing, and seconds later Alisha's reply appeared.

Not yet. You know me—brilliant ideas, zero execution skills.

Ellie shook her head. It was so like them to try to organize a last-minute event without actually organizing anything. Years ago, it was the same. The student council would meet and come up with great ideas, but then no one stepped up to do the actual work—besides her and a few others that no one gave credit to in the end when the events were a success.

Alisha hoped to do this in three weeks, and yet there was absolutely nothing planned yet. No venue, no discussion about food, no theme or decor... Ellie sighed.

"What's wrong?" Callum asked, handing her another book.

She studied the copy of Jane Austen's *Pride and Prejudice*, unable to fully appreciate it. Did she go to the reunion or didn't she? Would it make her feel better or worse about the direction her life had taken, catching up with her former classmates? "It's my ten-year high school reunion this year, and the populars are posting nonstop on the Facebook group page with updates."

Callum frowned. "The populars?"

"You know, the popular crowd in school. The ones who are still popular and want to show off how awesome their lives have turned out by forcing everyone to return to the scene of some of the most humiliating days of their lives and try to maintain chitchat while feeling the weight of judgment," she said.

What would they say about her? About the fact that, unlike so many of them, she hadn't become what her high school yearbook had claimed she'd wanted to be—a teacher. What would they whisper when she walked past?

Poor Ellie—still working in a bookstore.

Poor Ellie—not married, not engaged, not even having fantastic casual sex.

Poor Ellie—no kids yet. Didn't she say she wanted three?

Better get on with that life plan before her ovaries completely dry up.

"I always thought reunions were just a fun way to catch up with people you haven't seen in years," Callum said with a shrug.

She eyed him. "Of course that's what it would be for *you.*"

He faked a look of hurt. "What's that supposed to mean?"

"Look at you. You're gorgeous—tall, dark and handsome with muscles in places I didn't even think muscles could grow…or form…or whatever they do," she said casually. She wasn't hitting on him, just stating facts.

She knew better. Guys like Callum got the pretty girls, the athletic girls, the popular ones…like the ones she was wanting to avoid at this reunion. Ellie had been the book nerd even in high school. Not much had changed. Her idea of fun was a quiet night in, discussing a good book with close, like-minded friends while enjoying an amazing vintage wine. Going to an event to reminisce about the good old days with people who remembered high school a lot differently than she did wasn't her idea of an enjoyable time.

"You eyeballing me?" Callum asked, leaning against the shelf and flashing her his best flirty smile. She knew it was his best flirty smile because he used it on all the female customers, and their orders magically increased. As she was technically his boss—being the store manager—Ellie appreciated his sales abilities, but she knew not to read anything into the flirting.

"I'm saying that you wouldn't understand the intense pressure this event could have on a person," she said, taking the remaining books out of the box and shelving them without even opening the cover flaps to check for inscriptions. A serious sign that this whole reunion thing was stressing her out.

"What pressure? Explain it to me," Callum said, taking the empty box from her and breaking it down.

She sighed. "If I go, everyone will know that my life is just as boring now as it was back in high school. So, my choices are to skip it or go and invent a more exciting existence."

He frowned. "I thought you loved your life here in Wild River."

She did. It just wasn't newsworthy. Running the small bookstore on Main Street, living in the apartment upstairs wasn't exactly how she'd expected her life to turn out. Not that she had anything to prove or that there was anything wrong with her lifestyle…if she didn't know for a fact that Brent was a commercial pilot whose most recent serious relationship had been a six-month affair with a flight attendant who'd missed her calling as a Victoria's Secret model. Ellie had consumed countless tubs of ice cream while cyberstalking the two of them on Instagram.

Brent had been her first boyfriend and one true love. They'd started out as friends when she was assigned as his English tutor. At first she'd thought he would be just another jock who'd expect her to do his assignments for him, but he'd surprised her. He was actually interested in literature, he'd just suffered from assignment anxiety. Writer's block of sorts.

During their time together, she'd fallen hard and fast, and he'd surprised her again with a spontaneous kiss and then asking her out on a date when he got a B in English on his midterm report card. The two had been inseparable until graduation, when Brent had made it clear he was planning on going away for university and flight school. It was his dream to become a commercial pilot and suddenly Ellie hadn't been a part of the future he saw for himself.

He'd left. She'd stayed.

He'd moved on. And she was still stuck in a heartbroken limbo of wanting to get over him and secretly hoping someday he'd come back to Wild River and tell her he still loved her.

Pathetic, but that's where she was.

"I do love my life." Most days. "I'm just dreading seeing certain people, that's all," she said honestly.

"Your ex Brent?"

She frowned. "How'd you know?"

"Because you talk about him as though you'd marry him and have a dozen children given the chance."

"Well, I would, but that's not going to happen because..." She opened her Instagram app and turned the phone toward Callum. "He's currently dating her." This new one was a waitress from Hawaii—beautiful, blonde, tanned with a breathtaking smile and perfect teeth. Apparently, flying commercial flights to the beach destination had more perks than just the round trips to paradise.

Callum squinted through his dark-rimmed glasses. "You're cuter."

She scoffed. "You're not getting a raise, so you can quit the compliments."

"I don't need a raise."

That's right. Callum was independently wealthy. His family were hotel owners, and the poshest hotel in Alaska was here in Wild River. It didn't quite fit the rest of the remote resort town's rugged mountain esthetic, but it catered to a different kind of tourist—one with lots of money. The Wild River Resort was located near the ski slopes and offered guests panoramic views of the mountains. A luxury spa and five-star restaurant were additional offerings that even had movie stars visiting the town. Or in the recent case of Selena Hudson, finding refuge from a stalker.

Callum didn't talk about his family much, but she could sense he wanted nothing to do with the hospitality industry or following in his father's and grandfather's footsteps of hotel ownership. He worked in the bookstore because he enjoyed books, and he hadn't told her, but she knew he donated his paycheck to the local animal shelter and the local school's love of reading program.

How he was still single, she had no idea.

Maybe it was hard for him to trust whether a woman was interested in him for himself or his trust fund and family status. Ellie thought he had nothing to worry about—he could be dirt poor, living in a van, and women would still crave his attention.

"Anyway, I think you're worrying for nothing. He's probably off jetting around the world and won't even show up."

He hadn't RSVP'd one way or another yet, so Callum might be right. Brent rarely returned to Wild River now that both his parents had moved to Arizona to retire, and as an only child, he didn't have any other family to visit.

"Maybe," she said. She didn't want to go to the reunion, so why was she secretly hoping that Brent would say yes? If he did, there was no way she could *not* go. There hadn't been an opportunity to see him since he'd left Wild River. She wouldn't turn down the chance that maybe...

He'd see her and confess his undying love. Yeah, right.

Maybe it was time to lay off the romantic comedies for a while.

CHAPTER TWO

THE BLINKING CURSOR on Callum's laptop screen taunted him. It had for days. He'd been flying through his manuscript, the thoughts and ideas and perfect wording flowing from his mind to his fingertips… Then it had stopped. The dreaded saggy middle, as he'd heard some bestselling authors refer to it, was a real thing.

And now he understood the frustration. His first attempt at compiling his prose into a full-length work of creative nonfiction, after years of reading craft books and taking online courses, wasn't exactly going as he'd imagined. Maybe short stories were all he'd ever successfully complete.

"More coffee?" Gillian, his usual waitress at Carla's Diner, asked, approaching his booth in the corner with her pot of coffee. The owner's daughter worked the night shift every day. She was raising money for her backpacking trip across Europe the following year.

Therefore, after tip, Callum's several pots of coffee cost almost as much as if he harvested the beans himself. He liked to support other people's dreams.

"You know most people go on dates on Saturday nights," she said as she leaned one hip against the table.

There was only one woman in town he wanted to date and she was completely oblivious. Callum was in love with his coworker. Head over heels, can't eat, can't sleep, give-up-the-lifeboat in love with her. But Ellie wouldn't notice if he spelled it out with old pages of the classic books she lovingly placed on the bookstore shelves every day.

It was one of the reasons he worked at Flippin' Pages. Getting to see her in her element every day, to see her passion for the works of literature she cared about so vehemently, was inspiring.

And right now, Callum could use some inspiration. Anything at all.

He lifted his half-empty cup for a top-up and smiled. "I'll keep that in mind."

Gillian flushed as though she'd happily accommodate and glanced at the laptop. "What are you always working on so intently, anyway?"

He closed the file and shrugged. "Nothing exciting." He'd never told anyone about his passion for writing. Not his parents, not his friends… The only person who might not be surprised to learn he was writing a book was his high school English teacher who'd encouraged him to write more, claiming she saw potential in his short stories and essays.

Probably the worst thing to happen to someone with big dreams—having one person encourage them.

"You're still not going to tell me, huh?"

She asked all the time, and it was tempting to actually tell someone. If for no other reason than to put it out there and put more pressure on himself to finish the damn thing. But he wasn't prepared to call himself a writer just yet. He wasn't even sure what he planned to do with the work in progress. It wasn't like he could really publish it. "I think I'll keep my secret a little longer," he said with a smile.

"Okay, well, if you need anything other than coffee, let me know," she said with a wink, and a new sway of her hips appeared as she walked away. She had great hips and a great ass and a great smile. There was literally nothing not great about Gillian.

Except that she wasn't Ellie.

But he had to be careful. Coming into the diner to write all the time might be giving Gillian the wrong idea, especially when their casual chitchat bordered on flirting. He didn't want to lead her on.

The truth was, he couldn't write at home. His apartment was too quiet, and he ended up getting distracted by chores or the baseball game on TV. Here, he'd learned to appreciate the background noise of other customers, the clanging of dishes, the ring of the old-fashioned cash register, the chime of the door as people came and went. It was all ambience, a soundtrack he didn't really hear, but it helped to drown out his own random, everyday thoughts that interrupted his creativity.

His cell chimed with a new text message, and he groaned inwardly seeing his brother Sean's name on the display screen. He hadn't responded to his father's message that day, so now he was siccing his brother on him.

Picking it up, he read, Monthly meeting tomorrow at 9 a.m. in the Chugach Ballroom. It's mandatory.

Mandatory. Meaning if he didn't attend the hotel management meeting, he could kiss his access to his trust fund goodbye. His father refused to believe that he had zero interest in the hotel business or in joining forces with his brother to take over running the Wild River Resort Hotel someday. He'd walk away from the fund if there was a way to do so and still be able to give to the charities he supported. He'd hate to stop donating because he suddenly needed the money he made at the bookstore, but he wasn't sure how much longer he could keep this up.

He had his own goals…

Ones that were taking a little longer than he'd hoped.

But if he could finish this book and grow a set of balls big enough to actually submit his work to publishers, then maybe he wouldn't need his family's money anymore. It would also most likely mean severing all ties with his family.

If walking away permanently from the family business would be seen as a direct insult to his father, this creative nonfiction project, which was only a thinly veiled account of their family's personal life stories, would be even worse. His father would never understand Callum's need to write about his childhood and young adult experiences as a way to move through them, just like he'd never understood the damage he'd caused to their family over the years.

Maybe it wasn't writer's block but a realization of what this project meant that had him stalling. He stared at the last paragraph he'd written, desperate for a muse to start talking to him again. Unfortunately, the only being that seemed interested in communicating with him was the pretty waitress staring at him from across the diner.

WALKING INTO THE Wild River Resort Hotel the next morning, Callum braced himself for two hours of mind-numbingly boring stats and figures regarding tourism traffic, projected revenue for the upcoming season and updates from each hotel department. Every month it was the same dull slide show presentation and a lot of patting one another on the back. He wasn't sure how many more of these he could handle. He really had no business even being there, and everyone knew it. He'd never worked inside the hotel. As a teenager, he'd loved to hang out there—use the pool and spa facilities and the state-of-the-art workout room—but he hadn't developed a passion for the tourism industry the way his father had hoped. Maybe if Callum's grandfather had still been running things, he might have. His grandfather had been an amazing businessman who'd claimed his greatest resource was his employees. He'd treated everyone who worked for one of his hotels like family. He'd known every single person by name and had a way of making everyone feel special. He'd hosted employee family events, even closing the resorts for a week once a year and offering the facilities to staff for staycations. Callum's grandfather had made running the hotels seem fun and exciting, but when his father took over the string of McKendrick properties, any interest Callum had felt vanished. His father cared about bottom lines and profit. Full stop. And it was evident to everyone who attended these monthly meetings.

Unfortunately, Callum had been ambushed.

Inside the ballroom, his father and his brother, Sean, sat alone at the long mahogany boardroom table. That was it. No managers, no staff, no board of directors. Just his family members staring at him, annoyed that he was late.

Callum sighed as he approached the table. "Dad, Sean... Not such a great turnout today, huh?"

"I moved the meeting to this afternoon," his father, Alan, said, either missing or ignoring Callum's sarcasm as he gestured for him to sit. "Have a seat."

The stern tone left no room for argument. It never had. Growing up, he and his brother had quickly learned that things had to be Alan's way or no way at all. The relationship between father and sons had been strained at best. *Damaged* was the word their family therapist had used on more than one occasion when Callum's mother had been successful in dragging Alan to the sessions. After several years of trying and failing to get her husband to realize his demanding, workaholic ways and unrealistic expectations were destroying the family, Callum's mother, Carolyn, had finally given up.

She'd been able to walk away from the unhealthy marriage, but unfortunately, he and Sean were still left in the trenches.

"What's going on?" He unbuttoned his suit jacket as he sat.

His brother avoided his eyes, his hands flicking a series of elastic bands on his wrist beneath his own suit jacket. Under the table, his knee bounced.

Great. Whatever this was, it wasn't good.

His father wasted no time launching into his attack. "As you know, I'm retiring next year and I want you to get serious about your life."

This again. It had been almost three months since the last time his father had delivered this particular lecture, so he should have expected it.

"I am serious." And besides that, his father's definition of retiring was very different from most people's. He'd be retiring in theory only, based on pressure from the board to bring in fresh blood and new ideas. The Wild River Resort Hotel had always been known for its luxury accommodations in the ski resort town, but recent focus groups had revealed that young travelers often found the place "stuffy" with its brown leather furnishings throughout the common areas and "cigar smoking, boy's club" vibe. The plan for the following year was to redecorate and rebrand slightly, with the current generation of McKendricks at the helm.

Of course, his father would hand off the business, but he'd still have a finger on the pulse of things. And working alongside him was something Callum would never survive, even if he was the least bit interested in the hospitality industry.

His father wasn't the type of leader who encouraged collaboration and ideas. He was more dictatorial in his management style and treated those below him as hired help. He didn't try to get to know his staff, and he certainly didn't have an open door policy. Callum and his father were far too different and would only butt heads at every turn.

"Working at a bookstore?" Alan said. "That's your idea of serious? Come on, Callum, you have an Ivy League education. Is stacking books really what you see for yourself?" His disappointed look was the biggest kick to the gut. As though he was questioning how he'd failed so greatly with his younger son.

Amazing that it still landed its mark with sniper precision.

"No, the bookstore isn't the only thing..." But there was no way he was telling his father the truth. Trying to become a writer would be seen as a pipe dream. Unattainable. In his father's mind there were different levels of dreams. Owning a luxury hotel was achievable because it could be done by practical means—a good education, a strong support system and investors, a safe risk assessment and hard work. Becoming a published author was like wishing on a shooting star. "I'm working on some things," he said, simply.

"What things?" Alan folded his hands on the table and leaned forward. The look of interest on the older man's face was a trick. This was his father's way of convincing himself he was open-minded. If Callum could present another option for his future—one his dad approved of—he'd hear him out.

But that wasn't the case at all. Anything Callum proposed right now, his father would find a reason to dismiss. "Why don't we just cut to the chase, Dad? You obviously have an agenda with this meeting, so let's get to it."

Next to him, Sean stared at his hands and remained silent. This was the way it always was. While Callum continuously battled with his father, Sean knew there was no point in even trying, so he stayed quiet.

Just once, it would be nice to have his older brother's backing.

"I want you to take over running the hotel," Alan said.

"And I've told you I'm not interested." Several times. It continued to fall on deaf ears. His father firmly believed that Callum owed him this. That being born into a life of privilege came with responsibilities.

"Well, you haven't really expressed an interest in anything," Alan said, moving quickly to the ultimatum part of his speech. "I'm not funding this lifestyle of yours forever."

How many times had he heard that threat?

"I've never asked you to." Access to his trust fund had been given to him when he'd turned eighteen on the agreement that he continue his education and complete the MBA program. His only passion and interest had been writing, so he hadn't argued with the agreement. He'd studied hard, kept his perfect GPA and used his electives to take creative writing classes. It had worked. But now things were different. He couldn't keep putting off the inevitable since he was no longer at university.

"I want a decision in thirty days," his father said, confirming Callum's thought. "If you're going to take over running the hotel, you need to start your official training next month."

Official training. Under him. Was there a worse fate?

His father stared straight into his eyes as he delivered his next blow. "You're either in this family or you're not."

Hearing the dismissal, Callum stood and pushed the chair back in. It hit against the table a little too abruptly and he kicked himself for allowing his father to see that he'd gotten to him.

His brother's voice calling after him as he left the room made him stop and turn in the hotel hallway. "Could have warned me," he said.

Sean looked stressed as he ran a hand through his short, dark hair. His eyes were bloodshot and he was definitely thinner than the last time Callum had seen him weeks before. His navy suit jacket seemed to hang on a skeletal frame. "I'm sorry, man. I had no idea that's what this was about."

Callum put his hands on his hips and fought to calm his thundering pulse. His father knew how to get under his skin like no one else. "I just don't get it. How many times do I have to tell him I'm not interested in running the hotel?"

"You should take it as a compliment," Sean said.

His brother would feel that way. Sean would give anything for their father to be so adamant about him taking over. As the oldest, Sean would be the logical choice. Unfortunately, his brother suffered from extreme anxiety issues... It didn't take a therapist to understand where those issues had come from. But despite the damage their father had inflicted on him, Sean was fiercely loyal to the old man. Callum knew he'd turned down several offers from competing hotel chains over the last few years. His experience and knowledge made him an appealing candidate to others.

And it devastated his older brother that their father didn't see him as the one to take over the family business, when even strangers could see his work ethic and potential. Just as it devastated Callum that he was seen as the obligatory choice.

"Look, he needs to see that you are the better man for this," he said, touching Sean's shoulder. His brother may be three years his senior, but Callum had always been more of the protector, the one who looked out for him. His brother's confidence had been shaken by their father's disregard for years, and it added to Callum's frustration with the man.

"He's never going to trust me the way he trusts you," Sean said.

"Well, he should. You know the business better than he does." His brother hadn't completed university, but he'd been on the ground, learning the business for years. He'd shadowed every position in the hotel from housekeeping to catering to the front desk. He knew it inside out, and more than anything he wanted to take over. He enjoyed working with the staff and the managers, and everyone liked and respected Sean.

Except the person who mattered most.

"Thanks, man…" Sean said, staring at the ground. "But I need to face reality. His first choice is you, and after that there's a list of others he'd consider before me." The snapping of the elastic bands at his wrist resumed.

Callum sighed, knowing there was no point in disagreeing. Sean was right. Their father had zero faith in his older son and he made no secret about it. He treated Sean as a workhorse but refused to fully trust him with big decisions or responsibilities.

Callum tapped his brother on the shoulder. "Hey, I've

got a few hours before I have to go to work. Want to grab a drink?"

Sean checked his watch. "It's 9:30 a.m."

"Got something better to do?"

Sean shook his head. "Lead the way."

CHAPTER THREE

"STORMY, COME EAT," Ellie called as she set the food dish on the counter. While cats were common as bookstore fixtures, Flippin' Pages had its own resident fox, and the bookstore's new four-legged "employee" was as close as Ellie would get to owning a pet herself. She fed the arctic marble fox, cleaned the litter box, took her to all of her vet appointments, but she'd drawn the line at actually living with her upstairs in her apartment. It would be the last step into spinsterhood, one Ellie wasn't quite ready to make just yet.

Stormy gracefully jumped up onto the counter and started to eat. Her gray-and-white coat and striking resemblance to a husky always made Ellie smile. At least the fox was living her best life, surrounded by books and customers who spoiled her after a tough year trying to survive in the wild where Levi, the grandson of the bookstore's owner, Meredith Grayson, had rescued her while on a wildfire call. Domesticating her had been surprisingly easy as her temperament was more catlike.

That morning was a quiet one. Sunday mornings usually were, with people attending church services or weekend brunch. The afternoon would pick up with mostly browsers, an occasional sale, but the morning was normally Ellie's favorite part of the day.

Leaning against the counter with her coffee in one hand, she scrolled through social media on her phone. Pictures of family vacations and weddings and honeymoons filled her feed and her breathing grew more and more labored the longer she looked. By age twenty-nine she'd assumed she would have the things she'd always wanted—a great career teaching at the elementary school, a devoted, smart, handsome husband and at least one adorable child of her own.

Life goals.

Recipe for disappointment was more like it.

She shook her head. It had to be the upcoming reunion making her feel this way. A few weeks ago she hadn't felt like her life was slipping past, and she certainly hadn't viewed it as a failure. But seeing everyone else's life, seeing what they'd accomplished in ten years was starting to take its toll.

A social media hiatus would be the smart thing to do until she cleared this dark cloud that loomed over her.

She sipped her coffee, and the liquid stuck in her throat as a new notification popped up.

Brent Lanigan RSVP'd "YES" to Wild River High Class of 2011 Reunion.

Ellie's heart raced. He was online right now at the same time she was. She clicked on the group page and stared at the photo of him in his pilot's uniform, standing in front of a commercial plane on the Anchorage airport airstrip. He looked so handsome—the casual smile that had filled all her teenage fantasies now filled her heart with a longing she couldn't quite shake.

For her, it had always been Brent. He was good-looking, polished, kind and ambitious. He'd been a fantastic kisser, and he'd never been afraid of showing his emotions for her. He was honest and straightforward and stood up for the things he believed in. She'd respected that about him. She'd never doubted her feelings for him and had always been able to picture a life together. He'd valued family as much as she did and they'd both wanted a solid, long-lasting marriage, a safe place to raise the children they both dreamed of having. Their morals had aligned, and Ellie always knew that with Brent she wouldn't have to worry about ever being alone. No one else had ever measured up to him. He'd set a standard that no other man she'd dated could live up to. And now he'd be back in Wild River at the reunion.

If there was ever going to be a chance that they could reconnect, maybe this was it.

She sipped the coffee and stared at the RSVP button on the page. Without overthinking it, she hit YES, and just like that she was going to the reunion.

And an hour later, she was somehow involved in the planning of it.

Her polite, friendly message to Alisha asking if there was anything she could do to help had been met with a full to-do list that Ellie was somehow now in charge of.

You're so good at this stuff.

Alisha's praise had made her feel good for about thirty seconds before the list of things to do had appeared.

Contact the Wild River High School to see if the auditorium was available that night for the event, call around to local caterers for pricing and availability, come up with a theme (nothing cheesy), plan and buy the decorations, and follow up with the attendees once all the details were confirmed.

Sure, no problem. Ellie could pull off an event in less than three weeks.

And this was good. She wanted Brent to notice her, right? What better way than to be a key player in the reunion? It gave her a legitimate reason to reach out. And there was no time like the present.

She took a deep breath and posted for the first time in the group page.

Hey, everyone! I'm really excited to see everyone at the reunion.

So, maybe stretching a little—there was really only one person she was excited to see.

Alisha has entrusted me with some of the planning for the event.

Or all of it.

If anyone has any special requests or dietary restrictions, please let me know as soon as possible.

Then she sat back and waited.
Within seconds someone was typing.
Her heart raced seeing Brent's comment appear.

I'm sure you remember my dairy allergy. You were always so great at finding lactose-free desserts whenever we went out.

Ellie rode the high of his comment all morning as she worked. It might seem like a casual comment, but there was definitely a hint of flirtatiousness to it. Like he wanted her to remember the past and how close they once were.

As if she could forget.

She was instantly feeling better about her decision to

attend, and she wasn't the least bit bothered when Alisha continued to send her more things to take care of.

Unfortunately, her coworker was in less than a good mood. Entering the store a half hour late in a suit that was obviously custom-made, Callum's expression was…intense, which was definitely off-brand.

"Let me guess, mandatory hotel board meeting?" It was the only time Ellie ever saw him in a bad mood.

He nodded, yanking the tie off from around his neck and removing the jacket. "Yeah," he mumbled. "Only not really. It was more of an intervention," he said, unbuttoning and rolling the sleeves of his dress shirt.

"What do you mean?" she asked, looking up from the latest update from Alisha.

"It was just Dad and Sean, and basically I've been given an ultimatum. Either join the family business or be disowned."

Ellie cocked her head to the side as she put her cell phone away. "Disowned? Dramatic much?"

Callum's laugh held zero humor. "You really need to meet my family sometime so you can see the level of assholery for yourself."

"Well, what does your dad want?"

"For me to start getting serious about my life." He bent and lifted several boxes of publisher new releases with ease and carried them to the shelves.

Ellie bit her tongue. She didn't want to make him feel worse with her honesty, but she too wondered why he was kinda just coasting through life. He seemed happy working in the bookstore, and not that there was anything wrong with the job, but didn't he want something more? He was certainly capable of so much more. The guy had an MBA. He could be climbing any corporate ladder he wanted, even if he didn't want to work for his father in the hospitality industry.

Had his privileged upbringing made him less motivated? She couldn't claim to fully understand him. But she liked and respected him enough not to judge. Families could be complicated, and she didn't know the whole story, so she kept her opinions to herself.

Unfortunately, he could read her expression.

"You think he's right?" Callum asked.

Ellie sighed and hesitated before answering. "Do you want honesty or someone to agree with you?"

"I guess that answers the question," he grumbled, tearing violently into the boxes with the box cutter.

Fearful for the fate of the book covers inside, Ellie took the knife from him and took his hands in hers.

Callum's expression immediately softened as his gaze dropped to their joined hands, and his eyes held a look she couldn't quite decipher when they met hers again.

Ellie awkwardly let go and cleared her throat. "I just think maybe you're not living up to your potential, working here, that's all."

He scoffed. "Isn't being happy more important? I mean, I can appreciate how hard my father worked to get where he is, I really can, but the dude's miserable. He may have money and a reputation but he also has two failed marriages and kids who don't even really know him. He wasn't around much when we were growing up, and now he expects us to follow in his footsteps." Callum shook his head. "There's more to life."

She didn't disagree. She just wished she had the opportunities and the choices that he seemed to take for granted. Her parents had been in their late forties when they'd had Ellie. She'd been unplanned and unexpected, though not unloved. Sadly, they'd passed away from illnesses within months of one another the year she'd graduated high school, and before then they'd never really put any pressure on her or had any expectations.

While some people would find that freeing, Ellie had longed for a little more guidance and involvement from them. As free-spirited people, they hadn't been concerned about her education, wanting her to enjoy life and not work so hard. They also hadn't felt any pressure to ensure that there were college funds available when she graduated, feeling that she'd somehow make her own way, that the universe would take care of her. All she had to do was put that positive energy out there and things would miraculously work out. She didn't begrudge them that, but unfortunately fate had not intervened, and she'd never been able to get that funding figured out on her own. Her grades were good, but in her final year they'd slipped a little, just below the threshold for scholarship qualifications, and her jobs hadn't afforded her the luxury of saving enough.

Her cell chimed for the millionth time that morning and she took the phone from her pocket and clicked on the new notification in the group.

"Oh no." Her heart fell deep into her stomach as she read.

"What's wrong?"

"Brent just added a plus-one to his reunion RSVP."

Callum looked like he was over the whole reunion discussion, but he nodded. "Don't worry about it. I'm sure it's not anyone special," he said, a note of irritation in his voice as he placed the last book on the New Release shelf.

Ellie frowned. "What's that supposed to mean?"

"Don't get defensive. I'm just saying the guy doesn't seem to be long-term material." Callum broke down the empty box and headed toward the back.

Ellie followed him, on a mission. "Why would you say that? You don't even know him. He's totally long-term material. He just hasn't found the right one yet."

Callum swung back toward her and she nearly collided into his body. He steadied her. "What you mean is that he let the right one get away?"

Ellie shrugged. The thought had crossed her mind. The two of them had been perfect together. What more could Brent be searching for? "I'm just saying that maybe there's a reason neither of us has found anyone else to settle down with yet." It wasn't that she hadn't put herself out there... Or maybe in some ways it was. It was just difficult to trust in new relationships. Brent had been there for her when her parents had died, and he'd been the rock she'd relied on back then. That had bonded them in ways other people couldn't understand.

Callum nodded. "Yeah, there is. You're pining for him and he's living his best life dating a new woman every few months."

Her eyes narrowed. "Don't judge him."

Callum sighed. "Fine. Maybe you're right. Maybe he's still single because he hasn't found someone as incredible as you yet."

She scoffed, turning her attention back to her phone.

"That wasn't sarcasm, Ellie. You are incredible, and if this guy can't see that, then he's an idiot."

She was barely listening as she clicked on the profile of the woman Brent was planning to bring as his date. Tall, thin, dark hair, breasts that had to be medically enhanced... stunning but obviously she knew it. Why else would a grown woman post a photo of herself suggestively licking a lollipop? She sighed. Poor Brent. Always dating superficial women as a way to protect his heart.

"Look, if you don't want to see your ex with someone else, then just don't go," Callum said, opening the back door and tossing the cardboard into the recycle bin in the alley behind the store.

Ellie bit her lip as she held the door open for him. That ship had sailed. "Um, yeah… I kinda have to go."

Callum reentered and locked the back door, then turned to face her. "Why?"

"Because I agreed to help with the planning?"

"You mean you agreed to do *all* the planning." He shook his head and moved past her in the hall. "You really need to work on saying no."

She followed him back to the front of the store. "It's not a big deal. I'm good at that kind of thing." She shrugged.

"And you thought if you were on the planning committee, then Brent would have no other choice than to interact with you."

Damn, why was she so predictable? And how the hell did he know her so well? "Well, it worked," she said in a huff. Unfortunately, now she'd have to deal with the dietary restrictions of his plus-one, as well.

Although the woman looked like a plate of ice cubes might be all she'd eat. She flicked through the unlocked profile. Picture after picture of the woman loaded…each one more perfect than the last. Had Ellie ever taken even one photo that looked this good? Had to be some kind of filter…

"Fine, I'll go to the reunion with you," Callum said.

Ellie's head snapped up. "I'm sorry, what?"

"I'll be your plus-one," he said.

Her eyes narrowed. "Did I ask?"

"No, but you were hinting at it."

"No, I absolutely wasn't." She hadn't even considered bringing a date. Her mission had been to go alone, bump into Brent and then spend the rest of the night reminiscing about old times and getting him to fall back in love with her. Simple. Only now that plan had been derailed by Samantha.

"Fine, I made the executive decision that you need me," Callum said, picking up Stormy and petting her.

The fox curled into him and purred like a cat.

Ellie bit her lip. Maybe she should bring someone just in case… "I don't know. Bringing a hot guy friend might make me look even more pathetic. Like I couldn't get a real date so I brought my coworker who felt guilted into doing me a favor." The last thing she wanted was for everyone to think she had to bring a friend to events because she couldn't get a date. But admittedly, she didn't want to ask someone who might read something into the invite. The last guy she'd dated, a dental hygienist, would be more than willing to go with her, but she didn't want to lead him on. Greg was a nice guy—good-looking, smart and caring— but she hadn't felt a spark. The few times they'd gone out, the conversation had been somewhat forced, and whenever he'd touched her hand or kissed her cheek, it had felt more platonic than anything. Great relationships could develop from friendship first, but Ellie wanted passion, at least in the beginning. Her parents had been so passionately in love, even after years together, that it was hard to settle for less than the type of relationship they had role modeled.

"I don't feel guilted, and you could get a real date if you wanted one," Callum said. "In fact, we can just tell everyone that we're together," he continued casually.

She blinked. "Like pretend you're my boyfriend?" Was he serious?

He laughed, sounding slightly dejected. "You could do worse, you know."

She punched his shoulder playfully. "I could do a lot

worse." Sadly, every guy she even entertained the thought of dating was always compared to the one guy that no one could compare to.

She hesitated. Callum's solution might not be a terrible idea. He was certainly a head turner. No one would feel sorry for poor old Ellie Mitchell if she showed up with this amazing man…and it wouldn't be a real date with expectations and complications. Conversation with Callum wouldn't be strained or awkward, and he was a good dancer—she knew that from the store's four-person Christmas party where he'd spun her around The Drunk Tank's dance floor until 2:00 a.m. and they shut the place.

Maybe if she showed up with someone, Brent would even be jealous.

"So? What do you say? Let me take you to your reunion?" Callum asked.

A hot guy on her arm might ease the sting of seeing Brent with a supermodel a little, and if she felt really bad and got shit-faced, he could easily carry her out of the high school auditorium. "Fine. Okay." She paused. "Thank you."

He smiled.

"But, there're some ground rules."

Callum sighed, folding his arms across his chest, a look of amusement on his handsome face. "Right, because we couldn't just wing it," he said.

"Winging it will only lead to disaster," she said, completely serious. Ellie had not inherited her parents' "go with the flow of the universe" attitude. Maybe it was always feeling a little unsettled with their carefree way of life that had her desperate to live hers with more structure and familiarity.

"Okay. What are the rules?"

"No kissing…" That was an obvious and easy one. She

paused. "Well, maybe one but only if it's absolutely necessary to sell the idea that we're actually dating—and no tongue."

He nodded. "Not loving it, but okay."

She rolled her eyes. "No elaborate meet-cute story. If anyone asks how we met, we tell them the truth—we work together. I want to avoid lying as much as possible." Lying would only come back to bite them if their stories somehow got twisted throughout the night.

"Boring, but I can work with that."

"And third, we go, we mingle, we leave by ten before the karaoke starts."

Callum cocked his head to the side. "I love karaoke."

"I know you do, but I can't carry a tune." She refused to get up onstage and make a complete fool of herself. She'd argued against the activity ten minutes ago, claiming a photo booth was more than enough, but unfortunately she was outvoted in the decision, by the two other planning committee members—Alisha and Cheryl—who hadn't actually planned anything else so far.

Callum looked ready to argue. "One song? A duet and then we're out."

She shook her head. "These rules are not open to negotiation. No songs or we're not doing this."

Callum's sexy, smoldering stare down would break any other female on the planet, but Ellie wasn't conceding on this. It was her reunion, her shot at seeing her ex-boyfriend again, and she needed the night to go as easily as possible.

"Fine. Deal." Callum relented. He extended a hand and Ellie hesitated, staring at it, remembering the odd sensation that her previous touch had sparked.

"Please don't make me regret this," she said, reluctantly sliding her hand into his.

"I promise, you will not regret this."

Then why did she kinda regret it already?

CHAPTER FOUR

As THE REUNION got closer, Callum realized there was no way he was sticking to Ellie's rules.

Ellie might see this reunion as a way to show Brent all that he was missing, and he'd certainly help her accomplish that, but he also saw it as a chance to connect with her on a different level. For two years they'd worked together, and she'd never taken him seriously. She thought he was joking whenever he complimented her and refused to take him up on his offers for dinner or a real date. This was his one shot to change that. Help her see that he truly was interested in her, that she was the only woman in a long time who had caught his attention.

Two minutes late for his shift, he entered the Wild River Search and Rescue station in time to see three of his fellow crewmates getting into gear. He immediately reached for his own jacket and boots stored on the rack on the wall beside his name. "What do we have?" he asked Reed, the search team leader, as he pulled on his jacket.

Reed glanced up from lacing his boots. "A group of campers called for assistance after one of them stumbled into their fire…"

Summer season was in full swing. Locals and tourists hit the campsites and trails as much as possible while the weather was nice and mild. But despite ideal conditions, the S & R team had plenty of calls to keep them busy. Lost hikers and minor injuries were most common. And a lot of them had to do with wildfires. "Alcohol involved?"

Reed nodded. "I would think so."

Of course, if the group was underage, all evidence of it would have disappeared by the time they arrived. Callum suspected they'd waited until it was absolutely necessary before calling in for assistance.

Five minutes later, just before dawn, the crew hit the trails leading south along Snowcrest Peak, where the kids were camping, and Callum fell into step at the back of the group.

Diva, their four-legged team member, walked alongside him as usual. The husky seemed to always stick by him, almost as though sensing he was the one who might need her, being the least experienced member and the youngest on the crew. He liked the dog, but it was a little unnerving that she'd pegged him as the weak link.

"Hey, Tank, want to call your dog?" he shouted to the big six-foot-five dude at the front of the pack with Reed. The owner of the local watering hole was Diva's handler after all. They were a certified team, so shouldn't the dog be with the appropriately nicknamed man?

Tank turned and walked backward. "Nah, she's got a crush on you...like every other female in Wild River," he said teasingly before turning his attention back to the hike.

Diva glanced up at Callum with a smug expression on her gray-and-white face.

"What's it going to take for you to trust me? I got this," he whispered to the dog.

He'd been a member of the search and rescue crew for three years. He was currently a support member, but he took as many shifts at the station and went out on as many rescues as everyone else. He wasn't quite sure what held him back from applying to be a full member, but he wasn't ready to commit to the crew in a more permanent way yet as a full volunteer.

Damn, maybe he was drifting through life the way everyone assumed. He wanted to think that he still hadn't figured out his life path yet and that it was okay to continue weighing his options and exploring things, but maybe at twenty-six, it wasn't okay. Maybe he did need to decide on something… something a little more secure than a writing career.

As he trudged through the muddy trail toward the campsite, his muse chose that moment to talk to him. The sights and sounds and smells of the wilderness brought vivid descriptive imagery to mind as he watched the dark sky turn into the deep blue and purple hue of Blue Hour. This time just before Golden Hour, when the sun would break over the horizon, was one of the most beautiful times of day. This transition period from night to day cast a breathtaking natural illumination over the forest, dim enough to bring out the darkness, yet light enough to surround the forest in an almost surreal glow. Blue Hour never lasted long and most people never even noticed it, but those who paid attention recognized the powerful part it played in the breaking of a new day.

He grabbed a pen and paper from his bag and started writing notes as the thoughts came to him. Maybe it was the great outdoors, fresh air or just being away from the pressure of the keyboard and blank page, but he always did his best writing when he wasn't sitting at the desk or the diner table but out living life.

"Whatcha writing?" Erika, Reed's fiancée and one of his fellow crew members, asked, sneaking up next to him.

He tucked the paper out of sight. "Just remembered a

few things I need to do, so I wanted to write them down, that's all."

She grinned, not looking entirely convinced. "Yeah... So all those questions you were asking me at The Drunk Tank the other night about the long-term effect of blocking out childhood trauma and abuse—that was all just out of curiosity?"

He studied the brilliant ER surgeon. What did she think she knew? Was it worse to let her think he'd been asking for personal reasons? He shrugged. "I find that stuff fascinating, that's all," he said. He liked Erika—she was a no-bullshit kind of person who'd give it to him straight if his writing sucked. But he wasn't ready to tell anyone about his book yet, especially not the guys on the crew. And if he told Erika, she'd tell Reed and then everyone would know.

They wouldn't give him shit over it. Worse, they'd all be supportive—too supportive. They might even want to read it, and that wasn't happening.

"Okay, I'll pretend to buy that," she said, but she glanced at his right hand. More specifically, his right middle finger. "You know, I had a friend once who called bumps like the one you have on the side of your finger writer's bumps... from constantly holding a pen or pencil." She winked then walked on to rejoin Reed on the trail.

Callum absentmindedly ran his thumb over the bump as he climbed the incline on the trail behind the others. A writer's bump. He may not have a finished book, but he'd consider the bump a rite of passage of sorts.

Arriving at the campsite moments later, he put the paper and pen away as the doused firepit came into view. Five teenagers—three boys, two girls—sat around it, blankets wrapped around their shoulders, drinking from thermoses as they waited. Three tents were set up around the perimeter of the camp. Luckily they were next to a lake, and they'd been smart enough to treat the burn with cold water.

Reed glanced at the group. "Erika, you want to take this?" he asked.

She glanced at Callum with a grin. "I've already proven myself to Diva. Maybe Callum should do it."

"I'm on it," he said, grabbing the medical supply bag. He was one of the more highly trained members of the team when it came to medical emergencies. He approached the poor kid, who looked a lot less upset than he'd expected given the extent of the burn on his arm. Wearing shorts, sandals and a T-shirt with the edges singed, he held a cold compress to the injured arm. "Hey, T.J., right?" He squatted down in front of him and opened the kit.

"Yes, sir," the boy of about fifteen said.

"These your friends?" Callum nodded around the group, all high school age. He'd been camping alone with friends at that age, so he couldn't deliver the "you should have an adult present" speech without feeling like a hypocrite.

T.J. nodded. "And my brother A.J."

A taller boy stood up and approached. "I'm his brother."

"You were responsible for keeping an eye on him?" Callum asked the older boy.

The teen nodded. "Yes, sir." He shot his younger brother a glare. "But I didn't think he'd go do something so stupid," he grumbled.

"I have a brother too, so I get it." Though in his case, Sean was older, but it had never felt that way growing up.

He removed the compress and applied an ointment to the raw-looking wound that extended from the boy's palm all the way to midway up his forearm. It was a nasty burn. The boy flinched and mumbled a profanity under his breath.

"Why were you so close to the fire, anyway? Were you drinking?"

"No, sir." The teen's cheeks flushed, and his gaze shifted to one of the girls sitting on the log next to them. The pretty, petite blonde looked worried as she watched Callum treat the burn.

Ahhh...there was a girl.

T.J. cleared his throat. "Janeen dropped her charm bracelet near the fire," he mumbled as Callum wrapped the arm in gauze.

The young girl smiled at him as she played with the bracelet on her arm. Obviously he'd retrieved it. "So, you decided to be a hero?"

"Says a dude that looks like Superman," T.J. said with a grin.

The other teens laughed along with the other members of the S & R crew. Guess he'd walked straight into that one. "Well, next time, just buy her a new one, okay?" he told the teen, knowing he was wasting his breath. He'd walk into a fire for Ellie too. Men did stupid things to impress women.

He finished bandaging the burn and handed the boy some painkillers. "Keep it wrapped and take one of these every eight hours. No alcohol."

The teen nodded. "Thank you."

Callum gathered the medical kit and stood, then heading back down the trail, he turned to Diva. "We good now?"

The dog eyed him but then sauntered off toward Tank.

Looked like he'd finally passed the canine's test.

"Repeat after me... Hat, house, hammock." Ellie paused and gestured for her student to repeat the words starting with *H*.

On her computer screen, the young woman from a small

seaside town in Spain pronounced the words carefully. "At, ouse, ammock."

"Good…okay, but remember the *H* makes a sound in English."

"*Muy* confusing," Raquel said over the background noise of the waves of the Mediterranean Sea behind her on the screen. The twenty-two-year-old Spaniard was secretly learning English to move to Ohio to be with a man she'd met online. Her parents didn't know her plans yet. Ellie was desperate to ask how the two had formed a connection considering their language barrier, but she wasn't sure she was quite ready to hear the answer.

Maybe love really did have a language of its own?

Ellie laughed. "Agreed—English can be tricky." She checked the time on her wall clock. It was 2:58 a.m. Time to wrap up for the night. "Next class we will be focusing on verb conjugation for the verb 'to be.'"

Raquel groaned and looked ready to argue, but an older man exited the house behind her and she waved and disconnected the Skype connection quickly.

Ah, young, forbidden love. How exciting for Raquel. But maybe Ellie should also focus on teaching her emergency words just in case she arrived in Ohio and lover boy turned out to be a serial killer.

Ellie yawned as she shut her computer. These late night classes were starting to catch up with her, but with the time difference between Alaska and Spain, they were the only teaching slots available.

Completing her ESL-teaching certificate the year before, she'd signed on with Languages America to teach English to Spanish speakers looking to immigrate to the United States, hoping it would help fulfill her desire to be a teacher. While she enjoyed it, she didn't think it was the same as working in a school, in a classroom environment with eager children.

Her mother had always said that Ellie would make a great teacher. She'd told her stories about how Ellie had set up "classrooms" to teach her dolls when she was really little. How even then she'd liked the structure and discipline of the school system. Maybe that was why she'd enjoyed school so much. Children craved structure and support, and it wasn't always that way at home.

She stood and her phone chimed with a new message as she climbed back into bed. Opening it, she read the text from Callum.

How was class?

He always texted on Friday nights after her class. He must really be bored on his night shifts at the station, and she was the only one he knew who would be awake this time of night. But it was kinda nice to know someone else was awake.

Pronunciation day. How's the station?

Two small calls today. No major injuries. Have you decided what to wear to the reunion yet?

Nope.

And the reunion was the next evening. The last three weeks had been a blur with work and planning the event. Somehow she'd pulled it off so far. Deciding what to wear would almost be the biggest challenge. Everything she owned was too plain or too boring. But she hated shopping, so she dreaded having to go the next day to find something suitable that didn't make her look and feel like a fifty-year-old spinster.

Should I send you a dress?

She smiled, knowing he was kidding.

We can go over some details to make sure we can convince people we are in love.

Details are boring. Can't I just kiss you all night?

Her pulse quickened slightly at the thought. Remembering the odd sensation that had run through her the day in the bookstore a few weeks ago when she'd taken his hands in hers, the idea of a kiss had her sweating. She wasn't sure they could avoid a kiss the entire night if they were pretending to be an item…but maybe they were just one of those couples who didn't like PDAs. Maybe they liked to keep their relationship private.

She ignored his question as she responded.

Alisha is a nurse at the hospital and she's been dating Nick, a lawyer, for several months.

Why do I care?

Ellie sighed. Why on earth had she agreed to this? If she hadn't already RSVP'd a plus-one herself, she'd totally be reconsidering this decision. But Alisha had been curious, to say the least, about who Ellie was dating. Turned out everyone cyberstalked everyone…even the book nerd from high school, apparently.

Because if you and I are dating, I would have told you about my friends.

Friends. Were they really friends? She'd spent a lot of time with them in high school, but they were really Brent's friends. After her and Brent's relationship ended, she hadn't seen or heard from any of them. They didn't have much in common besides Brent.

Her phone chimed.

Okay, I've got a pen and paper, ready to take notes.

Ellie rolled her eyes at Callum's text, but continued to give him the basic info she thought would be important to know.

Cheryl and Mitch are recently married. They have a six-month-old baby. A girl, I think. She's a personal trainer and he's some fitness guru with his own start-up…

Unemployed, you mean?

Ellie grinned. Quite possibly. Cheryl's family were wealthy, so they really didn't need to worry about money. She worked as a trainer because she enjoyed it and it gave her the flexibility to make her own hours. She'd already reduced her client list since having the baby.

Instagram influencer or something.

She still wasn't quite sure what that was or how it translated to income. But Mitch seemed happy and he had a ton of followers.

Obsessed with his own muscles and wants everyone to worship him, got it.

If he was Cheryl's usual type, then that sounded about right.

Another chime of her phone before she could respond.

What about Brent? What do I need to know about your ex?

Ellie stared at the phone. Where did she start? What did Callum need to know? He was her first kiss, her first sexual experience, her first love. He'd also been her first heartbreak.

But it was late, and she already sensed that Callum thought her hang-up over Brent was ridiculous. She was worried enough about seeing her ex again—with someone else. She didn't need Callum's opinion on the whole thing making her even more stressed.

I think we can wing the rest.

I thought winging it would lead to disaster?

Her gut told her that there were a million things that could go wrong the next evening. Least of all, their fake relationship could be called out as a hoax.

We'll survive. Night, Callum.

Three dots as if he was typing, then…

Sweet dreams.

Ellie didn't know about sweet. Despite her exhaustion, she suspected her anxiety about the next evening's event would plague her with unsettling dreams.

CALLUM LAY ON the cot in the corner of the search and rescue cabin a few miles away from Ellie's apartment, anticipation of the following evening making him sweat a little…okay, a lot.

Ellie wanted to impress her friends, wanted them to see that her life was as amazing as she saw theirs. He wished she didn't feel the need to prove herself in any way, but he understood. There was a ton of societal pressure on people these days, women especially, to be a certain way, look a certain way…

He reread the notes about her friends. Alisha—nurse. Cheryl—personal trainer… He had this. By the end of the reunion events, he hoped to show Ellie that he was the kind of man she could count on. She'd been on her own since she was nineteen, with no real family or close friends around for support. He knew their boss, Meredith, the bookstore owner, was the closest Ellie had to a confidante and mentor, and he wanted to be someone else she could rely on. For anything.

So he couldn't mess this up.

His cell phone chimed and he smiled as he reached for it. Did she have more notes for him, or was she texting to say she'd reconsidered the kissing?

It wasn't Ellie. It was Sean.

His smile faded and his stomach twisted. A late-night text from his brother was never a good sign.

You awake?

He dialed his brother's number as he sat up and threw his legs over the side of the cot. Three rings later, Sean answered.

"Hey…sorry if I woke you."

"You didn't. It's my night at the station. What's up?" Callum asked.

"I'm working on the new marketing campaign for the winter, and it's just not coming together."

Callum heard the familiar strain in his brother's voice. He could hear the snapping of elastic bands and the steady thumping of Sean's footsteps as he paced on the other end of the call. If it was anyone else, he'd tell them to step away from the project, sleep on it… But that didn't work with someone who lived with high-functioning anxiety. Sean couldn't walk away and come back to it in the morning with fresh eyes. His overactive brain would have him stressing over it all night and doubting his abilities. The further he got from the project, the more he'd convince himself of the reasons to give up, which would then lead to a depression spiral. Callum had seen it enough times.

For Sean, it was always better to push through. Which meant Callum was pushing through his tiredness a little longer.

"Okay, walk me through what you have."

"It's shit. It's all shit."

Damn, they'd already reached that stage. Why hadn't Sean called him hours ago? "I'm sure it's not. You just need another perspective. You're too close to the work. What have you got so far?"

"Dad wanted fresh and unique."

Their father only used buzzwords like *fresh* and *unique* to impress the board. Sean should know that by now. "Seriously, bro, you know he doesn't. Give him the same campaign as last year—just revise the wording and the graphics."

Sean was silent for a long moment. "Can I come by?"

Callum repressed a sigh. If his brother needed his help, there was no way he could turn him down. "Of course."

"Be there in ten," Sean said, and he could hear the sound of a door closing before his brother disconnected the call.

Callum blinked the sudden exhaustion from his eyes. No matter how hard he tried to escape the family business, he kept getting pulled in.

He ran a hand through his hair as he made a pot of coffee and waited for Sean's truck headlights to pull into the station parking lot.

It was going to be a long night.

CHAPTER FIVE

THE NEXT EVENING, the Wild River High School gymnasium looked exactly the way it had on prom night.

And Ellie felt just as nauseous as she walked in.

You're not the self-conscious book nerd who just got dumped by her boyfriend anymore.

Callum squeezed her arm and bent to whisper, "You're not the self-conscious book nerd who just got dumped by her douchebag boyfriend anymore."

"Get out of my head," she said.

"And you look absolutely amazing," he said, his gaze drifting over her. It had several times already since he'd picked her up for the reunion. She vaguely remembered him complimenting her several times, as well, but she was far too nervous to really be paying attention.

Was the black, knee-length, formfitting strapless dress too much? It wasn't her usual style, but this evening she was trying to be a little less "her."

"I just hope I can keep this dress up," she said, yanking the fabric higher. She was fairly flat chested so there wasn't much to stop the fabric from sliding all the way to her ankles. She was putting a shit ton of trust in the tiny closure at the back meant to cinch it in around her body.

"Well, if it falls, you'll definitely catch Brent's attention. And every other man's in the room," Callum said with a grin.

"Not helpful," she said, rubbing her chest. Was her heart on the left side of her body or the right? The pain was kinda all over...

Callum took her hands and turned her to face him. "Stop stressing. You look amazing. *You* are amazing."

The tension eased a little from her shoulders as she stared at him. It was working. His words and overall calm presence was quieting her pulse a little. Of course, he had nothing to be freaking out about. But maybe she was over-reacting. It was just old familiar faces for a few hours.

The contracting of her chest subsiding, she pulled back and looked at Callum, really seeing him for the first time all evening. Dressed in a pair of charcoal dress pants and a salmon-colored button-down shirt, his hair gelled back, he looked as incredible as he always did, but something was different. "Did you get a haircut?"

"Yes, ma'am. Like it?"

He'd look gorgeous bald, but this new polished look was definitely working for him. As much as she thought the longer hair that always fell into his eyes was cute, this new style was manlier. More presentable as the man she was supposed to be in love with. It made him look a little older, which was good. She did not need to be labeled a cougar. "It's perfect," she said.

"'Perfect' as in my appearance won't embarrass you?"

"Exactly," she said.

"Oh my, I'd recognize those dark-rimmed glasses any-where," a booming female voice said behind them.

Callum's face looked slightly ashen as they both turned to face Mrs. Garnett, the high school English teacher who'd been teaching at the school for over thirty years. Ellie had enjoyed the woman's class—it had been one of her favor-ites. And she'd seen Mrs. Garnett at the bookstore for several book club events over the years, and they'd always had a great time discussing books long after the event was over and the store was closed. Avid readers were natural kindred spirits.

However, at that moment, the older woman was focused only on Callum.

"Hi, Mrs. Garnett," he said nervously, accepting a hug from her. She was only four foot ten so she seemed to only reach his waist, but she definitely squeezed a little longer than necessary.

Ellie watched with amusement as he slowly peeled her away, and the other woman beamed at him. "I haven't seen you in years. I keep missing you every time I'm in the bookstore."

Callum looked slightly guilty, and Ellie fought to remember those times...

Yep, he'd been there on a few occasions during the book club meetings. Always found an excuse to be in the back stockroom or on a break... Why? Why was he hiding from the nice old English teacher?

"Maybe I was off that day," he mumbled.

"Are you still writing?" Mrs. Garnett asked.

Ellie's eyes widened as she glanced at him. He used to write?

He was red around the collar, and he cleared his throat. "Nah, not really."

"What?" Mrs. Garnett frowned. "That's a shame. You were so talented."

He was?

"No, it was just something I did for fun back then," Callum mumbled, glancing around the gymnasium as though looking for an escape or a way to change the subject.

"You write?" Ellie asked, not willing to let this discussion drop just yet. This was a fun fact she hadn't known about her coworker. And it definitely needed more exploration, especially considering how uncomfortable it was making her usually calm and unfazed friend.

He shook his head, but Mrs. Garnett interjected. "Yes, he does. Amazing short stories that had the potential to be full-length novels and the most inspiring prose… In all my years teaching that English class, I've never had a more promising student."

Mrs. Garnett had taught a lot of students. That was a huge compliment coming from her. The teacher was a writer, as well, mostly ghostwriting memoirs for local legends and heroes. So she'd know talent.

Why hadn't Callum ever mentioned this? They talked about books all the time, were surrounded by them. Obviously he'd been intentionally keeping it a secret.

"Ah, thank you, but I'm sure that's not true." He glanced toward the food table. "Hey, anyone hungry?"

"I'm good," Ellie said.

"I could go for some punch and a pastry." Mrs. Garnett hooked her arm through Callum's. "You don't mind if I borrow him for a moment, do you, dear?"

"Borrow away," Ellie said with a smile.

Ellie watched him escort Mrs. Garnett to the concession table. This conversation definitely wasn't over. She'd be getting to the bottom of this closet writing thing one way or another.

A writer. Safe to say her mind was blown.

Alone, she took a breath as she scanned the auditorium. It was filling up with all of her former classmates and their spouses or significant others. They were expecting about fifty people that evening, and it looked like most had already arrived. A lot of them still lived in Wild River or in other parts of Alaska, but a few had flown in from other states.

In the far corner, Alisha was reminiscing with her old cheerleading squad. A group stood in a close circle around them as the women had ditched their heels and were attempting to create their old pyramid stunt to a round of applause.

Crazy that they could still remember their old routines. Or were still flexible and limber enough to pull them off.

Her gaze shifted toward the stage where the DJ had set up, ready to play the nostalgic playlist Cheryl had approved— her contribution to the planning.

And in the center of the gym, a group of former football players had broken into the equipment room and retrieved a football they were throwing around. Everyone seemed to be having a good time and reconnecting. She really should start mingling, but her palms sweat at the thought of approaching any of the groups that she'd never fully belonged to. The only person she'd ever really connected with in high school was Brent... She'd had a small group of close friends, but no one who'd fully understood her the way he had.

And there he was.

He had his back to her, but she'd recognize that sandy-blond hair, those broad shoulders, that strong back and tapered waist anywhere. He wore snug-fitting designer jeans, brown leather shoes and a light tan sports jacket that she recognized from an Instagram post of shopping with a girlfriend on a trip to Paris, but she wouldn't hold that against him. He had to buy new clothes, and from what she remembered, he struggled with fashion.

Her heart raced as her feet—on autopilot—slowly started shuffling in that direction. What was the right way to play this? Pretend not to notice him until he came to her? Would he? Bump into him? Would that appear casual? Strike up a conversation with one of the men standing next to him until he heard her voice?

Unfortunately, that would require actually knowing who those guys were, and she was totally drawing a blank scanning the faces of the nerdy group in *Big Bang Theory* T-shirts standing near Brent.

Brent was alone, casually sipping a drink from a red Solo cup and scanning the room.

She should just go for it. Approach him and be the one brave enough to initiate a conversation. He was by himself. She didn't see his supermodel-gorgeous date anywhere... Now was her chance. She needed to take it.

She took a deep breath as she crossed the rest of the auditorium. When she was close to him, she reached out and softly touched his shoulder. "Hi," she said as he turned around and those mesmerizing hazel eyes settled on her.

"Wow! If it isn't my Ellie," he said softly.

His Ellie. It had been years since she'd heard him call her that and yet it still had the same knee-weakening, "butterflies in the stomach" effect that it always had.

He hugged her tight, scooping her up and spinning her around. Just like always. If her heart hadn't already been locked up, waiting for him, it certainly belonged to him once again now. Looking at him, feeling his arms around her, it was as though no time at all had passed. And when he set her down again and gazed at her, she could tell he felt the same way. A mix of intrigue and attraction reflected in those eyes that had always seemed to look straight into her soul. "How are you?" he asked.

"I'm good. You?" Really? Years of envisioning this moment and that was all she could come up with?

He smiled. "I'm good too. Better now. I have to say I

wasn't sure coming was a good idea…you know, being away so long, losing touch, but I'm glad I decided to come."

"Me too."

He shook his head. "Wow, it's so great to see you again."

Her pulse was going crazy. "Yeah, you too." Oh my God. She sounded like a complete moron. It was going to take more than two-word sentences to reconnect with the love of her life.

"You did a great job organizing this." He looked around. "I can't believe all these familiar faces."

Funny, she still lived in Wild River with most of these people and barely recognized everyone. Despite his insistence of the contrary, he obviously kept in touch better than she did. Yet, the two of them had drifted apart over the years…

You weren't supposed to stay in contact with your ex. It didn't mean he hadn't wanted to. After all, she'd wanted to and hadn't. Maybe he hadn't been sure if she'd be happy to hear from him after he'd broken her heart.

"Thank you. It was really all Alisha," she said.

He laughed, glancing across the auditorium at the event's mastermind. "Yeah, right. Alisha is the queen of good ideas and delegating the work."

She laughed. "Okay, so I did a lot of the planning."

He nodded toward the punch bowl. "You wouldn't be serving anything stronger than that by any chance, would you?"

She could use a little liquid courage right now too, but she shook her head. "We couldn't get a liquor license because it's a high school."

"Didn't stop us before," he said with a wink.

He stared at her for a long moment, and she felt the heat rise across her neck and chest. When was the last time she'd felt so shy and slightly intimidated by a man? Probably the last time Brent had looked at her this way. He could always make her tongue-tied and put her off-balance.

"Man, I've missed you," he said.

Then why hadn't he reached out? She couldn't summon the courage to ask so she glanced downward. "Yeah, I've missed you too," she mumbled.

"You look amazing. I mean, you always did." His gaze soaked her in and when it settled on the neckline of the dress, she resisted the urge to yank the fabric higher again.

"Thank you." She cleared her throat. "Where's your date?" Did that sound casual?

He looked sheepish and slightly embarrassed as he said, "She dumped me."

Ellie's eyes widened as her pulse quickened in her veins. "So, you're here alone?"

"Yep. Stag once again."

Her heart soared, then pounded even louder as she caught sight of Callum out of the corner of her eye approaching from across the auditorium. Oh no. Bad timing. She needed to figure out a new game plan in light of this recent development. She had to stop Callum from saying they were more than just friends. She opened her eyes wide and shook her head in a tiny, frantic motion from behind Brent, hoping Callum would catch the hint.

He shot her a confused look as he stopped next to them. "Hi, I'm Callum," he said, extending a hand to Brent.

She couldn't breathe.

"I'm Ellie's plus-one."

Plus-one. Okay, that could mean anything.

But was it her imagination or did Brent look slightly jealous as he shook it. "Brent Lanigan. Ellie's *former* plus-one," he said casually, but there was definitely a hint of tension in his voice.

Ellie's laugh at the joking reminder that they used to be an item sounded strained even to her own ears.

"Well, I guess I have you to thank for setting this one free," Callum said, a slight edge in his voice that she'd never heard before.

She needed to clarify this situation and quickly. If she could just get Callum alone for a second, she could tell him his services that evening were unnecessary.

But before she could, Brent glanced back and forth between them. "You two are a couple?"

Callum wrapped an arm around her waist and held tight when she squirmed. "Engaged, actually."

And that was the moment Ellie's heart stopped.

As SOON AS the word slipped past Callum's lips, he knew he'd created a massive mess. The look on Ellie's face suggested she'd murder him the moment they were alone. And yet, he couldn't bring himself to regret it or retreat and say it was only a joke.

Brent's timing on taking a sip of his drink was regrettable as he was now coughing and sputtering. "Engaged?"

Ellie rushed to make sure he was all right. "You okay?"

Brent nodded and cleared his throat. "Yeah...that just went down the wrong way, that's all."

Obviously.

"Engaged," he repeated. "Wow."

"Well, it's um...complicated..." Ellie said.

"It's not exactly official yet," Callum said, coming to her defense.

She pinched his arm as she forced a strangled-sounding

laugh. "Right. We haven't really told many people yet." She shot him a glare.

He squeezed her into his body. "Sorry, I just want to scream it from the mountaintops, you know."

Ellie stepped on his foot and he sucked in his bottom lip.

"Then why the secrecy?" Brent asked, looking back and forth between the two of them.

"No secrecy, we just haven't been seeing one another very long," Callum said.

"Like a blink in time, really," Ellie mumbled through gritted teeth next to him. "And you know how people like to gossip around here."

"Oh my God, are you pregnant?" Brent looked mortified at the thought as his eyes dropped to her flat stomach.

Ellie wrapped her arms around her waist. "No!"

"We plan to get started on that right away though, right, El?" He was a dead man as soon as they left this school auditorium, but he didn't care. It was fun pretending to be her fiancé and so far she hadn't told Brent the truth... Besides, she was even more adorable when she was squirming like she had red ants in her underwear. Which he'd noticed were seamless and barely visible through the tight-fitting soft fabric of her stunning dress that evening.

She'd nearly knocked the wind from his lungs when he'd picked her up. He was used to seeing her in jeans and T-shirts, the occasional loose-fitting sundress and sandals in summer. Her light brown, wispy, shoulder-length hair was always getting in her eyes, and she blew it away with her bottom lip. Between the dress, the heels, the hair curled and pulled back away from her face—exposing her long, slim neck—and the heavier than usual but still subtle makeup, he'd barely recognized her.

Until she'd launched into her usual bossy recap of the rules of engagement for that evening.

"Wow. Well, I guess congratulations are in order," Brent said, raising his glass to them and taking a gulp of whatever was inside the cup. A solitary toast as neither of them had drinks.

The music started to play on the stage, drowning out Ellie's next words, and her eyes widened at the sound of the familiar slow-tempo love song that had once been the make-out song of their generation.

Brent's grin was wide as he glanced at her.

Great, the song must have meaning for them.

"Remember this one?" he asked Ellie.

"How could I forget?" she asked, looking like she'd been transported back in time to when this song was the backdrop to their teenage relationship. Callum's gut twisted as he thought about the two of them together back then. Young love, first love. One that Ellie had never gotten over. And now this nostalgia was playing into the emotions she'd been holding on to for years.

And the guy was here—apparently dateless, single and available. Fantastic.

"Shall we?" Brent nodded toward the dance floor where couples were already swaying to the slow beat. "For old times' sake?"

Ellie hesitated, looking at Callum. Was she waiting for permission? He'd love to be the one leading her out onto the dance floor, but he'd never prevent her from having this moment that she'd been waiting for, for so long. This was why they were at the reunion after all.

Brent turned to him. "You don't mind me borrowing your fiancée for one dance, do you?"

He smiled as casually as possible. "Not at all," he said,

but then he turned to Ellie and impulsively grabbed her hand as she started to walk away. "But first, a quick good-bye kiss."

Her eyes widened as he pulled her toward him. "What are you doing?" she muttered.

"Making it look good," he whispered, lowering his mouth toward hers. Slowly. Giving her ample opportunity and time to push him away.

He absolutely expected her to stop him right there and then. Stop the whole charade. After all, they didn't need to continue the hoax now that Brent was there alone. She could end it now. He could leave, and Ellie and her ex could pick up where they'd left off in high school if that's what they wanted. What *she* wanted.

Instead, she closed her eyes and lifted her chin expectantly.

Holy shit.

She was going to let him kiss her. But did she want him to kiss her?

Right now, he'd settle for her consent. He pulled her to his chest and tangled his fingers into her hair, drawing her face closer. She smelled sweet like honeysuckle. She always did, and somehow that made him feel even more drawn to her. She may be dressed up that evening but inside she was the same Ellie he spent hours with arguing over books and pop culture. The same book-obsessed girl next door with the big trusting heart and hopeless romantic soul whose smile always made his day better. The same Ellie he'd been torturously in love with for almost two years.

He had one shot at this. He had to get it right. Show Ellie exactly what she was missing by not taking his advances seriously. Show her how he really felt about her. In a five-second kiss before he had to let her go dance with the love of her life.

His mouth met hers and he savored the soft, full lips pressed to his. Ones he'd fantasized about kissing so many times it almost felt familiar in that moment. Her mouth was soft, warm, delicious, and if they weren't in a room full of her high school classmates with her ex staring at them, he might not be able to stop at the intended quick peck. Her body sank toward him and her hands held his forearms as though she was trying to steady herself, as though the kiss threw her off-balance. His entire body sprang to life as he gripped her tighter and pressed his mouth harder to hers, sealing the effect of the kiss before slowly releasing her.

Her eyes were full of surprise as she opened them and stumbled away.

The kiss had hit its mark.

"Enjoy your dance," he said, feeling much better as he stood back, hands in his pockets as Brent led her onto the dance floor. When she glanced over her shoulder and her gaze returned to his, her expression said that it was a kiss that one dance with her ex-boyfriend wasn't going to make her forget so easily.

SHE WAS SPINNING, and it wasn't from Brent turning her in circles out on the dance floor. What the hell had just happened? She'd let Callum kiss her. Was she insane? This dance should have been an opportunity to tell Brent the truth. She could have claimed that Callum was kidding, that it was just an elaborate joke that had lasted three minutes too long. But then he'd kissed her, and now she couldn't say they'd been faking without having to explain the kiss and why she'd gone through with it if they weren't actually a couple.

She barely heard the music or felt Brent's hands on her waist as she still reeled from the effect of the kiss.

Mind-blowing? Absolutely. But why? It was Callum. She didn't think of him that way, so why had the kiss impacted her like this? Why had the feel of his mouth against hers turned her legs to Jell-O? She wasn't romantically attracted to him.

It had to have been just the awkward nature of the moment. Kissing her coworker in front of her ex-boyfriend. Panic and anxiety was all it was, masking as sexual tension. The body must process those emotions the same way.

But if it had been awkward, why hadn't she wanted it to end?

"Hey, you okay?" Brent asked, bending slightly at the knees to peer into her eyes.

She forced a slow, silent breath and smiled up at him. She was supposed to be enjoying this moment with him. Not driving herself crazy wondering how her sneaky coworker had somehow had an effect on her. "Yes, I'm perfect. Why?"

Brent laughed. "Because I don't think you've heard anything I've said in the last minute and a half."

Guilty. Had he been talking? "Sorry...the music..." she said lamely. "What were you saying?"

"I asked if you were still working at the bookstore."

Still at the bookstore. The last place he'd left her in the small town. "Yes."

"Whatever happened to the teaching dream?" he asked. "Did you change your mind?"

She was simultaneously thrilled that he'd remembered that was her dream and embarrassed that she hadn't fulfilled it. "No, it's still a...goal. But well, life happened I guess." She shrugged. In less than a year she'd lost her parents and him. It had been one of the most challenging, darkest times in her life.

"I'm sorry, Ellie. I think you would have made a great teacher. You certainly helped me."

She smiled, releasing the pain of the past. "Well, there was the extra incentive with that situation."

He grinned. "Yeah, maybe those study sessions wouldn't have been so much fun with a different tutor."

She swallowed hard, remembering all of those after-school meetups that had usually dissolved into make-out sessions. So many passionate kisses as rewards for getting the answers right. So many nights curled up together in the back of his secondhand beater car, holding one another like they'd never let go… Or at least *she'd* been desperate to hold on.

Callum and his kiss had almost completely vanished from her mind as the song came to an end, but Brent held her a little longer, as though sensing the emotional toil he'd put her through when he left. He stared into her eyes and sighed. "Those were some good times."

They were. Was there a chance they'd ever get moments like that again? Right now, she thought maybe he would be interested…

"I guess I should get you back to your fiancé," he said, reluctantly releasing her.

Fiancé. Right. She nodded as she stepped away, confusion and regret mixing into a strangling ball in her chest.

How the hell had she allowed Callum to convince her this could ever be anything but a disaster?

WATCHING ELLIE IN Brent's arms was too much, so Callum turned his attention to the mixed bag of cliques all around him. The cheerleaders were obvious—the loud, pretty ones—the football stars were demonstrating they still had skills in the corner of the auditorium, the geeks were huddled around some game app on one of their phones and the outcasts looked like they might actually be considering spiking the punch.

When he imagined a high school reunion, this was exactly what he pictured.

The song ended and he turned his attention back to the dance floor where Brent still had an arm around Ellie, holding her close. The two looked caught up in the moment and in each other. Damn, how could he compete with the guy she thought was the one for her? Should he even try?

Thing was, he knew Ellie. He knew she'd tried too hard to fit in with these people years ago and had only been miserable for it. She'd told him how out of place she'd felt trying to keep up with their ideas of fun and how her lack of focus and priorities in high school had cost her a scholarship to college. She'd been young then, but he knew she would put herself through it again now for another chance with a guy who didn't deserve her. Ellie didn't seem to fit in with any of them. She was unique. If only she could appreciate that.

He stared at her now as she said something to Brent. The discussion looked intense, serious…

Was she telling him the truth? Was their entire charade over? It made the most sense for her to come clean now, since the man was here alone, no supermodel clinging to his arm…they could arrange to see one another while he was in town this week. Rekindle the spark the way Ellie wanted.

They headed toward him and he held his breath, ready to go along with whatever she'd decided to do.

"There you are, safe and sound," Brent said to him as though handing back a possession. The hair on Callum's arms stood up. No doubt that was how Brent viewed his relationships.

Ellie avoided Callum's gaze as she shifted from one foot to the other. Obviously, she hadn't come clean.

Why not? Did his kiss maybe have her second-guessing? Could he allow himself that hope?

"Hey, guys, best news," Alisha said, approaching them with an armful of red Solo cups. She handed one to each of them before continuing. "Cheryl's parents have offered the cottages for next week—five days at half the usual rate. We were thinking we should all go. This catching up has been so amazing, but one night is not nearly long enough."

Or too long.

Alisha turned her attention to them. "What do you think? There's space for two more couples. Cheryl and Mitch and Nick and I would love for you to join us. You did such an amazing job organizing the event, Ellie."

Ellie looked slightly panicked.

About which part, Callum wasn't sure. Was it the idea of spending five days with her old friends or in a cottage with him? *He* liked the idea…he only wished they'd be alone, not with this group. But he waited for her to answer.

"Oh, it sounds amazing, but…we have to work," she said, finally.

"I'm sure we could take some time off," he said with a grin. It was fun to watch her squirm a little. She was usually so in control and unfazed by things. This evening she was getting a crash course in how to roll with it.

"I also have my online English students," she said apologetically to Alisha.

"That's too bad." Alisha looked genuinely disappointed as she turned to Brent. "What about you?"

"Well, I'm stag, but I'll go and be the pathetic fifth wheel drowning his sorrows," Brent said with a laugh.

Beside him, Ellie looked like she was just realizing something. "Hey, actually I'm off next week, and I could always teach my class from there as long as there's a reliable internet connection." She glanced at Alisha.

Alisha nodded. "Trust me, there's Wi-Fi or I would not be going."

Ellie smiled. "Well, then, I might actually be able to go after all." She turned to him. "You have to work though, right?" she asked pointedly, straining to sound disappointed.

He should say yes. That was what she wanted. That was what she was expecting.

Instead he shook his head. "Nope. Free as a bird."

Daggers shot like laser beams from her eyes. "But what about the bookstore?" she asked tightly. "We can't close it for five days."

"I'm sure Mrs. Grayson can handle it. She's always telling us we need to take some time off together," he said for good measure. "And April's been asking for more volunteer hours for her college application, so I think they'd be okay without us for a few days." He was in now, and he was determined to see this through. Five days of them pretending to be in love might be just the thing Ellie needed to see him in a different light, and up against Brent, he was determined to be the one that had her attention by the end of the week.

"Well, that settles it," Alisha said, excitedly. "We're all in!"

Ellie shot him a murderous look behind her forced smile. "Yeah, I guess so."

Callum knew he should be feeling guilty or at least worried for his life after they were out of view of the group, but he wasn't. Even if things didn't go his way, even if Ellie didn't fall madly in love with him, at least he'd be there in case she needed him.

She might be infatuated with her ex-boyfriend, but Callum could see right through the guy, and he didn't like what he saw.

CHAPTER SIX

A FULL WEEK away with her former classmates was stressful enough. Adding a fake fiancé that she had to first convince everyone she was in love with and then stage a breakup with all within five days was giving Ellie pangs in her chest that she was certain had to be mini heart attacks. She pressed her hand to her chest and forced several deep breaths, but they only stuck in her throat.

Getting the time off work had been surprisingly easy. Meredith had been more than accommodating when Callum had announced they were going camping together. The woman had literally lit up at the idea of the two of them together. Not that they'd told her about their elaborate scheme—she thought they were going as friends though it was clear she hoped that friendship would develop into something more. It only made Ellie feel worse to think that their boss and friend, a mother figure to them both really, thought the two of them together in a romantic way was a good idea.

Disappointing Meredith when she, hopefully, reconnected with Brent wouldn't be a great feeling.

Packing her bag, she put things in and then took them out. What the hell should she take anyway? She wasn't a big camper, and the weather forecast for Wild River was reporting warm, sunny days, but the weather was often more unpredictable three hours away, closer to the coast.

One minute it could be hot and sunny, the next overcast with thunder and lightning.

Consulting Alisha's group message on Facebook was no help. The other woman had provided the directions to the cottages and said to be prepared for a fun, adventurous week full of surprises that Cheryl had planned.

Ellie wasn't a huge fan of surprises either. Not since her parents threw her a surprise party when she was sixteen and she'd ended up in the hospital with a broken arm after falling down the stairs in fright when everyone jumped out at her screaming "Surprise!"

Nope, that word literally gave her an involuntary twitch.

And besides, Ellie was a planner. She liked to be prepared, she liked having a heads-up. Winging it never went well, as had been recently confirmed, and she needed this week to go according to plan.

It would all be so much easier if she just told everyone the truth, but she was too far into the lie now. Pretending that Callum had to bail last minute wasn't a great idea either. She didn't want the others to think she was there flirting with Brent behind her fiancé's back. How would that make her look?

And being there with Callum might make Brent jealous. Of course, Ellie wanted him to want her back because he realized he still had feelings for her after spending time with her again, but a helpful nudge from the green-eyed monster could definitely help.

She picked up her cell phone and texted Callum.

We need to be on the road by noon tomorrow.

Then she deleted the last two words and wrote eleven thirty tomorrow instead. Always give a chronically late person a time a half hour earlier than you want them there, her mom always used to say.

Her gaze fell to the picture of her parents on her bedside table now. In it, they looked so happy, so proud. She sighed. What the hell would they think if they knew what she was up to? They would disapprove of the lying and they'd never particularly liked Brent… Her stomach twisted a little.

But they'd always said they just wanted her to be happy, and she hadn't truly been happy since she was with Brent. She'd yet to find someone she wanted to spend her time with the way she'd always wanted to be with him. Back then, her parents had worried because he was a teenage jock with a reputation for being a bit of a rebel. But if they could see him now and the success he'd made of himself, they'd have to reevaluate their opinion, wouldn't they?

Unfortunately, they weren't here, so she'd never really know. She would just have to go with her gut.

"Sorry, Mom and Dad, desperate times call for desperate measures."

MISSING HIKERS IN the Chugach Mountains in summer were one of the least complicated searches, but each one held its own unique challenges and surprises. Therefore, the search and rescue crew were always prepared for anything.

Though Callum was sure no one had really prepared for this particular search. A ninety-year-old man visiting from Texas had gone missing with his forty-year-old wife. The two were reportedly on their honeymoon.

"Is it obvious to anyone else that the woman might have been *trying* to get her new husband lost?" he asked Reed as they trudged slowly through the trails along the north side of the mountain as the sun started to dip low in the sky.

Reed laughed. "I'm pretty sure that's what we're all thinking."

Even Diva looked unimpressed to be hiking in the dead summer heat to look for two people who probably shouldn't have been out there in the first place.

"Stop being so judgmental," Tiffany, one of the other crew members, said behind them. "Maybe they really are in love."

Of course Tiffany would come to the couple's defense—she was dating a woman ten years older and was completely paranoid about what others thought about that. Coming out had been hard enough for her, but then announcing the age gap had added to her stress. They'd all known she was gay, and they were thrilled she'd found someone she cared about after a string of men who'd never made her happy. "Ten years is a lot different than fifty. Name one woman you know who'd like balls shriveled up like prunes," Callum said.

She laughed. "Okay, so maybe this age gap is a little suspicious…given the circumstances."

The circumstances being that the old man was a multimillionaire with no dependents. This was his fifth marriage, and his health wasn't so great.

Callum's phone chimed with a new text from Ellie, the "Could You Be Loved" ringtone he'd assigned to her contact garnering an eyebrow raise from Reed.

He ignored it as he read her message about pickup the next day. He quickly texted back.

I'll be there, my love.

Her emoji response of an unimpressed koala bear made him laugh as he tucked the phone away.

"I noticed your week-off request from the call list," Reed said. "You going on vacation?"

"Sort of… A few of Ellie's high school friends are heading to Birchwood Cottages for five days. They invited us along."

Reed raised an eyebrow. "Your coworker Ellie? Things heating up between you two?"

He hesitated. How much did he want to share about the situation? Reed would find the whole fake fiancé thing hilarious, but he didn't want anyone judging Ellie…and he was still holding out hope that maybe their situation wouldn't be as fake by the end of the trip. "We're just going together as friends. It's a couples thing and she didn't want to go alone."

Reed eyed him. "But obviously you're hoping to change the current status?"

Man, were his feelings for Ellie that obvious? He talked about her a lot. Maybe too much. But he wasn't trying to hide it. He did like her. "That would be the goal, yes." A goal he really hoped he could achieve.

CHAPTER SEVEN

IF SHE SURVIVED the week, it would be a miracle.

Ellie's juvenile asthma returned as she waited on her front step for Callum, her overnight bag in hand. She reached for her emergency inhaler, which she hadn't had to rely on in years. Fantastic timing for the ailment to reappear. She was sweating in the muggy humidity of the overcast day, and her heart raced as her mind overthought absolutely every little detail of the upcoming camping trip.

How were they supposed to fake a relationship all week while she was trying to get to know Brent again?

She'd been awake all night thinking about it, and the only thing she could come up with was that they'd have to stage a believable breakup at the end of the week if she and Brent were reconnecting, if there was any sign from him that he might still be in love with her and want to get back together. The way he'd looked at her at the reunion and the way he seemed disappointed to hear of her sudden engagement had her hoping...

"Come on, Callum." Ellie checked her watch. What a surprise, he was late. Everyone else was driving up together in Nick's six-seater SUV, and there would have been space for her, as well, if Callum wasn't tagging along. The extra man made it necessary for them to drive up on their own together.

Alone for the three-and-a-half-hour drive up the mountains. She'd be a huge ball of anxiety by the time they got there.

Seeing Callum's silver SUV turn the corner of her street, she lugged her heavy bag down the steps to meet him on the sidewalk as he parked and got out.

"Good morning," he said, looking relaxed and confident. No sign of the anxiety she was struggling with.

But why should there be? He was getting a fun week away. It was just *her* future happiness on the line.

"You're late."

"I would have been here faster if my phone wasn't blowing up with text messages from you asking me where I was every two minutes," he said, opening the trunk and taking her bag from her.

"I wouldn't have to text if you could be on time," she said as he opened the passenger door.

He grinned. "Look at us...our first lovers' quarrel."

She glared at him as she got into the car. "Not funny. Get in, we need a game plan."

He laughed as he closed the passenger door and walked around the front to climb back behind the wheel. He was in shorts and a T-shirt that day, and the way the sleeves of the shirt seemed to be struggling to accommodate his tanned, toned arms had her mind flashing back to the way she'd gripped them to balance herself when he'd kissed her at the reunion.

Her mouth went dry, and she looked away quickly.

She needed to focus and not get caught in that weird spiral of trying to figure out why that kiss had affected her again. She'd wasted far too many brain cells on it already.

"Ready?" he asked as he closed the door.

"As ready as I could ever be," she said. And as soon as he pulled away from the curb, she launched into her strategy.

"Okay, here's how we're going to do this. Today when we arrive, we act friendly to one another, but not over-the-top in love." She gave him a pointed look. "Meaning no more of those impulsive kisses."

"You think your friends will believe we're engaged if we don't kiss at all?"

It would be odd, but she couldn't risk another one. "Yes. It will be a sign of our 'rocky' relationship."

"My mother kissed my dad every morning before he went to work, even on the day she left his ass," Callum said.

Ellie's eyes widened at the rare mention of his mother. He talked about his dad a lot, but in all the time they'd been coworkers and friends, he'd only mentioned his mom a few times. She knew the woman was living in Colorado, but that was the extent of her knowledge. Until now, that apparently she'd kissed her husband goodbye every morning even when she'd fallen out of love.

"Anyway, go ahead…what were you saying?" Callum said, realizing he'd shared something personal.

What *was* she saying? Right, the gradual downward spiral of their relationship up to the believable breakup. "Tomorrow, we start to act like we're fighting, like maybe we've had a huge argument and are trying to hide it. Then you start acting jealous, controlling whenever I spend time talking to Brent…"

"Jealous I can handle but controlling—nope."

Ellie sighed. "Fine, just be believably jealous. Then we will have a big argument in front of everyone, you'll leave early and I'll tell everyone the engagement is off. And if everything goes to plan, I'll have two full days with Brent and head back into town with everyone else." Giving them an extra three hours in a car together to reminisce and reconnect. It wasn't the ideal situation, but it could work. It had to.

Callum sighed as he took the exit for the highway. "Okay, if that's what you want."

Ellie studied him. "Of course that's what I want." Why else would she be putting so much at risk? If this didn't work out, not only would she have lost her one shot with Brent, but she'd be a laughingstock in town. Everyone would think she was crazy and desperate. Callum would, of course, be let off the hook, seen as just the collateral damage in her insane ploy to get her ex-boyfriend back.

He shrugged one shoulder. "This dramatic, elaborate scheme just isn't really your style, that's all."

Was he serious right now? "You're right. It's not my style. I wouldn't be doing this at all, but *you* got us into this mess." Maybe the pretending to bicker part wouldn't be so difficult. All she had to do was remember that Callum had complicated the hell out of everything.

"Um, I'm pretty sure you had an opportunity to tell Brent the truth once you discovered he was at the reunion alone, and you didn't."

"You interrupted us before I had a chance."

"What about while you were dancing? That conversation looked pretty intimate," he said, a tinge of jealousy in his voice.

She stared at her hands as she shrugged. "We were too far in after that kiss," she mumbled. "But you could have bailed on this trip, and then I could have told them we'd broken up. It's not too late."

He shot her a look. "Okay, and how will you get there?"

Shit. Everyone else had left already and she didn't own a car. First time in her life she was regretting that choice. She sat back in the seat and sighed.

"What's so great about this guy, anyway?" Callum asked as a light rain started to fall. He turned on the windshield wipers and glanced her way. "I gotta say, I'm not impressed so far."

"You don't need to be impressed. I'm the one who wants to relight the spark between us." Callum's opinion of Brent didn't matter in the least. Still, it made her slightly uneasy that he disapproved after the first impression.

"Come on, humor me. What do you like about him?" he asked.

Ellie sighed. "He's smart, successful, good-looking and funny."

Callum shook his head. "Frat humor funny is not your thing. You find it immature and off-putting."

She refused to admit he was right. Brent's humor around the old gang consisted mainly of off-color jokes that did irritate her somewhat, but... "He doesn't act like that when we're alone."

"Okay, fine. What else?"

"What do you mean, what else? He's the total package. Any woman would be attracted to him."

"I mean specifics. A lot of men are smart, successful, good-looking and funny. Present company, prime example," he said, winking at her. "What's special about him? What does he do that gets you going? What makes him different, unique—the one?"

Ellie frowned. "Oh okay... Well, um..." She thought hard. There were so many things she liked about Brent, reasons he was the right person for her... Just nothing specific was immediately coming to mind. Callum had put her on the spot, that was all.

"It's not a trick question, Ellie," he said as though her delay was perfectly illustrating his point.

She snapped her fingers. "His hugs. They were always so great."

"My grandmother used to give great hugs too. What's different about his?"

"He'd let me hold him as long as I wanted." She shrugged. "It made me feel safe, I guess." Most of the guys in high school were only out for one thing once the relationship turned physical, but not Brent.

Callum scoffed.

"What?"

"Dude was trying to feel your breasts squeezed up against his body."

"He was not!"

"Oh right, I forgot, you have experience being a seventeen-year-old boy," he said sarcastically.

Ellie rolled her eyes. "Not all seventeen-year-old boys are hormonal pigs."

"They absolutely are," Callum said as the rain fell harder and he turned the wipers on full to clear the windshield.

"Agree to disagree," she said, leaning forward to scan the darkening sky. She loved storms. Too bad they weren't already at the lodge. Under different circumstances, she envisioned how romantic this could be. Curled up by the lodge fireplace with a good book and a glass of wine. Brent on one end of the sofa, her on the other, reading together, just being together...

Callum glanced at her. "You really love this weather, huh?"

"I really do." Living in Alaska provided the best of all seasons—the beautiful colors of fall, the snow-covered mountains in winter, mild springs when the flowers bloomed and hot, sunny days in summer—but her favorite was always the storms.

Thunder rumbled in the distance, followed by a large lightning bolt shooting across the sky to the right. "Wow, did you see that?" Callum asked, taking his eyes briefly off of the road.

"Amazing," Ellie said.

Their eyes met and held for a fraction of a second before something flashed on the side of the road and they both swung their attention forward.

The Kodiak bear seemed to appear out of nowhere in the middle of the road. Its dark brown fur and massive three-hundred-pound body blocked the vehicle, and its eyes were wide and menacing as it turned to stare at them. Unyielding. Terrifying.

Callum turned the wheel to prevent hitting the bear just in time, and the car jerked violently to one side. Ellie's shoulder slammed into the passenger door and an ache radiated down her arm. The vehicle spiraled on the slippery wet road, and Ellie shut her eyes tight and held on to the seat as Callum struggled to regain control. Her stomach plunged as though she was on a dizzying amusement ride, and the spinning seemed to last forever. She heard the loud pop of the tire blowing, and then the car came to a stop facing the opposite direction, safe on the shoulder of the road.

Thank God there hadn't been oncoming traffic.

"You okay?" Callum asked, reaching across to touch her white-knuckle grip on the fabric of the passenger seat.

Ellie slowly opened her eyes, slightly dazed, and looked outside. "Where did it go?"

"Ran off back into the woods. Uninjured," he said, releasing a slow, deep breath as though he'd been holding it.

"Wow, I've never seen one that close before." Her heart still raced and her hands shook slightly. She peered out the window, looking for the bear. She'd heard stories about how powerful and fearless the creatures were. Being stuck on the side of the road with one in the middle of a thunder and lightning storm wasn't exactly what she'd been hoping to do that day. The sky looked dark and menacing now, and the weather suddenly lost its appeal.

Callum touched her shoulder and she jumped. "Sorry," he said with a small laugh. "Don't worry, it's gone." He unbuckled his seat belt. "Unfortunately, we blew out a tire."

Ellie sighed. "Guess we'd better get started changing it." They'd be soaked to the bone, but he was only doing this trip because of her, so she felt compelled to help and not just sit in the car while he went out in the storm. Damsel in distress wasn't really her thing.

Callum looked slightly sheepish. "That actually was the spare."

Ellie looked at him in disbelief. "You've been driving on the spare? For how long?"

"A few months..."

"A few months?"

"Okay, more like a year."

"Callum!" Man, the guy seriously hadn't a care in the world. If it had been her car, she would have had the tire replaced the same day. But Callum seemed to like living without a safety net...or maybe his privileged upbringing was the net he thought would always catch him. Not today.

"What?" he asked innocently, like this was something that couldn't have been prevented. "It hasn't had a lot of wear—I don't drive much in Wild River unless the weather's horrible."

Ellie sighed as she pulled out her cell phone and opened a search for a local garage. "I'll call a tow truck."

As the call connected, she peered out the window at the ominous clouds overhead.

Please don't let us be stuck out here for too long.

ELLIE MIGHT BE annoyed at the predicted two-hour wait for the tow truck, but Callum was seeing it as a stroke of luck. More time alone with her before they joined the rest of the group at the cottages. So far that drive, they'd been focused on Brent. And unfortunately, their joint enjoyment of the stormy weather had been cut short by the crazy-ass bear that had nearly forced them off the road.

But they were stuck here now and the sound of the rain beating against the roof of the car was definitely a romantic sound. One he knew she loved. If he could get her to stop pouting and ignoring him, this unexpected dcrailment might be a blessing in disguise.

He cleared his throat to say something, but his phone ringing through the Bluetooth connection in the vehicle had him immediately reaching for the ignore call button on the dash, his father's ringtone—the Darth Vader soundtrack from *Star Wars*—interrupting his attempt at conversation.

Ellie shot him a look. "Your dad's not that bad."

"There's quite a resemblance." His mood quickly spiraled at the intrusion. His father and his family situation and the pressure he was under to make a decision was the last thing he wanted to think about this week.

"You can answer it."

He could. He just didn't want to. He shook his head. "It's not important. I know what he wants. It's always the same thing."

Ellie eyed him. "Why don't you want to go into the family business? You'd be good at it."

His jaw tightened. Just because a person could be suited

to a particular career didn't mean they should feel obligated to pursue it. Unfortunately, his family didn't share that perspective. Doing something for the love of it or out of passion was a foreign concept to his father. He knew Ellie would get it. "Thanks but it's really not my thing."

"Have we established what your *thing* actually is?"

Coming from anyone else, he'd find the question irritating, but Ellie could call him out on just about anything and he'd be okay with it. Explaining himself and his choices to her was something he was willing to do. "Can't it be as simple as working in the bookstore? That's your thing, right?"

She shook her head. "No. I mean, not really. I wanted to be a teacher, but life got in the way. I'm making the best of plan B."

"Well, maybe the bookstore is my plan A."

She turned in the seat to face him, her annoyance over their delay gone as she asked, "What about this mysterious writing talent Mrs. Garnett mentioned at the reunion…is that your thing?"

If there was ever anyone he'd confess to, it would be Ellie, and right now he felt the need to maybe try to show her that he wasn't completely without motivation. That he did have a passion for something. That he did have goals for himself and his future. He took a deep breath. "It's probably the closest thing to my thing, yeah."

Curiosity filled her expression. "So you do write?"

"I dabble in writing." Lately it was more staring at a blank page. The pressure his father had put on him to make a decision soon had completely messed with his creativity, and he'd struggled with the words all week.

"What kinds of things?" she asked.

Was he ready to fully confess? "Creative nonfiction and prose mostly."

She looked at him in shock. "You want to be an author?" Unlike any other person who could have found out, Ellie's reaction to the news was the one anyone hopeful of anything wanted to receive. Intrigue, respect, interest shone on her features for the first time ever when she stared at him now. He'd suspected his secret passion could be something to bring them closer, give them something to potentially bond over, but he'd feared that bond would be friend based, and he'd wanted her to be attracted to him on other levels first.

But his secret was out now. And it did feel good to tell someone. To tell Ellie.

He stared at the rain pouring down the windshield and the thick, dark clouds in the afternoon sky. "I know it's a long shot, but it's really the only thing I would be able to see myself being happy doing." The confession felt like a weight lifted from his shoulders.

"Have you actually written a book?" Ellie asked, kicking off her shoes and tucking her leg under her on the seat.

"Still working on it. Before, it was just short stories. A full book is proving much more challenging."

"What is it about?"

This was the hardest part. Telling Ellie that he was essentially journaling his upbringing. "Um…it's mainly about my family—what it was like to grow up with my father, a narcissistic overachiever with impossible standards for us to live up to…" He paused. "And the effects that had on Sean and our entire family unit." It sounded so lame to him saying it out loud. Everyone had family issues. Why did he think his were special? Or worthy to write about? "It's more therapeutic than anything else," he added quickly.

She looked at him in awe. "That's so incredible. Why haven't you told me this before?" Her tone edged on scolding.

He shrugged. "I haven't told anyone. Until now."

Their gazes met and held for a long moment. Her expression changed from one of casual interest to understanding what this moment meant to him. She was his confidante, the person he trusted with this secret. He longed to tell her the other secrets he'd been keeping to himself. What would she say if he told her right now that he was in love with her? Could he take that chance amidst this craziness they found themselves in? Would she consider giving him a chance or would it only make things even more awkward and complicated between them that week? His heart pounded in his chest as he stared in the light blue eyes he could stare into forever, and his mouth felt dry.

But before he could decide, she cleared her throat and grinned. "So, when do I get to read something?"

How'd he know that question was coming?

"Why don't we survive this week and then we'll see," he said with a wink, the idea of showing Ellie his work making him far more nervous than pretending to pretend to be in love with her for five days.

CHAPTER EIGHT

ARRIVING AT THE cottages long after everyone else, Ellie was desperate to shower and head to the main lodge where everyone was gathered for drinks. They'd wasted far too much time already stranded on the side of the road. Although, it hadn't exactly been horrible.

After all, she'd discovered Callum's secret.

He really was a writer. It wasn't just something he'd done in high school. She actually shouldn't be so surprised. He was a man in his midtwenties from a very wealthy family, and he could be an underwear model, but he was working in a small town bookstore. Obviously his love of literature extended beyond just reading and stocking shelves with old classics.

As he pulled his SUV into the gravel parking space in front of cottage number four, she unbuckled her seat belt and opened the door before he could even cut the engine. "In a hurry?" he asked, meeting her at the back of the vehicle.

"Yes. We're so late. Which may be on brand for you, but I like being on time," she said, dancing anxiously back and forth. He opened the trunk of the car and she reached for her bag.

He brushed her hand away and grabbed both of their bags and laptop cases, then slammed the trunk.

"Be careful, I have books in there," she said.

"Of course you do," he said with a chuckle. "Hope you also remembered to pack clothes."

She ignored the teasing as she followed him up the trail toward the door, her neck straining to see the lodge behind it. The lights were on, and she could hear voices and laughter.

Damn, they'd started without them.

Was Brent in there? She squinted hard to try to see in through the windows.

Her body lurched forward as her foot snagged in a tree root extended across the stone steps, and Callum's arm reached out to prevent her face-plant just in time.

Heart racing from the near fall, she gulped as he steadied her. "Watch yourself," he said, his voice slightly husky. His eyes held a slight intensity as they burned into hers, and that same uneasiness she'd felt after his kiss at the reunion enveloped her.

It was nothing. This whole situation had her on edge, that was all. And she'd nearly taken a spill.

Ellie removed his arm from around her waist. "*You* watch yourself," she said, hiding her embarrassment over her clumsiness and attempting to douse the slight spark simmering between them.

Callum grinned as he shrugged and picked up their bags off the ground. "No problem, next time I'll let you fall."

Ellie sighed with relief as the universe seemed to right itself again with his sarcasm. She moved past him to unlock the cottage door with the key the host had given them at the check-in desk, and pushing the door open, her eyes widened in surprise.

When Birchwood Cottages claimed to be "high-end" and "luxurious," they weren't kidding. From the outside, they looked small and cute, but inside, with the vaulted ceilings and exposed wood beams, the floor-to-ceiling windows allowing the dusk sunlight to shine through and providing a beautiful view of the nature surrounding them, the place looked much bigger. The hardwood floor with a large fake-bearskin rug in front of the small wood-burning fireplace and soft ivory curtains and furniture filled the space. Against the dark stained wood, the contrast was clean and elegant. Not at all "rustic cabin in the woods."

But the thing that drew her attention was the queen-size bed in the center of the room...covered in rose petals, a bottle of champagne and a basket of assorted chocolates, with a note that read, "Welcome to the romance cottage."

She groaned inwardly. Alisha had obviously told the lodge hosts that they were engaged. This lie was getting out of hand already...though the chocolate definitely wouldn't go to waste.

"Wow. That's...cozy," Callum said, coming up behind her. He picked up the bottle of champagne and read the label. "This is good stuff. The Wild River Resort bars don't even stock this particular brand."

"Yeah, too bad it's wasted on us." Maybe after their staged breakup she could share this chocolate and champagne with...

Pop!

The champagne cork hit the wall behind her head, making her jump, and liquid spilled over the side of the bottle.

Guess they were drinking it now.

"Want a glass?" Callum asked, reaching for a champagne flute from the basket and pouring some.

Ellie sighed. "May as well since it's open." She glanced around the room, biting her lower lip as she accepted the glass of expensive bubbly from him. "These sleeping arrangements might be tricky." She wasn't planning on sleep-

ing with him. She'd hoped they'd get a cabin with two
double beds instead. If the bed was bigger and they could
build a wall of pillows between them, maybe...but that
wouldn't be possible in this one.

"Don't worry, I'll sleep on the chaise lounge," Callum
said, nodding toward it in the corner of the room. It was
barely five feet long and definitely not wide enough to accommodate his body comfortably, but Ellie wasn't sure
what else to suggest. The Jacuzzi tub, maybe?

She nodded as she checked her watch. "Okay, I'm going
to shower quickly so we can join the others."

"Yep," Callum said, taking a big gulp of champagne
and then brushing all the rose petals off the bed and col-
lapsing onto it. "I'll nap because I doubt I'll be getting any
real sleep on that thing."

Ellie carried her champagne into the bathroom and
closed the door. The small but modern room had a two-
person Jacuzzi, a shower stall, self-flushing toilet with a
control panel on the wall and double sinks. Yep, they definitely were not roughing it this week.

She surveyed the selection of bath soaps, shampoo and
conditioner in the basket on the counter and picked out what
she needed. Another bottle caught her eye.

Sensual massage lotion.

They would definitely *not* be needing that. Taking it,
she hid it in the small drawer that held the hair dryer. She
didn't want Callum getting any crazy ideas.

DRIFTING OFF, IN A STATE of not quite awake and not quite
asleep, Callum heard the water turn on in the bathroom.

Just a door away, Ellie was getting undressed...

The bed was amazingly comfortable with the soft, down-
filled comforter. His head felt heavy against the silk pillow-

case, and the sound of Ellie humming off tune seemed to drift farther away. Then he was spinning.

Or at least the car was. The bear. The rain. The spiraling into the other lane and then coming to a stop at the side of the road. The entire moment out on the highway flashed in his dreamlike state.

He quit fighting the slumber and allowed the dream to sweep him away.

Ellie's eyes were closed. Her hands gripped the fabric of the passenger seat. Her chest was rising and falling in a quick, slightly frantic pace. He could hear her heart beat in time with the patter of rain on the roof. He touched her hand gently and her eyes flew open.

But instead of fear, there was only attraction in those deep, gorgeous eyes. Lust that called to him and couldn't be denied.

He dropped the driver's seat back and reached for her. Picking her up, he pulled her into his lap. She didn't resist as she straddled his body and her hands roamed his chest. He gripped her face between his hands and kissed her hard, feeling his body stiffen with the pressure of her body tight against his. Her tongue separated his lips and met his hungrily, desperately, as though she'd been waiting for this moment too.

His fingers tangled in her soft hair as he deepened the kiss, unable to fully satisfy his craving for her. She tasted like champagne and honeysuckle lip gloss—an intoxicating combination.

Her hands were unbuckling his jeans, and he raised his hips to allow her to pull the fabric down. She freed his erect cock, and he groaned as her hand wrapped around him. Her gaze met his as she stroked slow and hard, torturing him with the pleasurable sensation.

He needed her. He needed to be inside of her.

"Ellie..." It was more of a whispered groan escaping his lips.

She simply nodded.

He undid her pants and she shimmied out of them and lowered herself down over him, her wet, tight body taking the length of him deep and slow. Her hands slid beneath his T-shirt and her nails dug into his chest, dragging the length of his body.

She rode him up and down as she kissed him. He could barely breathe as his orgasm quickly rose and her mouth was relentless against his. Her eagerness and passion had him toppling over the edge in no time at all. He gripped her ass, digging his fingers into her flesh as she pressed her pelvis toward him, as she slowly rode him up and down, clenching her muscles around his cock as she came.

Her body collapsed against his and their breathing was in perfect synchronicity as he held her close, never wanting to let go.

The rain on the rooftop of the car sounded real.

"Callum!"

He moaned, fighting to hold on to the moment that was fading behind his closed lids.

"Callum, wake up." Ellie stood over him as he opened his eyes, and for a brief second he thought maybe it had all been real. Her face hovered above him, framed in an almost angelic glow—a stark contrast to what she'd been doing in his dream.

"I'm ready. Get up," she said.

Yep, definitely just a dream. "Just let me shower quickly," he said, jumping up off the bed and heading toward the bathroom that still smelled like her perfume and shampoo, still slightly steamed from her shower.

"Oh my God, are you serious? You're fine."

"Come closer and tell me that," he said. Six hours in the car in this muggy, wet, humid weather and the sweat pooling on his back now from the sensual dream he'd just had definitely had him smelling slightly rank.

Ellie wrinkled her nose and nodded. "Okay, but hurry," she said in annoyance as he closed the bathroom door.

He turned on the water and stepped inside the streaming spray. He closed his eyes and rested his head against the cool shower stall wall. His body was still reacting to the dream—his semi-hard-on wasn't going to be easy to get rid of.

Damn, somehow he had to make these erotic dreams a reality. And soon.

"CALLUM, COME ON!" Ellie paced in the room twenty minutes later. How long did the guy take to shower? She'd been in and out in fifteen minutes and she'd had to wash her hair and shave her legs. What the hell was he doing in there?

Alisha had texted to ask where they were and Ellie's FOMO was reaching an unhealthy level.

She banged on the door. "Callum!"

The water shut off. "I'll be five minutes," he called through the bathroom door.

"Why don't I meet you up there?"

The bathroom door swung open, and Ellie's mouth gaped as Callum exited, a far-too-tiny towel wrapped around his waist. The stomach and chest muscles were even more impressive than she'd ever imagined. Not that she imagined her coworker naked at all, but she had wondered what he looked like from time to time, especially when he wore his old, thin, almost threadbare fanfic T-shirts. She was only human after all. The biceps and forearms were muscles on top of muscles, and apparently it was the same throughout his entire body.

How did one get those shoulder and neck muscles? Were there specific exercises for that?

Callum's expression was full-on amusement when her gaze finally got around to his face.

She flushed and looked away. "Why is your towel so small?"

"There was only one big one and you used it," he said, walking across the room toward his bag.

Ellie desperately wanted to avert her gaze from the shape of his ass in the towel, but her eyes didn't seem to give a shit about what was best for her, as they were on their own viewing-pleasure mission.

"Well, please hurry," she said, checking her watch. She was desperate to join the others but even more desperate to get out of this romantic cottage—which seemed a lot smaller all of a sudden—and not be alone with her sexy-as-hell coworker.

He'd always been sexy. Why was it only now having an unsettling effect on her? Must be the stress combined with the champagne she'd consumed while he was taking the longest shower in history.

"Okay." He dropped the towel, and her eyes widened even further as he stepped into fresh underwear and turned to face her as he pulled them up over his ass. He looked like an underwear model from her teenage magazines. His bulging thigh muscles looked as if they'd been chiseled out of marble, like the statue of a Greek god. How often did the guy work out? "Enjoying the view?" he asked.

She turned away quickly. "I should give you some privacy."

"Kinda late now, don't you think?" he asked, reaching for his shirt.

Ellie headed for the door. "I'll just wait outside," she said with another quick glance at him as he pulled the tight shirt over his head and struggled to pull it down over the contours of his abs.

Damn, her coworker was hot as hell.

Outside the cottage, she sucked in a huge breath of cooling night air. Overheated, she appreciated the slight breeze that blew her hair into her face. She'd always known Callum was attractive, but in the context of working together, it was easy to brush it aside. She'd thought of him as a coworker and friend for so long that thinking about him in a sexual manner hadn't really entered her mind.

This week would be different. Close quarters. Sharing personal space.

Shit, how had she not really thought about what this meant before now? She'd been too preoccupied thinking about Brent and winning him back to focus much on the logistics side of spending time with Callum.

He'd see her in her pajamas and with her overnight face cream on...discover her secret night guard... Maybe she'd skip her usual routine for a few nights.

And he'd see her first thing in the morning with her crazy messy pillow hair and bad breath.

Clearly, she hadn't thought this whole thing through.

"Okay, I'm ready," he said, joining her on the step.

She swung to face him. "Do you think this is really necessary? Maybe you should go now and I'll tell everyone you had to head back...for an emergency."

"A bookstore emergency?" he asked with a smirk.

She sighed. "Okay, fine. But I'm not sure how long I can keep this up."

He ran a hand through his still-wet hair, slicking it back away from his face. "Pretending to be attracted to me? Shouldn't be hard based on the way you were drooling over the sight of my body five minutes ago."

"I was not drooling."

He teasingly ran a finger below her bottom lip and winked at her. "You sure about that?"

Okay, maybe now she was drooling.

The gesture had stopped her heart, and she was quite literally frozen on the spot.

"Let's go. You're making us late," he said with a grin to her openmouthed expression, grabbing her hand and leading the way to the lodge.

CHAPTER NINE

IT WASN'T HARD to see why these cottages normally cost over four hundred dollars a night. If Callum had thought their individual cottage was impressive, the lodge and shared areas of the campgrounds were even more so. The outside space had tennis courts, a basketball court, an infinity pool and two large hot tubs with breathtaking views of the surrounding mountains. Nestled in the valley, with wildlife and trails all around them, it was an outdoor enthusiast's dream vacation.

Over four thousand square feet, the log cabin–style main lodge contained a restaurant and kitchen for meals, an expansive dining room, a games room, a library—which he was certain Ellie had been tempted to visit—a small lounge with a bar and piano, and a great room with a double-sided fireplace where the rest of their group were waiting for them.

"Ah, there are the lovebirds now," Alisha said as they entered. Dressed in a pair of jean cutoffs, a plaid button-up shirt knotted at her waist and hiking boots, she had this camping fashion thing figured out.

Beside Callum, Ellie glanced at her sundress. He suspected this is what always happened around this group—she was constantly second-guessing and reevaluating herself. He wished she didn't feel the need to compare herself to the others. Maybe by the end of the week, he could show her how they didn't even compare to her.

Callum grinned and tightened his grip on her hand when she instinctively tried to pull away. He sent her a look that said, *That's what we're trying to make them think, remember?*

She forced a smile as she addressed the group. "Sorry we're so late. Car troubles."

Nick winked over a glass of Scotch. "Car troubles. Sure. We'll buy that."

Ellie blushed, and it took all of Callum's strength not to allow everyone to think that car troubles was a euphemism and they were late because they'd been busy having wild sex all afternoon, having to pull to the side of the highway multiple times because they just couldn't keep their hands off of one another.

Instead, he came to her rescue. "Actually," he added for good measure and because it was true, "we did have a slight accident on the way here."

"Oh no... Well, you guys are okay, obviously, that's a relief. What happened?" Alisha asked.

"A bear," he said.

"A Kodiak ran right out into the road. Callum swerved and luckily missed him, but we blew out a tire."

"Didn't know how to change it?" Brent joined the group from the other room, looking like a puffed-up version of himself.

Callum's spine stiffened as he saw the flush of color the other man's appearance brought to Ellie's cheeks. Not so unlike the flush of color she'd had seeing him in a tiny towel. Unfortunately, he knew she'd blame the latter on embarrassment over the awkward situation.

"Someone was driving on the spare already," Ellie said chastisingly.

A slight irritation crept up the back of his neck. He didn't like it when couples berated one another in front of their friends. His father used to do it to his mother all the time at family events and parties, and it definitely had helped to chip away at their marriage. And sure, he and Ellie weren't actually a couple, and sure, they were supposed to start acting like there was trouble in paradise, but it still didn't feel right to him. And Ellie wasn't the type to make someone else feel less than, so he knew this was all for show.

"Guilty," he said, but then turned to her. He wasn't ready to move on to part two of their plan just yet. He brought her hand to his lips and stared into her eyes as he said, "But it was actually nice. Sitting there together, listening to the rain on the roof of the car. Just the two of us."

Ellie's look was a mix of annoyance and a hint of confusion, as though sensing there was truth in his words and not quite sure what to do about it.

"Awww..." Alisha said, tipping her head to the side. Then she slapped Nick playfully. "Why don't you say nice things like that?"

"'Cause I'm a dude," Nick mumbled.

Ellie forced a laugh and tugged her hand away. "Anyway, we made it." She crossed the room and sat in a chair near Brent.

There were no more available seats, except one across the room from her—too far away—so Callum sat on the floor at her feet.

"Yes, and you guys are just in time," Cheryl said.

"For what?"

"We were just about to play some board games."

Alisha turned to the game shelf in the lodge. She grabbed the Couples Trivia box. "Let's play this one. It will be fun."

Cheryl nodded. "I love this game."

"Sounds like a great way to end up in the doghouse to me," her husband, Mitch, said. "Amirite?" he asked Callum.

Callum nodded his good-natured agreement, but he reached for Ellie's ankles and wrapped her feet around his body, gently massaging her arches. He felt her stiffen slightly at first, then relax her feet.

No lady could resist his massages. Magic hands, he'd been told on more than one occasion. The night of their staff party, he'd massaged Ellie's feet in a corner booth at The Drunk Tank after hours of dancing. She hadn't complained that night either.

"You're in the doghouse because you don't rub my feet like that anymore," Cheryl told her husband.

Nick shot him a look. "Seriously, man, stop making us look bad."

If the other men appeared lacking because Callum knew how to take care of a woman and treat her the way she should be treated, that was on them.

"Okay, so couples partner up. And, Brent, I guess you can be the host since you're on your own?" Alisha asked him as she opened the game box and took out the whiteboards where they'd each write their answers. She handed them out, and Ellie removed her feet from his lap and tucked her legs under her on the chair.

He knew Ellie would rather be playing this game with Brent… She'd claim they knew each other so well, and maybe they had. But he knew her well too—the Ellie she was now. This game might give him a chance to prove just how much he did know about her, how much he paid attention when she spoke and how much he cared.

She may have a game plan for the week, but he also had one of his own.

AS THE GAME STARTED, Ellie took a moment to check out Brent. Wearing khaki shorts and a light blue polo shirt, his slightly longer hair combed to one side and his face free of any scruff along his jawline, he looked just like the preppy, popular jock she'd fallen in love with years before. He'd barely aged at all. Except for a few lines around the corners of his eyes, he was the mirror image of his high school self. He was still incredibly hot. Hot enough to erase the image of Callum's partially naked body from her mind.

That was it. She just needed to focus on Brent. Callum's body and the kiss that had replayed in her mind since the reunion would vanish from her thoughts the more attention and time she spent with her former flame.

And as long as Callum quit doing all of this extra-attention stuff like massaging her feet. Because damn, that had felt good. Too good.

Maybe once all of this was over, they could be better friends. Ones who exchanged midday break room foot massages?

She watched as Brent got up and approached Alisha, taking the game cards from her. His sandy hair fell into his eyes, and she remembered how she loved when he'd look at her through that messy hair and how she'd brush it away from his face right before she'd kiss him.

Yep, Callum who?

"Okay, rules of the game," Brent said. "If you get an answer right, we go to the next question, presented to the partner who didn't answer the first one. Game play moves on once we hit a mismatch."

Everyone nodded their agreement.

"Who's up first? Alisha and Nick?" he asked the group as he wrote their names on the large whiteboard behind him.

Ellie stared at the board. It should be their names up there—Ellie and Brent—instead of hers and Callum's. Brent had spelled Calum with one *l*.

On purpose maybe? She didn't want to get her hopes up, but there'd definitely been jealousy in his gaze the night of the reunion when Callum had lied and said they were engaged. And when Callum had grabbed her for a kiss…

If Callum noticed, he didn't say anything.

Alisha sat on Nick's lap and nodded. "We're ready."

Brent took the first question from the box. "Okay, ladies first. Alisha, what is Nick's alcoholic drink of choice?" He flipped the sand timer on the table.

Alisha and Nick scribbled their answers on the white-boards.

That would have been an easy one. Callum hated any-thing fruity or sweet. Tequila was his favorite. Straight, on the rocks. Expensive brands. He'd spouted the health benefits of the alcoholic drink numerous times. Why couldn't she have gotten that question? Definitely something a couple should easily know about one another.

Brent looked at the timer as the sand ran out. "Reveal."

He was really good as the host. Then again, he'd always been comfortable in front of a crowd or in the spotlight. A sporty kid who wasn't afraid of exploring other interests, he'd been active in the drama club for two years, and his part as the lead in the senior play had been Oscar-worthy in her opinion. Of course she'd gone to see the young-adult romance/drama every night in the high school auditorium. Watching him kiss the female lead had been difficult, but it had been art…

"Martini on the rocks," Alisha said confidently, turn-ing her board around.

Nick frowned. "Since when?"

"Since always. It's what you always order when…" Alisha's voice trailed off as her eyes widened.

"You mean that's what Arron used to order," Nick said, a slightly annoyed but mostly amused grin on his face as he turned his own whiteboard around. "Gin and tonic is the correct answer, Pat."

Everyone laughed as Alisha snuggled into him. "Sorry, honey, you know I knew that."

New relationship. They were still getting to know one another…but six months seemed like a pretty good length of time to know a lot of things. Ellie's favorite part about relationships was just that—the long into-the-night conversations learning about one another, getting closer and sharing secrets… Knowing the little things about one another that no one else noticed, which meant you were paying attention, that you were truly invested.

It was the true intimacy part of being with someone that she was really missing right now. She could date around, but she wouldn't feel fulfilled. She was ready for a real relationship again…and there had only been one man who'd ever made the effort seem worth it.

The one turning his attention to them now. "You two ready?"

She nodded and Callum moved closer.

"We will start with the lady. Ellie, who is Callum's favorite author?"

"Not fair—they got an easy one. They work in a bookstore together," Nick said.

"Luck of the draw," Brent said with a shrug, flipping their timer.

It *was* an easy one. Ellie scribbled her answer on the whiteboard and a second later they revealed the same answer—Ernest Hemingway—to be the first team on the board.

"You pay attention," Callum said.

"Nick's right, we were basically given that one," she said.

"Okay, so we stay with you guys for the next one." Brent read the card and grinned. "Finally, an interesting one. Callum, what is Ellie's bra size?"

Her cheeks flushed, and she frowned seeing Callum immediately writing on his board. He knew that answer? He looked fairly confident as he sat there waiting for her to write on her own board.

Well, she wanted to think of herself as a good sport, but she wasn't revealing that detail to the group. She'd always been smaller than the other girls and it hadn't really bothered her, but this wasn't the moment she wanted to reveal her embarrassing "trapped between an A-cup and B-cup" dilemma that always made bra shopping a total nightmare. Especially when Brent's Instagram consisted of double D's.

Their team would lose this one. Fine with her. She scribbled her answer quickly before the timer ran out.

"Reveal," Brent said with a quick grin at her that said he knew this answer.

Her tongue felt swollen in her mouth as they turned the boards around, and then her mouth dropped open seeing Callum's response. Exactly what she'd written on her own board. "PASS."

The group laughed.

"That shouldn't count," Nick said.

"Yeah, they didn't answer the question," Cheryl said.

Brent shrugged as he picked up the game rule sheet. "Says here, the couple needs to have the same thing written on their whiteboards. They do. That is another point and back to Ellie for the next question."

She wiped her board clean, still slightly reeling from Callum's matching response. He was a respectful guy, she knew that, but this was just a silly game so she'd expected some smart-ass answer from him. He was really decent, and if they were actually dating or engaged, that gentlemanly response would definitely have earned him bonus points.

Which wasn't a good thing, given their circumstances.

What had happened to acting like things were rocky between them? He was acting like the perfect man instead. They needed to talk this evening. Get on the same page with her plan.

"Ellie, what is the one item of clothing that Callum hates to wear?" Brent asked.

A tie. Simple. He detested the things. Claimed they were metaphors for the business world. Choked the life out of people until they woke up dead one morning.

She started to write but then paused. Getting another right answer wasn't working in their favor. If the group thought their relationship was rock-solid, trying to convince everyone—especially Brent—that things were over in a couple of days would be much harder.

She wrote "dress shoes" instead, knowing Callum wouldn't completely know that she'd thrown this one. Dress shoes weren't his favorite either. He preferred to be barefoot. She often caught him walking around the bookstore that way when there were no customers in the store.

"Reveal," Brent said.

As she suspected, Callum had written a tie. "Oops, got this one wrong," she said, showing hers to the group. She avoided Callum's suspicious, unfooled look as she wiped her board clean and Brent turned to Mitch and Cheryl.

"You got that wrong on purpose," he whispered.

"Maybe I don't know you as well as you think I do,"

she said casually with a shrug, but they both knew she was lying. They knew one another very well, oddly well, but that was natural for coworkers who spent a lot of time together.

Hell, she spent more time with Callum than anyone else in her life.

That was what she was here to change. Her coworker couldn't be the one person in her life she could confide in or trust or depend on. She wanted to share that connection with a lover.

The next rounds continued on, and Nick finally scored a point for their team by knowing Alisha's favorite food—but Cheryl and Mitch still weren't on the board yet. Not many late-night conversations were happening at their house with a new baby.

The game returned to Ellie and Callum, and they were still in the lead.

"Okay, Callum… What is Ellie's most irrational fear?"

There was no way he was getting this one. And *she* wasn't about to be truthful anyway. She wasn't sharing it with the group. Like bra sizes, deep, dark fears were reserved for special people, not friends she barely knew anymore or ever really had.

She scribbled "Swallowing a spider in my sleep" on her whiteboard because she'd read somewhere that the average person swallows eight spiders in their life. Seemed like something most people would be afraid of, even though it was highly unlikely to be true. Whatever happened when she was asleep was none of her business.

"Okay, reveal," Brent said, sounding bored with the game already.

Callum hesitated, then turned his around. "Ellie's most irrational fear is not living a fulfilled, meaningful life."

Her mouth dropped. What the hell? He was right, but

seriously what the hell? She was terrified of that, but had she ever verbalized it to Callum? Or did he really just know her that well?

"That's deep," Nick said.

"Ellie, you need to reveal," Cheryl said, when she continued to clutch her whiteboard to her chest.

"Oh right." She turned hers around and the group laughed at her answer.

"That seems a helluva lot more plausible," Alisha said with a shudder. "In fact, I think I just got a new irrational fear."

Callum looked at Ellie with a quizzical expression, then he nodded. "Right. This one must have been my last girlfriend," he said, trying to make light of the moment.

The rest of the group laughed, and Ellie did her best to laugh along despite the odd, unsettled feeling in the pit of her stomach.

She was in for far more than she'd imagined this week.

SPIDERS CRAWLING DOWN her throat? No way. He'd seen Ellie eat freeze-dried crickets.

Of course, maybe revealing something personal and deep about her to her former friends had been the wrong choice, but he'd wanted to use the game as a wake-up call for her and maybe start to display his own feelings. Slowly. A full-on confession would make her retreat, but he couldn't just go along with the plan for this week without taking his own shot.

He'd never get another chance like this.

"Okay, now that it's been established that none of us know one another besides Ellie and Callum, who's up for reheating their relationship in the hot springs?" Alisha asked.

He wouldn't mind soaking his muscles. He could feel the

tightness and tension developing from the accident on the highway, and while he'd rather soak alone with Ellie, this was the next best thing. Unfortunately, she was looking at Brent, waiting for his answer.

Of course. That was why they were there.

"I think I'll pass for tonight," the other man said.

That was surprising. He'd definitely pegged the guy as the hot tub and drinking type. But he wasn't about to try to change Brent's mind.

"Yeah, I'm enjoying this cozy lodge," Ellie said. "But you go on ahead," she told Callum.

He swallowed hard. She wanted time with Brent and that was what he'd promised to give her. He nodded as he stood. "Okay, well you know where I'll be if you change your mind," he said, kissing the top of her head before leaving her alone to start reconnecting with the wrong guy.

"ANOTHER GLASS OF WINE?" Brent asked.

She'd already had two, plus the champagne in the cottage…but she was on vacation. "Sure, thank you," Ellie said, extending her glass to him.

As he went to refill, her gaze shifted out the window. Callum was removing his clothes down to his underwear and climbing into the hot springs with the others. He was smiling and laughing. Seemed to be having a good time. Hot springs at midnight was definitely his thing. It wasn't hers. And she'd been relieved that it wasn't Brent's. Anymore, anyway. She remembered a lot of hot tub parties in high school. They'd always made her uncomfortable and self-conscious. Too much drinking and fooling around.

He returned with her wineglass, and she smiled up at him as she accepted it. "Thank you."

He sat next to her on the couch, and her hands sweat

slightly. Why was she so nervous? This was the guy she'd confessed her teenage secrets to, shared her hopes and dreams with, had her first sexual experience with. Losing her virginity to him was something she'd never regretted. She'd loved him and that first time had been special. She knew it wasn't his first time, but she'd refused to let that bother her. Maybe that was more than enough reason to be nervous. There was a lot of history between them and, for her, a lot of unresolved feelings.

"So...have you read any good books lately?" she asked. It was one of the things they'd always talked about. He preferred sci-fi novels over the classics, but she wasn't a genre snob. As long as people were reading, they shouldn't be shamed for their preference of material.

He laughed. "Geez, I actually can't remember the last time I read a book at all."

That was a little disappointing. But he had a busy life.

"What about you?" he asked, restoring her positive vibe. He was interested. That was a good sign. A lot of adults couldn't find time to read—didn't mean they didn't want to. And so what if he didn't? Why was she so hung up on that?

She turned to face him, tucking a leg under her on the couch. "I just finished a series of memoirs by three women who lived through the Second World War. Each perspective was incredibly different based on their social and economic status, and it was fascinating to read about things the history books have casually—or purposely—omitted," she said, feeling her own passion filling her chest.

Brent listened intently, his steady gaze making her blush slightly, and all the warm sensations she'd always felt around him came flooding back.

"I'd forgotten how light blue your eyes were," he said.

She blinked. Her eyes? Okay...had he actually even

heard anything she'd just said? Not everyone was interested in history, and he was flirting with her—that was a
good thing. But the memoirs were so fascinating...

Get over the book thing, Ellie!

"So, are you still volunteering with at-risk youth?" Years
before, he had volunteered at the after-school community
program for young teens. It had been one of the many things
she'd admired about him. How eager he was to help others
and his commitment to the program. He'd been there three
or four times a week.

He shook his head. "Nah, that was part of the extra-
credit requirement to apply to colleges and flight school."

Her heart sank a little. Why was she being so judgy?
He was busy. He had a full-time career. Not everyone had
time to volunteer. It had to be just that she was sensing a
little disconnect between them that had her feeling uneasy.
So far, nothing from their past had served as a launching
off point to get the conversation flowing. But they didn't
have to reconnect based on their old habits and likes. They
were adults now. They'd find new things in common and
have more mature discussions.

"I mean, don't get me wrong," Brent said quickly. "I'd
like to, but I just don't have the time."

She nodded. "Totally understandable."

Brent laughed. "Yeah, right. I heard the judging in that
brilliant mind of yours. And you're right. I should make
time to give back to the community. I will. I'll do better."

That did make her feel slightly better. The charitable
guy she'd once known was still in there.

"How long have you and Callum been together?" he
asked.

She hesitated. She really should just tell him the truth,
but how would he react? Most likely, he'd rightfully think

she was pathetic to have to make up a fiancé. He'd wonder why she'd lied, and how could he trust her if they based their rekindling on a lie? She cleared her throat. She and Callum hadn't really discussed the fake facts of their "relationship," so anything she told Brent, she'd have to relay to Callum to keep their story straight. "A few years."

"You work together at the bookstore?"

"Yes." Giving simple, truthful answers was best wherever possible. No more, no less.

Brent peered out the window at the hot tub and shook his head.

"What?"

"Nothing."

"No really, what?"

"Seems odd, that's all. A dude his age working in an old, small town bookstore."

She frowned. Was it also odd that a woman her age was doing the same? "What's odd about it?"

Brent shrugged. "Nothing I guess. I just would have thought he'd be running the resort."

How did he know who Callum was?

He looked slightly sheepish seeing her confused look. "Full disclosure, I may have googled him. I wanted to make sure the man my Ellie was about to marry was good enough for her."

His Ellie. She'd like to focus on that part. Unfortunately, the idea of him judging Callum and checking up on him to confirm his worthiness didn't have the heartwarming effect he was obviously intending. "He's not interested in the hospitality industry. It's not a career he wants to pursue."

"It's his family legacy though," Brent said with a shrug. "Does he really have a choice?"

"Everyone has a choice," she said. "Obligation shouldn't

play a role in life decisions. People should do what makes them happy." Callum had said something similar, and she hadn't completely bought it then—she did now. Maybe it was knowing he wanted to write that had her changing her perception? Either way, he'd been right.

"So, what makes him happy? Other than you, obviously?" Brent asked.

That wasn't something she'd share. "He has some things going on," she said simply.

"Well, as long as you're happy, Ellie. That's what matters," Brent said, sipping his drink.

Ellie drew in a long, slow breath. She was there with Brent, desperate to keep the focus on the two of them, and yet the conversation had mostly revolved around Callum.

Her gaze met his through the lodge window and she swallowed hard, that unsettling unease reappearing in the pit of her stomach. She'd seen him almost every day for the last two years, so why did it feel as though she was only actually seeing him right then, in that moment?

CALLUM LAY ON the chaise lounge in the cottage an hour later, listening to Ellie in the bathroom. In the hot tub, watching through the window of the lodge, he couldn't tell if the conversation with Brent was going well or not. She'd seemed to be enjoying it, but when his gaze had locked with hers, there'd been something in her expression that hadn't been there before…

It wasn't the lust-filled look she'd had when she'd seen him mostly naked or the admiration and respect she'd shown when he'd revealed his secret about writing in the car. It was a different look completely. Interest maybe?

The bathroom door opened and she emerged in a pair

of pink pajama shorts and a matching tank top, her hair braided and her glasses on.

Damn, she looked so cute. All of the time in the hot tub, he'd been counting the seconds until they all called it a night. Being in the cottage with Ellie without the rest of them around was definitely better.

"Bathroom's all yours," she said as she climbed into bed, her book under her arm.

Always with a book. He knew she liked to read every night in bed and so did he. Just another way their lives could fit well together. He imagined Brent had a seventy-inch flat screen in his bedroom, that he'd binge-watch episodes of the latest Netflix series and fall asleep with the TV on. Ellie would hate that. She didn't even own a television.

He stood and headed into the bathroom, where the smell of her body lotion lingered. That honeysuckle smell that always tempted him. He quickly brushed his teeth, and when he set his toothbrush back in the holder next to hers, he sighed.

Even their toothbrushes looked good together.

Man, he was such a lovestruck wimp when it came to Ellie. Maybe that was the problem. He was too full-on, too attentive… Still, he wasn't willing to pretend to be someone he wasn't. If Ellie would just give him the time of day, he'd cherish her the way a woman should be cherished.

He opened the door and went back into the bedroom. She was sunk low in the bed, surrounded by cushions, her book in front of her face.

He removed his shirt and shorts and slid under his blanket on the chaise lounge. He turned on his side, but the shape of the lounge was uncomfortable, so he lay on his back and reached for his own book. He opened to the chapter where he'd left off and read a few lines…and then read the same few lines again.

He lowered the book. "So, how did your chat with Brent go?" He had to know. It was driving him crazy.

"It was good," she said from behind the book.

"Just good?"

She lowered the book. "Yes, just good. He thinks I'm engaged, remember?"

"Was there a spark at least?"

"I think so," she said, but he caught a note of uncertainty in her voice.

"Well, I'm happy for you if you're happy," he said, feeling a tug at his chest. He did want her to be happy. That was the tough part. If at the end of the week, she walked away with Brent but she was happy, then he'd learn to live with it.

"That's kinda what Brent said about you," she said.

"Do you think everyone believes we're a couple?" he asked.

"I can't imagine they wouldn't given your performance up there," she said, flipping the page of her book quickly.

"It wasn't all a performance," he dared to say. He couldn't let her think that he was acting. She had to know genuine affection when she received it. So, she was obviously choosing to ignore it.

She sighed and put her book away, then checked the time. "Maybe we should get some sleep?"

Discussion was over. Of course. Right when they might potentially get somewhere.

He nodded, putting his own book away. "Yeah, it is getting late." He reached for the light switch on the wall behind him, turning off the main cottage lights.

Ellie turned off the bedside lamp and everything went dark.

"Night, Callum," she said softly.

"Night, Ellie."

Silence fell over the dark room, and as his eyes adjusted to the lack of light, he stared at the ceiling. He wanted to talk to her, but he didn't know what to say. If they were just friends and coworkers, he'd be happy to strategize with her about ways to get Brent back, but that wasn't the case. And he sensed Ellie was starting to sense that too.

"Callum?"

"Yeah?"

"You were right about my deepest fear," she said softly.

His heart ached as he released a slow, deep breath. "I know."

THE MOON ILLUMINATED Ellie's shapely curves as she removed the robe to reveal a sexy black two-piece that accentuated her thin waist and hips. As if in slow motion, she stepped into the hot tub and lowered her body into the water.

Callum swallowed hard as the lower half of his body reacted instantly. She was so beautiful...

She moved toward him and he tensed as her arms encircled his neck. His hands gripped her waist, pulling her in closer. Her light blue eyes burned into his, an intense passion he only saw in his dreams. He lifted her body so that she straddled him, and he cupped her ass, holding her against his hard erection beneath the water.

He kissed her neck, savoring the taste of her, his lips roaming over her shoulder and collarbone, down her arm. Her head fell back and he kissed the hollow of her neck before moving to the other side. He captured her earlobe between his teeth and she moaned as he pulled her upper body closer, her breasts pressed against his chest.

Her hands massaged his shoulders and moved down his

chest, dipping below the water to his thighs. She ran her hands upward, teasingly, seductively and slid them up the legs of his swim trunks. Her fingers tickled his balls and he groaned, feeling himself grow even thicker under her touch. So close, so gorgeous, so sexy, so tempting... She was driving him insane.

He reached around to untie the knot of her bikini top, letting it fall forward, exposing her breasts. The perky, erect nipples were ripened buds, desperately aching to be touched. He massaged the mounds gently, then rougher as her breathing quickened and she slid her hands down into the waistband of his shorts, pushing them down, off of his waist. Her hand wrapped around him and he sucked in a breath at her touch.

It always felt like the first time anyone had ever touched him that way whenever he was with her. She stroked the length of him and he muffled a groan into her neck as his fingers pinched her nipples. Her tiny shriek only turned him on more. He knew she liked it, so he pinched even harder.

"Callum, I want you inside of me," she whispered into his ear.

He lowered one hand into the water and between her legs, sliding the fabric of her bikini bottom to the side, giving him access to her body. He stroked along the folds of her opening—so soft, so wet, so swollen and ready. She shivered and held him tighter with one arm as she quickened her pace on him with the other hand.

She was trying to get him to move faster, trying to create a desperate urge for release in him so he'd take her faster, harder...

But these moments didn't last long enough, so he took his time. One finger in and out slowly...then the second one entering the tight, intoxicatingly sexy space between her legs.

His thumb rolled over her clit, and with the other hand, he reached around the backside of her ass and pressed a thumb between her ass cheeks. Pressure on all the right places. He found her G-spot with his fingers, and she cried out in pleasure, stroking him harder and faster, pumping him.

"Please get inside of me, Callum..." she begged.

He loved when she pleaded with him, when the pleasure mounting was so strong within her that she was desperate and at his mercy. Her release was all up to him. He removed his fingers and lifted her slightly, positioning her over his erect cock before lowering her body down over it. She moaned as every inch of him filled the tight space.

He ached for a quick release, but he needed this moment to last.

He lifted her up and down slowly. Her arms wrapped around his neck held tight as she lowered her mouth to his. The taste of mint and vanilla mixed together on her tongue, and he didn't think he'd ever get enough of the taste of her, the feel of her. She ground her hips closer, moving faster as her arousal mounted. Her kisses were desperate and frantic and tiny moans escaped her lips pressed to his.

He held her ass as he moved her body up and down over him, daring to press his thumb farther between her ass cheeks. Her breasts bobbed on the surface of the water and his fingers dug into her flesh.

Her breathing grew labored and he knew she was close so he halted the motion, holding her still, her folds tightening and clenching around his cock, and he throbbed, filling the space inside her body so fully.

"Callum, please..."

"Have patience, Ellie... Feel the pressure, let it mount."
His own pleasure was rising, tipping over the edge, but he

prevented any movement. Just stillness, gripping one an-other, feeling the ache grow to an unbearable height.

She took a deep breath and nearly whimpered as she clung to him. "Callum, please let me come."

"Not yet," he whispered against her mouth. He captured her bottom lip with his teeth and bit.

She moaned and her nails dug into the flesh at his shoul-ders.

He was so close but he couldn't let it end...

"Callum, please, I'm begging you..."

Instead, he pulled himself out, slowly until only the tip of him was inside of her. The action nearly killed him, but he needed this moment to last. He slowly moved in again and he felt the ripples of pleasure start within her as she clenched tight around him.

He pulled out again, just to the tip, pressing it hard into her. Then he slowly plunged back inside...

He might have one more in him before he was going to erupt.

Ellie moaned and panted as she pleaded for release. "Callum, you're killing me...it's too intense."

"Okay, ready?"

She nodded.

Holding her tight against him with one arm wrapped around her lower back, he reached between their bodies and pinched her clit as he plunged as deep as he could in-side of her and held as the orgasm made him dizzy.

Ellie let out a cry of release as her body stiffened, shud-dered and collapsed against him. His own release was so in-tense, he thought he might have blacked out for a second. He held on to her, knowing in a second, it would all be over...all be gone. He gripped her face between his hands and kissed her passionately, and as his eyes closed...

His eyes opened. His breathing was labored and sweat beaded his entire body. He scanned his surroundings, taking a moment to remember where he was, then he collapsed back against the pillow.

Yep, still on the chaise lounge.

CHAPTER TEN

THE UNGODLY HOUR Cheryl had requested they all meet on the trail that morning came far too soon. He wasn't a morning person the best of days, and the uncomfortable sleeping arrangements had made shut-eye almost impossible— except for a few blissful minutes, when he couldn't claim to be getting restful sleep. His fantasy about Ellie had been that much more real and intense due to the close quarters. Had he mumbled her name in his sleep? That would be hard to explain.

She was already up and dressed by the time the smell of coffee brewing roused him from his half-awake slumber. No surprise there. She *was* a morning person. She was always eager and ready to start the day. But it was barely sunrise. Had she set her alarm extra early to get up and be ready before he woke up so that he wouldn't see her first thing in the morning?

He felt like he'd been robbed.

Seeing her all messed up and sleepy was a perk he'd been looking forward to. Maybe he'd set his own alarm the next morning.

As he sat up and threw his legs over the side of the chaise lounge, he saw her sitting on the small deck, a coffee cup cradled in her hands as she rocked on the double porch swing. He wanted to join her, but she looked happy and at peace, and if he went out there, she'd only spring into action demanding he get ready fast, or launch into a game plan to fool her friends that day.

So instead, he folded the blankets and placed everything on the chair, then poured his own cup of coffee and headed into the shower.

Better get that day's activities underway.

He'd barely wrapped the towel around his waist before she was tapping on the door. "We're going to be late," came her voice from the other side.

He opened it and, unfortunately, this time she must have been expecting it because she had her back turned. Obviously she couldn't control herself at the sight of his body. "I wouldn't have slept so late if someone hadn't kept me awake all night talking in her sleep," he said.

She whipped around. "I don't talk in my sleep."

"How would you know?"

She folded her arms across her chest as she turned to the side to give him privacy, but her gaze shifted to look at him out of the corner of her eye. So she *did* like what she saw. That was a start... "Okay, well what did I say?" she asked.

"Wouldn't you like to know," he said, reaching for a pair of shorts from his bag. Dropping the towel, he stepped into them.

"Aren't you going to wear underwear?" Ellie asked.

Normally he would, but he'd forgotten to pack enough. He shrugged. "I prefer to let the boys breathe. Better for fertility," he said.

She sighed, ignoring the comment. "Come on, just tell me. What did I say in my sleep?"

He yanked a shirt on and grinned at her. "It really bothers you that I might know some deep dark secret, doesn't it?"

"I don't have any deep dark secrets...except the ones you already know about."

"Well, then, I guess you have nothing to worry about."
He sat on the chair and pulled on his socks and running
shoes.

"Callum, come on. Stop being a jerk."

He stood and walked toward her. Stopping just an inch
away. He saw her gulp as her eyes flitted back and forth
between his. "Fine. You said that you were insanely attracted to me and you weren't sure how much longer you
were going to be able to keep your hands to yourself."

She rolled her eyes and slapped his arm. "Nice try. Now
I know you're lying," she said, but her tone held a slight
waver of uncertainty that maybe her subconscious had really betrayed her like that.

THE EARLY MORNING sun was bright and intense as the group
disembarked from the Birchwood Cottages' shuttle in front
of a big warehouse in the middle of a twenty-acre field half
an hour later. Ellie squinted through her sunglasses to read
the name on the building.

Paintball? Seriously?

Her pulse thundered in her veins as she scanned the outdoor facility. Paint-splattered barricades, hay bales and old
tires positioned as hiding places, big bull's-eye targets all
strategically placed in the field. It all looked intimidating.

The owners of the outdoor sporting center stood in front
of them, dressed in paintball coveralls that were military
print. They looked like they were ex-marines—big, bulky,
muscular and mean-looking as they "welcomed" the group
to the war zone and explained the rules of engagement. Ellie
wasn't listening. What excuse could she use to get out of
this? Saying she wasn't feeling well wouldn't really be a lie.

"Questions?" one of the owners, Dutch, asked the group.

Nick raised a hand. "Are the bullets low impact?"

Dutch just stared at him until Nick retreated behind Alisha. "Never mind. I'll grow a set," he mumbled.

"Any other questions?" Dutch asked, sounding like the only right answer was "no."

The group shook their heads, and the two men led the way inside the warehouse to the equipment room where they were given their coveralls, guns and buckets of different-colored paintballs for each person.

The pale pink color of her bucket of balls did not fool her. These things were going to sting like crazy.

"Suit up! Be outside in three minutes," the other man, Frank, told them.

Ellie slid into her coveralls reluctantly. Scanning the group, she saw that they all looked excited and eager. Was she really the only one not thrilled about this activity?

Mitch and Brent were reminiscing about a high school paintball field trip as though it had been the highlight of their high school career. Ellie had skipped that one. She'd prefer to skip it again now, but she didn't want to look like a deadbeat.

It wasn't like she was allergic to fun, she just had a different definition of it than the rest of them. She glanced at Callum suiting up next to her. He seemed okay with it… Hell, the coveralls fit him perfectly. Hers were baggy and awkward. "Have you done this before?" she whispered to him as she laced the slightly too large, rented steel-toe boots.

"A few times. It's not that bad," he said reassuringly, picking up his gun and peering through the aim hole thingy…

Easy for him to say. She'd never shot a gun in her life. Real or otherwise. It felt big and awkward in her hands when she picked it up. "I think I'll just run and hide behind something," she said to Callum.

"And be a sitting duck?" Callum shook his head. "These may not be real bullets, but they sting like a mother. You're going to want to defend yourself and fight back."

"I don't want to do this at all," she hissed.

He put his gun down and finished zipping her suit up to her neck. Then he reached for her helmet, put it on her head and buckled it, his fingers grazing her chin tenderly. Her spine tingled, and she was overheated in the extra clothing. "You've got this," he said.

She most certainly did not have this, but she put on a brave face as she followed everyone outside. The backpack was heavy and uncomfortable. If she could just survive five minutes to earn their team a point and not get too many paintballs to the body in the meantime, she'd call it a victory.

"So we are going to divide you all into two groups. Any preferences to teams?" Dutch said.

There was an odd number. Ellie clung to a glimmer of hope. Maybe she'd have to sit this out. She'd happily volunteer.

"Men versus women," Alisha said, jumping from one foot to the other.

She was really into this. Ellie would have thought that as a nurse Alisha would be anti-violence. Turned out, she was up for inflicting bodily harm.

Cheryl nodded her agreement as she stretched her long, thin body to one side, then the other, warming up. "And we will take the extra man—Brent—to keep things fair."

Brent faked an "I'm honored" look as he moved to stand next to Alisha and Cheryl, wrapping an arm around each of them and nodding for her to come join them.

Well, at least he'd be on her team. She'd stick next to

him, and it would give them some time together without Callum on her hip.

It made the whole idea of getting shot at least slightly more appealing.

THE IDEA OF TAKING out Ellie's ex with a paintball was appealing.

Unfortunately, Callum had been hoping to be out in the field with her, helping her have a good time and keeping her as protected as possible.

Now that honor would go to a guy who didn't deserve it.

He shifted his paintball pack on his shoulders and scanned the field as they walked out to take their positions on home base. Nick and Mitch looked jacked and way too pumped about wielding a fake automatic weapon.

"Okay, here's the plan," Nick said, assuming command. "We each take a corner and move inward. If we can get them retreating toward the center of the field and we stay on the perimeter, we can block them in and they won't have anywhere to go."

Mitch nodded and Callum shrugged. Sounded like a bad idea to him, but he wasn't about to argue. This was their thing.

He glanced across the field to where Cheryl had taken control of Ellie's group, and she was talking and gesturing to the internal sections of the field. They were obviously planning the opposite—forcing Callum's team to the outskirts of the field where there were less barricades and places to hide. Smart. That's what Callum would have done.

"Okay, move out!" Nick ordered, and Callum jogged off toward his corner and took up a post high in a tower to get a better vantage point. He'd act as a sniper to give the other men a fighting chance to move inward.

He rested the gun on the ledge of the lookout and peered through the lens. At first he saw no one as they took up positions in the interior. The field was massive with dozens of mazelike paths. But then his gaze settled on Ellie and Brent hiding together behind a wall in one of the old structures in the very center of the battlefield. His heart raced as he watched them talk and laugh. Her face lit up as she listened and nodded to whatever Brent was saying, her oversize helmet bobbing into her face.

That should be him down there with her.

Not being with Ellie when he knew he could be the right man for her was frustrating, but actually seeing her with someone else was torture. They seemed to be picking up where they'd left off. If Brent was still that into her, why hadn't he reached out to her over the years? Why hadn't he realized sooner that he'd made a mistake letting her go? That there was no one better for him out there among the women he dated?

Or was he just interested because Ellie was here this week? He hated to think that the guy could be that douchey, but he wouldn't be shocked if Brent was seizing opportunities when they suited him with no intention of following through or making any kind of commitment.

He studied Brent now, looking for any sign of insincerity, but the dude seemed to be hanging on Ellie's every word. Could be an act, or maybe he really was realizing what he'd given up years before.

Callum's gut tightened.

What was the other guy thinking about all of this? Was he okay flirting with a woman who was supposed to be engaged? Trying to steal her away? How could Ellie seriously want to be with a guy who would do that?

He was seeing a different side of her this week. Only he knew it wasn't really her. She was totally blinded by her previous attraction to Brent—only seeing what used to be there, what they used to have. And she seemed willing to do anything to get that back.

He saw Mitch moving closer to where they were hiding, and he held his breath as the other man snuck around the side of the structure. Unfortunately, he was going in the wrong direction. As soon as he rounded the corner, Brent shot him before he could fire off a round, and then he and Ellie ran off before the mandatory thirty-second delay had ended for Mitch to try to retaliate and get a point for their team.

Callum sighed as he lost sight of Ellie and Brent. Probably for the best. If he wanted to avoid welts the size of golf balls, he'd best keep his mind in the game.

PAINTBALLS FLEW THROUGH the air in all directions.

Both teams had made their way to the center of the field now, and the hunting had officially begun. So far, their team had taken out Mitch and Nick—the other team's strategy to move in from the outside leaving them vulnerable, with less places to hide. Cheryl was out, having sacrificed herself to save Alisha moments before, and then Alisha was taken out only seconds later. There were only the three of them left—Brent, Ellie and Callum.

Sticking with Brent, Ellie was lasting a lot longer than she'd thought she would.

From her perch behind a hay bale, she saw Callum approach. He'd been on fire that day, single-handedly taking out Cheryl and Alisha. He was definitely impressive with that paintball gun. He and Brent had two shots, as did she. Next one of them to get hit was out. If it was Callum, the game would be over with her team taking the win. She wasn't uber competitive, but she was feeling confident they had this one if she and Brent worked together.

"I see that freckled nose, hiding behind the hay bale," Callum called out.

Ellie laughed as she dived behind a wall instead. At least she was having fun. She hadn't expected to, and she wouldn't necessarily be rushing out to do this again, but it wasn't horrible. She had Brent to thank for that. He was being super attentive and making sure she wasn't left behind.

Hearing Callum approach, she plastered her back to the wall, sucking her body in tight and holding her gun high and close to her body the way Brent had taught her. She glanced left and right but didn't see him. She was on her own. Could she take the shot before Callum could take his?

She took a deep breath and made a run for it as she saw him round the corner. She was almost behind the safety of a stack of monster truck–size tires when she felt the bullet hit the back of her leg. A light sting radiated from her hip to the ankle.

Her eyes widened as she turned around to face him. "Did you just shoot me?"

He shrugged. "It was either you or me," he said with a grin. Then seeing a flash of Brent's coveralls to the right of them, he turned and hurried off.

Callum had actually shot her. Taken her out of the game. "Unbelievable," Ellie mumbled as she headed off the field to the viewing "safe" zone where the others were watching. And she'd been doing so well. More importantly, she and Brent had been working well together as a team and having fun.

Ellie sighed as she joined the others and removed her backpack and helmet.

"You did awesome," Alisha said, paint smeared all over her coveralls. She'd been hit in the shoulder, the arm and the ass by Nick.

"Thanks. Who knew I had such gunman skills," Ellie said with a laugh.

"It's like *The Hunger Games* out there," Nick said as he watched Callum and Brent stalk one another out in the field.

"I didn't realize Brent was so competitive," Alisha said. "I guess with the right motivation..." She let the rest of her sentence trail off, but she shot Ellie a knowing look.

Were the others sensing there were lingering feelings between the two of them? Had they all seen the connection redeveloping between her and Brent? Had Brent said anything to the group?

"Yeah, apparently Callum is too," she said, despite knowing it was untrue. She had to at least appear to be rooting for her fiancé, didn't she?

But she knew normally Callum couldn't care less about winning. At this point, he'd basically forfeit and call it a day. So, why was he doing this? Why didn't he just give up and surrender? What was he trying to prove?

That he was the better man? In general...or for her?

THIS WAS DUMB. They'd been out here for almost an hour after everyone else had been taken out. He should just wave the white flag and be done. He was soaked in sweat and the boots felt like they'd molded to his feet. The blazing sun threatened to set the field on fire, and he'd kill for a bottle of water.

Still, his pride refused to give up.

Brent was doing this to try to prove something to Ellie, and Callum refused to let him win without a real challenge. Ellie deserved a guy to fight for her, and kudos to Brent for doing just that, but the other man also thought that Ellie was engaged, so why was he trying so hard to impress her? Would he actually try to steal Ellie away?

Either way, this game had to end soon. They were nearing their two-hour time limit on the field, and Brent had to be weakening by now too. He knew the guy couldn't be too far. They'd been stalking one another for a long time now. Whenever one of them got a clear shot, the other found somewhere to hide.

Callum crept along the side of a row of old crushed vehicles. He spotted Brent a few feet away. The guy's back was turned as he was peering around the side of the hay bales. He had an easy shot...

But damn, he didn't want to win that way.

He didn't want to win Ellie's heart that way either. And unfortunately, right now, he knew making the kill shot at Brent would only annoy her. His gaze settled on her now, sitting in the viewing area next to the others. She looked adorably hot, her hair messed up from the helmet and paint smears on her forehead and cheeks. She'd unzipped the coveralls, and the swell of her breasts was visible over the tight, white tank top she wore underneath. Damn she was sexy.

A paintball hit him square in the back and he stumbled forward slightly.

The other members of the opposite team cheered and everyone else seemed relieved the game was finally over as he turned to see Brent. He hadn't noticed the other man creeping up behind him. Obviously, Brent had no problem taking an unheroic back shot.

Callum extended a hand. "Great game," he said.

"Yeah, good hustle…" Brent's cocky grin returned as he shook Callum's hand firmly. "You had me worried for a minute there," he said, his gaze purposely drifting across the field and settling on Ellie.

CHAPTER ELEVEN

BACK AT THE COTTAGES, Ellie and Callum raced for the bathroom as soon as the door opened.

She was slightly ahead before she felt his arms wrap around her waist and swing her around, dropping her back to her feet before he dived inside. "Callum!"

He smiled at her annoyed look. "I'm kidding. Ladies first." He moved aside to allow her to enter the bathroom.

"Thank you," she said, turning on the taps. "I can't remember the last time I was this sweaty." The hot sun had been relentless out on the field and even without the coveralls, she was seriously overheating. They'd all retreated to their cottages for a shower before meeting up for what Cheryl had called "couples yoga" that afternoon. She claimed it was a great way to reconnect and rebalance the spiritual connection, especially after shooting at one another all morning. Obviously, Ellie would rather participate with Brent, but how could she ditch her fiancé and not have it seem completely inappropriate?

Maybe Callum could pretend to be sick?

"Need help peeling that tank top off?" he asked, leaning against the doorframe, arms folded, taking in the soaked fabric that was pressed against her skin and slightly see-through now that it was wet. Thank God she'd worn a bra today. Being as small as she was, she didn't always.

"I think I can handle it," she said, pushing him out of

the bathroom and shutting the door. A glance in the mirror revealed that even the bra had been soaked with sweat, so it wasn't doing much to provide coverage.

She reached for the base of the shirt and lifted it up over her head, but then it stopped, refusing to go any farther. It was snagged on the back of her bra. She tugged, but it only tangled her up even more. She tried pulling it back down, but her arms were stuck in the tight fabric and she couldn't get her elbows back down through the hole. She yanked a little more and tried twisting her body, but it was no use. Her face was trapped inside the shirt and the smell was too much. The damp fabric against her cheek was making her gag.

Shit.

"Callum!"

Instantly, he was outside the door. "You okay?"

"Um...not exactly. Can you come in?" she asked through clenched teeth.

"You sure?"

She sighed. No. But she also didn't want to be permanently trapped inside her tank top all day. "I just need a hand with something," she said through gritted teeth.

The bathroom door opened and she could practically hear the smirk, even though she couldn't see it.

"So, you actually do need help with that shirt?" he asked.

"Just get me out of here. I'm holding my breath and I'm going to pass out," she said, turning around so that he could untangle the fabric from the bra hook.

He laughed as his hands touched her back at the base of her bra. "Hang tight."

This was mortifying. At least it was just Callum...not one of the others catching her in this position. In high school, she was known for her slightly awkward moments. Nothing too embarrassing, just little things like being clumsy or having bad luck that often made her a source of entertainment for the others.

This would definitely be filed in that category.

She could feel Callum's cool breath against her warm skin, and she shivered as his fingers struggled with the fabric. "What's going on?"

"It's really stuck on the lacy trim of the shirt. It would be better if I just unclasp the bra and untangle it when it's not on you," he said, his voice sounding slightly hoarse.

"Really? You're not just saying that so that I'll take my bra off?"

"Believe me, I'm not hating that additional perk, but no, it really is stuck. I can rip it..."

This was her favorite tank top. It was soft and feminine-looking and had cost more than she'd normally spend on one piece of clothing. "No, that's fine. Go ahead and unclasp it," she said, feeling her cheeks grow even warmer. The heat combined with the arms-overhead position had her close to passing out.

Unfortunately, she wouldn't even be able to shield herself once the bra and shirt were removed from her body.

She heard Callum move away from her. "Where are you going?"

"Don't worry. Not far," he said as she felt a towel wrap around her body and knot at the back. "A shield," he added as he reached up under the towel to unclasp the bra.

A second later, he'd lifted the shirt and tangled bra off over her head and she was free and not at all exposed. Huh. "Thank you," she mumbled.

"You're welcome," he said. "Enjoy your shower, and I'll get this sorted out." He held up the tangled clothing as he closed the bathroom door behind him.

Ellie stood there for a second staring at it. He'd had a

chance to catch a glimpse of her exposed and he hadn't taken it. She knew it wasn't because he didn't want to see her naked—he was a guy after all.

A really good guy.

Would Brent have made the same call?

THE SIGHT OF ELLIE trapped in her tank top would forever be etched in his mind. The thin waist, sexy rib cage and enhanced cleavage—thanks to the arms-overhead pose she'd been stuck in—had been both hilarious and seductive.

Callum sat on the edge of the bed and carefully removed the bra clasp from the lace at the base of the shirt. A hint of honeysuckle hit him, and he groaned at his self-restraint. For once, why couldn't he be that guy who took advantage of a situation? Giving Ellie the towel for privacy had been the right thing to do, but damn if he hadn't been tempted to be the bad guy for once.

He stood and draped the tank top and bra over the edge of a chair as his cell phone chimed in his shorts pocket. He glanced at it and saw a new email message from Chateau Resorts.

Must be that time of year again.

Chateau Resorts was one of his father's biggest competitors with six luxury, high-end resorts in Alaska and the Northwest Territories. They'd opened their first hotel the same year Callum's grandfather had opened the Wild River Resort. The other company knew of the rocky relationship he and Sean had with their dad, mainly due to Callum's refusal to take over. At least once a year since they were eighteen, the major resort chain had reached out to them to try to recruit them. He always declined and so did Sean, but he wondered if his brother had ever considered accepting their offer.

Once again, they'd both been copied on the request for a meeting with the senior VP of Chateau Resorts, a Mrs. Sarah Mileman. Callum had met her a few times when their dad had dragged them to hotel sales conferences. Nice woman. Ran a very successful hotel chain.

Maybe his brother should consider their offer. Working for Sarah would be much better than working for their father. Nevertheless, Sean's decline on the invitation was almost instantaneous, and Callum sighed as he sent his own.

The bathroom door opened and Ellie appeared. "Okay, you're up," she said.

He nodded absentmindedly.

"Everything okay?" she asked.

"Yeah…just Chateau Resorts trying to recruit Sean and me again," he said as he set his phone on the charger.

"I know you're not interested, but do you think Sean would ever consider it?" she asked, towel drying her hair.

"I wish he would, but he's far too loyal to our father," Callum said. He shouldn't have opened the email. He'd been doing a good job keeping his family out of his thoughts that day, but now the stress was lingering there on his shoulders again.

"You okay?" Ellie asked, touching his arm.

He forced a smile as he grabbed his discarded towel from that morning. "Absolutely." He paused. "Hey, if you want me to bail on this couples yoga…" He didn't want to. Right now he could definitely use the relaxation, and the idea of participating in a reconnecting ritual with Ellie sounded like the perfect afternoon, but she obviously wanted to do this with Brent. "I can go up there, claim to be sick and insist that you still partake."

She studied him, hesitating. "You'd do that?"

Not happily. "That's what we're here for, right?" he

asked, staring deep into her eyes. Was it his imagination or was that same flicker of interest he'd caught the night before there again? Things were definitely changing between them, but he couldn't be certain in what capacity.

She shrugged. "I think maybe I spent too much time with him already today. It might be coming across a little weird."

"So you want me to do yoga with you?" His mood picked up slightly again as he waited for her reply.

She seemed to be contemplating it for a long time. "I think we should, yes," she said, finally. "Just for appearances' sake."

"Okay. But only for appearances' sake," he said with a wink.

Brent may have beat him at paintball in more ways than one, but Ellie had just given him a chance to redeem himself.

"DEEP BREATH IN. Deep breath out."

The group inhaled and exhaled as Cheryl started the class from the center of the yoga-mat circle they'd formed on the tennis courts near the lodge. As a certified fitness instructor, she taught all kinds of classes at the community center in Wild River and had an impressive client list as a personal trainer.

But she had her work cut out for her if she hoped to make this a relaxing experience for Ellie. Her heart pounded in her ears as she sat cross-legged on her mat next to Callum's. Brent was sitting this one out, but he was watching from a lawn chair near the pool, a cooler of beer beside him.

Ellie didn't remember him being much of a day drinker, but they were on vacation.

"Arms up, overhead and slowly lower," Cheryl was saying. "Okay, everyone stand and face your partner."

Ellie got to her feet and turned toward Callum. He was wearing just his shorts and his bare body was definitely an added distraction. Cheryl had insisted that they wear as little as possible for traction against one another in some of the more challenging poses.

Traction. Wonderful. She wasn't eager to create any sparks between her and her coworker.

"The first pose is the double swan," Cheryl said. "All you need to do is lean forward toward your partner, arms extended, and slowly lift your right leg straight into the air behind you. As you lean, stretch and lengthen your spine, and hold hands as you lower your head and relax your neck." Cheryl demonstrated the move with Mitch, who seamlessly perfected the move like this wasn't his first time.

Ellie glanced at Callum and he shrugged, moving through the motions. She did the same, and when their hands connected, she fought to control an odd sensation that extended through her arms, down her spine. A tingling that had her nerve endings on alert.

"We will hold this pose for a full minute. Allow your energy to flow to your partner. Support one another through the hold, keep your balance, focus on your core…"

All Ellie could focus on was her hands interconnected with Callum's. They were just touching hands and yet it did feel intimate. How the hell was she supposed to go through the other, more challenging poses?

It was a shame this activity was being wasted on her friend. This would obviously be better with Brent. There was no way she and Callum would find a true connection this way. They were faking it after all.

"And three, two, one… Slowly release your hands and return to a standing position," Cheryl said.

Ellie let go quickly and tipped slightly off-balance before dropping her leg back to the mat. Beside her, Callum looked more relaxed than he had in the cottage. At least he was getting that benefit of the yoga. She suspected the email from Chateau Resorts had rattled him more than he'd let on. He might not want to work in hospitality, but she knew he'd like to see his brother secure and working in a healthier environment.

"The next pose is the superman. Men, please lie on your back on your mat and bring your knees into your chest," Cheryl said, walking around the circle.

Callum lay on his mat and did as instructed.

"Ladies, we are simply going to place our stomachs against the heels of their feet like this," Cheryl said, lying on Mitch's feet. "And, as we hold their hands for support, they will lift up, extend their legs, and we will assume the superman pose."

Ellie eyed the position and hesitated. Alisha attempted it and laughed as she was raised into the air on Nick's heels.

It did look kinda fun.

"We doing this?" Callum asked.

"Why not?" Ellie placed her bare stomach on his feet and pressed her palms to his as he extended his legs and she was lifted into the air. "Whoa." The head rush threw her slightly off-balance and her upper body fell forward, and she nearly bumped her forehead on Callum's nose.

"Don't worry, I got you," Callum said, steadying her.

He did have her. She felt oddly safe in the pose with him. He wouldn't let her fall, she was certain of that.

"When you feel ready, secure…you can let go of your partner's hands and extend your arms to the sides. Balance with just the connection of feet and stomach and trust in one another," Cheryl said, demonstrating the move.

Yeah, she wasn't so sure about that. Letting go of Callum's hands seemed a little too risky. She glanced at Alisha and Nick and watched as they made a successful transition. Alisha's face lit up as she slowly extended her arms and indeed looked like she was experiencing the freeing sensation of flight. From the ground, Nick looked pretty damn proud of himself too.

"You can let go," Callum told her.

She stared down at him for a long moment, their gazes locking and holding for an intimate beat.

"Come on, I promise I got you," he said.

Ellie took a deep breath, and on her exhale she tightened her core against his feet and slowly released his hands. She wavered slightly and reached for his hands again, but he moved them out of reach. "Trust yourself."

She struggled to balance, staying focused by keeping her gaze locked on his as she extended her arms to the sides. Her body stabilized and she was balancing.

She was doing it.

They were doing it.

"Great work, partners," Cheryl said.

Ellie's smile was wide as the liberating sensation flowed through her as they held the pose. She was steady, secure and strong. The only thing threatening to throw her off-balance was the connection forming between her and her fake fiancé.

THEY WERE KILLING THIS.

Together they were naturals at this couples yoga thing. They were moving through even the more challenging poses by working together and trusting in one another. Right now, Callum was balancing on Ellie's thighs as she crouched in a chair pose and their extended arms were only connected by their fingertips, and he had complete trust. He'd never felt more relaxed and centered. Whole.

No wonder couples did this. If more couples did, the divorce rate in the country might not be so high.

Not only was it a way to reconnect spiritually, but it was also erotic as hell. Ellie's short shorts and bra top had had him salivating from the moment they'd stepped onto their mats, but the more they'd balanced against one another, supported one another's weight, joined their bodies together in the series of poses, the more turned on he was by her. Her soft, slightly sweaty skin against his was the most intoxicating experience he'd ever shared with a woman.

And now that she'd relaxed and gotten into it, she seemed to be enjoying it, as well.

Enjoying it and not wishing she was doing it with Brent?

He wasn't sure, but maybe for right now she'd forgotten all about her ex, who was watching intently from across the yard…and about their mission this week.

"Okay, and relax and release," Cheryl said as Mitch placed his feet back on the ground and she returned to a standing position.

The others did the same.

"Well, those were the poses. Well done, everyone," Cheryl said, and Callum was slightly disappointed that it was over already.

Ellie sent him a sidelong look, and he could tell she felt the same way.

"Okay, now for the meditation part," Cheryl said.

Meditation? That would be impossible with the semi-hard-on he was fighting to control the whole time.

"Everyone sit comfortably on your mats and face your partner," Cheryl said, sitting and facing Mitch.

Ellie sat without hesitation and smiled at him when he

sat across from her. He'd expected more reluctance from her, but when Cheryl reached for Mitch's hands, she immediately reached for his again. The hope rising in his chest was going to hurt like a son of a bitch if she went back into "getting Brent back" mode as soon as this was over, but for now, he'd allow himself this time with her.

Their hands connected again and he stared across at her. She was so beautiful. Sweat pouring down the side of her face, tendrils of hair escaping the messy bun at the top of her head, her expression serene and peaceful.

What did he look like to her? Could he dare hope that she was seeing him in a different light?

"Deep breath in, deep breath out," Cheryl said.

He watched as Ellie's chest rose and fell in a deep, slow rhythm that was in perfect sync with his own. They were breathing as one.

"Keep staring into your partner's eyes. Really look beyond the surface. Go deeper with your connection," Cheryl said, her voice calm and steady, almost hypnotizing.

He continued to stare at Ellie and she didn't look away. He felt her gazing straight into his soul, and he could stay here, sitting across from her, holding her hands this way forever. The moment couldn't last long enough.

"Deep breath in, deep breath out."

Inhale. Exhale.

"And namaste," Cheryl said far too soon.

"Namaste," they said together, and maybe it was his imagination, but Ellie held on to his hands longer than the other women held their partners' hands.

WHAT THE HELL had just happened?

As Ellie showered for the third time that day, her mind

reeled. That couples yoga was dangerous. They shouldn't let just anyone do that shit together.

For an hour out there, she'd actually believed that she and Callum were connecting in some mystical way. Their bodies had been touching, but it had also felt as though their souls were one.

She didn't really believe in all of that cosmic, karma stuff. Yet, moments before she'd felt closer to Callum than anyone else in her life. She'd actually completely forgotten about Brent and the reason she was here this week. She wasn't sure she would have felt as relaxed and comfortable doing it with Brent. She would have been self-conscious and wondering what everyone else thought… But today, she'd almost forgotten anyone else was there as she'd breathed through the poses with Callum.

She took a deep breath as the cool water cascaded down her back.

It had to be just that they were friends—there was nothing more to their relationship than that. Of course she was comfortable and able to relax around Callum, there wasn't any sexual tension between them.

Or she was lying to herself. He certainly seemed… aroused.

She sighed. No more couples yoga.

THE YOGA HAD DONE more than solidify his feelings for Ellie. All of a sudden, Callum's muse was back.

Sitting on the deck of the cottage with his laptop, his fingers flew over the keyboard. The fresh air, the setting sun, the light breeze rustling through the trees all around them and the faraway sound of waves lapping against the lakeshore were all contributing to his best writing sprint in a long time.

The relaxation exercise had opened up his emotional side, allowing him to dig deeper than ever. Raw vulnerability spilled from his memories onto the pages. Even events he'd somewhat repressed because they were too painful to recall or write about were finding their way into the book. It was both terrifying and exhilarating.

Times of peace and calm when his father was away were stories he hadn't even thought to include, but he realized they were essential to balancing the rest of the book. Highlighting the impact his father's absence had on the family only further enhanced the damaging effects when he was there.

They would smile. His brother, his mother and he. That was the thing that struck him the most. Smiles were forced or held no real joy when Alan was home, but Callum remembered actually laughing around the table with his mom and brother whenever their father's seat was empty.

He was so caught up in the work that he didn't hear Ellie exit the cottage. He jumped, noticing her reading over his shoulder. He quickly minimized the screen and turned to face her. "That's not ready for your eyes yet," he said. But damn, was she a sight for his.

Dressed in a light blue, ankle-length, bohemian-style sundress—flowy and loose but low-cut and sexy as hell—she made his mouth go dry. Her hair was loose and curled around her shoulders and her face was makeup-free, except for the most seductively shiny lip gloss that made her mouth more tempting than ever. "You look beautiful," he said.

"Thank you," she said, glancing down at the dress.

"I don't think I've seen that dress before." He would have remembered if he had.

"It's new. I bought it for this trip."

For Brent. Right. He nodded as he shut down his laptop. "Ready to meet up with the others?"

She hesitated, looking slightly apprehensive, and his heart fell. Their connection earlier that day was over. Either she hadn't felt it too or she had and it had terrified her. Either way, she was pulling back from him again. Sticking to her goal. "I thought maybe I'd go up there alone... You know, start the whole 'trouble in paradise' phase..."

She didn't sound very confident, but he couldn't tell if it was because she was struggling with her decision or if she was just afraid of hurting his feelings. Did she want him to argue? Show that he too thought things were changing between them? She was impossible to read, so he nodded. "Yeah, okay. I could use the time to write, anyway."

She smiled but it didn't quite reach her eyes, making him immediately regret not insisting that he tag along. "Great," she said as she descended the stairs, but then she stopped and turned back.

Had she changed her mind? His hopes foolishly soared.

"And by the way, your time keeping that writing to yourself is running out."

She headed up the trail and Callum watched her go.

Time was indeed running out.

CHAPTER TWELVE

THE SOUND OF her phone alarm playing a Spanish beat woke her at 2:30 a.m. and Ellie rushed to turn it off before it could wake Callum. He'd been passed out on the chaise lounge when she'd gotten back to the cottage just before midnight. His laptop had been on his lap, but unfortunately, the screen saver had blocked any peek she might have gotten of his writing as she put the laptop away and covered him with a blanket.

He continued to snore softly now as she quietly got out of bed and grabbed her own laptop. She tiptoed across the floor and turned the knob slowly. The door creaked a little as it opened and she glanced back over her shoulder. Still sleeping. One arm stretched overhead, the other dangling over the side of the chaise lounge, his long legs draped over the side. She really should let him sleep in the bed...but that day's yoga had stirred some weird stuff inside of her that she hadn't completely shaken off yet.

Best to keep their distance.

She went out onto the deck and closed the door behind her, then sitting on the swing, she logged into the online class site and dialed her student's computer.

A second later Raquel appeared on the screen. *"Hola!"* Ellie said and forced any sign of tiredness from her expression and voice.

"Hello," Raquel said, but it came out more of a sob.

"Everything okay?" Ellie asked.

"No...*mi padre*, my father, found out about Leo," she said over a loud sniff.

Ellie wanted to feel bad for Raquel, but she was more relieved. The idea of the young woman moving around the world for a stranger she'd met online had been a little terrifying to her. And she'd always felt like an accomplice to Raquel's plan. "Sorry to hear that," she said.

Raquel blew her nose and wiped her eyes. *"Sin pre-ocupaciones,"* she said, waving a hand. "I find new love in Italy."

Italy?

"So...do you still want to learn English?"

"Oh yes. *Mi amore* in Italy is American."

Phew! Thought she'd lost her client for a second there. But alas, Raquel's attraction to Americans persisted. "Okay, let's get started," she said.

An hour later, she shut the laptop and yawned as she stood. "So the rule about *i* before *e* is actually kinda bullshit." Callum's voice made her jump, and her hand went to her heart as she turned to see him standing in the cottage doorway.

"How long have you been standing there?"

"Long enough to learn a few choice words in *Español*," he said with a wink.

Ellie laughed. "Raquel has quite a potty mouth and doesn't love it when she's not getting something right. Did I wake you?"

He shook his head. "My alarm did."

She frowned. "You set your alarm for the middle of the night?"

"Only on the nights you teach," he said, holding the door open for her to enter.

That was weird. He always texted her, but she'd thought he was up anyway on those nights. "Why?"

"I don't know. I guess I can't sleep knowing you're awake. I feel guilty for sleeping."

She laughed. "That's ridiculous." But it warmed her slightly. Enough that she avoided his gaze as she put her laptop away.

"You are a really great teacher," he said. "Where did you learn how?"

"It's not hard to get certified to teach English as a native English speaker. Just a few grammar tests and a two hundred–hour online course."

"I think you're underestimating how hard it is to actually teach. Especially in an online setting. Not a lot of people can do that," he said.

She shrugged. "I guess it does take a natural ability to want to share knowledge, and I get off on seeing someone grasp a new skill or concept."

"So you've always had that knack… I mean you used to tutor in high school, right? That's how you and Brent got together."

She nodded, but at the moment she wasn't really in the mood to talk about Brent. "It probably started even before that," she said as she zipped her laptop case. "I used to set up chairs in our basement and sit all my dolls on them, and then I'd stand at the front of the 'class' with an old chalkboard my mom found at a garage sale and I'd teach them stuff." Her cheeks flushed. Why the hell was she telling him that? It was embarrassing.

But he smiled. "I can see little Ellie doing that."

"Anyway, it's just something I enjoy."

"Have you thought more about going back to school to get a teaching degree?"

She shrugged as she climbed back into bed. "I don't know. I'll be thirty soon." That ship was slowly sailing away each year. At first, she'd been motivated to keep saving for that possibility, but when the reality of how long it would take for her to pay off her parents' medical bills set in, the dream had seemed too unreachable to keep her motivation strong enough.

"What does age have to do with anything?"

"Asks the twenty-five-year-old."

He laughed as he tried to get comfortable on the chaise lounge. "Twenty-six and a half. Stop making it sound like there's a huge gap between us. It's only three years."

Three long years. Ellie felt so much older than twenty-nine. Having had to grow up quickly and face the world on her own at a young age made her feel twice her age some days. She hadn't had the chance to grow into herself, to take a year off after graduation and travel a little or spend time figuring out what she wanted for her future once going to university hadn't been an option financially. She'd fallen into the routine of surviving day-to-day. Like most people.

"I'm just not sure going back to school is the best option," she said with another yawn.

"You could complete the courses online."

She'd thought of that several times over the years. Had even decided on the school she'd like to attend. But she'd always backed out at the last minute. "I don't know. Financially, I'm not sure it really makes sense." She'd saved money, but was it worth investing in a new career? That money could go toward her retirement plans instead. But it was kinda depressing to think she was closer to the end of her life than the beginning.

"I could loan you the money. Hell, I could *give* you the money."

She laughed. "Not a chance."

"Offer's always on the table," he said.

She'd never accept it. But it was so like him to not even think twice about helping her like that. His generosity was never in question. She saw him buy books for kids who came into the store without money all the time, and his "private" charitable donations helped support some organizations in Wild River.

She watched as he fluffed the pillow under his arm then tossed it on the floor instead.

He was really struggling. She sighed as she yanked back the bedsheets on the other side. "Get in."

His eyes widened in surprise and he started to get up, then stopped. "Are you sure?"

"You don't fit on that thing. You're going to have neck cramps."

He studied her for a long moment, then eyed the comfy-looking bed before shaking his head. "Nah, I'm good. The bed is yours."

Her jaw gaped slightly. He was turning down the comfort of the bed? Because he knew she wasn't comfortable with sharing it and because he was a really great guy.

Damn, now she kinda wanted him in the bed with her.

"Night, Ellie," he said, tucking his arm under his head.

"Night, Callum," she said, turning off the bedside lamp.

"And think about the online courses," he said in the dark. "It's never too late."

At that moment, her dream of teaching was the farthest thing from Ellie's mind.

CALLUM LAY AWAKE in the dark cottage, his gaze on Ellie in the queen-size bed only three feet away. She looked so small, lost in the mound of soft, oversize pillows and tangle of bedsheets. One leg had escaped the sheets, and the light from the window illuminated the shapely calf and thigh and delicate-looking ankle.

She'd invited him in and he'd basically panicked. In a span of ten seconds, he'd gone full circle between wanting to say yes and knowing he should say no. Lying in bed with her would feel too personal, too intimate, and while he craved that, he wasn't sure he wanted the first time he slept next to Ellie to be just because she felt bad for him.

He sighed as he saw her roll onto her side. The bedsheet lifted, exposing her bare shoulders and upper back. Her skin looked like silk—and he knew from touching her today that it felt just as soft.

Maybe joining her wouldn't be such a bad idea.

The yoga that day had definitely made the earth around them shift a little... And what if she mistook his refusal as rejection? As in, he didn't want to sleep next to her? Wasn't interested?

Shit. What if the invitation had been based on more than just sympathy for his uncomfortable sleeping situation? What if she'd been trying to hint at something? Not sex obviously, but maybe she'd wanted his body in bed with her?

He wasn't sleeping tonight. Between the uncomfortable chaise lounge and overthinking, he'd be wide-awake until sunrise. Unless, he climbed into bed with her...

He sat up and threw off the blanket, then grabbing the pillow from the floor, he walked toward the bed. She must have heard him approach, as her eyes opened, and she looked at him with such a sexy sleepy expression it took all his strength not to dive onto the bed and take her into his arms.

"Callum?"

"I...uh..." His cell phone vibrating on the table interrupted him, and he sighed as he reached for it quickly. Sean's number lit up the display and his gut turned. "I have to get this. I'll take it outside," he said, heading for the door. "Get a good sleep."

Ellie's quizzical look held a trace of disappointment, and it was the first time in years that Callum was tempted to ignore his brother's call.

CHAPTER THIRTEEN

CHERYL WAS KEEPING the next day's activities close to her chest, and it made Ellie more than a little uneasy as she got dressed the next morning for what had simply been called Surprise Adventure Number One. She suspected she had a very different definition of *adventure* than Cheryl, but she had survived paintball and yoga the day before, so maybe it wouldn't be so bad.

"You ready?" Callum asked, popping his head around the bathroom door.

That morning he'd been awake before her, showered and ready and writing out on the deck. She'd been exhausted after the late-night English lesson and had almost slept in. She couldn't miss that day's outings, despite how tired she was. She'd gotten a slight cold-shoulder vibe off of Brent the evening before at dinner, and she could only assume it was because of the couples yoga. She needed to do damage control and quickly, before the entire week went off the rails and she lost this shot with him.

The shot she definitely still wanted. Right?

"Yeah...ready as I'll ever be." She grabbed a ponytail holder and wrapped it around her wrist. "And remember, if it's anything requiring pairs or couples, opt out so I'll be paired with Brent." The night before, away from Callum, she'd realized that the connection between them during the couples yoga had been nothing serious. Hell, it had essentially been a trust exercise. Had she been paired with anyone in the group, there might have been a resulting "bonding," but it didn't mean anything. But then back at the cottage, near him again, there had been a moment after her online lesson…

And, of course, he wasn't making it easy for her to brush him off. "What if it's something I want to do?"

"We have an agreement, remember?"

He grinned. "I didn't sign anything."

"Callum…"

"I'm just saying, we had fun together yesterday, didn't we?"

Maybe too much fun. Obviously Brent had noticed their connection, as well, which was why he'd backed off. He couldn't exactly make a play for an unavailable woman without looking like a jerk. "I think it's time to move into the next phase."

"The bickering and fighting," he said, looking disappointed.

She nodded. "Yes. The way we discussed it." Why was he suddenly not on board? Had he thought things had changed between them the day before? They hadn't. They absolutely hadn't…

"Fine. I'll miss out on the fun so you can reconnect with Brent," he said, opening the cottage door and grabbing his backpack.

She ignored his pout as she walked past him out of the cottage. "Thank you."

As the group hiked the side of Willow Mountain an hour later, Ellie's legs burned. She'd done more exercise so far that week than she'd done all year. Even muscles she hadn't known existed were aching from the yoga, and it was embarrassing how winded she was propelling her body forward up the trail.

Brent was leading the group and making the trek look easy. Unfortunately, there was no way she could keep pace with him without passing out.

"Water?" Callum asked, handing her a bottle from the backpack he carried with ease.

She accepted it and chugged half before saying, "This is not at all challenging for you?" He was bringing up the rear with her, despite the fact that he looked like he could jog the incline.

"I'm on the S & R crew, and contrary to popular belief, these muscles don't maintain themselves," he said, flexing a bicep.

Ellie rolled her eyes, but it was actually a very impressive bicep. "I always assumed it was from carrying boxes of books," she said. That's where her exercise typically came from.

Callum laughed, putting the water bottle back. "Well, anytime you want to work out…"

An image of Callum's body appeared in her mind—wet hair, sweat droplets on his skin from the yoga. Nope. Working out together again was probably not the best idea.

She turned her gaze across the trail toward Brent. He was chatting with Nick, but his gaze met hers and he smiled. A small, secret smile. One she knew well and one that set her pulse racing. They'd definitely been flirting out on the paintball field, and she wasn't great when it came to reading men, but she could sense that he might be interested in seeing where something between them could lead… Too bad he thought she was engaged. That's why he'd pulled away the night before.

And while she wanted to let him know that she was

open to the possibility of the two of them together again, she needed to be careful not to look as though she'd happily betray Callum. What man wanted a girlfriend that could be so easily swayed? No, she needed to change focus a little and continue to show Brent what he was missing out on. How amazing she could be as a girlfriend.

Turning back to Callum, she reached for his hand. His surprised look almost made her stumble on the trail. "What's happening?" he whispered.

"Slight change of plans. We're moving on to jealousy-invoking strategies," she mumbled under her breath.

He looked slightly annoyed to be used as a pawn in her game, but he'd signed up for this. In fact, this was his doing, so he really had no other choice than to nod and squeeze her hand. "Okay, well, let's see how he reacts to this," he said, stopping on the trail and pulling her into his body.

Their slightly sweat-damp shirts connected, and their hearts pounded against one another as he released her hand and cupped her face instead. His gaze burned into hers, and her breath caught and held as his head lowered toward hers.

"What are you doing?"

"Invoking jealousy," he said with a quick sideways glance toward Brent. "And believe me, it's working, so just go with it."

Just go with it. Okay. If it was going to ultimately help with her "get her ex-boyfriend back" mission, she'd allow it. "Okay, but just a small one," she whispered as she stood on her tiptoes and her lips met his.

Her eyes closed, and he held her face to his as he kissed her softly at first, then with more intensity, more passion… like the kiss at the reunion. His hands moved to her hips, and he held her firmly as he deepened the kiss even more, stealing her already labored breath.

Damn, he was a good kisser. She hadn't imagined it.

Her arms encircled his neck and her body pressed close to his. A soft moan escaped her, surprising both of them, as they both opened their eyes at the sound.

"Hey, you two, would you like us to come back for you later?" Nick called out.

Ellie stepped back out of Callum's embrace, her heart thudding in her chest. Shit, she'd totally lost herself there for a moment. The other kiss had messed with her a little, but that was just from lack of kissing in the last few years and the added pressure of their lie. This one had definitely been different.

And she wasn't quite sure what that meant.

But it wasn't good.

She forced a laugh. "No, I think we can keep our hands and lips off one another to make it the rest of the way."

"Speak for yourself," Callum said, his voice slightly husky next to her.

Ellie swallowed hard. Maybe the kiss had been too much. Maybe they'd gone too far. But a quick glance at Brent reassured her that her plan was working. Her ex was definitely wishing he'd been on the other side of that kiss.

THE SOUND OF Ellie's moan was on repeat in Callum's mind as he continued the steep hike up the side of Willow Mountain. This kiss had definitely been different. Before, he'd been kissing her. This time, she'd definitely been kissing back.

To make Brent jealous, she'd said. He knew better. He'd kissed women in the past who were just casually interested. Ellie's kiss had reinforced the connection that had developed between them the day before.

"We made it," Cheryl said as they moved through a

clearing in the trees and the view of the mountain's edge and valley below came into sight. Lush wilderness spread out before them, and the bright, cloudless day provided the perfect conditions to see far into the distance.

"Wow." Ellie's eyes widened as she took in the breath-taking scenery. "This is incredible."

Her flushed cheeks and the slight heaving of her chest beneath the tight tank top were incredible. He wished they were alone up here on the side of the mountain. This week would be so much better if it was just the two of them.

Could he grab her and kiss her again? Blame it on their quest to make Brent jealous? Or would she push him off the edge?

"So, here's the surprise," Cheryl said, opening her back-pack. "We're not going down the same way we came up." She took out a rappel harness and held it up.

Cool. He hadn't been rappelling in years.

A quick glance at Ellie revealed she wasn't as thrilled. Heights weren't her favorite thing. "Don't worry, it will be fine."

"Those harnesses don't look very strong," she said.

He laughed. "You're the lightest one here. You are the last person who should be worried about that."

"Are we even allowed to do this? Don't we need a certi-fied person or something?"

Cheryl raised her hand. "That's me. I'm the certified person."

Callum nodded. "Yeah, me too."

Ellie swung to look at him. "You are?"

"Search and rescue crew, remember?" One major perk of being a support member was all of the unique and inter-esting training he got to participate in. Living in Alaska, certain survival traits were necessary if people wanted to explore the outback regions. Every month, the crew had a new training day focused on some aspect of rescue and safety.

"Don't know everything about each other after all, huh?" Brent asked as he accepted a harness from Alisha.

The guy was getting on Callum's last nerve. He alternated between flirting with Ellie and giving her the cold shoulder. Mixed signals. Of course, Ellie wasn't exactly innocent in all of this, but Callum didn't like the way Brent was disrespecting both of them. "Every relationship needs some mystery," he said, accepting two harnesses from Cheryl.

When he turned to Ellie, she'd gone pale. Barely listening, she was moving farther away from the edge. Would she actually go through with the descent? He sighed. Maybe if he opted out and she could go with Brent, she'd find the courage. He approached her and said quietly, "I can opt out and meet you at the bottom if you'd like."

Her eyes widened and she shook her head. "No. If I'm doing this, I'm going to need you with me."

Hiding his pleasure was nearly impossible. "Okay. You got it." For the first time that week, Ellie was choosing him, realizing he was the one she could depend on.

And Callum wouldn't let her down.

"Okay, everyone is harnessed, so we can get started. Two at a time we will make our way down the side of the rock face," Cheryl told the group.

Ellie's palms sweat as she peered over the edge of the mountain. The rocks below looked jagged and it had to be a million-foot drop. There was no way she could do this. She didn't even like looking over the railing in the upper story of the Wild River Mall. If a fall didn't kill her, a heart attack would.

But how was she supposed to refuse and not look like a wimp?

Just like old times...

This wasn't the first time she'd gone outside her comfort zone to fit in or impress this group. Was it brave or was she simply not being true to herself by going along with things she had no interest in or desire to do? And would that always be the way if she were with Brent? Always having to compromise? Or was it that she was growing as a person each time she took on a new challenge like this?

At this point, she wasn't sure.

Cheryl and Mitch went first to show the group how it was done. They may not know trivia answers about one another, but they were certainly well matched as far as their adventurous spirit and energy level went. Maybe that was more important in a relationship—compatibility.

Ellie watched, trying to learn quickly as they approached the edge and turned around.

"Just sit back, plant your feet against the rock wall and release the cable a little at a time," Cheryl instructed.

Sit back, feet against the rock, release cable.

Seemed simple enough. Too simple. That was all that was required to keep her from dying?

Why was there no air up here? The high altitude was definitely affecting her breathing. Damn, where was her emergency inhaler when she needed it?

"You don't have to do this," Callum whispered as he tugged at her harness, making sure it was secure.

Didn't she?

Looking at Cheryl and Mitch reach the bottom and then Alisha and Nick talking one another through it...everyone encouraging Brent on his lone trek down the side—it didn't feel like there was any other choice.

"I'm okay. Let's just get this over with." They were up next. Everyone else was already at the bottom. Maybe she should have volunteered to go first, gotten it over with quickly and not had an audience.

She took a deep breath. No one else had had any issues. Maybe it wasn't such a big deal.

"Ready?" Callum asked as they slowly moved toward the edge.

Five minutes and it would be over. She'd be proud of herself for doing it. Better to do something you fear and be proud than chicken out and feel regret. Her old high school motto was back.

At the edge, her breath caught as she glanced down. Had the distance to the ground gotten farther since the last time she looked?

"Better not to look down," Callum said as he gently turned her around so she would be facing the cliff wall. "Just stare straight ahead as we descend, and we will be at the bottom before we know it."

She moved her feet backward until they couldn't go any farther.

What had Cheryl said?

Sit back, feet against the rock and release the cable. Don't look down and don't die.

"Okay, let's lean back. Just like you're sitting," Callum said, demonstrating.

He looked so comfortable perched against the side of the cliff. He'd no doubt make this look effortless. No matter what she did she was going to look terrified and awkward.

"Don't worry about how it looks, just get to the bottom," Callum said.

Damn, the guy was always in her head.

But he was right. The goal was just to survive this.

"Come on, you got this!" Alisha's voice echoed throughout the valley, and Ellie sighed as she slowly sat back, placing her weight and all her trust into the harness. Her feet pressed against the wall of the cliff and she waited for the free fall, but instead, she was dangling.

She glanced at Callum. "I'm doing it."

He laughed. "Yes, you are. Now let's try moving."

Moving. Right. She nodded.

"Release the cable slowly. Just small movements," Callum said, releasing his cable and dropping slightly lower down the rock wall.

Yep. He made it look easy. She took a breath and released her own cable. Her body lowered. About two inches, but at least it was something.

"Great! Now do it again," Callum said.

She did, and this time she dropped a little farther. She was level with him again. The harness was supporting her weight and her feet were planted against the side of the cliff. She was actually rappelling. She wouldn't lie and say she was enjoying it, but at least she was doing it.

"Okay, now we just keep going," he said, dropping lower.

Ellie released her cable and caught up with him. Not too bad. She dropped lower, gaining more courage with every few inches.

"See. Nothing to it," Callum said, smiling down at her. His look of admiration did make her feel good. Making him proud was definitely giving her a warm sensation. One she hadn't expected. "This scenery is breathtaking," he said softly, his gaze burning into hers.

"You're not looking at the scenery. You're looking at me," she said.

"I know."

Her heart raced and she looked away quickly. Unfortunately, she looked down. A wave of nausea hit her hard and dizziness threw her slightly off-balance. Her feet slipped against the rock wall and her knees bent. Her form compromised, she started to sway.

Oh no.

Unable to correct herself, Ellie gripped the cables and closed her eyes as her body crashed into the side of the rock face. Breathing immediately became difficult and her anxiety skyrocketed. What did she do now? She was dangling on the side of a cliff. She was stuck. She couldn't move. Her body felt completely paralyzed as she hung there.

The voices calling out instructions and encouragement seemed far away…almost dreamlike as she struggled to not black out. Why had she done this? She wasn't a teenager desperate for friends, desperate for acceptance anymore. She didn't enjoy these kinds of things, so why was she changing herself?

"Fancy meeting you here," Callum said.

She slowly opened her eyes to see him next to her. His grin looked slightly forced, and it didn't hide his concern.

"Is everyone staring?" she whispered.

"Nah, they all went for drinks," he said.

She shot him a look, but instantly her breathing relaxed a little. "I can't move. I'm stuck. This is where I live now."

"You're not stuck. You're just afraid. And while this would be a pretty cool place to live, it would get kinda cold in winter."

"I'm literally paralyzed. I can't feel my legs." She was gripping the cables so tightly, the cords started digging into the flesh of her palms. The heat of the sun radiating off the rock face felt like it could torch her skin, and sweat pooled on her lower back. The harness was definitely cutting off circulation.

"I'm here, and we're going to get to the bottom together," he said.

She made the mistake of glancing down again and shook her head, the valley swirling around her. "Can't we go up?" Down was another forty or fifty feet...up was quicker.

"Unfortunately, the rappel doesn't work that way, and besides, everyone is waiting at the bottom to hike back."

She sighed. "I don't think I can do it." She wasn't sure what was worse, having to complete the downward trek or facing everyone once she reached the bottom.

"Yes, you can."

"Says the man who has never been afraid of anything in his life."

His face clouded. "I'm afraid of things."

"Like what?"

"My father."

She blinked and momentarily her mind wasn't on her own fear. The shock of his confession worked to distract her. "Why?"

"Growing up he was abusive...not physically but mentally and emotionally. That's why my mom left. She'd had enough." He motioned toward her feet. "Lift your knees and place your feet against the rocks."

She did, painfully slowly. But a minute later she was back in position.

"After Mom left, things got worse," Callum said. "Dad was a workaholic, but now he was also angry. Being left with two kids wasn't the life he'd wanted. But then as soon as we were old enough to start going into work with him on summer breaks, he turned his anger into militant training. Suddenly, we were no longer a family but coworkers of sorts." He paused. "Slowly lift up and feed the cable through," he said.

She did and they moved several inches down the rock face.

"He's made it no secret that he doesn't approve of my lifestyle and that the only acceptable future is to take over the hotel." He paused. "The worst part is that I'm also afraid that maybe he's right. Maybe I am coasting through life," he said.

Ellie shook her head. "No. You have your writing."

"But what if I'm just hiding behind that because I know it's a long shot, but it's my excuse not to do anything else?" He nodded toward her cable. "Release a little more."

She dropped lower as she argued, "That's definitely not it."

"How do you know?" he asked as they went even lower.

"Because Mrs. Garnett said you were really talented… and because I believe in you."

"You haven't even read my writing yet," he said with a smile as they moved lower down the rock face.

"Maybe it's time we changed that," she said.

He laughed. "Make it to the bottom, and we can talk."

She nodded, more motivated than ever. She dared a glance down and saw they were only about ten feet from the ground. The group were all watching and nodding their encouragement and Ellie took a deep breath and kept going.

Within minutes, her feet were once again firmly planted on the ground.

Oh thank God. Relief rushed through her as Callum unhooked her harness. "There. See. Nothing to it."

She stared at him with gratitude. "Thank you." The words didn't even come close to capturing how she felt. Her emotions were undecipherable as she struggled to fight the overwhelming lingering anxiety. She was safe. Because of him. He'd been there for her when she'd needed him.

He always was.

He nodded, his gaze burning deep into hers as he removed her helmet and smoothed her hair. "Anytime."

She didn't even question that it was true. He was more than just her coworker and her friend…her fake fiancé and current partner in crime. He was the one person in her life that she knew she could always count on, and that realization was only becoming clearer the more time they spent together.

And the unsettling effect that knowledge had on her was something she was going to have to figure out. Fast.

Opening up to Ellie had been a bad idea.

Before this week, he'd had some hope of keeping the pieces of his heart from shattering if at the end of the week she still wanted to go through with the staged breakup. But now he was doomed. He'd shared things with her up on the rock face that he'd never told anyone.

Being vulnerable was new for him. Growing up, he'd learned to hide his emotions and fears. Once his mother left, he'd had no one he could depend on for support or encouragement. He'd always had to be the strong one for Sean.

Staring at Ellie now as she was showered with praise from the others, his heart pounded in his chest. Seeing her scared and pale up on the side of the mountain had had his protective instincts kicking into full gear. Ellie was always so confident and strong. He'd wanted to take her into his arms as soon as they were on the ground.

Brent was teasing her about her fear of heights and she was laughing good-naturedly, but she didn't look as enthralled with the guy as she had at the reunion…or a few hours ago.

Her gaze met his and there was definitely no denying the spark of interest reflecting in those deep dark pools now.

Was it wishful thinking or was Ellie finally realizing she was chasing something she didn't really want?

CHAPTER FOURTEEN

BOATING. NOW, THIS was an activity Ellie could get on board with.

In fact, anything that didn't require her fearfully clinging to the side of a mountain was acceptable.

Cheryl's family boat was a blue-and-white, forty-foot, open-deck Bayliner with a full bedroom and bathroom underneath. Sleek and stylish, the expensive boat looked like it might have been used once, bobbing at the end of the dock as the midday sun glistened against the lake. Ellie loved being out on the water, and it was just the relaxing activity she needed after that morning.

"That's impressive," Callum said next to her as they walked along the wooden planks.

"Doesn't your dad have a plane?" she whispered, shaking her head. She was currently surrounded by people whose families were richer than Ellie could even fathom. She'd grown up comfortable, but she'd never known the luxurious lifestyles that Callum and Cheryl had.

Callum nodded. "Yes, he does."

Ellie caught a tightness in his voice, and she immediately regretted bringing up his father, even in the casual way. His confession on the side of the mountain that morning was still causing her conflict. Money obviously couldn't buy happiness. Callum's life may have been full of private planes and big houses, but it didn't sound like a happy upbringing. She'd known his father was a jerk, but to hear that Callum had feared him as a child—and now feared his lack of approval—had shattered the misconception Ellie'd had about her friend.

And damned if they hadn't moved far beyond that this week.

They hadn't talked much as they'd trailed behind the others on the hike back to the cottages a few hours before, and Ellie had sensed an apprehension in him. He'd seemed lost in thought, as though processing what he'd told her on the mountain. Maybe regretting the vulnerability he'd displayed?

She was getting to know so much more about him this week, and it was definitely making her realize that she'd misjudged him. Dismissed him when maybe she shouldn't have. For the first time, she was looking forward to spending more time enjoying this trip with him. Brent wasn't the focus for her right now. She had no idea what that meant, only that she wanted to get to know Callum a bit more. Really get to know him.

Cheryl and Mitch climbed on board first and Mitch immediately took the captain's seat.

"Oh my God, Cheryl, why haven't we been on this boat all week?" Alisha said, stretching out on the large sun lounging area at the front of the boat. In her sailor-striped shorts and white bikini top, oversize sunhat and sunglasses, and wedge-heeled sandals, she looked like she belonged on the boat...or was at least photoshoot ready.

Ellie's jean shorts and tank top and flip-flops couldn't come close to the perfect look, but she was tired of comparing herself to the other women.

Nick and Brent carried a large cooler on board and began filling the under-seat cooler spaces with drinks.

"Looks like they're expecting a party," Callum whispered as the amount of alcohol being loaded onto the boat looked like enough for twenty people.

Ellie wasn't planning on drinking. She knew her water safety. Worst-case scenario, she'd figure out how to get the boat back to the dock if no one else kept their wits about them.

Callum climbed on board and extended a hand to help her. The same tingling rush of sensation coursed through her at the touch. "Thank you," she said.

He glanced around at the boat and pointed to a spot in the rear. "Um… I'll, uh, just hang out back there. Give you some space."

Ellie frowned. Was he saying that because he thought that was what she wanted or because he needed some space? She'd felt him retreat slightly since their moment on the mountain, and she couldn't quite figure out the cause. Was he embarrassed? Because he really shouldn't be. She'd been seeing more dimension and sides to him in the last few days than she'd ever imagined. And she was liking everything she was learning.

"I'll hang out back there with you," she said.

His expression was full of surprise as he nodded toward Brent at the front of the boat. "You sure you wouldn't rather join him? He's alone," Callum said.

Ellie glanced toward Brent. Dressed in white sailing shorts and a blue polo shirt, his light hair blowing in the breeze, his sunglasses on and a beer already in hand, he was the picture of everything she thought she wanted in a man—smooth sophistication. And two days before, she'd have jumped at the idea of joining him, trying to imagine herself in that picture-perfect image. But now she wasn't so eager. She wasn't sure how she felt about her conflicted state, but this was where she was.

She shrugged. "Maybe later. I mean, I'm supposed to be here with you, remember?"

His face clouded slightly and she wished she'd been honest. But what exactly could she say? That she was starting to not be so sure that Brent was what she wanted? That the connection developing between her and Callum was unexpected but not completely unappealing? That she'd like to explore it a little more?

Fear of rejection from him had her looking away from his gaze. "Do you want a drink?"

"Sure. Just water," he said.

She opened the seat and took out two bottles, then followed him to the rear of the boat. They sat on the soft padded seat and she moved slightly closer until their thighs were touching.

He gave her a quizzical look.

Obviously this had to be confusing to him. It was confusing to her.

Up until the day before, she'd been hell-bent on one thing—reconnecting with Brent. She'd wanted Callum to stay out of the way and give her space. They'd been planning the next stage of the week, leading up to the breakup.

Now she was sitting close to him and wanting him to sense her interest.

"Are you sure you wouldn't rather talk to Brent?"

"Do you want me to go talk to Brent?" Did he want to be alone? Was he not feeling the connection between them? Or had the rappelling incident really upset him and now he was retreating into his own emotions, dealing with his own past that had resurfaced that day?

He hesitated but then shook his head. "No. I want you to stay right here," he said, wrapping an arm around her.

A warmness flowed through her, until she saw Brent noticing them.

Shit. Was Callum's action just for show? She couldn't tell anymore. And it was her fault. "We don't need to put on a show..."

He pulled her into him, turning his body so that she could rest against his chest. "I'm not."

She sighed in relief as she settled into him. Then her pulse immediately started to race. So neither of them was acting anymore. She was cuddled into him because she wanted to, and he was holding her tight because he wanted to.

What the hell did it mean?

Had they somehow crossed over from fake fiancé to the start of a real relationship? How the hell...? And was that what she wanted? She'd thought she was sure she wanted Brent.

Damn, she was conflicted.

The boat started to pull away from the dock and Ellie stared out into the distance, trying to make sense of her emotions. Which ones were real?

She turned slightly to look at Callum and found him staring at her. "What?" she asked, feeling her cheeks flush with heat.

"Just enjoying the view," he said.

She cleared her throat, unsure how to completely fall into this moment with him and needing to keep the vibe less intense. "Hey, was that your brother calling last night?"

He nodded. "Yeah." He paused and didn't seem to have any plans of continuing.

"Everything okay?" she asked. She wasn't a nosy person by nature, but he'd opened up about his family, and now she was more than a little curious—especially after the early-morning phone call.

"Yeah, it's coming up on the end of the quarter, so he just gets a little extra stressed, that's all."

It didn't sound like that was all, but she didn't press, sensing the topic might be a touchy one. "Does he call a lot in the middle of the night?"

Callum nodded. "He's a bit of an insomniac. I'm not even sure he realizes it's the middle of the night."

"Do you always answer?" she asked with a suggestive eyebrow raise.

He laughed, but answered seriously, "Yes."

"Even if you're…otherwise engaged?"

His arm around her tightened even more. "Last night I thought twice," he said, brushing his lips gently against the side of her cheek.

She swallowed hard. What was happening to her? The heat radiating through her was off the charts, and it had nothing to do with the hot, blazing sun beating down on them.

Alisha approached them and grabbed Ellie's hand as the boat slowed in the middle of the lake. "I'm stealing her away."

Ellie reluctantly stood, with a glance back at Callum. "What are we doing?"

"Getting in the water," Alisha said, removing her sandals.

Ellie hesitated. "Oh, I'm not sure. I'm kinda loving this heat." She was loving her time with Callum.

"Oh come on. You'll get a better tan if you get wet first," Alisha said.

Ellie sighed, but she'd already realized it was pointless

arguing with these women. She removed her tank top and she could feel Callum's eyes on her as she unbuckled her jean shorts and slid them off over her hips.

Okay, that was definitely lust in his expression.

She turned around and lifted her hair. "Callum, do you think you could retie these straps? They feel a little loose." Where the hell had the courage to do that come from? Now she was flirting with her fake fiancé?

He got up, and his breath was warm against the back of her neck as he stood close behind her. "My pleasure," he murmured against her skin.

Goose bumps surfaced on every inch of her body and heat radiated through her.

His fingers tickled her flesh as he untied the straps, then tied them tighter. His hands rested on her shoulders and slowly slid down her arms. "There you go."

She swallowed hard as she turned to face him. "Thank you."

"You're welcome," he said, his gaze locked on hers stealing her breath.

Shit. Shit. Shit.

Things had just gotten even more complicated.

Damn, Ellie's body was amazing.

But what the hell was her game? Twenty-four hours ago she'd been set on getting Brent back. Now she was flirting with him? Was it real? Or was it just for show. They were in phase two of the plan—make Brent jealous. So that might be all it was. Yet, since their moment on the mountain, she seemed different. She was more attentive to him, wanted to be around him… Had his vulnerability brought them closer together?

Or was this all still part of the act?

Behind his dark sunglasses, he watched her swim with Cheryl and Alisha. Her firm, thin body in the modest yet sexy black bikini had him salivating. The way her breasts bobbed on the surface of the water and her legs threaded the current below, he was desperate to join her.

She looked up at him as she pushed her wet hair back away from her face, and the temptation to dive in, grab her and kiss those tantalizing lips until they were both sure that what was happening was real, until there was no more confusion about where they stood, was overwhelming.

"Hey, Callum, want a beer?" Mitch asked, joining him on the plush seat. He extended one toward him, the longneck covered in condensation.

Callum took it. "Thanks." Beer wasn't his thing, but he needed something to cool off.

"Having a good time?" the other guy asked.

He nodded. "This is great."

Mitch nodded toward Brent chatting with Nick at the front of the boat. "Gotta say, you are a bigger man than me. I'm not sure I'd be on board to spend a week with my girl's ex."

Callum shrugged. "Ah, that was high school. A long time ago," he said, taking a swig of his beer and glancing toward Ellie in the water.

Mitch didn't look convinced. "It wasn't that long ago."

Callum turned to him. "What are you saying?"

"Just that I'd be careful, that's all. Ellie's an amazing woman, and sometimes people don't realize what they have until it's gone." Mitch tapped his shoulder as he stood and removed his shirt. "Anyway, I'm sweating my balls off," he said before diving into the water and immediately swimming toward Cheryl.

Callum took another swig of his beer as he stared at Ellie laughing and enjoying the water with the others.

Unfortunately, he wasn't the only one. Brent was watching her intently, as well. Mitch's words echoed in his brain, and his gut tightened.

What was happening between him and Ellie? He needed to find out before it was too late.

ELLIE CLIMBED THE metal stairs back onto the boat and scanned it for Callum.

"I think he went down below," Brent said, coming up behind her with a towel. His gaze swept over her, and she quickly wrapped the towel around her body.

"Oh okay."

"Yeah, I think he wasn't feeling great." He lowered his voice. "A little tipsy maybe."

Tipsy? She'd been in the water less than an hour. He'd been drinking water with her. Had he started drinking beer with the other men? Callum didn't like beer. But there was a distinct scent of the alcohol coming from Brent, so maybe they had all indulged. "Maybe I should go check on him."

Brent laughed. "Are you his fiancée or his mother?"

Ellie's spine stiffened.

"I'm just kidding," Brent said, then his gaze dropped. "Sorry, that was a jerk comment. Jealousy's getting the better of me."

So he *was* jealous of her and Callum.

She wasn't sure how she felt about it, but she wasn't completely hating it. For years, she'd pined over Brent, longed for an opportunity to see him again and see if there was still something between them. She'd had to endure countless photos of him with other women on social media… If it was his turn to feel that, then so be it.

Unfortunately, she didn't know how far the jealousy should go. Did she want Brent to make a play for her still? Or was it enough to know that maybe he was regretting his decision years ago to let her go? A validation she really shouldn't need so badly.

"I have to admit, Ellie, it's not easy seeing you with someone else."

Of course, he'd never had to before. But what did that mean? Was jealousy a strong enough basis to think there might be another chance for them? Did she want him to want her just because he thought he couldn't have her?

"But I guess that's on me," he said in her silence. "Hey, what do you say we take a ride on the Sea-Doo while Callum sleeps off the day drinking?"

There was no malice in his tone, and Ellie was irritated that Callum would actually drink so much that he'd need to take a nap. Just when she thought her feelings for him were developing… She wasn't sure that was the kind of relationship she wanted.

It was unlike him though. Maybe it was more the combination of the drinks, the sway of the boat and the hot sun that had him not feeling so great.

"Um…" She eyed the Sea-Doo as Cheryl and Mitch pulled up to the boat, their ride on it done. It did look like fun.

Brent eyed her. "I know that look. Come on, you know you want to."

She offered a small smile and glanced around again. Callum was still downstairs. She'd rather go with him, but… "Okay, sure, why not?"

Brent smiled as he took her hand and led the way to the back of the boat. She tried to pull her hand back, but he held tight. "We're next!"

Cheryl frowned, looking slightly concerned. "You're going with Brent?" she asked her.

Ellie nodded casually. "Callum won't mind."

"Yeah, no of course not," Cheryl said, removing her life jacket and handing it to Ellie. "This might be a little big on you." The concern was back in her tone.

Ellie slid into it, but even pulled tight, it was far too big for her. "It's not fitting…"

"Sorry, Ellie, we don't have anything smaller," Mitch said, checking the life jacket supply on the boat.

Brent waved a hand as he buckled into his own. "It will be fine." He climbed onto the Sea-Doo. "We're not planning on falling in."

She nodded. He was right. And she could swim.

"You sure, Ellie?" Cheryl asked.

"Positive," she said, but her gut twisted. She moved past Cheryl, and Mitch extended a hand to help her climb down the boat ladder and throw her leg over the Sea-Doo behind Brent.

"Hold on to me," Brent said.

Her arms wrapped around his waist, her thighs clenching his legs, Ellie forced several deep breaths. Now that she was on the machine, her confidence wavered slightly. The machine vibrated on the surface of the water and the waves out on the lake looked a little rockier than they had from the boat.

This was going to be fine. Fun.

Brent had asked her to go for the ride. That meant he wanted to spend time with her. Be alone with her. He was jealous of her relationship with Callum. This was all good. It was what she'd wanted from the week, right?

Callum's touch as he retied her bikini and his lust-filled

gaze when he'd watched her swim in the water flashed in her mind and she desperately pushed them aside.

She tapped Brent on the shoulder. "Hey, were you drinking too?"

"I only had a couple."

She swallowed hard. Alcohol and motorized water sports didn't mix. Maybe this was a bad idea.

No, Brent was fine. He seemed completely in control. Still, "Don't go too fast, okay?"

He grinned as he glanced back at her. "Hold on tight."

There were other ways she'd envisioned having her arms around him over the years, but she wanted to show him that she wasn't a complete wimp. And this would be fun.

He started the machine and waved to the others on the boat deck as they pulled away. Ellie glanced back over her shoulder in time to see Callum return to the upper deck. Her gaze met his briefly, before the water spray coming from the back of the Sea-Doo blocked her view and they picked up speed.

The wind blew her wet hair away from her face as she held on to Brent's life jacket and they cruised along the lake, farther away from the boat. They hit the waves hard and Ellie's butt lifted off the seat with each crested wave. She smiled as the breeze and lake spray cooled her hot skin.

She'd forgotten how fun being out on the lake was.

Brent glanced at her over his shoulder and they shared a smile. Her heart twisted slightly and she remembered why she'd gone through all this trouble in the first place. Brent was the man she'd always loved. And it must have been just all the tense situations they'd found themselves in that week that had Ellie thinking that maybe she had real feelings for Callum.

That was crazy. If she'd been interested in Callum, wouldn't her feelings have developed before now?

They picked up speed, and Ellie gripped Brent tighter, struggling to get traction on the wet life jacket. "Maybe slow down a little," she yelled over the noise of the machine's engine.

He either didn't hear her or he ignored her as the Sea-Doo whipped over the lake.

He was going too fast. Ellie struggled to hold on as they hit the water harder and faster. Her laughter died and she shut her eyes tight. It wasn't fun anymore. "Brent, slow down!" she called over the wind. The water spray hitting her face and the wind whipping past almost stole her breath, her words getting swept away on the wind.

Brent went faster. Ellie glanced back toward the boat fading in the distance and saw Callum and the others waving frantically. They were telling them to slow down. Unfortunately, Brent wasn't paying any attention.

Her heart pounded in her chest as the machine seemed to catch even more air and Brent lost all control.

Callum's face miles away was the last thing Ellie saw before she was flying backward into the air and then crashing hard into the cold lake.

HE DIDN'T EVEN stop to think. Removing his shirt and glasses quickly, Callum dived into the water.

"Callum! Wait!" Alisha's voice faded as he plunged under the water and swam as fast as he could toward the last place he'd seen Ellie floating before she'd disappeared.

The image of the Sea-Doo flying over the waves, Brent losing control and Ellie flying off the back and crashing into the lake had terrified him. The impact of the hit alone could have knocked her out or winded her enough that she would be unable to catch a breath even when she did re-surface.

He swam hard against the waves, coming up for air, then going below again to peer through the murky water. He heard the motor of the Sea-Doo before he saw it bobbing on its side on the lake a few feet away. It had stalled, as Brent had fallen off, releasing the key from the ignition.

He looked around the surface, but he didn't see either of them.

A life jacket floating on the water had his heart falling deep into his gut. Cheryl had mentioned that Ellie's life jacket had been too big.

Damn it! Why the hell had she gotten on that thing with Brent? The guy wasn't exactly responsible at the best of times, let alone when he'd consumed half a dozen beers in two hours.

Taking a deep breath, Callum dived beneath the surface again and scanned frantically. Where was she?

The sound of the boat's motor drew closer, and he re-surfaced and saw the others scanning the waters, as well, from different positions on the deck. His gaze met Mitch's but the other guy shook his head. He inhaled as much air as possible and dived again.

This time he saw her. Ten feet away, she was slowly sinking deeper, lower into the water. Her arms outstretched, her hair billowing out all around her, her legs limp, he knew she was knocked out.

He reached her in record time and, wrapping one arm around her waist, he started the trek to the surface, moving upward, painfully slowly through the water. His legs were jelly and his lungs were desperate for air as he lifted Ellie's body to the surface and raised his own head seconds later.

He inhaled and a quick glance in both directions revealed he was closer to the shore than the boat, so ignoring the calls from the others on the boat he swam toward the safety of land.

ELLIE'S EYES OPENED and she knew two things. She was safely on land and the bright sun was trying to do what the lake hadn't as the piercing light made her head throb with such intensity, she thought it might explode.

She felt a heavy push on her sternum and water nearly choked her as it resurfaced out of her lungs and she started coughing.

Immediately Callum's face was above hers and he was lifting her head and turning her body to the side. "Oh thank God," she heard him say as he helped her evacuate the remaining water.

Had she swallowed the entire lake? She sputtered and coughed for what felt like forever, until she finally was able to take in a huge breath of air.

"You're okay," Callum said, rubbing her arms. "You're okay. Just relax and try to breathe in and out."

She didn't feel okay. She felt like she'd been hit by a freight train. Her arms and legs were numb and achy, her chest and rib cage felt bruised. Even her ass hurt beneath her.

She rolled onto her back, and Callum helped her into a sitting position. "Don't lie down," he said.

She tried to scan her surroundings, but the motion made her head throb. A wave of dizziness had her mouth filling with saliva and she fought to control the bile rising in the back of her throat. "The boat?"

He shook his head. "We're on the side of the lake. It was faster," he said, taking her face between his hands and staring into her eyes. Looking for a sign of concussion? He sighed heavily. "God, I thought I'd lost you."

Her eyes filled with tears as she stared at the unconcealed concern in his. It had been a close call. His devastated expression told her just how close it had been. "He was going too fast," she said, her voice sounding hoarse. That was the last thing she remembered. Begging him to slow down. Holding on tight...not tight enough. Soaring through the air and hitting the surface of the lake so hard it felt like hitting concrete.

Then darkness.

Callum ran a frustrated hand through his hair. "He should never have been driving. He'd had far too much to drink. What were you thinking getting on that thing with him?"

She blinked. This was her fault? "You were drinking too."

"That what he told you?" he asked, sounding a lot annoyed and not the least bit drunk. Ellie swallowed hard as she nodded. Maybe Brent had gotten his story wrong. Callum looked completely sober now.

She looked around but didn't see him. "Where is he?"

"On the boat," Callum said, his voice hard as he released her face and collapsed onto the ground next to her. "The others were able to get him. His life jacket stayed on."

Hers had been too big. Callum had dived in to save her. She'd been knocked out by the impact. There was no way she would have been able to save herself. What if the others hadn't been able to get to them? What if he hadn't been there?

She saw his hands trembling as he draped his arms over his bent knees and he lowered his head, taking long, deep breaths. "Thank you," she whispered.

He raised his pained gaze toward her, and she could hear his heart pounding in his chest. Or was it hers?

"I'd never let anything happen to you," he said softly, and she heard the conviction in his voice.

She was going to need to figure out the conflicting emotions raging through her and fast. She couldn't continue to expect Callum to keep saving her from herself and her decisions.

CHAPTER FIFTEEN

ONCE THE INITIAL shock and fear subsided, a new adrenaline coursed through Callum. Climbing back onto the boat, he helped Ellie to a comfortable safe spot, then he advanced on Brent in the downstairs bedroom.

"What the hell were you doing out there?" he demanded.

The others shrank away, giving the two men space to hash this out.

"Just having some fun, man, relax," Brent said. He winced as he touched the bandage on his head that Alisha had just finished applying. The guy was going to have more than just a head gash to deal with if he didn't take this seriously.

"Relax? You could have killed both of you. If you want to take risks like that with your own life, go ahead, but not with Ellie's." He couldn't remember ever feeling the intensity of the rage flowing through him now. His hands clenched at his sides, and he might not be showing so much mercy and restraint if the guy hadn't almost drowned.

"Stop exaggerating. It was an accident."

Was the guy fucking with him right now? Could he really not see the danger he'd put them in? His reckless behavior? "Ellie's life jacket wasn't on her and she was knocked out," he said through clenched teeth.

The others sent Brent varying degrees of disapproving

stares, and finally the guy had the decency to look remorseful. He looked past Callum. "I'm so sorry, Ellie."

"Callum, I'm okay," Ellie said, joining them, her voice still scratchy.

She was okay, but it had been a close one. If it had taken even a few minutes more to reach her, the day could have turned out a lot different. He could have lost her.

"Look, in hindsight, I shouldn't have been driving," Brent said. "I'm sorry, man." He extended his hand and Callum ignored it as he left the room under the boat and took the stairs two at a time to the upper deck.

If he didn't put some distance there, he was going to lose it. No one, besides his brother, had ever meant as much to him before. Ellie was everything. He'd always known the extent of his feelings for her, but that day had only confirmed it even further. He hated the idea of her with someone else. He wasn't sure if he was imagining their connection, but he felt closer to her that week than ever before, and he couldn't keep pretending that he was okay with just being her friend.

If he'd lost her today…

Downstairs, he could hear Alisha checking her out, asking a series of questions to ensure that she was okay.

His hands still shook as he leaned against the railing, staring out at the lake that wasn't so breathtakingly majestic anymore.

He ran a hand through his hair as he sighed, feeling every muscle in his body contract. He'd been operating on pure adrenaline before, and now that he was coming down off of the high, his body ached.

A long moment later, he felt Ellie's hand on his shoulder. "Hey, you okay?" she asked softly.

She'd nearly drowned and she was asking if he was okay.

"He put your life at risk," he said, gruffly. That was the guy she wanted to be with? A reckless, careless guy who'd let her down far too many times?

"And thank God you were there," she said softly, caressing his cheek. Her touch was gentle, her words loaded with so many emotions.

Love? Was there love in there, as well, or was it simply gratitude?

CONFLICTED, HER HEAD still slightly woozy, Ellie descended the stairs to the lower deck as they approached the dock an hour later.

Callum had saved her life. Alisha's account of his actions had only multiplied Ellie's gratitude tenfold. He'd dived in and swum to her. He'd searched underwater until he'd found her and then he'd swum the crazy distance to shore, making sure she stayed safely above the water the entire way. And then his quick actions and knowledge of CPR had saved her life. She'd almost died. She shivered at the thought. Because of Brent's recklessness and her own lack of judgment she'd been in danger.

She swallowed hard as she went to sit next to Brent. He still looked a light shade of blue, and the gash on his forehead from hitting some rocks had obviously reopened, because the blood seeping through the bandage around his head made her wince.

Alisha would definitely need to stitch him up once she got the first aid kit back at the cottages. She'd done what she could with the limited first aid kit on board the boat. Looking at him was a grim reminder that the enjoyable day had gone south quickly. They'd all been having a great time, and then they'd ruined the day for everyone. No one had any interest going out on the Sea-Doo after they'd had their accident and the machine had been retrieved from the middle of the lake. The somber mood on the boat as they'd turned back early was really depressing. It was made even worse by the blistering sun in the cloudless sky that seemed to mock them for being so careless.

She stared at Brent, his eyes closed as he lay on the bed, his breathing sounding hoarse and slightly strained. A slight pang of sympathy washed over her, diluting her anger a little.

He could have died. They both could have…

What the hell had he been thinking driving so fast? And under the influence? And why had she gotten on the machine with someone who'd been drinking? It wasn't like her to make such a bad judgment call.

He opened his eyes, and the pained, remorseful expression helped to dampen her anger even more. He hadn't meant for them to get hurt. It didn't change the fact that they'd made a terrible choice that could have ended so much worse. "I'm sorry, Ellie."

She nodded. "I know," she said as she sat on the edge of the bed. "I'm not completely faultless here either."

He sighed as he stared at the ceiling. "My drinking has gotten out of control. It's been a problem for a little while now."

She was surprised to hear it. He'd always drunk responsibly when they were teens. He was the one who'd always been the designated driver, who'd always made sure everyone got home safe after parties. He'd been so focused on all of his sports and other extracurricular activities that he hadn't even stayed very long at events. He'd been the good guy who would never have harmed anyone—on purpose or otherwise. So conscientious. It was one of the things she'd loved about him.

Obviously he wasn't exactly the guy she remembered.

Then again, she wasn't the same person either.

"It's partially the job. It can be stressful, so a cocktail after work helps to calm me. At first it was one, then it was two... When we are on resorts, we drink." He shrugged. "There's no excuse. I have to take responsibility for my own actions."

She nodded. At least he was realizing he had a problem. Didn't they say that was the first step in healing? "But why did you say Callum had been drinking?" She still couldn't understand that part. Was he trying to make Callum look bad in her eyes?

"I thought he had been," he said with a shrug. "Guess it was just me."

She swallowed hard, unsure whether or not she believed him. But given the circumstances and everything that had happened that day, she wasn't sure if it really mattered. A lot had been put into perspective in the last few hours. But there was still a lack of clarity regarding her feelings for both men.

She stood slowly. "I guess I should let you rest."

He reached for her hand, and the pleading look on his face weakened her. "Please don't go yet."

She sighed, then sat back down on the bed. Brent's hand held tightly to hers as he closed his eyes. Conflicted, Ellie stared at their conjoined hands, waiting for the sensation she got at Callum's touch to appear.

It didn't.

Unfortunately, *he* did. "Hey, Ellie, are you..." He paused on the third step, seeing her and Brent together, and his gaze fell to their hands joined on the bed. "Sorry to interrupt. We are about to dock," he said, his voice cold as he turned and headed back up the stairs.

Ellie sighed as she slipped her hand out of Brent's.

Too late.

CHAPTER SIXTEEN

THE ATMOSPHERE WAS tense in the lodge as Ellie joined the others for dinner. Alone. Callum hadn't been in any mood to try to pretend that everything was okay.

Ellie was still rattled too but she was trying not to make an even bigger deal of what had happened. After all, she'd gotten on that Sea-Doo. No one had forced her. Callum was acting as though Brent had abducted her. She was alternating between her own anger at and sympathy for Brent and just an overall relief that they were all okay.

That was what was important, right?

"Hey, how are you feeling?" Alisha asked as she took a seat next to her at the otherwise-empty, long dining room table. The concern on her face had Ellie rushing to reassure her she was okay.

"I'm fine. Just a little sore." *Little* was an understatement. Her entire body felt as though she'd spent twenty-four hours powerlifting at the gym. Her arms and legs felt tight, but it was her chest and ribs that ached the most. Partly from the inhalation of water and partly from the CPR Callum had performed.

"No doubt every muscle in your body tensed upon impact with the water." Alisha studied her closely. "Any headaches or blackouts? Trouble breathing?"

"No. Nothing like that." A few waves of dizziness and a couple of coughing spells but they were subsiding. She and Brent had refused a trip to the hospital, claiming to be okay. Ellie hadn't wanted to make a fuss and ruin everyone's week, more than she may have already.

"Good. Well, let me know, okay?"

She nodded. "Where's Brent?" she asked, looking around.

"Sleeping still," Alisha said. "I keep waking him every half hour looking for signs of concussion. So far I'm not seeing anything to be concerned about, but he hit his head really bad." She paused. "He's pretty shaken up. He feels horrible."

Ellie nodded as she picked up her glass of water, then rethinking it, set it back down.

"I guess his drinking is a little out of control," Alisha said quietly as the others carried their plates of food into the dining room. "I would have warned you, had I known."

"It's no one's fault. That's why they call it an accident, right?" Keeping her tone light was the only way through this. She didn't hold anyone responsible, and she hated that once again, she was the odd man out who had put a damper on the day. Brent hadn't done it on purpose and they were all okay.

"I'm thinking Callum's not seeing it that way," Alisha said, sounding like she understood his point.

"For the record, no one is blaming him at all for being upset. If Alisha had been the one on that Sea-Doo, I'm not sure I'd be able to resist kicking Brent's ass right now," Nick said, setting his plate and Alisha's on the table. "I'll get you some food."

"Oh no, it's okay. I can get it," Ellie started to protest.

Nick touched her shoulder gently as she went to get up. "Sit tight."

She hated everyone fussing over her but she nodded. "Thank you."

Cheryl sat on the other side of her and gave her a quick hug. "So relieved you are okay." She held out a hand that trembled slightly. "I'm still shaking. I don't know how you're not still freaked out."

Maybe because everything had happened so quickly. One minute she was on the Sea-Doo, the next she was in the water and everything was black. There hadn't been time to be afraid or worried. She hadn't struggled for air the way others do when they are drowning because she was already out cold the minute she hit the water.

"That fiancé of yours an Olympic swimmer?" Mitch asked, pouring a glass of Scotch at the bar before joining them.

"Not that I know of." But who knows? She was discovering so much about Callum that week that nothing would surprise her. Maybe she should have stayed at the cabin with him. He seemed to be okay once the boat had docked, but he hadn't really said much to her after seeing her below deck with Brent. He'd obviously misread that situation and was upset, but she had no idea what to do now or what to say. They'd been connecting on the boat before the accident, but where were they now?

Where did she want them to be?

"Well, if not, he should be. I have never seen anyone swim that fast," Mitch said.

Alisha nodded. "True story. As soon as you hit the water, he was diving off the boat without a second's hesitation." She shook her head and shivered. "You were so far away and then when you went under without the life jacket on, we totally lost sight of you. Apparently not Callum. I don't think anyone else could have gotten to you so quickly."

Nick nodded as he returned with Ellie's plate of food and set it in front of her. "With both of you landing in the water so far apart, I know there's no way we could have gotten to you both."

A silence fell over the table and Ellie's appetite was gone as the reality of that day's events hit her. She hadn't fully processed everything clearly until now. The boat had been closer to Brent. He'd been injured, but alert and bobbing on the surface. She'd gone under. Brent would have been the one they could have gotten to. He would have been the one they rescued first.

If Callum hadn't been there, if he hadn't dived into the water to save her, the rest of the group may have completely lost sight of her and been unable to locate her beneath the surface of the lake. Without consciousness, without a way to try to save herself, Ellie would have drowned. Without Callum's quick thinking and heroic actions, she would have died today.

THE ONLY GOOD thing to come out of today's events was the inspiration for his writing. All afternoon the words had flowed out of him, anger fueling each word. If his hands could just stop shaking, he might actually have one of those words without a squiggly red line underneath.

Ellie had gone to the lodge to join the others for dinner. She didn't want anyone thinking she was upset or holding them responsible for what had happened. Callum didn't care if they thought he was upset. He was. And he was holding Brent a hundred percent responsible for what had happened.

It annoyed him that Ellie wasn't.

He still didn't know what was going on. On the boat, she'd clearly chosen him over Brent to spend time with. Then he'd gone below to answer a frantic call from Sean and somehow she'd ended up on that Sea-Doo...

The worst part was seeing her holding Brent's hand. It

was right up there with the image of her flying through the air and crashing into the lake.

He sighed and ran a hand through his hair. There was no way to save the rest of the week. He wanted to leave, but he knew if he did, he'd be leaving alone. And he couldn't do that to her.

Ellie entered the cottage, and Callum glanced up from his laptop. She carried a plate of food and set it down on the table. "You didn't come up for dinner, so…"

"Thanks," he said, returning to the keyboard. It hurt to look at her. Every time he did, his heart raced and his palms sweat. He'd come so close to losing her that day. Not just to Brent, but for real.

"Everyone asked where you were," she said.

He ignored her and kept typing. Incoherent sentences, probably, but he wasn't ready to discuss things with her. He had no idea where they stood. He had no idea what she wanted from him. If she still even needed him here. Maybe it was time to just come clean.

"Are you getting much writing done?" she asked, sitting on the edge of the bed.

He sighed and nodded once.

"Will you please talk to me?" she asked, sounding exasperated with him.

Exasperated with him.

He set the laptop aside and stood. "What do you want me to say, Ellie?"

"I don't know. I just don't know why you're so upset with me."

She didn't know why he was upset? "Seriously? Because I don't even recognize you this week. All of these activities aren't your thing, yet you're going along with the group as though you've suddenly lost your own voice. Your ability to speak up."

"So, now stepping outside my comfort zone and trying new things is a bad thing?" she countered.

He raised an eyebrow. "That's just a new bullshit way of peer pressuring people into things. If you wanted to do these things and were simply afraid, that's one thing. But you have no interest in any of these adventure activities. You'd rather be curled up in the lodge reading or sitting out on the deck swing…"

She sighed. "Fine. You're right. But this was a vacation. It's not like they do this stuff every day."

So she was still contemplating a life with Brent. Thinking about how everyday life would look with him. He shook his head and stared at the floor.

"What?"

"Nothing." There was no point saying anything. If the connection forming between them wasn't enough for her to start having a change of heart, him criticizing Brent wouldn't get him very far.

"No, what is it? You obviously have something to say," she said.

"Fine." He took several steps toward her. "You are so blinded by past feelings that you aren't seeing what's really in front of you. You're not seeing who Brent is now and that maybe the things that connected you in the past don't anymore."

She stood slowly. "How would I know that after a few days? We are just getting to know one another again, and it's very difficult when he thinks I'm engaged."

"So this is my fault?"

"You were the one who got us into this mess by saying you are my fiancé." She started to pace the room. "I still don't know what the hell you were thinking. This is such a disaster." She massaged her temples and his gut turned. He hated seeing her upset. He wanted to wrap his arms around her and hold her. Make her feel safe and secure.

"I wasn't thinking," he said. Then shook his head. Time to be honest. "Or maybe I was. Maybe I was hoping that if you were forced to pretend to like me, be attracted to me, you might just look beyond your prejudices against me and realize there could be something there," he said softly and paused. "Between us."

Her mouth dropped. "For real? Like a real relationship?"

"Yes, Ellie, and don't look so surprised. I've only been crazy about you for two years." Now he was exasperated. He ran a hand over his face and sighed.

"Crazy about me?"

His shoulders slumped and he released a slow, deep breath. "Seeing you every day at the store is the highlight of my day. Highlight of my life, really." Couldn't say it any clearer than that.

Ellie strode across the room and stopped just inches from him. She reached up and gripped the back of his head, pulling his face toward hers.

A momentary shock had him paralyzed, but then his arms went around her and he deepened the kiss. The stress and tension and fear of that day all came out in the kiss as he pulled her into him. Every emotion he'd been hiding, repressing for two years poured out in this one moment.

If he'd lost her that day...

He kissed her even harder, needing the feel of her, the taste of her. He breathed in the sweet honeysuckle scent he couldn't get enough of as his hands dug into her rib cage.

When she pulled back a long second later, he inhaled

deeply as he rested his forehead against hers. His heart thudded in his chest. "What was that?"

"My attempt to show you that there's no spark between us," she said, her voice quivering slightly.

"How'd that work out for you?"

"It may have backfired."

"You bet your ass it backfired," he said. There was no way she could deny their connection now. "So, what do we do about it?"

She hesitated, moving slowly away. "I don't know. I mean all of this—" she gestured between them "—is kinda unexpected."

"It shouldn't be. I've only been flirting with you for two years."

"I didn't think you were serious," she said, sitting on the edge of the bed.

"Why not?"

"Look at you. You're like a chiseled Greek god. You could have anyone you want."

"I only wanted you. I still only want you," he said, his courage growing. His secret was out. She knew he was serious. Now the ball was in her court.

Man, he'd really put himself out there today. But he didn't regret it.

"I guess now the question is, what do you want?"

She was quiet for a long time as she stared at him. He didn't move. He didn't speak.

"I think I want to read your work," she said, finally.

He frowned. "What? Now?" They were kind of in the middle of something important.

"Yep. You promised if I made it to the bottom of the rock face, I could read your work," she said. She sat back against the bed cushions and reached out her arms. "Lap-top, please."

Wow. Okay. Guess they were doing that instead of figuring out where they went with their relationship. He sighed as he reached for his laptop case. "The work in progress is still off-limits, but you can read these revised pages." He hesitated, then reluctantly handed her the printed version of the first six chapters of the book.

She took them with a huge smile, her excitement only making him that much more nervous. But what the hell, he'd already been vulnerable twice that day, may as well go for the hat trick.

An hour later, Callum paced the room, shooting a glance at Ellie. She was a speed reader, often consuming a book in less than a day. What was taking her so long? Her expression was unreadable as her eyes flew over the words in his manuscript pages. "They are still really rough…"

"Shhh…"

"Sorry." He sat in the chair near the window and scrolled through his cell phone. Seeing a text from Sean, he ignored it, putting the phone aside. There was no way he could deal with his family after the day he'd had. The call earlier that day had stolen his attention and look what had happened. His brother could deal with things without him for a few hours. He couldn't do much from three hours away anyway, and didn't he deserve a vacation? Some time to forget about his family issues. He'd have to face it all again far too soon.

He stood and took out a bottle of water from the mini-fridge and chugged it loudly.

Ellie glared at him.

"Sorry… You know what, I'm just going to head out-side."

She simply nodded and waved him away. He was tempted

to go in for a quick goodbye kiss, but now that shit between them was getting real, he was too nervous. Instead,
he quickly escaped outside, where the early evening sun
was starting to cast shadows over the wilderness.

He looked toward the lodge and saw the group inside.
He wasn't going there. He'd eventually join all of them
again. By the next morning, he hoped he could see Brent
without wanting to punch him in the throat, but right now,
it was still too soon.

Maybe a run might ease some of the anxiety. He'd never
let anyone read his work before, not since his creative writing teacher, and this was absolute torture.

How was he ever going to send it out to agents or editors?
Having people all over the world read his stuff someday...
worse, his family. He wasn't sure he could ever do it.

Leaving the cottage deck, he headed down the nearest
trail in a sprint. He trusted Ellie more than anyone. She'd
give it to him straight. If she said it was good, he'd believe
her. If she said it was bad, he'd give it up and go work for
the hotel.

That idea made him completely nauseous. Having grown
up around the industry, he knew for certain it wasn't what
he'd be happy doing with his life. He often wished it was.
Life would be easier. He wouldn't have to feel like such a
failure in his father's eyes or leave all of the responsibility to Sean.

His mother's love of books and her passion for writing
had obviously been the genes he'd inherited. But had he
inherited her talent?

Sweaty and exhausted but still a ball of nerves, Callum
reentered the cottage an hour later. Ellie sat on the bed, the
pages of the manuscript beside her.

"Well?" He was fairly certain he stopped breathing as he waited for her answer.

"They were amazing."

His shoulders slumped in relief. "You're telling me the truth?"

"I'd never lie to you about something this important."

He sat on the bed and removed his running shoes, needing the distraction to hide his pleasure and pride at her words. She liked his writing. Now, if only he could get a straightforward, honest answer from her about whether or not she liked him.

"Can I read you my favorite part?" she asked, her eyes lighting up.

She had a favorite part? His mouth went dry. "Uh…" That would be almost torture. Rereading his own work was often challenging, impostor syndrome an ugly beast. Hearing her read the words out loud would be terrifying.

But she didn't give him a choice. Not waiting for him to answer, she flipped the pages to somewhere in the middle. She cleared her throat and read, "'Six bedrooms in this mansion of a prison and four remain empty, while this one contains two sides. I feel as though I'm split in half, like a multiple personality.'"

It was the scene from the point of view of their childhood home. Particularly the walls that formed the corners of his side of the bedroom. Callum swallowed hard. He'd shared a room with Sean because of his brother's night terrors. That scene had both poured out of him with ease and taken every ounce of vulnerability. Ellie continued reading and his heart pounded harder as she drew closer to the climax of the scene.

"'Across from me, the foundations shake and twist, paint peels away and beams start to break. I'm still standing.

Why am I not crumbling? The same storms rage against my beams, my drywall, my paint, yet the vibrant blue only deepens, the tiny cracks hold together and I feel indestructible.'"

Callum bit his lip, struggling to watch Ellie's emotional expression as she read, but unable to tear his gaze away. His words coming from her mouth seemed surreal, held more depth, made him realize just how impactful his past was on his future. He continued to be the strong one, and he could never allow his world to crumble.

"'Was I built stronger? Or have I simply learned to resist? Have the beatings of my environment only instilled a desire to last? To persevere? And how can I save the rest of this shelter without compromising the integrity within and risking it all falling down?'" She stopped reading with a deep sigh. "Wow."

Wow was right. He was both vibrating with the anxiousness of having her read his work out loud and paralyzed as to what to say or do next.

"That was completely captivating...and it's not just that scene but the entire work so far."

"Thank you."

"I can't believe you kept this talent to yourself all this time," she said.

This was the secret she was amazed he'd kept from her? Not the fact that he was in love with her and wanted to be more than just coworkers and friends. Much more.

"Well, what are you going to do next? Have you submitted anything to agents or publishers yet?"

Now that she knew about this, he knew she wouldn't let him put off that decision much longer. "No. It's not done and most want a completed manuscript from new authors."

She smiled and her entire face lit up, despite the lingering paleness from the accident earlier that day. "New author. I like the sound of that."

"Well, not that I'm really an author. I told you, this is just more...therapeutic than anything else."

"But you're going to publish it, right?"

He sighed. "I don't know. It's super personal and it talks about my family..." His father would kill him, and he wasn't sure Sean would be pleased about his own personal issues being put into a book.

"You could publish under a pen name. The stories in here could be about any family going through these challenges. You've written it in such a beautifully moving way that I think it would resonate with a lot of people."

"Really?"

"Yes really!" She shook her head. "I still don't get why you've never told anyone?"

"Who would I tell?"

"Well, your father for a start. Maybe if he knew you had another ambition, he'd leave you alone about the hotel."

Callum shook his head. "Nope. It would only enrage him even further."

"Even if the subject matter wasn't about him?" Ellie asked.

He nodded.

"What? Why?"

He sat on the edge of the bed and ran a hand through his hair. "Dad doesn't exactly appreciate the arts or anything that can't be quantitated with numbers and a bottom line. Success to him equals money and reputation." He paused before going all in. "My mom is a writer."

Ellie's eyes widened. "I feel like I've never really known you at all."

Maybe in some ways she hadn't. She'd never seen beyond the surface, anyway. And that was only partially her fault. He'd done a good job keeping his life private. How had he expected her to fall for him when he'd never shown her who he really was? Or at least who he could be? Wanted to be?

"I don't talk about her much. I try not to think about her much either. It's too hard, I guess." He'd been so close to his mom. Her leaving had been hard on Sean, but it had devastated him. "When she first met my father, she was working at a successful accounting firm, but she hated every second of the job. Her passion was writing. When she had my brother, she went on maternity leave and didn't go back." He paused. "Which my father never understood."

"She wanted to write?"

He nodded. "And she did. Which created even more fights and tension when my dad found out that she'd given up a lucrative career to chase a pipe dream."   .

"It's not like your family needed the money."

Callum shook his head. "Believe me, to my dad there's no such thing as ever having too much money. But I don't really believe it was about that. I think it was more that he felt like she'd betrayed him somehow, tricked him into thinking she was as career-minded as he was. And he didn't see writing as a viable career."

"Maybe he should stop by some author events at the store sometime."

Callum's laugh was humorless. "If you can get my father into a bookstore, you will have done the impossible. Anyway, Mom hid her writing from him after that. She even went back to the accounting firm after she had me in an effort to stop the fighting and try to regain some of their relationship for our sake, but she wasn't happy."

"When a mom's not happy, no one's happy," Ellie said softly.

"That's so true. My brother and I felt the tension between them and heard the fights. We knew Mom was miserable, but Dad was callous and oblivious to it. As long as she did what he wanted her to do, he didn't care."

Ellie sent him an apologetic look. "So, you really can't tell him about this without making things worse between you two?"

"Nope. And honestly, I don't care. I tried for years to bridge the gap between us. Mom gave up. Sean is still desperately trying, fighting for Dad's approval. I'm stuck in the in-between of either giving Dad what he wants or walking away." He released a deep sigh. He'd never admitted all of this out loud or told anyone about his past before. Opening up to Ellie felt liberating but also terrifying. What if she continued to reject him? He'd shared so much of himself today.

"I'm sorry, Callum. I wish you had his support." She picked up the manuscript pages, her passion returning to her voice. "But this is really good. I don't think you should give in to your dad. Your mom didn't. You shouldn't. And I think your mom would be proud of you."

His jaw clenched. "If she cared about us, maybe."

Ellie touched his shoulder gently. "I'm sure she does. Have you reached out to her? Does she know you inherited her passion and talent?"

"Not in years." She had used to reach out on Christmas and birthdays, but she'd gotten remarried in recent years and had adopted a child with her new husband. He wasn't ready to divulge all of that and the impact it had had on him to Ellie just yet. "She'd be happy, but I'm not ready to give her that, you know. I'm still pissed that she left, not for my sake, but for Sean's. She should have at least taken him with her."

Ellie nodded slowly. "I get it. I mean, at least I do now. Thank you for confiding in me and trusting me with this." She hugged his manuscript to her chest the way he'd seen her hug her favorite, precious books. And no matter how much turmoil he might have dug up regarding his family that day, or the way he was dangling out on a limb all on his own regarding his feelings, Ellie's admiration in this one respect helped to soften his uneasiness.

"What comes next?" she asked, curling her legs under her on the bed.

"In the book?" he asked, almost surprised that she was interested enough to want to know.

"Yes, in the book! You've left me hanging." She tossed a pillow at him and he caught it.

He laughed as he climbed onto the bed next to her and put the pillow behind his back to sit against the bed frame. "This is okay?" he asked. He didn't want to cross any boundaries, and she'd made it quite clear that they weren't sharing the bed. But after the intensely intimate kisses they'd been sharing lately, him sitting next to her on the bed seemed hardly something to worry about...

"Of course," she said.

He settled in and tried to relax his tense muscles. "I'm not sure. I've hit that dreaded saggy middle section that writers always talk about. I know some of the stories I still want to tell, but I'm running out of ways to tell them. Some are too close to the surface still, maybe... I have mad respect for anyone who has ever successfully completed a book."

Ellie bit her lip. "Well, what about writing those more difficult scenes in a different perspective?"

"Like Sean's?"

She hesitated. "I was thinking more like your dad's perspective."

He frowned. "He wasn't there for the particular scenes I'm thinking about." Mainly they were scenes of him helping his brother during the more challenging times. His father had never been around to witness those times. Which had probably been for the best, in hindsight. Callum had been angry that he'd been the one left supporting Sean on his own—just a teen himself—and that his father hadn't been there. But now he knew that would have only made everything worse.

"Then, that would make it all the more interesting and impactful," Ellie said softly. "What would it have been like if he had been? What would he have thought? How would he have reacted? How would it have made you both feel?"

Callum nodded. It would definitely add another dimension to the prose. He wasn't sure he could actually do it, but… "I'll think about it." He paused. "Thank you. It's a good idea."

Ellie nodded. "Do you know how you want it to end?"

"Yes. I do have that part figured out already." He wanted the book to be real, to be authentic, but he also wanted it to inspire and provide hope.

Ellie continued to stare at him. "So?"

"So what?"

She let out an exasperated sigh. "How does it end?"

He grinned. "You'll have to wait and find out."

She pouted, and it was so incredibly irresistible that it took all his strength not to kiss her. "Fine," she said. "But know that I plan to ride your ass every day to finish this now so I can read it."

He swallowed hard. Having her support, having her encouragement, having her ride his ass was renewing his motivation for the project. It sucked that he'd never had this before, but he was happy he was getting it now. From her. It meant so much more coming from someone he truly cared about.

His eyes dropped to her lips, then returned to her eyes. "Thanks, Ellie," he said, his voice slightly husky.

She nodded. "Of course, Callum. I'm here for you," she said, and her voice sounded slightly strained as an intensity filled the space around them.

Sharing so much with her had his emotions so close to the surface. He cared about her. He was in love with her. She was the closest person in his life… He slowly reached out and touched her cheek.

He still expected her to pull away, but instead she turned her face into his palm, and her gaze was hesitant as it met his. He ran his thumb along her jawline and then over her bottom lip, and he saw her swallow hard.

He moved closer, his face inching toward hers, giving her plenty of time to stop him or back away. She had kissed him a few hours ago to try to prove a point. Maybe now it was his turn?

"Ellie, I'm sorry if I've completely freaked you out with what I said, but after everything that happened today, I needed you to know." Life was precious. And short. Things could be ripped away in an instant. He couldn't risk another day of her not knowing how he felt. He wasn't expecting anything in return…just maybe a chance to show her how great they could be together.

She stared into his eyes, and the conflict he saw in hers made his chest ache. He didn't want to make this hard on her or complicate things…but he knew he was the better man for her.

He moved closer and wrapped his arms around her. She moved into him willingly, and when she lifted her face upward and closed her eyes, he kissed her.

Soft. Gentle. Teasing.

Not like her full-on, intense, passion-filled kiss earlier.

He wrapped his hands around the back of her neck and let his fingers tangle in her soft hair as he held her face to his. He tipped his head to the side and allowed his lips to move away from hers, kissing along her jawline and down the side of her neck.

He felt her swallow hard, and her hands knotted in the fabric of his T-shirt. "Callum…" she whispered.

He brought his lips back to hers and his tongue teased hers open. He kissed her harder this time before moving away to kiss the other side of her neck. The smell of her skin was driving him crazy. He wanted to leave kisses like this all over her.

She took his face into her hands and kissed him on the mouth again. Desperate, needy, as though searching for the answers to her conflicted heart.

He continued to kiss her for a long time. He wouldn't stop if she didn't. He was afraid to. Afraid of what awaited on the other side. Afraid he'd never get this chance again.

Finally, she pulled back, slowly, looking slightly dazed when her gaze met his. "I'm going to go get some air," she said, releasing his shirt and scampering toward the end of the bed. She didn't seem to be running away…more like looking for a way to process. "And you should write some more," she said, grabbing her sweater and running shoes and leaving the cottage quickly.

Callum sighed, but his heart soared with hope. Those kisses had been everything he'd been longing for from her. It wasn't one-sided. It was deep and raw and full of emotion—from both of them.

He grabbed his laptop and, heading out onto the deck, opened his work in progress. Now more than ever, he wanted to finish it.

CHAPTER SEVENTEEN

SHE'D NEEDED TO ESCAPE.

So why was she tempted to turn around and head back to the cottage and continue the make-out session with Callum? His touch, his kiss, the way he'd looked at her, his confession of feelings were all confusing as hell.

Maybe she had suffered a worse injury that day? Maybe she'd actually drowned and none of this was real. Or maybe she was still lying unconscious on the side of the lake... Unfortunately, no amount of pinching herself had her waking up from this mess of emotions she was caught in like a bug in a spider's web.

Everything had gotten so out of control. She never should have gone along with this idea. She'd been hoping to connect with Brent not Callum, but now she wasn't sure what she wanted. Brent was struggling through some things, and her old love for him had her wanting to be there for him... if he wanted her to be.

But her unexpected attraction to Callum was definitely stealing her focus. He was an amazing guy—sweet, thoughtful, gorgeous, the hero of the day, and he could write!

And not just kinda well, passable or a decent first attempt, but *really* well. Why he'd hide a talent like this had been a mystery, but now that he'd opened up about his family, she understood. And it only angered her further that his father was the way he was. Callum should be able to be proud of his talents, pursue his dreams with support and encouragement.

But if Mr. McKendrick had never given that to his wife, he'd never give it to his son.

Ellie loved to read and she'd dabbled in poetry as a teen, but that's where her lettering career ended. She'd always wished she had the talent, but her creative writing attempts all fell flat. But she could spot good writing, and her own difficulty with it only enhanced her respect for writers.

She'd be lying if she said Callum's talent wasn't a huge turn-on for her. That week she'd peeled back more layers to him. His writing was just another element of vulnerability and trust that he'd shown, and it was sexy as hell.

Not to mention he'd literally saved her life today.

What the hell was she doing out here? She must be insane. What she really wanted was to be back in the cottage with him.

"Hey, what are you doing out here by yourself?" Brent's voice on the trail behind her made her stomach twist. She'd needed some time to clear her head. Put distance between her and Callum to sort out the thoughts and emotions she was struggling with. Seeing Brent now that she'd just that instant sorta, kinda figured things out only made everything confusing again.

Was fate trying to tell her something?

"Just thought I'd go for a walk," she said with a forced smile. Damn, she should be happy to see him. Be thrilled for some time alone with him, but his presence was just frustrating right now. If that day's accident hadn't happened, would she be feeling this way? If Callum hadn't admitted to having feelings for her, if she wasn't starting to think she might return those feelings, would she be as conflicted?

"Everything okay in paradise?" Brent asked, and she heard the jealousy he'd admitted to in his voice. As if he wasn't even attempting to hide it anymore.

"Yeah, of course…" Maybe too okay.

"I understand if Callum's still pissed. I would be too if someone put your safety at risk," he said, his remorse evident.

"He'll come around." She glanced back down the trail toward the cottages.

"Do you mind if I join you?" he asked.

She hesitated. She'd been planning on heading back… But maybe this was what she needed to put things back into perspective. Spending time with Brent, reminding herself that he was the one she'd always had feelings for. Comparing how she felt with him to how she felt with Callum might help give her the clarity she was seeking. Help her figure out if this newfound attraction to Callum was real or simply the result of the whirlwind of emotions she'd spiraled through that day. "Sure," she said as they fell into step with one another.

"So, crazy day, huh?" he asked.

"It's been…eventful. The whole week has actually." In more ways than he could ever know.

"All of this adventure stuff really isn't your thing?"

"Not really," she said honestly. Didn't he remember that about her? Should he remember every little detail of their relationship, the way she did? Or was she expecting too much?

"I really am sorry about the boating accident. I can't possibly apologize enough." He shook his head and looked genuinely devastated. "I was an idiot, and I hope you know how bad I feel."

"It was a bad decision, that's all." One that could have cost them their lives.

"I seem to make a lot of those," he said regretfully. He paused on the trail and touched her arm.

She stopped, and her heart raced seeing his conflicted, emotion-filled expression.

"Seeing you again has brought up a lot of old feelings, Ellie."

She swallowed hard. For her too, but that week had also left her with a lot of questions about whether or not some things are best left in the past, if sometimes rose-colored glasses could truly block reality.

"My life is fantastic, but I haven't had a real connection with anyone since you," Brent continued. "But I guess I'm too late."

His hazel eyes burned into hers, challenging her, questioning...

Ellie's chest tightened. All of this had gone on long enough. Things had gotten out of hand. She took a deep breath. "I have a confession to make." Damn, this was harder than she'd expected. But she had to come clean. She had to tell him the truth. Especially now. "Callum and I aren't engaged. We were never engaged."

He frowned, wrinkling the new bandages wrapped around his head. "What?"

She studied her hands. "He pretended to be my boyfriend—my fiancé—to help me save face at the reunion." Wow, it sounded so lame saying it out loud.

"Why would you need that?" Brent looked genuinely confused.

"Because everyone always expected bigger things from me. They all expected me to go on to teach and leave Wild River the way I always planned. But instead, ten years later, I'm still living in town, working the same job I've had since graduation."

"But you're happy doing that, right?"

"Most days…some days," she said truthfully. "But it was more about feeling like my life didn't measure up to everyone else's. Look at you—a big-shot pilot, living your dream. Alisha wanted to be a nurse and she is. And Cheryl was always athletic, so it's no surprise where she ended up. Everyone else just seemed to have it all figured out…"

"So, you and Callum made up the relationship?" He still looked confused about that part and she couldn't blame him. Making up a fake career might have made more sense. Why hadn't she thought of that?

Now came the truly pathetic confession. "I didn't want to show up at the reunion alone when you were supposed to be there with a supermodel."

"Ah…" He was silent for a long moment. "So you…?"

She nodded. "I may have been struggling with old feelings, as well." She'd never admit for how long, but he deserved to know at least that much.

He was silent as he stared at her for a long, increasingly awkward beat. The ground beneath her could open up and swallow her anytime now. Though, given the week she'd been having, she probably shouldn't tempt fate.

"Say something." Even if he laughed at her, it would be better than this silence.

He smiled and his shoulders sagged in visible relief. "This is the best news I've heard all week."

"Really?"

"Yeah, really." He reached for her hands and took them in his.

She fought the unexpected urge to pull away.

"Ellie, I'd like to get to know you again. Better. For real.

Now that I know I don't have to hide my feelings because you're engaged," he said, his smile growing even wider.

She returned it, but her heart was conflicted. Why hadn't she just come clean at the reunion? Or at the first night in the lodge? She could have shown up on her own and explained everything before things got complicated. Before her feelings for Callum had gotten twisted and complex. She and Brent could have gotten to know one another without the complications, without the games and the jealousy and competitiveness between the two men.

This news should have had her heart soaring, but now things were different.

"Do you really think after all this time apart, we could get back what we had?" It was a legitimate question. One she'd been desperate for an answer to.

Brent squeezed her hands. "All I know is that I was the greatest version of myself when we were together. You brought out the best in me. Made me want things for myself. You gave me the strength and ambition to go after the future I wanted."

One that hadn't included her. Could she simply just forget about that? Blame it on the fact that they'd been young and first loves rarely last? "I don't think I can take credit for all of that," she said. Brent had been motivated and driven all on his own.

"You can." He lowered his head. "The thing is, I know I have a lot of work to do on myself, Ellie. I have some changes to make, and I could really use a friend through all of that. You were always such a steady rock for me."

So, he needed her again. Was that all it was? What happened when things turned around and he felt confident again? And could she really help him with his plan to get sober? How could she say no to someone who'd once meant everything to her when he was asking for help?

"So, what do you say? Can we try again? I booked two weeks off, so I don't need to head back to Anchorage for another week. I'd like to spend it with you when we get back to Wild River."

Why was this a tough decision? Brent was asking to spend more time with her. He wanted to give "them" another shot. Now as adults...

Damn, this should be so easy. It was all she'd wanted for the last ten years. Why wasn't the word *yes* coming from her lips?

Callum's touch, his kiss, his opening up that week, her own developing feelings were all too new, too sudden to jeopardize this opportunity with Brent. But could she risk what was happening with Callum? Could she disappoint him now that she knew his feelings for her went beyond friendship?

"Ellie, you still with me?" Brent asked in her silence.

Was she?

Ellie reluctantly nodded, guilt wrapping around her conflicted heart. "Of course I'll spend the week with you. I'd like that." This was what she'd wanted. This was the goal. The thing she'd been waiting for since they'd broken up... The reason she'd gone along with Callum's crazy idea and all the crap that week.

So why was her stomach telling her it may not be what she wanted any longer.

ELLIE WAS GONE for a really long time.

Callum paced the cottage and glanced out the window. She'd wanted time and space and he wanted to give her that, but she had had a near-death experience today, and he was starting to worry about her. It was getting dark and she could easily get turned around on these unfamiliar trails.

Grabbing his sweater, he left the cottage and headed up to the lodge. Maybe she'd stopped in there on the way back. His cell phone rang as he approached the lodge, and glancing at the call display, he saw Sean's number lighting up his phone.

Shit.

He sighed as he answered the call on the third ring. "Hey, man…"

"Callum?"

"Yeah, Sean?" Static filled the connection and his brother's words came in choppy bursts. "Sean, I'm having trouble hearing you. I'm out of town still…bad reception." He listened, but only more undecipherable words mixed with the static, before the call disconnected.

Callum hit Redial on the number and moved higher up the trail. The call went straight to voice mail. He sighed and sent a quick text to him instead.

Hey, man, bad reception. I'll call you from the main lodge.

Inside, he saw the group in the piano bar area and headed that way. Mitch sat at the piano playing some old rock song and the others belted out the lyrics. He was a fan of karaoke, but that evening, their off-key sing-along hurt his ears. Popping his head around the doorframe, he scanned the room for Ellie. He didn't see her inside.

Or Brent.

"Hey, Callum! Join us!" Cheryl motioned him toward the piano, but he shook his head. He suspected copious amounts of alcohol had been consumed by the four of them, and he wanted no part of it.

"Just wanted to see if Ellie was here," he said.

Alisha glanced at Nick, but he sipped his Scotch on the rocks, not saying anything. In fact, everyone avoided his gaze.

Wonderful.

"She went out for a walk about an hour ago," he said.

He didn't need Alisha to confirm what he already knew. "Brent left about the same time," she said almost sympathetically.

Right. He shouldn't be worried. She was with Brent.

CHAPTER EIGHTEEN

WALKING UP THE path to the cottage an hour later had to be what walking the green mile must feel like. She may not be on death row, but the moment she told Callum that she'd told Brent the truth and had agreed to spend time getting to know him again, it would definitely be the end of something.

But what exactly? The budding feelings between them? The connection? Their friendship?

Her chest hurt, but she couldn't figure out the depths of the pain. Was she just sad because she knew telling Callum would most likely put their friendship at stake? Or was it more than that?

After only a few days seeing her fake fiancé in this new light, it was impossible to know.

She swallowed hard as she entered. In the dusk of the late evening, only the desk lamp illuminated the cottage, creating a warm and inviting glow inside, but Ellie almost shivered as a chill ran through her. This was not a conversation she was looking forward to, and a strange foreboding hung thick in the air.

Callum sat at the desk, typing on his laptop. He held up a finger and typed a few more sentences quickly, then turned to her. "How was your walk?" he asked, a hopeful hesitancy in his voice.

That made this so much worse. No doubt he was hoping

that the walk would only solidify her emotions, help her realize there was a spark between them, realize maybe her feelings were far more than just friendship.

Unfortunately, things were even more complicated.

And seeing him only compounded the complexity. At first on the trail with Brent, she'd been still thinking about Callum, still wondering about the kiss and whether or not they should explore things further. Then the longer she was with Brent, talking and reminiscing about old times, and he'd started looking at her again with the same interest and affection that his gaze had held when they were teenagers so much in love, she'd started to feel as though the cloud over her emotions had lifted... Now she wasn't so sure again.

Damn it!

"It was...um...okay," she said, sitting on the chaise lounge and removing her running shoes.

"You sure?"

Shit. He knew something was up. She avoided his gaze. "Brent found me on the trail and walked with me for a bit."

"I thought you wanted to be alone."

"I did. I guess I wasn't sure how to say no." That was her problem with most things. She was incapable of disappointing people. She had a hard time saying no to anything, even if it meant jeopardizing her own happiness. She needed to get stronger in that regard.

Right now, she needed the strength to tell Callum the news. Weirdly enough, it had been easier to tell Brent the truth than it was to tell Callum that she'd confessed. "I told him the truth. About us." Blurting it out was the best way to say it.

"You did?" Callum looked apprehensive as he studied her. "What did he say?"

This was the really hard part. Disappointing Callum,

hurting Callum, was not something she was eager to do. Especially after today and the moments they'd shared.

Damn, why had she kissed him? Why had she let him kiss her? Why had she given him a sign that a confession of his own feelings would be a good thing, something she'd be open to hearing? She was there to connect with an old flame that week, not fall in love with her coworker. Allowing Callum to get close, playing with his emotions, using him to get to Brent had been unfair. Even if it had been his idea, she'd taken things way too far. This was on her.

And yet, she wasn't sure if she regretted getting close to him or if maybe she should continue to do so.

What was wrong with her? It was as though she leaned toward the person standing in front of her at any given time and she was unable to trust in her own gut, her own feelings to know what was real and what wasn't.

She took a deep breath. "He said he wanted the opportunity to get to know me again. He wants to spend the week with me once we get back to Wild River."

Callum's face was neutral, and Ellie scanned it for any sign of how he might feel about what she'd said. He'd told her he was crazy about her, but…

"What do you think about that?" she asked, feeling even more pathetic for asking. Why couldn't she just make up her own mind? Go with what she wanted? She didn't need Callum's permission or his approval.

But it was more than that. If he fought for her, would she reconsider?

"I don't think it matters what I think," he said. "It matters what you think. Is that what you want?"

Was it? It had been. But she wasn't sure anymore. She'd always seen Callum as her coworker and friend. Nothing more. Now they'd gone and messed all that up by kissing and getting to know one another. She liked him a lot more than she did before... But Brent had been her one true love for so long. A few days with Callum couldn't have changed all of that, right? She sighed. "I don't know."

He looked slightly hopeful as he took a step closer. Those mesmerizing eyes were deep pools, drawing her in. Had she felt this pull out on the trail with Brent? Had there been this simmering chemistry and desire? An urge to kiss him?

"I thought that was the point of all of this," Callum said.

"It was, but..." Was he pushing her toward Brent or testing her?

"But what?"

"Things got complicated." Her irritation increased. This should be an easy decision. She wanted to be with Brent, didn't she?

Callum stared straight into her soul. "Things got real, you mean."

Was that what she meant? "How do I know this—" she gestured between them "—whatever we have happening between us...is real? It's sudden and unexpected and maybe that's all it is, just a temporary lust."

"I guess you won't know until we explore it further," he said, moving even closer.

Her heart pounded against her chest. Exploring things with Callum meant not exploring things with Brent. If she took this leap of faith with him, she'd be risking any chance she'd ever have at a second chance with her ex-boyfriend. This opportunity wouldn't present itself again, and could she just let it go without seeing where things could lead? The last few days had been a roller-coaster ride, messing with her clarity. But before the last few days, she'd been so sure of what she wanted. Without both men pulling her heart in opposite directions, her focus had been on Brent and getting him back. But if she chose Brent, that would mean never knowing if there could be a real connection with Callum.

Devil you know versus the devil you don't?

"What's going on in that beautiful mind, Ellie?" Callum asked, sounding as though he knew the answer already. A slight disappointed defeat radiated from his body language as he tucked his hands deep into his jeans pockets.

And instantly, she was once again reaching for him, metaphorically, as though the minute he retreated, backed away, took the pressure off, she leaned into him, not wanting him to just give up. So unfair. "I'm not sure I can explore things with you."

"Because of Brent and what he wants?"

She nodded.

He searched her expression. "What do *you* want, Ellie?"

"I don't know!" Damn, if she knew that, she wouldn't be standing here torn between the urge to dive into his arms and see where things could lead and the urge to run out of the cottage and find Brent to help put things back in focus.

Was this dizzying back-and-forth a sign that maybe she just shouldn't be with either of them right now? Maybe she needed time to sort out her own thoughts and emotions away from both of them.

"What is your heart telling you?" he asked gently, obviously sensing her turmoil.

It only made things worse. Why was he always putting her feelings first? Why couldn't he demand that she make a decision? And help her do it by either pushing her away for her indecisiveness or taking her into his arms, stealing the decision from her?

Again, it was unfair to expect, but this patient non-aggressiveness wasn't helping anyone.

She rubbed her temple as pain radiated across her forehead. "Damn it, Callum. It's not that simple."

"If you really wanted to be with Brent, you wouldn't be questioning it. You wouldn't be second-guessing if he was the right one for you," he said, resting his hands on her shoulders and bending low at the knees to look into her eyes.

Now that he was fighting for a chance again, she immediately took the defensive. "I'm questioning things because of you! You've made all of this complicated with your kisses and your touches and your knowing everything about me!" She brushed his hands away and started to pace the room.

"I'm not sorry about that. I know we could be amazing together. I've known it for a long time. If you're finally starting to realize it too, then good. It's about damn time!" Exasperated, he ran a hand through his hair. "Look, I don't want to pressure you, but I need to know where we stand. I know how I feel, but if there's still hope in your heart that things could work out with Brent, then you need to explore that. I don't want to be with you if you will only be left wondering 'what if?' If part of your heart will always be longing for him."

She swallowed hard, her pulse pounding in her veins. It was decision time. Callum was right. She couldn't keep yo-yoing back and forth between them. It wasn't fair to either of them. Or herself.

She stared at him for a long, silent moment.

These feelings for him were too new. They couldn't be real. They couldn't possibly compete with the ten years of longing and anticipation she had for Brent. Callum had been right there in front of her all this time and she'd never considered him as more than a friend—an amazing friend.

But if she loved him, if she was in love with him, she would have known before now, wouldn't she?

She released a deep sigh. "Everyone knows the truth now," she said quietly. "We don't have to stage a breakup... I think you should just head back to Wild River."

He nodded, but she caught the tightening in his jaw as he said, "If that's what you want, that's what I'll do."

That wasn't what she wanted. Not even close. But until she could figure out what the hell she did want, letting him go seemed like the only fair thing to do.

SITTING AROUND THE warmth of the firepit by the lake that evening, Ellie still felt cold. Her argument with Callum weighed heavy on her mind, and the conflicted decision she'd made was making it impossible to feel happy and excited, despite sitting next to Brent on the carved log, a blanket draped over their legs. It wasn't even an argument really. It had been more like a breakup, but it shouldn't have been. They'd been planning a fake one, but she'd never expected to have to let him down for real.

Brent's smile, his lingering gazes, his full attention... everything she'd been dreaming about for years, craving for years, were suddenly all hers and damn Callum for making it impossible for her to enjoy any of it.

All she could think about was whether or not she'd done the right thing asking him to leave.

Right decisions were supposed to feel better, weren't they?

"Hey, you okay?" Brent asked, touching her knee.

Ellie blinked, snapped back to the moment as she turned to him with a forced smile. "Of course. Why?"

He nodded toward the unrecognizable lump at the end of the long stick in her hand. She wouldn't be eating that marshmallow. Not that she had much appetite for the sweet snack anyway. Since Callum had left and she'd apologized for the ruse to the rest of her high school classmates, she hadn't had much of an appetite or desire to participate in the evening's events. She would have preferred to read her book alone in the cottage, but she was hoping that being around the rest of them, around Brent, would eventually pull her out of the slump she was fighting.

"Well, I guess I ruined that one, huh?" she asked.

Brent sent her a sympathetic look as he used his marshmallow to make a s'more for her. He handed it to her and leaned closer. "Listen, if you're feeling weird or embarrassed about the Callum thing, don't. No one is upset that you were lying to them. I think they think it's amusing."

She swallowed hard. Amusing. Right. She'd always been a form of amusement for the rest of them. Shy, nervous, introverted Ellie who didn't quite fit in... This was a mess.

And it shouldn't be a mess. She should be enjoying Brent's time and his arm wrapped around her shoulders—not thinking about the fact that she'd hurt Callum or wondering if he'd made it back to Wild River all right...

She should be laughing at Mitch's jokes and singing along to Nick's guitar playing, not wishing she was sitting in a car on the side of the highway listening to the rain with Callum.

It wasn't even raining, not a cloud in the damn sky. So why was she remembering that drive with him, thinking it had been a great day? At the time she'd been eager to get to the cottages to see Brent.

Now, maybe if she could do it again...

She sighed. A little too loudly.

"Hey, why don't we call it a night?" Brent whispered. "You've had a long day."

Long day about summed it up. A near-drowning experience followed by making an impossible choice between two men about whom she really had no idea how she felt. Hard to believe it had all happened within the last twelve hours. It felt like a lifetime. "I think I definitely could use an early night."

He removed the blanket from their laps and stood, extending a hand to her.

She took it and got to her feet.

"I think we're going to turn in," Brent told the others as they looked their way.

Curiosity, interest…maybe a little judgment and concern reflected in the eyes of the others, and again it just filled Ellie's chest with dread. Why hadn't she just been honest? What had been so wrong with her life that she'd had to create a fake one?

"Good night," Alisha said. "Brent, make sure to set your alarm for every couple of hours, okay? A late onset concussion is possible."

He mock saluted her. "You got it."

Ellie waved to the others as she headed toward her cottage. Brent walked alongside her. "You don't have to walk with me," she said.

"I want to. If that's okay."

She nodded. Of course it was okay. This was exactly what she wanted. Above them, the night sky was clear, millions of stars visible. A cool breeze rustled through the trees, and the scent of smoke from the fire lingered on their clothing. It was the perfect summer evening. And she was walking next to her high school sweetheart, who wanted to give their relationship another try.

This moment should be everything.

They walked in silence, and when they reached the

cabin, Brent gently touched her hand. "I know it's been an...interesting day," he said. "But I promise tomorrow will be better. I meant what I said about old feelings, Ellie. Seeing you again after so long...it feels as if a missing piece of my puzzle has finally been found again."

If he felt that way...the same way she'd always felt—as though something was missing without him—then that had to mean something, right?

Slightly reassured, she smiled. "I'm happy we have this chance to get to know one another again." That was all they were doing. This didn't mean they had to rush into anything or start seeing one another again right away. It was just a second chance to see what could happen.

Exhaustion made her yawn and she covered it with a small laugh. "Well, I guess this is good night."

Brent lingered, his hazel eyes burrowing into hers, looking anything but tired. "I thought maybe I could spend the night in your cottage. With you."

Her mouth was dry and her pulse raced. It had been years since she'd been with Brent. They'd been kids back then. They were adults now. A week ago, she'd fantasized about this opportunity. Now the thought made her stomach twist.

Nerves. That was all.

Of course she was nervous to be with him again. She hadn't been with anyone in a long time. That didn't mean she shouldn't do it... And they didn't have to do anything. They could talk.

"Just thought maybe I shouldn't be alone tonight... impending concussion and all," he said with a coaxing grin. "But only if you want me to."

He was right—he probably shouldn't be alone. She nodded and led the way inside.

Brent closed the door behind them and immediately his

arms were pulling her closer and his mouth was approaching hers.

Whoa! What was he doing?

His eyes closed but Ellie's only grew wider as panic set in. Brent was about to kiss her. What did she do? The split second felt agonizingly long as her heart flip-flopped back and forth.

Just enjoy this! You want this!

So why the hell couldn't she erase Callum and his disappointed look from her mind when Brent's puckered lips were just millimeters from hers?

She couldn't do this. Not this quickly. There had to be a limitation on how many men she could kiss in one day. She pushed against his chest slowly and he sent her a slightly annoyed, quizzical look. "What's wrong?"

"Nothing... I'm just... Can we just...um...take it a little slower?"

He grinned as though he found her perceived coyness amusing as he nodded. "Of course."

Great. Now he thought she was playing hard to get.

He kept his arms around her and she sighed as she moved closer and snuggled into him. This was it. This was definitely better. This was where she'd find answers. In his hug was where she'd feel their old connection, his love, the safety and security to allow her heart to reopen to him. Her arms encircled his waist and she rested her head on his chest.

She breathed in and tried to let his familiar scent envelop her like it used to, but something seemed a little off. It was too harsh, too strong, too perfumy... Not the manly, clean soapy smell that Callum had.

Stop thinking about Callum!

Brent tried to move away but she held tighter.

He laughed. "You okay?"

"Yeah... I just, I've always loved hugging you." He had to remember their long hugs. They were one of the things she'd always missed.

"I remember how rock-hard your breasts used to make me... Still do," he said, a trace of lust in his voice.

That completely destroyed the moment for Ellie. Her gut twisted and she slowly released him, the hug no longer holding the same meaning.

Unfortunately Brent mistook it as her readiness to move beyond a hug. Taking her hand, he headed toward the bed, but she resisted, leading them back outside onto the deck instead. "It's such a nice night. We should enjoy it," she said, trying to keep the mood light.

Brent's annoyance was evident, but he sat on the swing beside her. He kicked his foot, moving the swing back and forth, and his gaze settled on the trees in the distance.

Shit, he was irritated with her. Why wouldn't he be? What the hell was wrong with her? She'd admitted to going through the trouble of inventing a fake fiancé to save face when she saw him at the reunion. She'd gone ahead with this crazy, elaborate scheme for three days...and now she was practically giving him the cold shoulder?

She turned and grabbed Brent's face, kissing him fast and hard. Their teeth clanged together and he looked wide-eyed, surprised and slightly put off at her attack. She pulled back and wiped her mouth with the back of her hand. "Sorry."

Brent grinned. "It's okay. I like an assertive woman. Just caught me by surprise, that's all." He reached for her again, and his hand immediately started sliding up her shirt as he leaned in for another kiss.

What the hell? What happened to slow? "Nope. Sorry..."

She stood and folded her arms across her chest. "I'm sorry, I can't do this. Not tonight, anyway." Maybe this was ridiculous. She was a grown-ass woman, not a teenager anymore. She'd been with Brent dozens of times in the past. Maybe he was right to think that they could skip a lot of the foreplay and getting to know one another and jump straight into the physical... Maybe she should want that too.

Was the fact that she didn't a sign?

Brent's jaw tightened, but he nodded as he stood. "Okay. No pressure. This is at your pace." He kissed her cheek and headed down the deck stairs.

"You're leaving?"

"No sense staying the night if you're...uncomfortable."

If she wasn't going to put out. Wow, how could she never have seen what an ass he could be? All of these years she'd been blinded by the past, by her first real relationship with the popular boy in school, the best-looking guy that every girl wanted. She'd thought her feelings were real back then, and maybe in a way they were. Young love.

But she wasn't young anymore. And maybe what she felt for Brent wasn't love anymore either, she thought as she watched him walk away.

CALLUM'S HANDS GRIPPED the steering wheel and he struggled to keep his eyes open as he approached the final hour of the drive back to town. He'd resisted the temptation to turn around at least a dozen times. He couldn't fight for something only he wanted. He couldn't fight for a woman who didn't want to be fought for.

Unfortunately, he struggled with believing that was true. He knew Ellie had feelings for him. He'd felt the change in how she looked at him, touched him... Her kiss had revealed so much.

Of course she was fighting it. It had caught her by surprise and she was scared. Too scared to take a chance on something new with him. So she was running back to the comfort of something familiar…even if it wasn't the right thing for her. Even if it wasn't something she still wanted.

Before that week, his unrequited emotions had been tough but survivable. Now, knowing that they'd had a connection—a real one, not the fake, nostalgic bullshit she was harboring for Brent—and that she refused to acknowledge it, was torture.

Not knowing Brent had definitely made Ellie's hang-up on him more tolerable. But since he'd met the guy, Callum was even more disappointed that she was so caught up in memories of her first love that she wasn't seeing the man Brent actually was. And if she *was* seeing it and was still in love with him, then Callum had been way off in who he believed her to be.

Watching her try to be someone she wasn't all week, just to impress a guy that didn't deserve her attention, had bothered him.

Would Brent have been interested in rekindling the relationship if Ellie had been single and available? Or had it been about the chase, the challenge, the idea that someone else had what he'd let go of?

Callum didn't trust the guy's motives, and he could only hope Ellie saw through any bullshit before it was too late and she got her heart broken again.

He dialed his brother's cell phone number using the Bluetooth connection on the car's dash. Three rings, then Sean's voice mail.

Callum sighed. He hadn't been able to reach him since the bad reception call. He hoped everything was okay. His brother had a way of going off the grid sometimes—for days, weeks or sometimes months. He would ignore any attempts to reach him…and often he just needed space to pull through whatever darkness he was lost in. But knowing there was support on the other end was important, so Callum left a message after the beep.

"Hey, bro, call me if you need me. I'm back in town now. Anytime. Whatever you need."

Seeing the exit for Wild River, he disconnected the call and turned off of the highway. Pulling onto Main Street moments later, he slowed his speed to the limit as the bright neon lights of The Drunk Tank caught his eye, and instead of going left onto his street, he pulled into the bar's parking lot and got out.

Drinking was definitely not the answer to his heartache, but Callum was willing to give it a try.

As he entered the bar, he knew it would take more than one tequila shot to settle the heavy uneasiness weighing on him. Ellie had wanted him to leave. She'd chosen Brent and she'd told everyone the truth.

Still, he was nervous about having left her there. After the boating accident, he didn't trust her "friends." What else were they getting up to that could endanger Ellie's life or at the very least make her uncomfortable?

He knew she'd been waiting for him to make the decision for her earlier that day in the cottage, but he couldn't do it. She had to make her own choices, and if Brent and the lifestyle with that group was what she wanted, then there was nothing he could do about it. And he wouldn't stand in her way.

He just wanted her to be happy. Even if that wasn't with him.

"Hey, man, what are you drinking?" Tank asked as he leaned against the bar, his six-foot-five, all-muscle frame looking like it could snap the wood in half. He glanced at Callum and shook his head. "Never mind. I know what you need." He poured two tequila shots and handed one to Callum.

Bartender clairvoyance from years of seeing different expressions from those sitting on these bar stools.

They tapped glasses and downed the liquid.

A warm sensation coursed through Callum, but it barely took the edge off. "Thanks, man. I'll take two more of those and a beer."

"I take it the time at the cottages didn't go as planned?" Tank asked, already looking slightly squirmy about the prospect of having to talk about emotions or some shit. He filled two shot glasses and poured the beer.

"It was going well…" one shot "…then not so much." Second shot.

"You're back early."

"Yep."

"She stayed?"

"She did indeed." A gulp of beer and he was finally feeling a little less raw.

"Sorry, man. I know you had your heart set on that one." Apparently he was worse at hiding his feelings for Ellie than he'd thought, if Tank had picked up on it. The beast of a bartender wasn't exactly tuned in to emotions.

"Yeah, well, I'm not sure how many times I needed to hear that she wasn't interested." He slumped on a stool and rested his head in his hand, self-pity setting in. Then it was immediately replaced with irritation. "But you know, it's bullshit, because there was definite interest on both sides, and the spark in that kiss could have set the cottage on fire."

Tank raised an eyebrow as though realizing that things had escalated to heartbreak level. "You kissed her?"

"It was more than once and more than just a kiss."

Tank's eyebrows would have touched his hairline if he'd had hair.

Callum shook his head. "Nah, not like that, man… We just connected on a real deep level. That shit doesn't happen every day."

Tank nodded. "Should I grab the darts?"

Darts. Tank's way of dealing with emotions was to throw pointy things at his personal dartboard in his office. Words of wisdom just made him queasy.

At this point, Callum would take any form of bartender therapy Tank was offering. "I want the red ones."

CHAPTER NINETEEN

SUNLIGHT STREAMING THROUGH the window of the cottage the next morning had Ellie's eyes opening far too early. She sat up and glanced at the chaise lounge before remembering Callum wasn't there. She lay back against her pillows and sighed. The night before had been a troublesome sleep—tossing and turning long into the night and then nightmares when slumber finally did take over.

Images of drowning, sinking deeper and deeper into the cold lake, had plagued her…and in the dreams, Callum wasn't there to save her. It didn't take a psychology degree to figure out what her subconscious had been telling her.

Unfortunately, there was little clarity regarding everything else.

Things between them had gotten so complicated so fast. She had no idea how she felt about him or if her feelings even mattered anymore. By sending him back to Wild River early, she'd essentially told him that she was choosing Brent, so she wasn't sure how they came back from all of this. Or if they ever could. How were they supposed to work together now? Could they go back to being friends?

Did she want that?

She had no idea what she wanted anymore.

The night before with Brent had been disappointing. Were the memories she had of their time together enough of a foundation to build a new relationship on?

Brent might be different now, but then maybe so was she. It had been foolish to think that just because her life hadn't changed much in the last ten years, she was still the same person. Maybe some things weren't meant to have a second chance.

Would she be feeling this way if things hadn't changed between her and Callum? If she hadn't started to be attracted to him? Have feelings deeper than friendship for him? Or would she have come to the same conclusion after having spent this time with her ex-boyfriend?

Guess she'd never really know.

She rolled over in the bed and reached for her cell phone. No new messages or calls from Callum. What had she expected? He was obviously upset by the way things had turned out. She hoped he'd made it back to Wild River okay. Maybe a quick text would be good...just to check.

She put the phone away. He would have texted if he wanted to talk to her.

She stared out the window and forced several deep breaths.

The day before had been a nightmare. Things had gotten out of hand and complicated. Her feelings and emotions had been a mess, and connecting with Brent had been almost impossible. She had been looking at him with the critical eye of someone just having made a choice. But now that the dust had settled and Callum was gone, it was just her and Brent that she needed to focus on. Maybe now things could be put into better perspective.

Today would be better.

A new day. A new start.

Tossing the sheets aside, she climbed out of bed and into the shower. The hot water and the invigorating, spicy scented soap made her feel a little better, and by the time she was dressed, she did believe things would be okay.

That feeling quickly vanished as they arrived at the site of that day's "adventure." Peering over the breathtaking view of the Alaska wilderness tree line, all Ellie saw was her body tangled in the evergreen branches.

Zip-lining was probably as close to hell as she thought she'd ever get.

Other people might love that rush of adrenaline as they soared over the beautiful scenery attached to a thin cord, supported only by a harness, but Ellie couldn't appreciate the experience. After the rappelling incident, she was terrified about how this would go. At least with the rock face, she'd had some control over her fate. With this, she'd be at the mercy of the cables. And after her near-death experience in the lake, she wasn't eager to tempt fate again so soon.

Huddled in the tiny wooden structure at one end of the line, the operator—a guy barely past puberty with, obviously, no sense of mortality—explained the operating instructions for the harness and what to do at the other end. He said something about pulling a brake…but Ellie wasn't listening.

Could she do this? No doubt they all expected her to bail. Or at least be scared stupid.

Well, they were right. But what did she care? So what if she only confirmed what they thought of her? All week she'd found herself back in the same place she'd been in high school—trying desperately to impress a bunch of people that she shouldn't need to prove anything to. Back then, it was excusable. Now it was pathetic and unnecessary.

"So, everyone's taking a turn?" the young guy asked, handing out helmets.

Ellie shook her head. "I think I'll sit this one out."

"Oh come on," Nick said, buckling his helmet under his chin as the guy helped him into a harness. "It's going to be amazing."

"Yeah, don't let fear hold you back, El," Alisha said.

Callum was right. Peer pressure was the same, even if the wording used as adults was different. "It's not fear, it's just a knowledge of myself and my interests."

She was older and wiser now. May as well go with it. They could say she wasn't living in the moment and taking chances; she saw it as knowing her limitations. Maybe someday she'd feel differently or want to experience this. Today was not that day, and that was okay.

"You'll love it once you get over the canyon," Cheryl said.

"Nope." Simple and firm. She wasn't doing it. They were wasting their breath.

"Well, there's a hiking trail along the east side of the canyon you can take to the other side to meet up with the group," the operator said. "It has really great scenery and a waterfall at the bottom."

Ellie nodded. "Great, I'll see you all there. Have fun."

She turned to leave, but a few steps away, Brent joined her. "Hey, wait up."

"What are you doing?"

"I'm going with you."

He was? He was giving up an amazing experience, that she knew he wanted, to be with her instead? "You don't have to miss out."

"I'm not missing out on anything," he said, taking her hand in his. "Shall we?"

"Sure. Let's go."

Reaching the edge of the waterfall a half hour later, Ellie was proud of the way she'd finally stood up for herself. It was a small victory, but a step in the right direction of growing the backbone she'd always wanted.

In the distance, she could see the others soaring over the treetops, the sound of laughter and several squeals echoing through the valley.

Removing her shoes and socks, she sat on the edge of a large rock and put her feet into the cool, running water. The sound of the waterfall in the distance was soothing, and the light breeze blowing through her hair was refreshing after the hike. She lifted her hair off of her neck and secured it in a loose bun on top of her head.

This was definitely more her speed, and it was a relief to know that Brent was capable of slowing down, taking a breath and not needing the constant adrenaline high.

She closed her eyes and inhaled deeply, determined to live in this moment. No more thinking about the past or the future. She would just be here in this moment with Brent and then see if she wanted to experience the next one with him.

She opened her eyes as Brent sat on the rock next to her. "It's so beautiful out here," she said.

"It really is. I've seen a lot of beaches in some of the most beautiful parts of the world, but I have to say, nothing compares to the views here in Alaska."

She turned toward him. "So, you've really been all over the world?"

He nodded. "Just about, yeah. All over Europe and South America, Asia, Australia…"

She'd never been outside of Alaska. Her parents had done all of their traveling and seeing the world before they'd had her and had been perfectly content not to leave the state in their retirement years. She supposed she could be traveling now, but the idea of going alone didn't appeal to her, and she wanted to hold off experiencing the world until she could embark on the journey with someone special. "That's so exciting. It's what you always dreamed of doing."

"Yeah," he said, sounding less thrilled than she would have expected. "It's great. It's just different than what I imagined." He brushed his foot up against hers in the water, and a slight tingle sizzled between them.

Finally. The spark. Was it because he was being a little vulnerable and real with her for the first time that week? "Different how?"

"Well, it sounds glamorous—and sometimes it can be when there's an opportunity to see the sights and take some time off. But more often, I fly into a place, sleep in the airport hotel and then get back on another flight heading somewhere else the next day. It's a lot of airports, hotels and cockpits."

Was he regretting his lifestyle choice? She didn't really hear regret, just maybe boredom. "Do you still enjoy it?"

He paused, weighing his answer. "Let's just say, I wouldn't want to do anything else." He turned to look at her. "Maybe if I had someone to travel with, it might get exciting again."

She swallowed hard and looked away as she said, "I bet you are fluent in a dozen languages by now."

He laughed as he shook his head. "Nope. Basic Spanish is about all I can fumble my way through."

She frowned as her head snapped back toward him. "But you were studying German, French and Japanese when we graduated. You wanted to be able to speak the language wherever you went."

"Turns out that was a little ambitious of my teenage self."

"I thought it was a fantastic aspiration to have." She'd

even taken basic courses online of each one...just in case. That was obviously for naught.

Nope, she wouldn't think like that. A language learned was something she'd always have.

But so much for the fantasy of raising multilingual children with him someday.

Brent shrugged as he kicked his feet through the water. "Well, I quickly discovered how difficult that was, and almost everywhere in the world they speak English now. I get along fine with some basic phrases."

She nodded. "Yeah, I guess that makes sense."

"You seem disappointed in me again," he said, tipping his head to the side to look at her.

"No!" She wasn't. Not really. It was more that she was realizing how much of her attraction for him had lingered over the years based on who she'd assumed he'd turned out to be rather than on reality. She'd watched his life through Instagram pictures and Facebook posts and then she'd just filled in the gaps herself with what she wanted to be real.

It was unfair to expect him to be living up to her imagined version.

"You know, you really should come on a trip with me," he said.

Her heart raced, but not in a good way. Could she really take more time off? Where would they go? She doubted they traveled the same way—from what she'd learned about him, she suspected he was a resort traveler, not really into exploring the less touristy parts of the world. And if she ever did travel, she wanted to go off the beaten paths, see places only the locals knew about.

Why was her immediate reaction to look for an excuse to say no? What was happening to her? This was something she'd only ever dreamed about. Now, here he was in the flesh, asking her to go on a trip, and all she could think about were reasons why it wouldn't be the best thing. "Yeah, maybe," she said.

He reached for her hand and held it.

The same tingle of excitement she'd gotten when Callum had held her hand didn't flare within her. Brent's hand felt clammy, awkward and heavy linked with hers. Not natural, right and comfortable the way Callum's had.

She missed him. She wished it were him sitting there with her, holding her hand. She couldn't do this. Couldn't keep trying to make things work with Brent when they just weren't. Her heart wasn't in it. Wasn't into him anymore. The realization hit hard, but it was better than moving forward, hoping for things to get better, holding on to that hope long after she should have let it go.

"Brent…" She went to pull her hand away but he beat her to it as his cell phone chimed in his pocket and he reached for it.

He smiled as he read a text message, and Ellie couldn't stop her gaze from dropping to the phone. The picture on the screen above the message was of the stunning woman in his latest set of Instagram photos.

I had a great time sexting last night. You free tonight?

Sexting?

He'd left her cottage after saying he wanted to try again, after making a play for her, and had gone to his own cottage to sext with the supermodel who had dumped him?

He caught Ellie's stare and tucked the phone away quickly without responding.

"You're still texting her?"

"It's nothing, just casual."

Sexting was casual? Maybe in his world, but certainly not in hers. How could she not have seen all of this? How different they both were now? How incompatible?

She had. She'd just chosen to ignore all of the things she didn't like about him…hoping the good qualities she'd admired when they were teens were still there. None of this was Brent's fault. It was all hers. He shouldn't have to try to be someone he wasn't, just as she couldn't try to be the person her high school friends wanted anymore.

Unfortunately, it only solidified what she already knew.

He wrapped an arm around her and she pulled away.

"What's wrong?"

"I don't think you and I are going to work," she said softly but firmly.

"Is this because of Samantha? 'Cause I can stop texting her."

"Ghost her?"

He shrugged. "Nah, just end it officially. It really was nothing, anyway."

"I don't think we are anything either," she said, removing her feet from the water and picking up her shoes. She knew in her heart, deep down, that they weren't. He had to know that too.

"You're wrong, Ellie. You're different. You're special," Brent said, getting to his feet. His slightly pleading look would normally have weakened her. Made her reconsider.

But the truth was, despite how Brent might feel about her or thought he felt about her, *he* was no longer special to her.

"I'm sorry, Brent. I don't think we can ever get back what we had in high school. Some things are just better left in the past," she said, walking away from the one man she'd thought she'd never walk away from.

HE'D BEEN RUNNING. Sweat glistened on Callum's tanned, sculpted chest and his dark hair looked wet as he entered the cottage. Ellie's body reacted to the sight in a way it never had before. The temptation to go to him and press her body to his was overwhelming. She longed to feel the heaving of his inhale and exhale against her, breathe in the scent of the outdoors and exertion on his skin, feel his tight muscles beneath her hands. But unsure if her advances would be welcomed, she stayed on the bed.

His gaze locked with hers above the book she pretended to read—full of passion, full of invitation before he turned and headed into the bathroom. The door closed but he didn't lock it.

Ellie put her book aside and slowly climbed out of bed. She walked toward the door, but her hand hesitated on the doorknob. Could she really do this? Could she go after what her body desired, even if she was unsure what her heart wanted?

She turned the knob and pushed the door open, entering slowly, her heartbeat echoing in her ears. Callum stood under the water spray, eyes closed, head back, his body shielded from sight from the steam on the glass shower door. She quickly removed her clothes, letting them fall to the floor with his. Then, before she could rethink it or overthink it or lose her nerve, she opened the shower door.

His surprise quickly melted away to intrigue then desire as his gaze took in her naked body.

"Can I join you?" she asked, happy that her voice sounded far stronger and more confident than she felt.

He ran his hands over his wet face and hair. "You sure you want to do that?" he asked gruffly, turning toward her. His erection was already on full display.

Was she? Absolutely not...but she was going to anyway. She nodded.

He stepped out of the spray and invited her in. She stepped under, the hot water stealing her breath and then Callum's arms around her making it catch in her chest as her body pressed up against his. "What do you want, Ellie?"

She had no idea. "Kiss me." Seemed like a good place to start.

Callum gripped the back of her neck and tilted her face upward as he slowly lowered his mouth to hers. He tasted salty from sweat and his lips were soft, but his kiss was hard, demanding. The kiss of a man who'd been thinking about this moment too long, had craved it and was now taking it. Ellie deepened the kiss, standing on tiptoes and wrapping her arms around his neck. His hard length against her leg made it all the more intoxicating as her tongue slid between his lips and explored his mouth.

He moaned as he held her tighter.

She pulled back, slightly breathless, and opened her eyes slowly. His gaze burned into hers. "Now what?" he asked.

"Touch me," she said.

"Where? Be specific."

"My breasts," she said, swallowing hard.

His hands moved down her neck, over her shoulders, down her chest until they cupped both breasts tenderly. Softly he massaged her wet skin, and the sensations tingling through her were intense as a desperate need arose inside of her. "Harder," she said.

He squeezed as he massaged, then moved his fingers toward the nipples, pinching gently at first, then with more pressure. She moaned as she felt herself grow wet between the legs. She couldn't remember the last time a man had touched her like this. It had been far too long. "Do you like this?" he asked.

She nodded.

"Where else do you want me to touch you?"

She moved away and leaned her body against the cool shower wall and spread her legs wide. She reached for his hand and pressed it against her mound. He moved close, sliding his fingers along her wet folds as he lowered his mouth toward hers again. The pressure of his fingers at her entry made her breathing slightly labored as she waited for him to kiss her. He didn't. Instead, he ran a thumb along her bottom lip seductively. "Can I kiss you?"

She nodded.

"Not here," he said, releasing her lip. "Here." He plunged a finger inside her body.

Holy shit. Her entire body twitched with desire as she nodded her agreement. "Yes, please."

Callum knelt in front of her and lifted her legs onto his shoulders; holding her ass, he buried his head between her legs. His warm breath against her skin made her shiver. His fingers dug into the flesh of her thighs as his tongue licked along the folds of her opening. She shut her eyes tight, savoring the pleasurable sensations coursing through her. It felt so incredible. So unbelievable. Callum was going down on her, and never in her wildest imagination had she seen this coming. He sucked her clit and her breathing grew ragged as her orgasm mounted. She gripped his shoulders tight as her head fell backward and she arched her back, desperate to get even closer to the pleasure. His tongue dipped inside of her body and she clenched her thighs tighter around his head. It wasn't nearly enough. She craved the pressure of him inside of her. Longed to feel him fill her. "Callum, I want you inside of me..."

He took his time lifting his head away from her and glancing up at her. "Now?"

She nodded urgently and he gently set her back on the shower stall floor, then scooped her up into his arms. He carried her out of the bathroom and placed her dripping wet body onto the bed, then his body fell on top of hers. He supported his weight on his arms and she once again marveled at the sculpted, sexy muscles of his upper body. He was the most beautiful man she'd ever laid eyes on. And she was the lucky one who had his attention, his gentle touch, his loving gaze, his patience and eagerness to please her.

She ran her hands over his arms and shoulders and chest, wanting to touch him everywhere. He felt so incredible, so strong, so real... He could have any woman he wanted, so how had she gotten so lucky to be here with him, like this?

"You are perfect, Ellie," he said, staring into her eyes, echoing the thoughts she had about him.

She couldn't wait any longer, her desire overwhelming her. She opened her legs for him and he wedged his lower body between them. He pressed his cock against her opening and buried his face into her neck. She held her breath as she felt the tip of him slide into her body, and she stilled, hesitating.

"What's wrong?" he murmured against her ear.

"Condom?"

Leaning on his elbows, he looked her in the eyes and smiled. "We don't need one. This is all just your fantasy, Ellie."

She blinked. And when her eyes opened, he was gone.

Breathing hard, she sat up in the bed and looked around the dark, empty cottage. A thin stream of moonlight cast a glow across the floor and chaise lounge near the window.

It too was empty. She was all alone. It had been a dream. An amazing fantasy of Callum. Never in her life had she had a dream so vivid, so real, so amazingly perfect. One that had left her body trembling with desire.

She groaned as she fell back into the pillows.

What the hell was happening to her? And why had she woken up just as things were getting good? Her body still ached with the unfulfilled craving and the image of Callum's naked body. The way he'd hungrily gone down on her, his passion and desire for her as he'd touched her and kissed her, and the way his body had felt pressed into hers, had her clenching her thighs together tight beneath the bedsheets.

Damn.

There was no denying her physical attraction for her coworker, and she now knew her emotions were there, as well. Things had changed between them that week—for her, anyway. Things had heated up on so many levels.

He'd claimed to have always had feelings for her. All the flirting, all the time they'd spent together in the bookstore, all the late-night check-in texts when he knew she was awake. He knew her better than anyone else in her life because he listened to her, respected her, cared about her. He was the one person in her life she'd always known she could count on. It was odd that she'd never questioned that. That she'd never taken the time to wonder why Callum had been that steady constant in her life all this time.

All of it made sense now. How had she never seen it before? How had she been so blind to what was right in front of her all along? Because she hadn't wanted to see it. She'd thought she'd known what she wanted all along in Brent, in a redo of the future she'd thought she'd missed out on.

She'd been so incredibly wrong.

Callum was the right man for her. He had been all along.

He'd known it and he'd sat back waiting patiently for her to realize it. He'd never asked her for anything. Never expected anything from her. He'd never given up on her even when he knew she was going after the wrong man.

She certainly was seeing everything so much clearer now, but she'd made a mess of things by pushing him away, by choosing Brent. Her heart dropped into her stomach and a new ache radiated through her body straight to her core. One full of apprehension and regret and longing. What she wouldn't give to have him there with her right now. To tell him how she felt. To apologize for hurting him and making the wrong choice.

She released a deep breath as she stared through the dark at the chaise lounge where she never should have asked him to sleep.

Was it too late to get her fake fiancé back?

HIS USUAL BOOTH in the diner. His usual waitress. His laptop open.

Same old routine. Why did it feel so much lonelier now?

He stared out the diner window at the darkness, but his reflection staring back at him in the glass was the only thing he saw. What was he going to do? Twenty-six hadn't seemed so old before. He hadn't been in a rush. He'd been enjoying his life and living it his way. But now a slight anxiety took hold when he thought of where he was in his life and his father's ultimatum.

He turned his attention to the laptop and that damn blinking cursor. What was he even doing with this book? He couldn't publish it. It was far too personal. Yet Ellie's advice on how to rewrite the scene that was troubling him had his mind stretching.

His father's point of view?

Hell, he'd written from the POV of inanimate objects before, this should be easier. In theory. However, it meant seeing a different side. One he'd never acknowledged existed.

He ran a hand through his hair and noticed his coffee cup was full again. Gillian must have refilled it when he was lost staring out the window. Even she must sense he wasn't in the best of places right now. There'd been no flirting that evening, and she'd left him alone in his thoughts.

He almost wished she wouldn't. He wasn't sure he'd find any comfort there, and maybe a little flirting could pull him out of the depressed state he'd been in since leaving the cottage.

His phone vibrated on the table, making him jump.

Sean?

He'd tried reaching his brother that day, but his calls had gone to voice mail and Sean still hadn't responded to his text. Nothing too unusual—especially at the end of the quarter when the resort workload doubled for him.

Picking the phone up, he felt his heart race at seeing a text from Ellie.

Any wildlife encounters on the way home?

The casual nature of the text just made his heart sink further. She was obviously trying to ignore the fact that there'd been something between them that week and slide back into the friend zone. But he couldn't do that. And he hated that she could.

Obviously things with Brent must be going well.

He wasn't looking for sympathy from her or an apology. He'd played the role of doting fiancé willingly, knowing the consequences, so he only had himself to blame for how he was feeling now, the way things had turned out. So, he wasn't sure what he was expecting from her or this first contact, but this wasn't it.

And a 1:00 a.m. message meant she was still awake. Immediately, disturbing images of her and Brent together—kissing, touching, lying in bed together in the cottage they'd shared—had his stomach turning.

What the hell, Ellie? Was she trying to torture him?

He turned the phone completely off and tossed it onto the table. The clatter caught Gillian's attention, and he nodded a silent apology. She sent him a sympathetic look, and he almost called it a night, but the blinking cursor taunted him.

Was there anything he wanted that was within reach?

He closed his eyes tight and tried to put himself in the shoes of the one man for whom he lacked all respect. Opening them again, he started to type.

Weakness. Failure. Waste of potential.

The only things I see when I look at my youngest son...

The wounds in his heart, those he'd thought were scabbed over, reopened as the words appeared on the page. He typed for hours, until he had to stop, not out of a lack of words but out of fear that if he continued, he might start to understand his father a little better.

CHAPTER TWENTY

COULD THE DRIVE back to Wild River the next morning be any more awkward? If there had been another way to get home, Ellie would have opted for it. Obviously the rest of the group could feel the strained vibe coming from her and Brent as he sat in the SUV's front passenger seat next to Nick and she sat in the far back, her gaze out the window.

The familiar scenery whizzed past, but nothing felt the same. So much had changed for her during the trip, and even though she was headed home, she felt like she was embarking on a new path. She needed to make some changes.

Had there ever been a time when she'd felt more embarrassed? If there had, she did not want to recall it. She'd spent the rest of the day before in her own cottage reading and had only popped into the main lodge to grab some food to go at dinnertime. She hadn't spoken much to the group, but she suspected Brent had filled them in on the current status quo.

They all must think she was so pathetic. First, inventing a fake boyfriend/fiancé to not look bad at the reunion. Then, falling back into the arms of her ex only to realize he wasn't the guy she thought he was or wanted.

Thank God for her dark sunglasses.

The worst part was that she'd hurt Callum. And for what?

She hadn't heard from him since he'd left two days before. He'd ignored her text, and as much as she wanted to continue to reach out, she couldn't have their next conversation be by text or over the phone. She needed to see him and tell him that she'd been wrong, she'd been a fool to let him go, and hope that there was still a chance for them.

Not that she deserved it.

She groaned inwardly.

How could she have been so blind to what she'd had right in front of her this whole time? How could she have held on to the past so long that it had prevented her from moving forward? How many potentially great relationships had she missed out on because she'd compared other men to Brent, when there shouldn't have been a comparison?

She'd spent far too much time living in the past, and that needed to stop. Unfortunately, now that she was ready to move forward, she may be too late to take a leap of faith with the man she really wanted.

"You okay?" Alisha whispered next to her.

She nodded, because she didn't trust her voice not to break if she tried to tell the truth.

IF HE DIDN'T NEED to open the bookstore that morning, Callum would have stayed in bed all day. His head throbbed and his stomach was unstable. He'd been out too late, drunk far too much coffee and knew that the woman he loved was probably curled up in bed, rekindling a spark with her ex boyfriend right now. Nothing could erase the troublesome images of Ellie and Brent from his mind.

Unlocking the door to the store an hour later, his chest was heavy with dread. This would likely be one of his final shifts at the store. He couldn't continue working here with Ellie now. Whatever happened or didn't happen between her and Brent, he couldn't see her every day, be around

her every day and go back to the way things had been before that week.

Nothing was the same.

He'd put himself out there and she'd rejected him.

But, damn, he'd miss working with her. Before, at least
he'd had the vague hope that someday things between them
would change. They certainly had, but not in the way he'd
wanted.

He'd miss the store too. For two years, working there
had been amazing. He loved being around the books, feeling the inspiration from decades of creation. He'd just have
to spend more time at the library.

He sighed as he tossed his keys onto the counter, noticing a stack of boxes of a new release in the center aisle.
Grabbing a box cutter, he carefully opened the top one. It
would help ease his guilt over quitting if he could at least
get a lot of work done first.

But after opening the box, his heart ached even more.
The new release from Amelia Dash. His mother's pen name.
She only released a book every few years, and she was far
from a famous, bestselling author, yet every time Callum
saw a new book with her name on it, his emotions battled
between a strong sense of pride and happiness that she'd
fulfilled her dream and hurt and disappointment that he
couldn't reach out and tell her.

What would she say if she knew he had inherited her
passion? Would she be proud of him?

He turned the book over in his hands and stared at the
author photo. She looked years younger than she had the
last time he'd seen her, and she looked happy. That made
him feel better at least. He read the bio on the back…

"Married, mother of four, living in Colorado…"

Mother of four, but only ever really a mother to two. Not that he held her responsible for that.

His cell phone rang, and seeing his father's number on call display, he silenced it and sent it to voice mail. He'd have to talk to his father soon…but this morning he just couldn't deal with the bullshit and pressure to make a decision.

He finished unpacking the new books and made sure to turn them face out on the shelf. Grabbing a copy for himself, he stashed it behind the counter. Then he broke down the empty cardboard boxes and carried them out back to the recycle bin.

As he turned on the lights and flipped the sign to Open, his cell phone rang again. An unknown number. Probably his father trying to trick him into answering. Wouldn't be the first time.

He frowned and sighed. It could be Ellie. And damn, he was a fool for wanting it to be and knowing if it was and she needed him, he'd go to her rescue without thinking twice.

He answered on the fourth ring, before the call went to voice mail. "Hello?"

"Callum?"

"Yes." His heart picked up pace at that tone. It was serious and slightly authoritative—never a good sign.

"This is Erika."

He relaxed a little. "Oh hey, I didn't recognize the number. It's not your cell."

"No, it's my office number," she said. "At the hospital."

Now his heart raced. Ellie. He should never have left her there with that irresponsible asshole. If anything bad had happened to her…

He was jumping to conclusions. Erika might simply

need him to cover her shift at the search and rescue station that night.

"Everything okay?" he asked, trying to keep the fear from his voice.

"I'm afraid not. Your brother was admitted late last night. He's doing okay, but..." She paused. "Can you come in? I'd rather talk in person."

He didn't need any more information. He grabbed his keys from the counter as he said, "Yeah, I'll be there right away."

A quick call to a very understanding Mrs. Grayson and Callum was locking the store and heading toward Wild River Community Hospital. His palms sweat against the steering wheel, and he could barely focus on his surroundings as he drove quickly down Main Street.

His brother had tried calling him and Callum had been unreachable. He'd tried him a few times in the last few days, but his mind hadn't really been on Sean or whatever might be going on with him. He'd been distracted by his own problems. With Ellie.

He should have tried harder or gone to the hotel.

He pulled into the parking lot of the hospital and headed inside. At the triage station, he saw Erika talking to several nurses. She glanced his way and approached.

"Where is he?" he asked.

"He's in ICU. He overdosed on some antidepressants and antianxiety meds. He's stable, but so far he's been unresponsive," she said. "We have him on fluids, and we're monitoring him for any signs of change, but right now it's too soon to predict..." Her voice trailed off.

Predict whether or not his brother would come out of this. And what things would look like if he did. Callum swallowed hard, tasting vomit rising in the back of his throat. Why the hell hadn't he gone to the hotel or to his brother's apartment? He'd known something was up, but he hadn't thought things were this bad. "Can I see him?" he asked, his voice hoarse with emotion.

Erika nodded. "Heads up—your dad's in there."

His hands clenched at his sides and his jaw tightened.

Erika noticed the reaction and touched his shoulder. "I had to call him first. He was listed as next of kin, but say the word and I'll ask him to leave."

Her understanding had tears burning the back of his eyelids. He nodded, and she led the way down the hall to his brother's room. His legs felt slightly wobbly as they stopped in front of the door. "We are doing everything we can, and if you need anything, let me know, okay?"

"Thanks, Erika," he said, pushing through the door.

His brother lay in the hospital bed, looking pale and thin, hooked to monitors and IVs. The pale blue hospital gown seemed to match the slightly translucent shade of his skin, and his eyes were closed, but they flitted somewhat frantically as though desperate to open or looking for a way out.

His brother had been looking for a way out of the darkness too.

He swallowed the lump in his throat as his gaze fell on his father, back to him as he stood at the window. Dressed in a suit and dress shoes, hands in his pockets, he looked cold and unemotional as he turned. Not at all like a concerned, distraught father. "I see Dr. Sheraton had better luck reaching you," he said.

Callum's chest hardened. "You usually only call about one thing." Business.

"And now that I have your attention, we do need to discuss that."

Was his father serious right now? He shook his head.

"Not now, Dad." He glanced at Sean and his brother's body seemed to stiffen as though sensing the thick tension in the hospital room. "How is he?" he asked, hoping his father could show some level of decorum or care about his son.

"Dr. Sheraton said no change since he was brought in."

"Did you find him?" he asked, moving closer to the bed.

"No. Housekeeping at the resort. He was in the ballroom." His displeasure was obvious, and Callum fought for patience.

Couldn't his father see that this was a cry for help and approval? Sean hadn't wanted to kill himself. If he had, he wouldn't have overdosed in the ballroom where he knew he'd be found. Where he'd hoped his father would find him?

Callum's heart felt like it had been run over that week and now it was being trampled on. How much pain must his brother be going through to have attempted something like this? It killed him to think his brother saw no other way.

"This is the person you think is capable of running my resort?" his father asked.

Callum's gaze shot up to meet his old man's. "Dad, this is not the time," he said through clenched teeth.

"When is the time, Callum? You've been putting this off for years, and I'm done waiting for you to realize that Sean is not capable the way you are."

Callum grabbed his father's arm and shoved him outside the hospital room. He took three long strides down the hall, forcing a calming breath before stalking back toward his father.

"Sean is clinging to his life in there right now and you want to make this about the resort?" Anger had his entire body trembling.

"I want you to use this incident to realize what I have, that Sean is not capable of taking on the pressures of running the family business. The littlest bit of stress causes him to lose it."

A little bit of stress? Was his father really that oblivious to the source of his brother's problems? Could he really not accept part of the blame for it? Or did he truly not care? "I wonder where that stress comes from?"

"Keep blaming me for your brother's problems all you want, but he's a grown man now. Time to take responsibility for his actions, to move on from the 'childhood trauma' that resulted from me wanting to raise successful, strong men," his father said in his usual stern, calm manner that was absolutely infuriating.

"You didn't raise us. You belittled us, tormented us, abused us…"

He scoffed. "It was called the school of hard knocks when I was growing up with my old man. Now it's abuse if you don't praise your children for every insignificant accomplishment. Do you think I would be where I am if my father had coddled me?" He shook his head. "Your grandfather had a zero-tolerance policy and I have the belt scars to prove it. Mistakes and excuses weren't acceptable. Parents have lost all control because they are afraid of their kids."

Callum released a slow, deep breath. There was no point arguing with him. His father had never listened to anything any of them had to say. If the sight of Sean lying in a hospital bed couldn't soften the man's heart—make him realize that he'd made some mistakes, make him want to change things, fix things—then Callum was certain nothing could. And he was done wasting his breath and energy. "Well, Dad, you shouldn't be afraid of your children. But you could at least be afraid of losing them," he said before heading back into the hospital room, leaving his father standing in the hallway. A few seconds later, he heard the unmistakable sound of his dad's heavy footsteps moving farther away down the hall.

CHAPTER TWENTY-ONE

THROWING HER DIRTY laundry from the week into the washing machine hours later, Ellie shut the door, turned the washer on and then leaned against it.

Her apartment felt cold and empty. She'd never minded living alone before, but suddenly the hollow silence seemed to be screaming how much she'd missed, how many opportunities she'd let slip by while she was clinging to the past and an imagined future.

Maybe she should go down to the bookstore and bring Stormy upstairs with her for the night so she wouldn't be so alone.

She sighed. That would be unfair to the fox.

Going into the kitchen, she made a pot of coffee, and then carrying a mug into the small living room, she sat on the couch and curled her legs under her. She picked up Callum's manuscript pages, which he'd left behind at the cottage, and read them again. The words jumped off the page and resonated even more with her this time. She knew him better now, knew the source of his inspiration and knew the depth of his passion for the subject he was writing about.

Callum was full of depth and passion.

She sighed, hugging the pages to her chest and breathing in deeply, hoping his scent still lingered on the pages and desperate to feel closer to him, or at least this very personal part of him.

He had to do something with this amazing talent of his. It would be such a shame if he let fear or hesitation prevent him from going after what he wanted.

Kinda like she was?

She'd told Callum he should pursue his dreams, but wasn't she being hypocritical when she wasn't actively pursuing hers?

He'd told her she'd make a great teacher, and damn it, she knew in her heart that she would. A lack of funding had prevented her from doing it before, but now what was her excuse? She'd been teaching English online, saving for her future… Well, maybe now was her future, and if she didn't spend the money chasing the career she desperately wanted, what was even the point?

She sighed as she set the manuscript pages aside and reached for her laptop. Opening it, she took a deep breath as she opened a search engine and typed in online degrees.

She couldn't expect Callum to follow his heart if she wasn't willing to.

And registering for an online learning program was just the first step for her. From now on, she refused to let her deepest fear of not achieving the fulfilled life she wanted become a reality. She'd start that evening by taking control of her professional future, and then tomorrow she'd go after the love she really wanted.

DISAPPOINTING MRS. GRAYSON was going to be tough, Callum thought, looking around the bookstore. The older woman had been like a grandmother to him for years. She'd given him the opportunity to work among the books he loved, and unlike everyone else, never questioned his choice to not redeem his birthright place on the resort ownership throne.

But he had no other choice. He couldn't continue to leave

the pressure of the family business on Sean. His brother had shouldered that burden far too long, and Callum needed to step up and help. Not for their father, but for his brother. He'd agree to his father's terms and take over running the day-to-day operations with Sean, and maybe someday he'd be able to hand the responsibility over to his brother full-time. But in the meantime, the obligation was something he needed to take on.

Erika's update that afternoon was that Sean had woken several times throughout the night, and while he'd been loopy and unable to communicate, she was hopeful and optimistic about a recovery. Callum was heading to the hospital next, but first he needed to give his notice to Mrs. Grayson.

He bent to pet Stormy, curled up in her bed in the hallway, and fought the emotions welling up inside of him. She was just a fox. She wasn't going anywhere. He could visit her anytime.

As he entered the office in the back of the bookstore at the end of his shift, the older woman glanced up with a sad smile. "You're leaving me, aren't you?"

Obviously there was nothing wrong with her grandmotherly instincts. "How'd you know?"

She laughed. "You have been sweating all day and going well above and beyond, and you were actually on time this morning, so call it a hunch."

He sat in the chair across from her and ran a sweaty hand through his hair. At least he hadn't had to verbalize it. She'd made it easy on him. "I know I'm supposed to give two weeks…" This was the other difficult part. How could he work out his notice next to Ellie and even focus on the job at all with his brother and the decision he'd made weighing heavily on his mind, preoccupying him.

Behind her oversize dark-rimmed glasses, she sent him an understanding look. "It's okay, darling. I understand you have a lot going on."

"No, I want to fulfill that obligation. Honestly, I'm not quite ready to let go just yet." He hated to admit this part of his life was over. Hated to think he wouldn't walk through those doors—late—and see Ellie almost every day. "I was thinking I could do inventory or stock the shelves after hours for a few days this week…" Anything to help and also transition from the job he enjoyed. He just couldn't be in the store with Ellie…

Mrs. Grayson studied him. "Is this just because of your family? Or is there more to it?"

The older woman would have to have been blind or oblivious not to have noticed his love for Ellie. And she was neither. "I think you know the answer to that." He still had no idea what he was going to do with the unrequited feelings that had skyrocketed to an even more devastating level.

"I take it the time away didn't go as well as you'd hoped?"

"That would be an accurate assumption."

Mrs. Grayson sighed as she shook her head. "That girl is one of the most brilliant people I know when it comes to books… Emotions may not be her strong suit."

Her emotions had been on full display that week. There had been no hiding them when she'd kissed him…or when she'd returned his kiss.

Damn, the memory of it tore him up. The idea that he'd never get that chance again frustrated the hell out of him. She wasn't just someone he loved—he was in love with her, and that week had only solidified his confidence in his feelings.

He nodded. "Anyway, this isn't just about Ellie. I think

it's time to get serious about my own future, and as much as I love working here…my father's right." The words nearly choked him. "The family business is where I should be."

Meredith gave him a sincere, sympathetic look. One that said her heart was breaking watching the life he wanted for himself slip away. "I hope you're making this decision because you believe it's the right one for yourself."

Of course she wasn't fooled. He'd never made any secret that the hospitality industry wasn't for him. His "change of heart" now was simply because he had no other choice. "Sometimes a person isn't given that luxury," he said as he stood. "Thanks for everything, Mrs. Grayson."

"Good luck, dear," she said as he closed the office door behind him.

CALLUM HAD GIVEN his notice.

That hurt, but what had she been expecting? Obviously, he thought they couldn't continue to work together after everything that had happened, that the tension and awkwardness between them would be too much. She'd texted him that morning when he hadn't shown up for their first shift together after the weekend, but her *Hey, get your butt to work or you're fired* text had gone unanswered. He was avoiding her and she couldn't fault him for that. She just wished he'd give her time to explain that she hadn't reconciled with Brent…because she was falling in love with Callum.

Maybe it didn't matter anymore.

Their friendship was ruined, their working relationship was ruined and it was her fault. Ellie's chest ached as she stacked a bookshelf full of the memoir from a debut author scheduled for release that day.

A debut author. Would Callum submit his book to publishers? What was his plan now? Would he work at the resort? Take the offer from his father?

Working there without him wouldn't be the same. Not seeing him almost every day would be torture. She hadn't realized just how much she depended on seeing his goofy grin as he casually strolled in late... How much she'd miss their book discussions and debates. How much she'd miss laughing with him or watching him flirt with the customers.

Having him flirt with her.

The memories of his kisses were absolute torture. In her mind, she'd replayed them over and over. She didn't know it was possible to crave someone's lips so terribly. And it wasn't just his lips she missed, but every part of him. His smile, his heart, his hot-as-hell body, his kindness...

The lump in her throat nearly strangled her. Why was the ache in her heart so strong when she'd only been falling for him for a few days? The pain of her breakup with Brent years before paled in comparison, and he was completely out of her mind and heart now.

It made no sense, but then maybe love wasn't supposed to. Maybe she needed to abandon reasoning and common sense and just go with her gut. If Callum refused to answer her calls and texts and was going out of his way to avoid her, she'd go to him and give him no other choice than to acknowledge her. She was ready to take control of all aspects of her life, including her love life, she reminded herself.

As she reentered through the back door after taking the box to the recycle bin, she heard the store phone ringing and ran to the front to answer. She cleared her throat. "Flippin' Pages. How may I help you?" she asked breathlessly into the phone.

"Hi, my name is Claire Rodet. I was hoping to speak

with Ellie Mitchell, the store manager," a polished female voice said.

"This is Ellie. How can I help you, Claire?"

"I'm an editor at Lakeside Publishing, and I believe your store is stocking copies of Darla Henshaw's memoir, *When the Lights Go Out*?"

"We are, yes. I just finished stocking the shelves actually," she said. Shoot, hopefully there hadn't been a printing mistake or a shipping issue. Pulling them off the shelves would be a pain in the butt, and they'd had posters designed advertising the upcoming release date hung in the store for two months. This was a highly anticipated book written by an Alaska resident, and the readers in Wild River—especially the book club folk—wouldn't be impressed if they had to wait or buy the digital copy. "Is there a problem?"

"The books are completely fine, but I have a sort of emergency request that I'm hoping you can help me with," Claire said, indeed sounding slightly desperate.

"Of course…"

"One of our live signings scheduled for Saturday canceled last minute and we need a replacement while the author is still touring through Alaska. Would your store have any openings this weekend?"

"Let me check…" Ellie scrolled through the events scheduled for that weekend on their site. It would mean rescheduling their weekend read-along, but she could accommodate the request. A surprise author signing announcement would have all the bookworms in town lining up around the block. "I can do Saturday afternoon around two. Does that work?"

"Perfect! We will make it work," Claire said, sounding relieved. "Thank you so much, Ellie."

"No problem at all. Would you like to email me the details and arrange for more copies to be sent to the store?"

"I'll do that right away. Thanks again."

Ellie disconnected the call and adjusted the weekend event schedule. As she opened her email, Mrs. Grayson carried chairs from the back room to set up for that evening's book club chat. Ellie rushed to take them from her. "I told you I'd set up."

Meredith waved a hand, almost as though insulted that she was thought too old to carry a few chairs. She set them down and started positioning them in a circle. "Did I hear you book an event, dear?"

"Yes, a little short notice, so I hope that's okay. It's for this Saturday—the new memoir, *When the Lights Go Out*."

"Oh wow! I'd been hoping to get Darla Henshaw into the store. We went to school together, and her life story is truly fascinating. She was one of the first women working in the Coal Harbor mines. She's survived a violent marriage and three rounds with cancer and is a huge advocate for women's rights. The woman is incredible."

Ellie nodded. "I can't wait to read the book. I stashed one behind the counter already. Oh, and I also found a copy of Amelia Dash's latest back there. Were you holding it for someone or can I reshelve it?"

"I think it's Callum's," she said.

Ellie frowned. Callum wanted the latest chick-lit book club title? "Really?"

Meredith nodded. "I think he may know the author," she said somewhat cryptically, and Ellie's eyes widened.

"That's his mom?"

Meredith just shrugged as though she would reveal nothing, but it was too late. It totally made sense that he'd want a copy. And how could she have missed the family resemblance between Callum and the woman on the back of the book. He may have gotten his height and chiseled features from his father, but the jet-black hair and blue eyes were the same as those of Amelia Dash...or Carolyn McKendrick.

Obviously, he was trying to support his mother's career, even in this small way, and even if she didn't know it.

"Are you staying for book club tonight?" Meredith asked.

"I don't think so... I didn't have time to finish the book." She had been planning on finishing the latest historical thriller the previous week. She'd even taken it to the cottages, but it just hadn't happened.

Meredith sent her a knowing look. "You didn't tell me how your week went with your old friends."

Ellie sighed. Talking about this was the last thing she wanted to do, but she couldn't be rude. "Um, it was interesting... The week was full of adventure, I'll say that much." She wouldn't mention the near-death experience. "Eye-opening," she said softly.

Meredith nodded. "Well, good news is now you can move forward with that certainty and not have to continue to wonder what might have been."

Only now she'd be wondering about a different man, a different possible future.

Ellie's smile was forced as she hesitated before asking, "So, Callum—did he say why he was leaving?" The older woman was like a grandmother figure to Callum. The two were close. Ellie knew quitting must have been hard on him. On both of them. And she was the cause.

Would he have told their boss the truth? That he couldn't work with her because she'd essentially used him and broken his heart by choosing the wrong guy?

"Your business is your business," Meredith said gently.

"But I suspect it had something to do with the enormous crush he's always had on you."

Ellie's cheeks flamed. Nothing got past the older woman. Guess you didn't live to be in your seventies without picking up on human nature. Too bad Ellie hadn't picked up on it sooner.

Would it have mattered? Or would she have continued to harbor unresolved feelings for Brent and never considered Callum anyway?

"Of course, I'm sure that wasn't the only reason," Meredith said. "He also mentioned that it was time to move on... get serious..."

Ellie's jaw clenched. "All his father's words." Callum had been happy working here, silently, secretly pursuing his own dream. It made her stomach hurt to think that because of what had happened between them, he now felt that the best choice was to accept his father's offer when that wasn't really what he wanted.

Damn, she'd really messed things up. Could she fix it? Would he give her that chance?

"Shame about his brother though."

Ellie's eyes widened. His brother? "What happened to Sean?"

Meredith looked at her in surprise. "I'm sorry, dear, I assumed you'd heard."

Ellie's heart raced. "No."

"Attempted overdose." Meredith shook her head sadly. "He's still in the hospital. That poor boy always struggled..."

"I had no idea," Ellie said quietly. She knew Sean had demons, especially after reading Callum's work, but she'd never thought he'd do something so tragic. He must be in so much pain to think that was the only option. And Callum...

She understood why he'd think that fulfilling his family obligation now was the right decision, even if it wasn't what he ultimately wanted. He was such a great man. Kind, considerate, talented—and the only one in a very long time to have her feeling something real and meaningful.

And the man she was falling in love with was hurting and dealing with so much, and she had no idea if he'd appreciate her reaching out.

Meredith seemed to read her thoughts. "Despite whatever happened…or didn't happen, you never turn your back on a friend," she said, tapping Ellie's shoulder gently before heading into the back of the store.

Her boss was right. She'd never turn her back on a friend, and Callum was so much more than that.

IN HIS BROTHER'S hospital room, Callum sat in the chair that he'd occupied for the last twenty-four hours. Erika had called to say that Sean was stable and showing signs of improvement and that they were hoping he would regain full consciousness soon. Callum had stayed by his brother's side, not wanting Sean to wake up alone. Sean had drifted in and out, mumbling incoherently and tossing and turning in his sleep. Callum hoped that when his brother finally did wake up fully, he'd feel a bit better.

His laptop open, Callum scanned the resort's latest board report. Numbers and stats about tourist traffic the previous year and marketing plans and budgeting all boring him to tears, but he needed to really pay attention to all of this stuff from now on. He couldn't just gloss over everything and leave it in Sean's hands.

He ran a hand over his face as he tried to focus, but his manuscript was calling to him. Especially now. The rawness of their current situation had his emotions so close to the surface that the words were desperate to escape onto the page. Writing had always been an outlet for him during challenging days with his family, but he didn't have time for that now.

Sean stirred on the bed and Callum glanced at him as his eyes fluttered open. When they stayed open and Sean scanned the hospital room, he put his laptop aside and stood. "Hey, look who's awake."

Sean looked slightly confused and disoriented as he continued to scan his surroundings and turned to look at Callum. "What happened? Where am I?"

He'd asked the same questions twice before, but obviously he hadn't been lucid enough to understand what was going on. His eyes looked clearer now and he seemed more alert. "Well, you are in the hospital, and I was hoping you could help me with the 'what happened' part," Callum said gently.

Sean slumped low in the bed as though wanting to sink all the way through. "Shit. I'm sorry, man," he whispered, his pained expression instantly full of remorse and regret.

Callum shook his head. "No, I'm sorry. I should have tried harder to reach out when we had trouble connecting."

"You shouldn't have to babysit me," Sean said. "You have your own life."

"It's not like that. We are family and I'm here for you, whatever you need. Sorry, I wasn't there this time." He ran a hand through his hair. "I had no idea the pressure was mounting so much…" He should have known. He shouldn't have constantly turned his back on the family obligations, leaving Sean to deal with it all alone. It had been selfish.

Sean shook his head. "Most days, I think I'm doing okay. The hotel is running smoothly, and I'm making plans for the upcoming seasons. I mean, not up to Dad's standards and expectations," he said, his voice hardening. "But I'm managing."

His brother was more than managing. He was doing a great job, and he'd be doing even better if he had confidence in himself. If their father could recognize the effort he was making and offer praise instead of constant criticism.

"Then some days, like the other night, something goes wrong. Then other things start to go off the rails—little things, but suddenly they feel insurmountable. I just can't take it all, you know. I start to think Dad is right and the pressure and anxiety mount to this unbearable level, and I don't see a way out." Sean released a deep sigh.

Callum should have been there to help his brother find that way. Mental illness wasn't something his brother should have to be battling on his own. Once they left the hospital, things would change. Callum took his brother's hand in his and squeezed tight. "I do know, or at least I'm trying to, and I'm sorry I wasn't here for you. I will be from now on."

Sean frowned. "What do you mean?" His voice was hoarse and his throat sounded dry.

Callum reached for the water jug on the table and poured his brother a glass. He handed it to him. "I'm going to help…"

Sean shook his head as he took the glass with a shaky hand. "No. That's not what you want."

"It's my responsibility too, and I've made a decision."

"No, Callum. I can't ask you to do that. You have your own plans…"

"You're not asking me to do anything. This is what I should have been doing all along." Maybe life really was about doing the right thing, even if it meant sacrificing his own happiness. When did anyone really get what they wanted? "We'll talk about it in a few days. Just rest and know that you won't have to deal with all of this—with Dad—on your own anymore. You never should have had to."

Sean looked relieved but mostly distraught. "Dude, I don't want you giving up your own life for this."

"I'm not giving anything up," he said, and it wasn't a lie since he didn't have anything real to give up anyway.

CHAPTER TWENTY-TWO

HOSPITALS HAD TO be the most anxiety-inducing places on earth. Ellie supposed no one really liked them, but for her especially, hospitals and funeral homes were two places she always felt nauseous entering. With her parents' illnesses, enough of her life had been spent in both. The smell of sickness and cleansers, the sterile cold-beige walls, and the buzz of doctors and nurses—so serious and often pulled in all directions—was an unsettling atmosphere for her.

She sat in her vehicle in the visitor parking lot of Wild River Community Hospital, staring at the building. She wanted to be here for Callum, in case he needed her. She knew he wouldn't reach out. He was too proud, and she'd hurt him with her rejection. But Mrs. Grayson was right. She'd never turn her back on him when he needed her. If only she could reassure him of that. He'd always been there for her, and she knew if she needed him again now, he would be.

She desperately wanted to apologize and make things right. Now wasn't the best time, but she hoped he'd at least let her be there for him and his family—even in just a small way that would show him how much she cared about him. And eventually, maybe they would get back to where they'd left off before she'd made the worst decision of her life.

Getting out of her car, she headed across the parking lot and pushed through the revolving doors. Ignoring the twisting sensation in her stomach, she approached the nurses' desk. She hadn't seen or spoken to Callum since he'd left the cottage. What if he didn't want to see her? What if her being there only made things worse?

She had to try. At least he'd know she cared, and right now that mattered more than anything.

But her heart dropped seeing Alisha at the desk talking to the triage nurse. She hadn't spoken to any of her former classmates since they'd dropped her home a few days before. Things would probably go back to the way they'd been before, with them all living in the same small town, seeing one another in passing, but Ellie continuing to be outside the circle, not really a friend. She doubted she'd hear from any of them again.

Brent had already unfriended her on Facebook and blocked her on Instagram. Guess that was his way of moving on and making a clean break.

She was okay with that. If he hadn't, she probably would have. No sense keeping in touch when they'd said all they needed to.

But this first run-in with Alisha was sure to be awkward. Would they have sided with Brent and think less of her now?

Damn, why did their opinion of her still matter so much?

"Ellie!"

Oh well, so much for Alisha not noticing her. She forced a small smile as she stopped at the desk. "Hi, Alisha... How are you?"

"Good...that time away was exactly what I needed to regroup, and now it's back to all the craziness around here." She smiled warmly. "How are you?"

Such a loaded question. That week at the cottages, she'd done a ton of soul-searching and had discovered things about herself that she'd never taken the time to uncover before. She'd opened old wounds, started to heal and then made more mistakes and created even more heartache. But she was also ready to start rebuilding and using her new self-awareness to make positive changes. How did she say that in five words or less? "I'm okay," she said simply. "I'm actually just here to see Callum… I think his brother is here." She knew he'd be here.

Alisha nodded sympathetically. "Yeah, he's here. Unfortunately, we don't allow visitors to that ward of the hospital. Family members only."

Right. Of course, that made sense. Had Callum's dad been by to see Sean? Was he here now? And what about Callum's mom? Did she know her son was in the hospital? Either way, this would all be awkward and tense for the family. Damn, she wished there was a way she could be there for Callum. "Okay…no problem. I should have called to check," she mumbled.

"I can let Callum know you stopped by though," Alisha said.

"Thank you." Ellie turned to leave.

"Hey, I'm about to take my break…want to grab a coffee?"

She didn't. She was hardly in the mood to chat or gossip casually with someone she'd realized she couldn't truly be friends with…but maybe not all friendships had to be super deep and meaningful. Maybe she and Alisha could be casual friends who met once a year for a coffee and catch-up if they ran into one another. And she didn't want to be rude, so she nodded. "Sure, okay."

She waited for Alisha near the hospital cafeteria doors, and a few minutes later, the two of them headed toward the coffee dispensers. "So did you have any fun last week?" Alisha asked, almost apologetically.

"Yes! I did…" It wasn't a lie. There had been several moments with Callum that had made the entire week worthwhile, that had brought them closer and had opened her eyes to who he was—to the fact that he was everything she'd ever wanted.

So, for that, she was grateful for the week away. She only wished it had ended differently. And she could have done without the near-death experience.

"Good. I still feel terrible about the accident." She shook her head. "Brent can be a little reckless. He was always that way—except when he was with you—and I think while alcohol definitely played a factor that day, so did jealousy. At that point, he still thought you and Callum were a thing," she said, reaching for two packets of sugar and ripping them open.

Ellie's cheeks flushed. Right. Her lie. Couldn't expect to get out of this visit without that being brought up again. "About that…again, I'm sorry about deceiving all of you."

Alisha laughed. "You two were really convincing. Especially Callum. I know Nick loves me, but I don't think he will ever look at me the way Callum looked at you. He missed his calling as an actor," she said, stirring the creamer in her coffee and putting on the lid.

Ellie gulped. Or he was really that much in love with her. And she'd blown it, blown any opportunity she had with him—to have a man that wonderful and special—because she was an idiot. "He's a great guy."

They carried their coffees to an empty table and sat.

"What about you and Brent?" She leaned forward and studied her. "Have you two spoken? Tried to work things out?"

"No. We decided us getting together again wasn't such a great idea," Ellie said. She'd decided this time.

"That's too bad. I remember you were so in love with him years ago, and he was relieved to hear that the fiancé thing was a hoax," she said, sipping her coffee. "And I saw him leave your cottage the other night." She raised an eyebrow suggestively over her coffee cup.

Ellie shook her head. "Nothing happened." Thank God. There'd be no way she could go back to Callum and ask for forgiveness and another chance if she'd gotten physical with Brent. "I just don't think we're the right fit, you know." She cradled her cup, wishing she'd said no to the catch-up. Talking about Brent and Callum only reminded her of the choice she'd made, how she'd ultimately hurt both men... in varying degrees.

Brent would immediately bounce back, and he'd probably already forgotten about her again. But Callum had so many other things going on right now, and she'd only compounded his stress and disappointment. "What we had was teenage love. That doesn't always work in adulthood." She knew that now. A little too late.

But she wouldn't keep beating herself up over lost time. All she could do was keep moving forward.

"Well, I'm sure things will work out when the time is right, with the right one for you," Alisha said, sipping her coffee. "And hey, a group of us are going camping in two weeks. You're welcome to join us," she said.

"Oh, I'm not sure…"

"No crazy adventures this time, I promise," Alisha said quickly. "Just maybe s'mores and reading by the lake?"

Ellie gave a small smile, for the first time feeling seen by the other woman. "Thanks, I'll think about it."

Unfortunately, there was only one person she wanted to spend her time with right now, and he wanted nothing to do with her.

So ELLIE WASN'T with Brent.

Sitting at a table, shielded by a large cookie display, Callum could hear Ellie and Alisha talking a few tables away. Ellie had decided Brent wasn't what she wanted after all. That thought gave him an irrational, momentary lift. Which was dumb. Ellie hadn't wanted him before Brent, she wouldn't want him now either. But at least knowing she was no longer trying to fit in with that group and be what Brent wanted made him feel better for one person he cared about.

And she obviously had heard about Sean and was here to offer support to him. He sighed. He couldn't accept that support. That was why he'd been ignoring her calls and texts the last few days. Her sympathy and kindness wasn't what he wanted. He wanted far too much from her, and he didn't want another stressful situation to be what drew them together. If Ellie wanted to be with him, she would have chosen him that night in the cottage when he'd opened himself up, been vulnerable and laid all of his cards on the table.

He was angry, but he was mostly just hurt and disappointed. Still, he was glad that she hadn't ended up with the other man either. She deserved so much more... He wanted to be the one who gave her everything, but that wasn't up to him.

He chugged his lukewarm coffee—the third one so far that day—and checked his watch. He had to get back to his brother. Getting up, he tossed his cup into the trash can and headed toward the door. He hesitated, seeing Ellie from a distance, smiling and talking to Alisha. She looked so beautiful in that blue sundress she'd worn at the cottage, her hair in soft waves around her shoulders, her wispy bangs refusing to stay out of her eyes.

He missed her. Missed seeing her. Missed talking to her. Missed touching her and kissing her.

Maybe he should say hi. Thank her for coming, even if that was as much support as he could take. Let her know he appreciated her reaching out.

He shook his head and pushed through the cafeteria doors.

Right now, he wasn't sure he could handle opening himself up to further disappointment.

CHAPTER TWENTY-THREE

FOUR UNANSWERED TEXT messages and three calls later, one thing was certain—Callum's silence was driving her insane.

In the two years that they'd known each other, they hadn't gone more than a day without talking. Most days they saw one another. It was true that people didn't realize what they had until it was gone. She felt hopeless and lost and desperate to just talk to him. If he refused to answer her calls and texts, there was only one thing left to do.

Ellie climbed the stairs to Callum's apartment the next morning, her heart ready to burst out of her chest. He couldn't avoid her if she was standing right in front of him. But what would he say to her? Would he be angry and annoyed that she was being this persistent or would he be happy she was making the effort?

She paused at the door.

Could she do this? Apologize and tell him how she felt? Hope that he could forgive her for hurting him?

The timing was really bad, but she needed him to know she was there for him and his family, whatever they needed. And she was afraid that if she let too much time pass without reaching out to him and telling him that she was falling in love with him, it might be too late when she finally did find the courage and strength.

She took a deep breath and knocked on the door. Silence. She peered in through the window and listened intently for the sound of footsteps or voices inside. Nothing. His car was in the driveway, and she knew visiting hours didn't start at the hospital for another two hours. She'd purposely chosen the early morning visit as her best chance of catching him. The thought that he might still be in bed added another level to her anxiety. She'd had a chance the week before to be in bed with him—in a beautiful setting with champagne and chocolates and rose petals—and she'd totally blown it.

She rang the doorbell. Nothing. Had he seen her from the window and decided to pretend not to be home? She knocked on the door again. "Come on, Callum, I just want to talk," she called out.

The next-door neighbor poked his head out through his living room curtain and she offered a small smile and wave.

"Two minutes. That's all I'm asking for!" She was bordering on stalker behavior, and she knew she must look odd standing out here so long, begging him to open the door, but she couldn't let Callum continue to avoid her. He had feelings for her and she was falling in love with him. They couldn't just let that go. She wasn't willing to let *him* go. At least not without a fight. "Callum!"

"Ellie?" his voice said behind her.

She winced. So he wasn't inside, ignoring her.

She turned and her mouth went dry, seeing him standing at the bottom of the stairs in just his running shorts and shoes. Shirtless, sweat glistening on his body, damp hair falling across his forehead and days-old stubble along his jawline, he had to be the hottest guy on the planet. The hottest guy on the planet, who had confessed his feelings for her, and she'd walked away. Making her the dumbest woman on the planet.

"What are you doing here?" he asked in her silence.

All of a sudden, she wasn't sure how to begin. What did she say now that she had his attention? "I needed to talk to you," she said. Her voice sounded strangled, unsure, so she cleared her throat. "I'm sorry to hear about your brother."

He nodded, taking deep breaths in and out. "Thank you. Alisha told me you stopped by the hospital. I appreciate that—I know hospitals aren't your thing."

"How is he?"

"Doing better every day. It's been a long battle and it will always be," he said sadly. "Erika has set him up with a therapist at the hospital, and Sean's agreed to continue to see him after he's released. She's adjusting his medication, and at least now I know that he may need more support than he admits."

This had to be so hard on him. He must be feeling so much pressure. "If there's anything I can do…" Her voice trailed away as her uncertainty rose. He didn't seem upset to see her, but he didn't look happy either.

"Thank you," he said.

She stared at him for a long beat, the tension-filled silence growing thicker around them with each passing second. "Callum, I made a mistake," she blurted out.

He placed his hands on his hips and stared at the ground. "I'm sorry things didn't work out between you and Brent."

So he knew she wasn't with Brent and still, he hadn't reached out or wanted to talk to her. Her confidence wavered even more. Had he really already shut the door on them? On her? "I'm not… I'm just sorry it took me so long to see what was in front of me. You." She paused. "You were always there with your support and friendship…and love. And I was so blinded by what I thought I wanted, needed, that I didn't know that that was you. All along."

She almost didn't recognize her own emotion-filled voice. When was the last time she'd felt so vulnerable? So exposed?

He took a deep breath, his gaze still on the ground. The silence went on for an excruciatingly long time.

What was he thinking? What was he feeling?

"Say something, please," she said softly.

His gaze rose to meet hers. Pain and disappointment and uncertainty reflecting in his eyes made her heart sink. "So much happened in the last week. So much changed between us. I opened myself up, I shared things with you."

She nodded. "I know. And all of that meant so much."

"Our physical connection was definitely there, and I thought maybe we were connecting on a deeper level. A meaningful level," he said.

"We were," she whispered. They had connected in so many ways, on so many levels. They'd both felt it.

"Then you chose Brent," Callum said, his voice hardening slightly as though steeling himself against further hurt.

Her shoulders sagged and a lump formed in the back of her throat.

"I'm sorry, Ellie, but I'm not okay with being second best."

"That's not what you are," she said quickly, taking several steps toward him. "I was just too stupid to see how amazing you are. It took that time together to realize it. It shouldn't have, but…damn, Callum, I'm sorry."

"I don't want an apology, Ellie. I want to go back to that moment of decision in the cottage in the woods and have you say my name. Choose me. I want to erase the pain and disappointment of you deciding that I wasn't enough."

Her heart shattered. "You are enough. More than enough. And I know I hurt you and I don't deserve another chance.

I can't go back in time and change things, but I'm hoping you can forgive me long enough to let me show you how much I care about you. I'm falling in love with you, Callum." There. She'd said it. Her heart was out there. Whether he'd accept it or not hung in the balance.

He stared at her, tormented, torn…as though processing her words yet not fully hearing them or believing them.

She dared another step closer and reached out for his hand. He didn't pull away but he didn't lock fingers with her either. She stood there, staring at him, waiting…holding her breath. She wanted to wrap her arms around him and cling to him tight until he believed her, trusted in her words. But all she could do was stand there, waiting.

He swallowed hard and slowly removed his hand from hers. "Ellie, I've got a lot going on right now. My brother… the job at the resort…"

All valid reasons why he couldn't think about "them" right now, but she knew they were really just excuses— a defense mechanism against more damage he obviously didn't think his heart could take.

She'd hurt him once. Why should he believe that she wouldn't do it again?

WHAT THE HELL did he say?

The woman he loved just told him she was falling in love with him. It should be the happiest moment of his life, yet his emotions seemed to be on lockdown. He stared at her, trying to find the words for a long time…too long.

"Right. I guess it's too late," she said, her disappointment crushing him. He wanted to reach out and hold her. Tell her everything was okay. That he didn't care about what had happened. He just wanted her. But what if this was all just because her emotions were a mess because of Brent.

Maybe she was clinging to the connection they'd had because of the one she'd lost. One she'd once thought was real.

How could he take a chance that, given the choice again, she'd pick him? What if she decided he wasn't the one she wanted either?

He really could use her support right now. He'd never trusted anyone in his life the way he trusted her, and not having her as a sounding board for the latest crisis he was going through was really hard.

They'd not only blown their shot at love, but he'd lost his best friend.

She reached into her oversize purse and took out a book. His mother's. The one he'd put behind the counter the day he'd gotten the call about Sean being in the hospital. He'd forgotten to get it. "Meredith said this was yours," she said.

He took it and nodded slowly. "Thank you. Amelia Dash is my mom," he said, though he suspected she already knew.

She nodded. "Well, it looks like a great book. I'll make sure to feature it for one of the book club events."

Her attempt to sound casual, unfazed when he could see through the false bravado and knew she was hurting as much as he was nearly broke him. But he had to stay strong.

"I guess I should let you go," she said, her gaze sweeping over him.

Her unconcealed attraction made him want to abandon all his common sense and self-preservation and take her inside and kiss her until he was sure she could no longer hurt him, but… "I'm sorry, Ellie, I just can't do this," he said. So much in his life was out of his control right now. He longed to hold her and feel safe and secure in one aspect of his life. But his brother was spiraling, and he needed to take care of his family. That was what he had to focus on right now.

She nodded, swallowing hard. Her pride obviously kicking in, she said, "Yeah. You're right. This isn't the best time and maybe that chance for us is gone. I have no one to blame but myself. I'm the one who let it slip away," she said, moving past him. And with a final wave, she disappeared down the street.

CHAPTER TWENTY-FOUR

BOOK SIGNINGS WERE normally her favorite events, but the next day, Ellie's smile was forced and her overall energy was low as she entered the bookstore to set up. Interacting with the long line of readers and pretending that she was okay was going to be exhausting. She already couldn't wait for the day to be over.

Stormy seemed to sense her mood and followed her around the store as she turned on the lights. The beautiful fox seemed to be wondering where Callum was the last few days, as well. She'd spent a lot of time sitting in the bookstore window, peering outside.

Ellie knew how she felt.

She bent to pet the soft gray-and-white fur as the crystal blue eyes stared up at her, sad and questioning. "It's my fault. I messed it all up."

The fox gave a tiny whiny sound and then retreated back to the windowsill.

In the back lunchroom, Ellie poured a mug of the dark, thick black coffee Meredith had brewed already and took a gulp, not caring that the liquid scorched her tongue. Hopefully the jolt of caffeine would help restore her motivation.

All day she'd replayed her conversation with Callum, her chest only tightening with disappointment the more she remembered his words and expression as he'd rejected her. He'd said he hadn't wanted to be second best, and while that was so far from the truth, what could she say? She had chosen Brent first.

More coffee. More regret.

Checking her watch, she sighed and squared her shoulders. She needed to pull it together. There was so much to do that day and hopefully staying busy would help keep her mind off Callum.

Hours later, the local author, Darla Henshaw, sat behind the signing table, which was decorated with her author signage, almost hidden behind the tall stacks of books as the line to meet her extended across the bookstore and down the street outside. Her editor, Claire Rodet, sat next to her. The polished professional in the gray pinstripe dress and two-inch red heels looked exactly the way Ellie envisioned when she thought about editors. Glamorous in a book-smart way, the gatekeepers of the literary world. Both intimidating and fascinating. Claire was friendly and polite as she opened the books to the signing page and chatted with the next people in line as they waited to meet the author.

Readers always had the most interesting questions. They wanted to know everything about the author, the process, the inspiration for the novel… Without Meredith politely ushering them away with their signed copy after the delegated thirty seconds, they would be there until Christmas.

Ellie stood behind the counter, ringing in the purchases, and within ten minutes the store had made its weekly target. The lineup at the counter was a never-ending stream of reading enthusiasts, and by the time they took a break, Ellie's feet were aching and her fingers hurt from working the register.

Unfortunately, it hadn't helped take her mind off Callum. If anything, it only had her thinking how incredible it would be for Callum to be signing his own book in the store someday.

He'd mentioned the new job—taking over the resort. No doubt he thought it was the responsible thing to do, the right thing. But would he still find time to write? Or would his father's expectations leave him no time to focus on anything but eighty hours a week working at a career he hated?

Whether it was her place or not, she loved him far too much to not try to save him from that fate.

Seeing Claire sitting alone in the nonfiction area of the bookstore, Ellie hesitated only briefly before approaching her.

"Hi, Claire. I'm Ellie, the store manager... We met earlier."

Claire smiled up at her as she kicked off her heels and tucked her legs under her on the comfy leather chair. "Yes, hi... Thanks again for putting the event together so quickly. The early release to get ahead of the upcoming competitor title made it almost impossible to organize live events, and they are so important to Darla and her readers," she said gratefully.

Just how grateful was she?

Ellie never bothered the authors and editors who visited the store, simply acted as a support system for a successful event. But this time she thought going out on a limb was worth it. The opportunity had presented itself, and she'd kick herself if she just let it go.

She'd learned a lot in the last few weeks—life was short and she needed to go after what she wanted, even if she sometimes fell flat on her face. She hoped this wouldn't be one of those lately too-frequent incidents.

"It was really no problem." She hesitated. "Um, I was

wondering—if an author wanted to submit to you, would they need an agent?"

Claire nodded, her short, whip-straight blond hair falling into her face. "Yes, unfortunately we get so many submissions every year that we'd never be able to respond to them all, so we only take vetted, agented work at the publishing house at this time."

Shoot. Ellie knew if Claire could read Callum's manuscript pages, she'd be impressed, but there were rules for acquisition for a reason, and as much as she wanted to, Ellie couldn't overstep or expect special treatment. But when would Callum get a chance to finish his book now, let alone start the querying process? She'd been hoping maybe Claire could help expedite that if she enjoyed his work. "I understand." At least she'd tried.

Claire studied her. "But I mean, I am here right now, and I might be able to fit in a few pages if there was a manuscript lying around."

Ellie's heart soared. "Really? That would be so incredible."

"Absolutely. I think I can make an exception for you since you did help us out, and I guess I'm not technically on company time since I'm on break," she said with a wink.

"Well, the manuscript is actually not mine, but believe me these opening chapters are brilliant—I read a lot of books," she said.

Claire laughed. "I imagine you do. Let me take a look."

Two minutes later, Ellie returned with Callum's manuscript pages and a fresh cup of coffee and a tray of cookies for Claire. She set the treats on the table beside her and then reluctantly handed over Callum's work in progress.

Stormy followed her and curled up on the back of Claire's chair.

"Okay, I'll let you know what I think," Claire said, settling in to read.

Ellie nodded, still standing there. Waiting.

Claire didn't glance up from the pages. "The fox can stay, but you have to go," she said as she shooed her away.

"Oh right. Enjoy," Ellie said, rushing off, a twisting in her gut at having kinda betrayed Callum's trust by allowing someone else to read the pages. But if Claire liked them, this could be the start of his career. One he actually wanted. One he deserved.

Callum, please don't kill me.

CALLUM TOOK A DEEP breath as he walked through the resort lobby, seeing it differently for the first time. It wasn't just his father's hotel anymore. It would now be his own future. His gut tightened.

Could there be a more depressing thought?

Maybe only that Ellie would be so disappointed that he was letting go of his own plans and goals he'd had for himself and giving in to Father. But right now, it seemed like the only future he could control. His brother needed him, and he'd focus on that to keep heart when the tie around his neck started to threaten his existence.

He steeled himself as he entered the Chugach Ballroom for the monthly meeting with the board and the faces around the table turned to look at him. His father's gaze met his, the one question he wanted answered reflecting in his own hard gaze.

Callum nodded once, sealing his fate with the nonverbal agreement to his father's offer.

His father's expression changed as he gestured to the empty seat next to him at the front of the room. For so long, Callum had longed to see that acceptance on his father's face. But for something *he* was proud of, as well. Earning it now just because his father had perceivably won the battle, broken his resolve, just made Callum feel like even more of a failure.

He sat in the empty chair next to his father, the one his brother usually occupied, and the weight of expectation hit him like a brick wall as the meeting resumed. For the first time, he actually had to pay attention.

Curious eyes of the board members studied him, questioning, judging. Why was he there? Why the sudden interest in the family resort? Could he live up to expectations or would the resort's success falter under his leadership?

He wished he could confidently say it wouldn't, but this wasn't his passion. He'd give it his all, work his hardest and do his best even if his heart wasn't in it.

Everyone had to know about Sean by now, and that was tough. They all loved and respected his brother, but Callum knew Sean would have a hard time coming back and facing everyone. He'd feel as though he'd failed somehow or that the staff may not have the same respect for him.

Callum would be there now to help, to restore confidence that the resort was being left in good hands. He would give that perception, anyway. Sean was the one everyone could trust to make sure the resort thrived long into future generations, but unfortunately Callum's presence would inspire that belief.

Tuning out the voices in his mind that screamed he was making the wrong decision, Callum actively participated in the meeting. His preparedness surprised and impressed everyone, including his father.

Again, it only made him feel sick that his father was seemingly gloating that this was the path he'd known Callum should take all along. And Callum's behaving like the heir he was expected to be was simply validation for the years of pressure his father had applied.

As the meeting wrapped up, Callum shook hands with the board executives, and with each welcome-on-board acceptance, he felt his own identity fading.

But this was the right thing to do. Life wasn't about getting what you wanted. Never had that been clearer than the last few weeks.

Moments later, everyone dispersed, and alone in the ballroom, his father approached. "Wasn't sure I'd see you here today."

He almost hadn't. "Well, I'm here," he said tightly. He didn't like it. But he'd step up and do the best job he could. For no other reason than his brother.

"Why the change of heart?" his father asked.

"It's more like a change of mind. This is the practical thing to do," he said tightly.

His father nodded as he extended a hand toward him. "I can live with that."

Callum stared at it. Maybe his father could, but could he?

CHAPTER TWENTY-FIVE

CLAIRE RODET HAD left the store on Saturday without commenting on the manuscript pages, and Ellie's disappointment was strong. Those pages were good. Claire and Lakeside Publishing weren't the only publishing companies Callum could submit to, but Ellie had been hoping for some validation from Claire to pass along to Callum. Anything to reassure him that he wasn't wasting his time, and that even if he did work at the resort, he might still keep his own dream alive.

She knew how important that was now more than ever. Staring at the acceptance email from the online university, Ellie's heart swelled with happiness and pride. She'd done it. She'd applied. She was registered, and that fall she'd be starting her teaching degree part-time.

Damn, she wished she could share her excitement and this moment with Callum. She'd never understood what a big part of her life he actually was until he was no longer there to share things with. She kept staring at the front door, expecting him to waltz in late with that gorgeous smile that used to brighten her day without her even realizing it.

The store felt colder and a lot less like home without him there.

The bookstore phone rang, and she tucked her cell phone away as she reached for it. "Flippin' Pages, how may I help you?"

"Ellie? This is Claire Rodet."

Ellie quietly took a breath. "Hi, Claire."

"I wanted to apologize for not talking to you before I left the store on Saturday, but it was a little chaotic toward the end of the day," she said.

"That's no problem." She held her breath as she waited.

"But I did want to tell you that you were right. Those pages were good. Really good. The author's writing is raw and real and the voice is captivating. The use of humor to balance the tough subject matter is done extremely well."

Ellie had thought so too.

"As I said, we usually don't accept unagented submissions…but I'd love to see the full manuscript once the author is ready to submit."

Ellie's mouth gaped and she shut her lips quickly and nodded.

"Ellie?"

"Oh, yes, sorry, I'm still here. Thank you so much, Claire. I know the author will be thrilled to hear it." If he wasn't majorly pissed that she'd shared his writing in the first place. She had to believe he wouldn't be. That he'd see it for the act of love and belief in him that it was.

"Great. Well, just be sure that they mention you and our connection in their query letter so I can be sure to connect the two," she said.

"I will let them know. Thanks again, Claire."

"Sure, I'm just kinda peeved that you've left me without more to read," she said with a laugh.

Ellie knew the feeling. "I'll be sure to tell the author to hurry up."

"Take care, Ellie."

As she disconnected the call her heart soared, and despite the pain of Callum's rejection, she felt happier and lighter and more hopeful than she had in days. He had amazing talent, and she hoped Claire's validation would give him the confidence to go after his dream.

But first she needed to stop him from making the biggest mistake of his life.

PAPERWORK ON TOP of paperwork. Callum had never seen so many legal documents in his entire life. His father's transition to "retirement" and the changing of the guard looked like it could take months. And if he was forced to make sense of all of this dull, dry reading for too much longer today, his head might explode. But this was what his life looked like now. Stacks of paper without a creative word in the lot.

He scanned the legal contracts his father had put in front of him. It was his official retirement contract that would secure the passing of the resort to Callum as the new acting owner. His father would still have his finger on things and would oversee operations from a distance...not far enough away for Callum's liking. He tapped the pen against the boardroom table, every fiber of his being resisting signing on the dotted line. Once he did, there would be no turning back, no changing his mind.

Could he really spend his entire life cooped up in rooms like this one, working on marketing and promotion campaigns, hiring and firing staff and walking these halls that had only ever caused his family pain?

Essentially he was signing away a life of any kind of happiness.

The ballroom door opened as his pen was poised above the signature line, and Sean entered, slightly out of breath. He looked a little thinner, but the color was back in his complexion and his eyes looked a lot clearer than they had the last time Callum had seen him in the hospital.

His father looked more than a little annoyed at the interruption. "Did the hospital release you?"

Sean nodded. "I signed the release papers this morning."

"Do you think that was a good idea? I thought we'd decided that it might be best to stay in for a few weeks," his father said, no concern just irritation in his voice, as though Sean was an intrusion he didn't want to deal with at the moment. As though the man who'd been responsible for the day-to-day operations of the resort for years shouldn't be a part of this, shouldn't have a say in this transition.

Callum was happy his brother was here. He hadn't been sure when Sean would feel up to returning, but his timing was perfect in Callum's opinion. He stood and walked toward him, grabbing him in a hug. "Great to see you doing better."

"I am. And the thing is, while I was lying there feeling hopeless and slightly lost, I came to a conclusion. I don't need more time in a facility. I just need time away from this place," Sean said.

The strength in his voice was something Callum had never heard before, and an overwhelming sense of pride wrapped around him as he watched his brother confront their father.

"Dad, I quit. You've won. You never wanted me to run the family business, you never believed in me or trusted me, so I'm out. I'm tired of killing myself—quite literally—trying to prove to you that I could handle all of this. Tired of the pressure and stress of never measuring up."

Yes! The resolve and confidence in his brother's voice had Callum smiling from ear to ear. His brother was finally doing what was in his own best interests—cutting his losses and moving on.

His father cleared his throat and nodded. "What do you plan to do instead?"

The fact that the man cared was a bit of a surprise, but Callum was curious too.

"I've accepted a position with Chateau Resorts."

Good for him. That was what he should have done years ago. Working for the competition might help heal years of damage caused by the tumultuous relationship with their father. The Wild River Resort would still thrive, but now Sean would have that chance, as well.

"Fine. Resignation accepted," their father said simply.

Right. Why would he fight to keep the best person he could hand the resort keys to? Man, the guy was so short-sighted. But, of course, now that he had Callum on the ropes, he no longer needed Sean. He was getting exactly what he'd always wanted—from both of them.

Sean turned to him. "Thank you. I couldn't have made this decision if it weren't for your threat of throwing your own life away to help me."

Callum frowned. A threat? "What do you mean?"

"I mean, now you're free too. You were only going to do this to protect me. To be here for me, take on this obligation out of a sense of brotherly duty. But this isn't what you want. So, don't do it," he said.

Callum stared at his brother. Could he actually be free of this obligation? He'd agreed to take on the role, but that was when he'd thought he couldn't leave Sean at the mercy of their father any longer.

Could they both finally walk away?

Or was it time for Callum to put aside his dreams and face reality?

Shit, she hoped she wasn't too late. If Callum had already signed his future away to the resort and the family business, Ellie's heart would break even further. He was a man of his word, and if he signed his father's agreement, he'd follow through.

She pushed through the revolving doors of the Wild River Resort Hotel and headed toward the desk. "Hi, I'm looking for Callum McKendrick. I believe he had a meeting here today?"

The desk clerk nodded, his eyes wide. "Yes, please tell me you're here to talk him out of working here."

The staff at the resort had insider knowledge of the family dynamics? Maybe they just knew what a tyrant Mr. McKendrick could be. She nodded. "I'm hoping."

"The Chugach Ballroom," the guy whispered. "Don't say I told you."

"My lips are sealed." Ellie hurried down the carpeted hall of the posh hotel, the spirally pattern combined with her nerves making her slightly dizzy. She paused for a breath as she stopped in front of the ballroom doors.

No backing out now. If Callum was upset with her for overstepping or for trying to stop him, she'd have to live with that, but right now she really had nothing to lose.

She opened the doors, and her heart pounded as she saw Callum sitting at the large boardroom table with his father. A multipage contract sat on the table in front of him, and the conversation looked slightly heated.

Please don't let him have signed it yet.

His gaze lifted to hers, and surprise registered on his handsome face as his scowl disappeared.

So handsome. She'd always seen how gorgeous he was, but it had been surface-level attraction to a great-looking guy—now that she knew him better, he was by far the most beautiful man on earth.

But he was also barely recognizable—clean-shaven, wearing an expensive tailored suit and tie that must be driving him batshit crazy, and with a new haircut that was professional and short... He'd already started the transition into becoming his dad, like it or not.

"Ellie? What are you doing here?" he asked.

"This is a private meeting..."

Callum held up a hand to stop his dad as he stood. "She's a...friend."

Damn, that hurt and yet simultaneously gave her hope. He hadn't said "the woman I'm in love with," but he hadn't said "former coworker" either, so she was clinging to that.

"Hi, Mr. McKendrick... Sorry to interrupt, but, Callum, could I talk to you for just a minute?"

He frowned, looking uncertain.

His father shook his head. "It'll have to wait. We are in the middle of something."

Ellie swallowed hard. Callum was right—his father was cold and harsh. Even as an adult she felt intimidated by him. She couldn't imagine what it must have been like growing up with the man. She straightened her shoulders and stood her ground. Callum needed all the facts before he made this huge decision.

"Actually, it can't wait," she said.

Callum looked worried, and she wanted to reassure him that it was all good news she was there to deliver, but she refused to say anything in front of his father.

"I'll be back," he said.

Mr. McKendrick slapped a palm down on the table. "Callum..."

"Dad, I said I'll be back," he said firmly. Then he turned

to her, and his expression was completely unreadable as he pushed the ballroom door open and held it for her as they walked back out into the hallway.

"I'm so sorry," she said. About so much. She wanted to hug him and kiss him and beg him to forgive her for everything, for never seeing what was in front of her. Never seeing him and how fantastic he was. How well they could fit together.

But she'd tried that already. Right now, she needed to tell him about the manuscript.

"It's fine. What's wrong?"

She took a deep breath. "Nothing's wrong. Except you are about to do something I know you'll regret."

He sighed and stared at his shoes. "Ellie... I've made a decision."

"It's the wrong one," she said quickly, before she could lose her nerve.

His head snapped up. "Weren't you also saying that I needed to think about my future? That I couldn't continue to waste these so-called talents and opportunities?"

She nodded. "I was wrong. Or partially wrong anyway. And I said those things before I read your work—your writing."

Callum glanced around quickly as though to make sure no one was within earshot.

She took a step toward him. "But I think you should be pursuing that dream. Your dream. Not someone else's. And not out of family obligation or fear that you might fail... because you won't."

His gaze softened, but then he shook his head. "It was a pipe dream, Ellie," he said, his voice hardened to hide the pain she could still hear.

"It wasn't. It's not," she said, taking a step closer. She

dared to reach out and touch his hand. He didn't pull away. "I may have done something that you'll be upset about, but I'm hoping you'll forgive me." For so many reasons, but she'd start with this.

He frowned. "What did you do?"

"I gave your manuscript pages to an editor at the book signing the other day," she said in a rush.

His mouth dropped. "You what?"

"I told you, you might be upset," she said, her heart racing. He looked pissed, but she couldn't regret the decision. It had been the right one.

"Damn right I am. I gave those to you in confidence. In private. I told you I wasn't ready to submit…"

"She loved them," she said quickly, her smile wide and full of pride, despite his annoyance. She couldn't help it. She was so happy for him…and he'd be happy too… Hopefully… Eventually… She held her breath, waiting for his response.

"Which editor?"

"Claire Rodet from Lakeside Publishing. She was there at the signing with her author. I helped them get the last-minute live event, so she said she'd read a few pages…and then I guess she must have taken them with her and she read them all."

His eyes widened. "Seriously?"

Ellie nodded, tears brimming. "Seriously. She loved it, and she wants you to submit the rest once it's done."

"She wants me to submit my manuscript to her?" He sounded as if he was in shock.

"Yes."

"But that's not how this industry works. Authors write for years and submit to countless agents and editors and collect a stack of rejection letters as thick as the manuscript itself before they ever get published. It doesn't happen like this."

"Maybe it does for you," Ellie said softly.

He shook his head. "I don't know."

"And you won't unless you finish the book."

Callum stared at her, then he stared at the ballroom door. A long moment of silence fell over them as he contemplated his future. It was the longest, toughest sixty seconds of Ellie's life.

"What about my father's contract?" he asked quietly.

"You should sign it if it's really what you want," she said gently. She'd interfered in his life, in his future, too much already. He needed to make this decision for himself. As much as she wanted to push him, figuratively and literally, out the front door of the resort, she couldn't force him. "But if it's not what you want, you should hold off until you've at least explored this opportunity."

He nodded slowly. "She loved them?"

"She loved them. Almost as much as I did," she said, her voice nearly breaking.

His face melted into a wide smile as he ran a hand through his hair. "Wow. This is unbelievable."

"It's so well deserved. That book is incredible, Callum." She paused. "You're incredible." All she wanted to do was dive into his arms and hold him, squeeze him, kiss him… But she held back. He was happy about the amazing news, but that didn't mean he forgave her.

His gaze burned into hers. "And you did this, for me?"

She nodded. She'd do so much for him. Anything it took to get a second chance. "The thing is, I loved your manuscript… but I love you even more."

He took a small step toward her and her pulse thundered in her veins. "You love me?"

"Very much so."

"How do you know?" he asked, taking her hands in his.

"Because I know what I thought was love, and it doesn't even come close to these feelings I have for you. This is real. What we have...had," she said, still unsure where they stood, afraid to let her hopes get too high.

"Have," he said, stepping toward her and drawing her into him. "This is definitely the real thing. I love you, Ellie, and I always have."

"I love you too," she said as she stepped into his arms and stood on tiptoes to kiss him. It was soft and long and everything in the world that mattered. It had taken her far too long to realize she had everything she could ever want right in front of her, and there was no way she was letting it go—letting him go—ever again.

He pulled back slightly, his gaze full of love as he stared down at her. "I can't believe you did this for me."

Her heart was full as she held him tight. "I figured you saved my life, the least I could do was save yours."

EPILOGUE

Six months later

"I'M SO NERVOUS. I feel like a ten-year-old," Ellie said, pacing in front of the counter of the bookstore, one eye on her laptop, where Callum sat refreshing the online university's page every few seconds. Her first-semester grades were scheduled to be posted any minute now and she clutched her emergency inhaler in her hand.

Callum smiled at her. "I promise not to ground you if it isn't straight As."

Ellie's shoulders relaxed. He was right. She'd worked hard that semester. She'd done her best. As long as she passed...

"They're here," Callum said, leaning toward the computer screen. Ellie rushed to stand next to him.

Oh please, God, be straight As.

It was hard enough learning these results on her own, but she wanted Callum to be proud of her, as well. The last few months had been busy and chaotic for them both—working at the store, her taking the online courses, him finishing his book...which Lakeside Publishing had bought...and moving in together, to her apartment above the bookstore. Life was fantastically busy.

He reached for her shaky hand and pulled her down onto his lap on the stool behind the counter. "Ready?"

She nodded, and he clicked on the link to the posted grades. Ellie closed her eyes. "Just tell me they aren't horrible."

"Let's see. Three As and a C—"

Her eyes flew open. "What? Which course was that?"

Callum laughed. "No course—you only took three."

Ellie playfully punched his shoulder as pride and relief washed over her. All As. Her hard work had paid off. "Well, that's good news."

Callum turned her so that she was straddling him on the stool. "I'm proud of you. I'm not surprised that you did so well." He kissed her nose, and she wrapped her arms around his neck.

"I think we should celebrate," she said seductively, pressing her body into his. Maybe they could put the "Be back in an hour" sign on the bookstore door...

He swallowed hard and his expression was full of desire for her as he nodded. "I was thinking the same thing."

They'd both been "celebrating" a lot lately. They couldn't get enough of one another. Ellie had to be the luckiest woman in the world. Living with Callum, loving Callum, starting a life with Callum was everything she never knew she needed and wanted.

She kissed him and he gently pulled back. "But we have work to do first," he said.

"Since when are you employee of the month?" she teased, pressing her pelvis against him and kissing his neck.

He reluctantly held her away. "There was a new box of books delivered today..."

She laughed. "Fine! I'll get back to work." She climbed off his lap, and he followed her to the aisle where two boxes of books sat waiting to be shelved. He'd already opened them, and her eyes widened, seeing the cover through the cardboard flaps. The image of a tree growing up through an old rusted 1950s Citroën DS had her heart racing. She recognized that image… "Oh my God…are those what I think they are?"

Callum beamed at her as she opened the box and took out the top copy of his book—*The Blue Hour*. Her fingers gently rolled over his embossed name on the front, pride and love swelling in her chest.

"Claire sent author copies," he said.

"Author copies." Callum was officially an author. "I love the sound of that." Ellie released a huge sigh of happiness as she hugged him tight. "I'm so proud of you. This is so amazing."

Callum took her face between his hands, and the love in his expression made all other good news that day pale in comparison. "I couldn't have done this without you."

"We make a good team," she said softly.

He cleared his throat. "So, I was thinking the next time we tell people we are engaged, maybe we could be telling the truth?"

Her heart soared as she stared at the man she loved. "Are you asking me to marry you?"

He nodded toward the book in her hands with a mischievous gleam in his eyes. "Why don't you see if it's inscribed?"

Ellie's hand trembled slightly as she opened the front cover. Callum's handwriting inside brought a batch of happy tears to her eyes as she read:

What do you say, Ellie? Me and you against the world?

She looked up at him and nodded. "Forever." She leaned forward, and when their lips met, Ellie was no longer afraid she could ever possibly live an unfulfilled life.

* * * * *

ACKNOWLEDGMENTS

Thank you to all my readers for continuing to visit Wild River with each new love story! I'm grateful for all the support, reviews and emails about this series. Thank you to my agent, Jill Marsal, and my editor, Dana Grimaldi— I couldn't live this amazing dream without either of you and your belief in me and my work. And thank you to the incredible art department at Harlequin for the most beautiful covers. I could never choose a favorite! Big hugs to my husband and son, who keep me sane during deadlines and give me the time and space to create. xo

Wild
Alaskan
Hearts

CHAPTER ONE

NICK HAD ACTUALLY unfriended her. And blocked her, judging by the slightly ominous disappearance of all his posts and comments from her social media sites. He'd even untagged himself from their photos together. Alisha Miller had been able to view her ex-boyfriend's Facebook profile long enough to see him change his status from "In a Relationship" to "Single," and notice that he'd "Liked" the Wild River Single Professionals dating page.

That hurt, but it was probably his intent, and how could she fault him for it? The breakup had been 100 percent her fault.

Who mixed up their current boyfriend's birthday with their ex's? Worse—who planned a surprise birthday party on the completely wrong day? She'd barely had the word "Surprise!" out of her mouth before the look on Nick's face made her realize the mistake. The sound of her apartment door slamming behind him had made it perfectly clear that things were over.

If only one of their friends could have prevented the mix-up… But Nick was a transplant to Wild River, so *her* friends had become *his* friends over the months they'd dated, and therefore, no one—not a close buddy of his or family member—could have prevented her massive blunder.

Alisha sighed as she shut down the site and tucked her

phone into the pocket of her scrubs. Getting dumped had been overdue actually. How many times had she messed things up and Nick had let it go? Even the sweet, patient, smart, successful lawyer had his breaking point. It was disappointing because she and Nick were compatible on so many levels. He was everything she claimed to look for in a man.

Unfortunately, he wasn't Arron.

She'd thought that after all this time, she'd have moved on. Healed from the breakup before this one. But Arron Bosch had somehow weaved his way into her heart so deeply that even a steady, reliable relationship with Nick hadn't been able to shake him loose.

Alisha left the break room at Wild River Community Hospital and suppressed a yawn as she headed toward the maternity ward. She paused in the hall outside the baby room and the familiar tug at her chest felt even stronger this time.

She wouldn't call the sensation the result of longing or a ticking clock—it was more a foreboding sense of not being sure whether she wanted children of her own. In three months, she was turning thirty, and she'd never felt the pressure to get married and start a family even when it seemed everyone around her was blissfully betrothed. But her lack of desire one way or another was worrisome. She'd heard of the inexorable biological clock and she'd expected it to be ringing or at least sending warning signs anytime now…

But nothing.

The babies were beautiful, precious, adorable. She could cuddle one or all of them for hours. But it was also just as easy to hand them back. Indecisiveness over something so big was the scariest part. How could she plan her future if she had no strong feelings when it came to something as important as children?

She continued down the hall and pushed through the door to Room 43, where her best friend, Cheryl Kingsly, was breastfeeding her new baby girl. Her second child in less than two years. Cheryl and her husband, Mitch, wanted a big family and they wanted the kids to be close in age. Cheryl and Mitch had a plan.

"How's Mom and baby Rose?" she asked quietly as she tiptoed toward the bed.

Cheryl was already showered and dressed, and looked fresh as a daisy only twelve hours after delivering the perfect little girl. Cheryl was a personal trainer and Alisha suspected she'd be back in the gym with her clients, baby Rose strapped to her chest, doing squats in record time.

"We're doing great. She's latching like a champ," Cheryl said with a smile as she swaddled the baby and put the sleeping child into the plastic crib next to the bed. When she turned back to Alisha, she frowned. "You don't look so great though. Everything okay?"

She was a terrible liar and Cheryl could always tell when something was up, so she said, "Nick has officially banned me from his life. I've been erased on social media now."

After the birthday incident, he'd refused to answer her calls and texts. He'd sent Mitch to collect his personal things from her apartment. Just a week earlier she'd been thinking his next move would be to bring *all* of his items in, as his own apartment lease was coming up for renewal. But there had been no opportunity to explain or apologize, and it killed her that at this point, she was concerned more with clearing the air and removing the awkwardness between them than with actually getting back together.

Since the breakup, she'd had to reluctantly admit it was

for the best. Still didn't stop her from missing him or the life they'd been sharing. But expecting him to still want to be her friend would be selfish.

Cheryl offered a sympathetic smile and said, "Look, I know you wanted Nick to be the one...but you can't force these things."

Right, but if Nick wasn't the one when he was absolutely perfect in every way, how would she ever find the one? An anxiety attack threatened, so she calmed herself by staring at the peaceful, sleeping baby.

"I didn't have to screw things up so badly though. I still can't believe I made such a crazy mistake. I know when Nick's birthday is. He's a Scorpio. It was one of those perfect things where the stars—the *actual* stars—aligned. We were astrologically compatible." It wasn't something she put a ton of stock in, but it certainly helped. "I don't know how I got the two dates confused."

Cheryl eyed her. "Because you've never gotten over Arron."

Alisha opened her mouth to argue but then slammed her lips shut again. No sense trying to bullshit Cheryl. She paced the room and resisted the urge to scream. Arron infuriated her. Any thought of him, any mention... The fact that he didn't infuriate her as much as he should infuriated her. "How could I? There was never any closure."

"What did happen between you two anyway? I was away at that yoga teacher training when things ended. You never did tell me. It was all kinda crazy, intense...then boom! Over."

Boom! Over. That pretty much summed it up. "Things *were* crazy and intense." Arron was one of those exciting men who swept a woman off her feet with the promise of life being a continuous adventure. He was a free-spirited free climber who was essentially living life one challenging mountain to another. As an adventure guide for SnowTrek Tours, he was living the life he'd always wanted.

Alisha had met him on a rock climbing team building exercise with the hospital staff and had fallen hard and fast. Their sense of adventure had been in sync. She loved to climb and surf and ski and all things outdoors that provided an adrenaline rush.

Arron had been one hell of an adrenaline rush.

She took a deep breath and continued. "Then his twin brother, Langdon, died of a brain aneurysm and Arron was devastated. He seemed lost and depressed one minute and almost manic the next. He quit his job at SnowTrek, sold off everything in a matter of days, bought an old Volkswagen sleeper van and decided to travel the world."

He didn't exactly ditch her. He'd asked her to go with him, and the memory of that moment continued to haunt her. At the time she'd thought he was asking the impossible. She had a career, an apartment, friends, family and a life in Wild River. They'd only been seeing each other three months. Giving it all up had seemed impulsive. His actions had appeared to be on the brink of reckless and the whole thing had terrified her. She had been unable to go with him and he'd left...but they'd never really ended things. They'd never talked about what happened next for the two of them. If there was a way to make things work...

"There was never any real closure." After he drove away, she'd never heard from him again. Pain and pride had prevented her from reaching out.

"Well, maybe it's time you get that," Cheryl said in her best life coach tone. Twelve hours after childbirth and she was already back in action as Alisha's best friend and sounding board.

Alisha's heart raced. She wasn't sure she wanted advice right now. Especially when it was obviously the right advice, which was notoriously difficult to follow. "How?"

"Call him. Right now. Say the things you didn't get to say and then tell him it's officially over." Cheryl's instructions made it sound so easy.

Alisha stared at the ground as she mumbled, "I don't even know if I still have his phone number."

"Bullshit."

She sighed. "Okay, so maybe it's still on my speed dial." Another thing that had pissed off Nick. The guy deserved a medal for sticking it out as long as he had.

"Well, do it. Like pulling off a Band-Aid."

Yeah, a sixteen-month-old Band-Aid that was likely covering an open wound.

Could she really do that? Call up the only man she couldn't stop thinking about, dreaming about, reminiscing about…and finally close the door on a relationship she obviously never wanted to be over?

Unfortunately, it seemed like it might be the only way she could ever move forward.

HIS THIRTIETH FREE CLIMB, to mark his thirtieth birthday, had to be epic. So, naturally, Arron Bosch was back in his hometown of Wild River, Alaska. Or more accurately thirty minutes outside town, staring up at the base of Denali Diamond. This mountain had always eluded him, with its menacing height and dangerous terrain, and while the goal wasn't to climb to its very peak, this free climb would be one of the very few attempted on this rock face.

This had been the plan for almost five years. The pact he'd made with his twin brother, Langdon. They'd been working their way up to this climb. Training for it, preparing for it. To mark their thirtieth birthday, they'd tackle one of the world's most formidable mountains with the most challenging climb of their lives.

Langdon was gone, but Arron was determined to fulfill the promise. A way of honoring his brother's memory. He'd spent the last sixteen months traveling the United States, climbing peaks from California to Colorado to Maine. Alone, in his old sleeper van, living on his savings and picking up an odd job here and there, he'd made his way from north to south, from east to west and now back home again.

He stared up at the mountain in front of him. This was it. He was ready.

No harness, no safety net. Just him and the rock face.

He took a deep breath, checked his gear and started his climb. His muscles were ready—he'd been endurance training for six months. His mind was ready—razor focus could mean the difference between life and death. Sound decisions, careful calculation, never taking a foothold or handhold for granted. There was a spiritual element to these climbs, a connection to nature, a respect for the danger these skyscraping mountains could evoke.

This climb would take over forty hours, so he paced himself as he went higher and higher. There was no rush. The goal was to complete the ascent, not break any records. And he wanted to enjoy it. His climb path would take several days and he'd be portaledge camping after the sun went down.

About two hours and two hundred feet from the bottom, he paused and took in the breathtaking view of the valley below and the snow-covered mountain peaks in the distance. Rivers and lakes reflected the sun's warm glow and midafternoon shadows fell over the forest areas. This sight never got old. Wild River had some of the best experiences and scenery in the world. Surreal majesty enveloped him as he continued the trek upward, letting his mind and body come together as he pushed through the more difficult aspects of the challenging climb.

This was living. And he was determined to do as much living as possible. Langdon had taught him the importance of not wasting a single moment.

His twin brother had been the adventurous one growing up—the daredevil, the wild child. Arron had been more afraid to try new things, but his brother always refused to do something if Arron didn't do it too. Langdon had helped him overcome his many fears, and after they both graduated college with matching physical education degrees, they'd moved to Alaska to operate their own free-climb clinics in partnership with SnowTrek Tours.

They were twins. They were brothers, so naturally they were close, but they were also best friends because they respected one another. They'd had each other's back.

Unfortunately, there was no fighting the brain aneurysm that had taken his brother's life. Langdon had led a life of activity, geared toward good health and body positivity. The one day he was at home with a minor head cold, chilling in front of Netflix, he'd died suddenly, without apparent cause. The autopsy report had shocked them all. How could someone so healthy, so full of life, just die?

Arron's life had changed in that split second. He hadn't known what to do. Fear unlike any he'd ever experienced had gripped him, making it hard to breathe, hard to focus, hard to sit still... He'd needed to escape the pain, so he'd left for the road trip of a lifetime, hoping to find peace in a world without his brother.

Whether it had been the right thing to do...maybe he'd

never know, but lately he'd found himself second-guessing his decision more than he'd like.

The sound of a ringtone came from his backpack—one that he hadn't heard in sixteen months. He attempted to take the next step upward but lost his footing. He frantically reached higher to try to steady himself against the rock face, but the ledge above him was too narrow. Without a firm grasp, his fingers slipped, and the one hand holding his body weight gave way.

A second later, he was free-falling.

CHAPTER TWO

ALISHA YAWNED AS she headed toward the locker room. Her last twenty-four-hour shift for the week was over, and she was looking forward to three days off. She needed time for self-care. An at-home spa day and maybe a new hairstyle would help her rebound from the breakup…and get her head on straight to prevent any more impulse dials to ex-boyfriends. As soon as she got home, she was deleting contact details for all former flames from her cell phone.

Thank God Arron hadn't answered her call. What the hell would she have said?

Cheryl was right—she did need some kind of closure if she was going to move on with her life. But maybe that closure had to come from within. Maybe the fact that they hadn't found their way back to each other after so much time was enough.

Did she really need to hear him say he didn't love her?

The thought made her stomach drop. She changed quickly, grabbed her purse and headed out of the locker room. Pizza, cheap Chardonnay, pajamas and a face mask held the cure to all her problems. And maybe she'd grab some cleansing herbs from the apothecary store on Main Street to reset the balance in her apartment.

As she approached the front doors, she waved to the staff at the triage desk and paused to rearrange the stack of magazines in the waiting room. For three days, this place would not be her problem. She'd unwind and relax and not give work a second —

The emergency doors swung open, and the sight of a stretcher being rolled in had her moving toward it. She wasn't sanitized or dressed to deal with the patient, but her oath as a nurse prevented her from simply leaving the hospital when she might be needed. "What do we have?" she asked one of the paramedics.

"Male. Late twenties. Climbing accident," he said. "Several broken bones for sure. Internal bleeding and concussion suspected."

Alisha glanced at the man. "Is he unconscious?"

"Induced. He was in a lot of pain."

She walked alongside the stretcher as they made their way down the hall toward surgery, and when she looked at his face, really looked this time, her heart stopped. The man she'd been trying to call an hour before was now lying there severely injured.

Fate had the worst sense of humor.

It was irrational to be mad at someone on a stretcher, but damned if she could control the feelings of rage flowing through her at the sight of Arron lying there damaged and broken. She wanted to yell at him for getting hurt. But in the next instant, she had to resist the urge to grab him and hug him in relief that it wasn't so much worse. Her stomach felt queasy as she forced a calming breath and tried to take in the situation as a professional caregiver and not a woman seeing the love of her life for the first time in months under terribly unfortunate circumstances. It was nearly impossible.

She swallowed hard and took a deep breath. "Thirty."

The paramedic frowned. "Excuse me?"

"Not late twenties. He's thirty. His birthday was a week ago today."

IF HE COULD just feel his toes, he'd know he was okay.

Unfortunately, Arron couldn't feel anything at all as he lay in the hospital bed, staring at the ceiling. The last thing he remembered was reaching for the rock face just barely wide enough for his fingertips, then free-falling. It was every climber's nightmare. Reaching for the mountain and feeling nothing but air.

The monitor next to him beeped and he slowed his breath. He was no stranger to hospitals, but that didn't mean they didn't stress him out. Between him and Langdon, his parents has been back and forth to the hospital dealing with broken bones and concussions at least once a month. There wasn't a bone in his body that he hadn't bruised or fractured at one point.

Unfortunately, the last time he was here hadn't been for one of his injuries. The day Langdon was taken in and pronounced dead on arrival was etched in his memory, and the sights, sounds and smells of the hospital made his chest ache. He couldn't determine how long he had been here. He felt as though he'd slept a long time.

The door opened, and Dr. Sheraton entered the room. He forced a relaxed smile as he asked, "How bad is it?"

"Not bad. Horrible," she said. He'd never been under her care before, but he'd heard the young head of surgery didn't exactly sugarcoat things. She was supposedly working on her bedside manner. If this was progress, he'd hate to have been a patient before.

"What's broken?" he asked.

"What's not?" she replied with an annoyed look. "Femur, wrist, ribs…"

"Okay, I get it, I'm basically Humpty-Dumpty."

She frowned, not getting the joke.

"Anyway, I'm alive, so that's a good thing."

"You may not feel that way once the morphine wears off," she said, checking his vitals.

Wow.

The door opened again and Alisha entered. His tongue seemed to swell in his mouth at the sight of her. She was dressed in her pale green hospital scrubs, her blond hair in a braid down her back and her face free of makeup but full of unconcealed concern. He struggled to find a breath. He hadn't seen her in sixteen months. Sixteen long months.

At least not in person. He'd cyberstalked her quite a bit. Whenever his heart could handle the sight of her with another guy anyway. When the photos of her and some guy named Nick had started to appear on her social media, he'd hoped it was just a fling, a rebound, revenge even for the way they'd left things, but then he'd realized that was all just ego. As months went by and the two seemed to fall more and more in love, he realized Alisha had found the real thing…and it wasn't him.

And now here he was lying there at her mercy.

"Hi," he said dumbly.

"Hello," she said coolly, barely glancing his way, then turned to Dr. Sheraton. "Mrs. Dorsey is ready for her foot surgery. I'll finish filling in the chart."

Dr. Sheraton nodded, and then, forcing what was obviously fake enthusiasm in the presence of a coworker, she touched his leg gently, briefly. "You're going to be fine."

"Thanks, Doc," he mumbled. After the door closed behind her, he turned to Alisha and whispered, "She wasn't that nice before you came in."

Unfortunately, it didn't earn him the laugh he'd been going for. In fact, her body language suggested she was pissed at him. This reunion wasn't exactly ideal. He hated that this was the way they were seeing one another for the first time in forever, but he couldn't help being happy to see her.

"She's the best surgeon in this hospital," Alisha said. "You can thank her for the fact that your hand will continue facing the right direction once the bones set and heal."

Was there a new tough love policy at Wild River Community? Maybe he couldn't expect sympathy when his accident was due to extreme sports. Or maybe he just couldn't expect sympathy from his ex-girlfriend. He cleared his throat. "How are you?"

"Not in a hospital bed," she said, avoiding his gaze as she wrote down his vitals in his chart.

Her skin was smooth as silk and her beautiful emerald eyes had him craving that they'd look his way. But she seemed intent on doing her job with as little interaction as possible. "How've you been, I mean?" If this was the only time he'd get to talk to her, he didn't want to waste it.

She closed the folder and turned to him. "I'm good. Great, actually."

He nodded. "Good. I'm happy to hear that," he said awkwardly. Then something hit him. "Wait, you were calling me." He remembered now what had caused him to lose focus. His phone ringing. Her ringtone.

She shook her head quickly. Too quickly. "No... I don't think..."

She was lying. She always licked the side of her upper lip when she was lying. "You were. When I was climbing."

She winced. "I don't recall that."

"Should we check my cell phone?"

She stared at her shoes and shrugged. "Must have pocket-dialed you," she said lamely.

He wasn't buying it. After over a year of no contact, he'd thought she had deleted his phone number. The prospect of calling and having her not know who it was had been the only thing preventing him from reaching out. That fear of having been forgotten.

He knew she was dating someone, and it was obviously serious, so out of respect, he'd let things just lie…but now, seeing her again, he knew he was far from over her. And suddenly he wasn't so okay with the way they'd just left things. Suddenly there was so much he wanted to clarify, so much he wanted to say.

Unfortunately, the right words refused to come to mind.

And she used his silence to change the subject. "Dr. Sheraton says they'd like to keep you in for a few days…"

He shook his head and immediately tried to get out of the bed. "No can do. My health insurance expired, and I suspect I'll be paying for my reset bones until they're six feet under, so I have to check out."

Her mouth gaped. "You do what you do and you don't have health coverage?"

"I usually don't fall," he said with a wry grin. He'd tried to get insured, but no company would touch him without insanely high premiums. He slowly inched toward the edge of the bed, scanning the room. This would be challenging, but what choice did he have?

"Wait. No. You can't be on your own yet…in your van…" She reached out to steady him when he nearly fell out of the bed.

Can't be on my own… His heart raced as his mind

reached an illogical conclusion. It was worth a shot. He shrugged casually. "Okay, you're right. I guess I'm rooming with you while I recover."

Her head shot up. She rapidly blinked several times as though her brain was trying to process what he'd just said. "Um…no. Why would you assume that would be okay?"

"I fell because of your call. So, technically this is your fault and you feel guilty."

"No, I don't. You shouldn't have had your cell phone on you."

"If I hadn't, I'd still be lying in a crumpled heap at the bottom of the cliff." His cell phone's screen had been shattered, but miraculously it had still worked to dial 911.

She winced.

He waited, watching her battle with her common sense and her emotions. He knew she'd agree. She was far too caring to allow him to be on his own, and his closest family was five hundred miles away. Her chest rose and fell in a deep sigh.

"Fine," she said, pointing a determined finger at him. "You can stay with me until you can take care of yourself, but not a second longer."

"Deal," he said, trying and failing to hide his pleasure.

These would be the slowest healing injuries he'd ever had.

CHAPTER THREE

THIS WAS A huge mistake.

Just seeing Arron again had knocked the air from her chest. Letting him stay in her apartment was going to be torture. It was a nine-hundred-square-foot space with one bedroom and one bathroom... Oh my God, how had it not occurred to her until this very second that she would have to help him into the shower?

He'd be bathing with his underwear on for the next few weeks.

She should never have agreed to this. But he was right. He had nowhere else to go. He couldn't live in his van in this condition. And she did feel responsible for what happened to him.

Damn, she never should have made that impulsive call. He could have gotten hurt far worse...or...nope, she wouldn't think of the worst-case scenario.

The current scenario that he was her roommate indefinitely—was bad enough. And the idea shouldn't be giving her butterflies like fluttering little beacons of hope in the pit of her stomach. Nothing would happen between them.

She unlocked the door and wheeled him inside with the chair she'd borrowed from the hospital.

As the door closed behind them, she fought to steady a

breath. Memories of the last time they were alone together in her apartment flooded back…

"I need to get away," he said, pacing the living room. He was a mess. Unshaven, with dark circles under his eyes, his fauxhawk a mess, and wearing the same clothes he'd worn to Langdon's funeral three days before. He smelled slightly of booze and she knew he'd basically been living at The Drunk Tank. She'd wanted to give him space and time to deal with his grief, unsure how much support was too much or not enough in a new relationship. Her heart had ached for him, but she was so terrified of the difference in the man standing in front of her.

She'd usually seen him so casual, so carefree…and this wound-up, on-edge version of him was someone she didn't even recognize. Losing his twin brother had him unraveling, naturally, and she was desperate for him to reach out, grab hold of her for comfort. Not push her away and claim he needed even more space. Not insisting on being with him the last several days had been a mistake.

"Where do you want to go?" she asked carefully. Maybe a short vacation would give him time to grieve. It obviously wouldn't be a fun getaway, just time to decompress, process and learn to start moving on. She could take a week off and go with him.

"Anywhere but here," he said, running a hand through his hair.

"We could go to a beach somewhere…or to a cabin in the mountains?"

He shook his head. "I'm talking longer than a week."

She swallowed hard. "How much longer?"

He collapsed onto her couch and stared up at her, his expression so full of pain she could barely breathe. The look in his eyes pleaded for her to understand what he was about to say.

"A while," he said, suddenly calm but eerily somber. "I gave notice on my apartment. I just can't be there..."

The one he and his brother shared. Again, she understood. "You could stay here. With me."

He looked like he didn't understand, and that hurt. They'd been dating only three months, but the relationship had been going so well. She'd hoped the next step would be moving in together eventually and not under these circumstances, but sometimes life gave you a new set of rules. "Not move in or anything," she said quickly, ignoring the jab to her heart. "Just until you feel better and find a new place."

He stood and paced again. "I'm not sick, Alisha. This isn't something I'm just going to recover from. Langdon is gone."

"I know. I'm so sorry you're going through all of this... I just mean I'm here. Whatever you need." She was desperate to help him, any way she could. Langdon had been his only family and she didn't want him to navigate this hollow despair by himself. Every day at the hospital she witnessed the pain of losing loved ones. This one was tragic and sad and it didn't make sense. People needed help to process that kind of loss.

He turned toward her and a look of hope glimmered in his eyes as he took her hands. "I bought a van. I want to travel around for a while."

He bought a van? When? "What about work?"

"I already told Cassie I need time off...indefinitely."

He had? He'd planned this road trip and discussed it

with his boss before telling her? She'd thought they were closer than that.

"Come with me."

"Come with you where?*" He was losing it and she understood, but he needed to think clearly about the huge life decision he was making. And asking her to make.*

"I don't know yet. Anywhere. Everywhere." He seemed almost delirious.

"What about my job?"

"Take a leave of absence."

She'd just gotten promoted. She was just settling into the new head nurse position. She loved her job and her life... Traveling around the world had never even crossed her mind. While she wanted to be with him, especially in his time of need, he needed to know how impulsive this idea was. She took a deep breath. "Arron, I think you need to take a few days. Think about this when things don't feel as heavy."

"When things don't..." He shook his head and released her hands. "Alisha, Langdon and I were closer than brothers. This..."

"Is complete shit, yes, I know." She reached out and touched his arm. "Sweetheart, I know. But I just think you're not thinking clearly right now."

He tensed. "Maybe not. But if I don't get away from here for a while, I'm not going to recover from this." He paused and stared at the floor. "Langdon had such big dreams, you know. So much he wanted to do. So much he won't ever get a chance to do. I feel like I owe it to him to try to live life to the fullest."

His words hurt more than they should have. It was impossible not to internalize them. She wasn't enough. A life here with her wasn't enough. She struggled not to make it about them—about her—but she was about to lose a person she desperately loved. Unless she went with him...

"So, what do you say? Will you come with me?" he asked, his gaze pleading.

The second of deliberation had felt like a lifetime. Give him up or derail all of her life plans for a man she'd been dating for only three months. Her heart wanted to say yes, but common sense had her shaking her head. It was too much of a risk to take. "I'm sorry, Arron..." she said over the lump in her throat.

He nodded slowly and shoved his hands deep into the pockets of his dress pants and cleared his throat. "It was a long shot. Take care, Alisha."

The loud slam of the door as he left had instantly made her reconsider, but it was too late.

She blinked as her apartment door shut behind them now and she turned to face Arron. He was staring at her expectantly, so obviously she'd missed something. "What?"

"I said, I hope your boyfriend won't mind me staying here."

She eyed him. That hadn't seemed to bother him when he suggested this idea. And it really didn't seem to bother him now, based on the mischievous glint in his eye. It was tempting to let him think she was still in a relationship, but her heart refused to lie.

"I don't think that will be an issue. We broke up."

SHE WAS SINGLE AGAIN.

He hadn't expected that. Was that why she'd called him? She wanted to try again? Reconnect? Despite his broken bones, he couldn't be too upset about his accident right now.

Maybe it was fate. If not for the call and the fall, who knew when they would've been in this situation? Together again. Alone.

He swallowed hard, realizing just how alone they were.

The last time he'd been in this apartment, he'd been on the verge of a breakdown. Then the compounded impact of losing her and his brother in a matter of days had him plummeting into despair so deep he hadn't thought he'd ever recover. She'd been his family and he'd felt the sting of her refusal as rejection. But it hadn't taken him long to realize she'd been right to say no. They'd only been dating a few months…and his request had been the unfair demand of a grieving man.

Unfortunately, that realization had come too late.

"I'll set you up in the bedroom," she said awkwardly, placing her purse and keys on the kitchen counter.

"No way. I'll take the couch." He wouldn't survive sleeping in her bed, with the smell of her on the pillow and sheets, remembering the last time he'd been with her…

She hesitated, but then nodded. "The pullout is actually more comfortable and it's closer to the bathroom anyway." She placed his bag on the floor next to the couch and he reached for her hand.

She flinched at his touch and he dropped his hand. "You still didn't tell me why you were calling," he said.

She cleared her throat and released a deep breath. "I was calling to tell you that it was officially over. You and I. That I've…moved on," she said, her voice strong and full of conviction.

And damned if he didn't believe it. And damned if it didn't hurt more than the crash at the end of his free fall.

CHAPTER FOUR

OF ALL THE nights for a thunderstorm...

Lying in her bed, Alisha stared at the ceiling, listening to the rolling thunder as the lightning illuminated her bedroom. Storms like this were her favorite.

Arron's too.

Sitting on her front porch under a blanket with him, watching the storms rage against the beautiful mountain in the distance, had been part of some of the best nights of her life. Every new storm after he'd left had brought back the memory of him, creating a bigger hole in her heart. She'd never been able to watch them with Nick, feeling as though it would be betraying Arron in some way. And maybe forcing her to admit that her feelings for Nick couldn't be as real as she'd wanted them to be if a storm caused her to wish she were with someone else.

Had Arron thought of her wherever he was when the sky opened up like this?

Was he awake now? Was he listening to it too? Remembering different nights...a world ago?

She sighed, rolled to her side and shut her eyes tight.

Telling him she'd moved on had been her only choice. She refused to allow him to think that she was still in love with him, pining over him, allowing her comparison of what they'd had together to destroy new relationships. They weren't meant to be together. She'd followed the old adage,

"If you love something, let it go," hoping Arron would come back to her, and he hadn't.

Her phone chimed with the distinct sound she'd set up for Arron's notifications, and her heart thudded in her chest. Reaching for it, she read the new message:

You awake?

Should she ignore it? Pretend she was sleeping? Not let him know that these storms still meant something to her? That they reminded her of nights falling in love with him? That would be the best idea. No good could come from reopening the past.

She put the phone aside and pounded her pillow before repositioning her head. She tossed and turned. This bed was seriously uncomfortable. Sleep was impossible. In the morning, she was buying a new bed. And new pillows and blankets. She shut her eyes, slowly counted to ten and ignored the pull of the text message.

What if he needed something? Her vow as a nurse prevented her from ignoring a person in need. She sat up and reached for the phone.

I'm awake. Do you need anything?

That's a loaded question, he replied.

Her pulse thundered in her veins. Right, maybe she should clarify...

Water? Bathroom break?

Dots appeared as he was typing.

Just thought it would be a shame to waste a perfectly good storm.

Oh shit. She took a deep breath. Nothing good could come from getting out of bed to go watch a storm with her ex, who was quite arguably the love of her life but would be leaving her heartbroken again soon enough.

Then again, nothing good could come from lying here thinking about him, wishing she was watching the storm with him. Either way, she would be heartbroken.

Grabbing her blanket, she got out of bed. Checking her reflection in the mirror quickly, she left the bedroom.

He was waiting by the front door in his wheelchair. How was he getting around so well on his own?

"I'm only doing this because you're right, it would be a shame to waste a perfectly good storm," she said.

"Yeah, me too," he said, but she could hear the emotion in his voice, and a new storm brewed in her chest.

She opened the door and they made their way to the front porch. She helped him onto the two-seater and sat next to him, draping the blanket over them. Their legs were touching and the small source of contact had her pulse racing. Familiarity washed over her as they sat in silence, watching together...remembering.

Regretting?

She was certainly regretting lost time, a lost connection. But he hadn't come back until now. He hadn't called. He hadn't texted. It couldn't have been clearer that he'd moved on, as well. But maybe now that he'd had his time exploring the world, now that he was back...with her...maybe...

A clap of thunder snapped her out of it.

Damn, why was she doing this to herself?

If Arron had loved her, he would have told her. In the

three months they'd dated, she'd heard versions of "I love you." *I love spending time with you. I love the freckles on your neck. I love that we have a lot in common...* But never *I love you.*

She hadn't said it either, but she'd been about to, before his life had taken a dark turn.

Next to her, he cleared his throat. "Colorado has the craziest lightning storms," he said. "You would have loved them."

She tensed at the mention of his adventures. "Were you there long?" she asked politely but tightly.

"A month. I climbed Longs Peak and Lizard Head. Incredible experiences," he said.

In another world, another situation, his adventures would sound exciting, intriguing, fascinating. She'd want to hear about them. But the path he'd chosen over her, over them, wasn't something she could get enthusiastic about. "That's great," she mumbled, staring off into the distance as a lightning bolt lit up the sky.

"Driving through Ohio and Wyoming, I saw some pretty fantastic storms, as well. Some nights, I'd climb up to the roof of the van and lie there for hours."

That sounded amazing, and the fact that she could have been there experiencing it too made her stomach twist and turn. How much had she missed by not going?

"I met a team of storm chasers in Texas. They were following a tornado—"

She cleared her throat. "Can we just watch the storm? In silence?"

He seemed surprised but then nodded. "Of course."

Unfortunately, now she was left with her own regretful thoughts.

HE WAS MESSING this up.

He'd just wanted to break the awkward silence, ease the tension that had been simmering between them since they'd left the hospital, but he was making things worse. Of course Alisha didn't want to hear about his journey when it had meant the end of the two of them.

"Sorry... I guess I'm just not sure what to say," he said.

She heaved an exasperated sigh.

Shut up. Got it.

Still... He had to say it. "I missed you."

She scoffed and his head whipped around toward her. "You don't believe me?"

"I thought we weren't going to talk."

"I just think if we're going to be living together..."

"We're *not* living together. You're staying here for a few weeks. Max."

He nodded. "Okay...since I'm staying here, I thought we should clear the air a little. So this isn't so awkward."

"I'm not awkward."

"I beg to differ."

She turned to face him, her expression even more intense than the electricity blazing through the night sky. Maybe he should have respected her request for silence. "Okay, you want to clear the air?" she asked.

"That's why you called, wasn't it?" he challenged. No turning back now, and he was curious about what she'd been planning on saying. Sixteen months was a hell of a long time to prepare a speech. One she deserved to deliver if it would make her feel better.

She nodded. "Yes. Okay. Here it is." She took a deep breath. "I was falling in love with you and life fell apart and you left. It's been over a year and I'm completely over it."

Bullshit. He could tell she was still struggling with feelings for him. Maybe they were no longer love, but there was definitely the same chemistry, the same spark there had always been. The way she'd looked at him in the hospital had told him everything he'd been longing to hear on those lonely nights when all he could think about was her. Even if she'd convinced herself otherwise.

"When someone is truly over something, they don't need closure," he said.

She flushed. "Fine. You want me to admit that I've thought of you a few times?" She shrugged, but it looked anything but casual. "Sure, I thought of you. But the biggest memory I have is of you leaving and never hearing from you again."

"I needed to get away. I know that's hard to understand."

She shook her head. "Nope. Not at all. You're an adventure seeker. You live for excitement and new challenges. New scenery. It was just a matter of time."

"So you think you have me all figured out, huh?" She didn't have a clue if that was what she thought. She was right about the adventure-seeker part, but he'd had no intention of going on those life-changing trips alone.

"You're thirty years old and live in a sleeper van and coast through life one adventure to another. There's not much to figure out."

Her casual dismissal of who he was hurt. But he knew it was just a defense mechanism. It actually gave him hope. "My sense of adventure was what originally attracted you to me."

"Yes, but…it…"

"Gets old," he finished.

She sighed. "I just need more stability, more predictability. Someone who stays in one place for a while."

He turned in the seat and moved closer. His face just

inches from hers. "How are those guys working out for you?"

She swallowed hard. "They are… I mean, things…"

"So good, then?" he asked with a small grin as he moved even closer.

She lifted her chin defiantly. "As a matter of fact, it *was* good."

"So why did you break up?" he asked, running his thumb along her jawline and down the side of her neck. How he missed kissing that neck…

"We weren't right for each other," she said, and her chest heaved.

"He was a bad kisser?" he asked, moving even closer.

Alisha's eyes dipped to his lips and she licked hers.

Thank God. The reaction, the confirmation he'd been hoping for. "Do you want to be reminded of what a real kiss feels like?" he asked. His tone was light and flirty, but his heart was pounding. So many nights in his van he'd dreamed of this moment. Fantasies of being with her had plagued him mercilessly.

She closed her eyes, and for a split second, he thought she might lean in. But then they snapped open again. "Are you seriously trying to kiss me right now?"

"I was thinking about it." Not anymore. He reluctantly moved back. "Sorry, I was going off a vibe…never mind."

"Are you high?"

He stiffened. Damn, was he really reading things wrong? Was she over him? His ego had him retreating. "I don't know. You're the one in charge of my meds," he mumbled.

She stood and grabbed the blanket. "Well, looks like the lightning has passed."

So had the moment he'd obviously imagined.

CHAPTER FIVE

"Why on earth won't this baby poop?" Cheryl sat on the edge of the hospital bed, looking ready to promise baby Rose a pony if she'd just have a bowel movement already so they could go home. "With Darcy, it was like ten hours from the first contraction to sending us on our way. I'm losing my mind here. I want to go home."

"I know..." Alisha tickled the baby's tummy. "But we can't rush these things, you know. They have to happen naturally. In due course. When people are ready for them. I mean, sure, sometimes things can take you by surprise, but those aren't necessarily the best moments, you know..."

Cheryl stared at her like she had eight heads. "We're not still talking about poop, are we?"

She sighed. "Arron tried to kiss me last night."

Cheryl blinked. "Arron. Tried. To. Kiss. You?" She looked seriously confused. "In a dream?"

Alisha needed to catch her friend up on the latest developments.

Three minutes later, Cheryl sat dumbfounded. "So your call almost killed him." She looked sheepish. "Apologize to him for my part in that, by the way... And now he's staying with you. You told him you *don't* have feelings for him anymore, even though you absolutely do. And then he tried to kiss you?"

Alisha nodded. "During the lightning storm." That part

shouldn't be left out. She'd been weakened by the moment. She'd almost let her guard down. Every minute since the almost kiss, she'd yo-yoed back and forth about whether rejecting it had been the right thing. The jury was still out, but she'd gone back to bed frustrated and even more confused. She'd escaped the apartment that morning before he'd woken up, to come talk to Cheryl.

Who looked even more confused now. "Right…okay. Um, why?"

"Why what?"

"Why didn't you kiss him?"

"Why *would* I have kissed him?"

"Oh, I don't know. Maybe because you've been so insanely in love with him for over a year that you sabotaged a great, mature, stable relationship with a lawyer!" Her usually zen best friend exploded.

"Okay, I'm gonna blame that outburst on post-baby hormones," Alisha said, but then she sighed and collapsed in the chair next to the bed. "I know. You're right. There is quite literally nothing in the world I've wanted more than a kiss with Arron since…the last time he kissed me. But I can't go down this path again. I know this isn't permanent. The minute he can drive, he'll be hitting the open road and I'll be left in the dust."

"How do you know?"

"Because it's who he is." She still couldn't believe he'd tried to engage her in conversation about his travels. As though it shouldn't bother her to hear about how great he'd been doing out there, alone, without her. Not once regretting his decision to leave.

A woman likes to hear that there have been regrets!

"You love that about him though," Cheryl said gently, opening Rose's diaper and taking another peek.

"I love his spirit. I don't love that he lacks the support structure for a lasting relationship."

"A relationship according to *your* rules," Cheryl said.

She frowned. "I think it's more like societal rules. People who decide to settle down, settle down. Living in a van is not exactly settling down. In fact, it's most probably the opposite of settling down."

"Do you want kids?" her best friend asked, surprising her.

She hesitated. "Someday. Maybe. I think. I don't know yet."

"Do you want to buy a house?"

"Again, maybe someday, but I'm more focused on saving money right now…" Her mother was an investment adviser, and she often said there were just as many downsides to investing in a home in the current climate as there were benefits. She eyed Cheryl, knowing where this line of questioning was leading.

"So, what's more cost-effective than a van with no rent?" Cheryl said with a grin.

"Cheryl, come on! You're telling me that you would actually consider that nomadic lifestyle?"

Her friend didn't even think about it. "Five years ago? Yes. With Mitch? Absolutely." She stood and picked up the baby as she started to cry. "Look, I think settling down means letting your heart stop wandering to other hearts. To settle on *one* heart for life. It doesn't have to mean in one place or one house or one country even."

Damn, she'd never thought of it that way. She cleared her throat, hating that Cheryl's words were ringing so loudly in her mind. "I don't know."

"You love him. You've always loved him. And if he does leave again, you'll still love him. So, what's worse? Loving him and not being with him? You've tried that already. Or trying this new life and being with the man you love?"

Okay, so her friend had a point, but… "He hasn't exactly asked me to go with him."

"He tried to kiss you though, right?"

She nodded.

"So, maybe next time—let him," she said with a grin, gently bouncing baby Rose on her shoulder.

Alisha sniffed the air and wrinkled her nose. "I think you might have poop in there."

Cheryl released a sigh of relief as she set the baby back in the plastic crib and tore open the diaper. "Yes!" She gave a victory dance. "I never thought I'd be so excited to change a dirty diaper. Let's go home."

Home.

Could Cheryl be right? Was home really where the heart was? Or was that just another adage that wouldn't apply to her?

HE HAD TO GO. Staying with Alisha while he recovered was a big mistake.

If last night was any indication, his long-repressed feelings for her were unreciprocated. He'd gotten his hopes up when she'd joined him to watch the storm, but trying to kiss her had completely backfired. He'd been caught up in a moment, and showing her how he still felt had seemed easier than vocalizing it. She'd shut that down, and despite the blow to his ego, kissing her was all he could think about. Better to leave on his own terms before she kicked him out.

With his good hand, he threw his clothes into his bag and then struggled to reach his shoes on the floor, nearly toppling the wheelchair over in the process. A wheelchair he'd need to bring back to the hospital immediately so he wouldn't be charged for borrowing it. He wasn't sure how he was going to pull this off exactly...

A key turning in the lock had his heart racing. Shit. He'd been hoping to make a clean getaway before she got back. Their last goodbye had already left a deep scar on his heart. Would he survive saying goodbye to her a second time?

The door opened and the smell of expensive aftershave hit him before a guy walked in. Dressed in a suit and tie, tan leather shoes, dark hair gelled neatly to one side and clean-shaven, the man had to be Nick—the lawyer. The one he'd seen in all of Alisha's photos. The one she'd broken up with.

Nick jumped back, seeing him. "Jesus. Who the hell are you? And why are you in my girlfriend's apartment?"

"Ex-girlfriend's apartment," Arron said tightly, feeling his spine stiffen. "Why are you here?"

Nick's eyes narrowed as he studied him. "Holy shit, it's you."

Obviously, Alisha had told her most recent ex about him. That made him uneasy. Had she said good things? Or bad things? Given the way their relationship had ended and her frosty reception to him the day before, he would put his money on bad things.

"I'm Arron," he said in the awkwardness.

Nick shook his head and gave a wry laugh. "Unbelievable. Actually, no, it's not..."

"What's that supposed to mean?"

"Nothing, man. I'll be out of your way in a minute. I just stopped by to grab my golf clubs." He walked past him toward the closet.

Arron had no idea what to do or say, so he busied himself with tying his shoe with one hand. He kept one eye on Nick as he grabbed a jacket and a baseball glove from the closet, as well.

It was hard to believe that Alisha had dated them both. He didn't think he'd have anything in common with this man.

Nick was a buttoned-up professional who spent his days in an office and his free time on a golf course. Arron would rather die than do either of those things. Nick was polished and put-together…and Arron was tattooed and a mess most of the time.

She'd claimed to want the stability that Nick presented, so what had happened to tear the two of them apart? Had Nick broken things off? Was that why Alisha seemed completely against any thought of reconciling with him?

More likely, it had everything to do with Arron not being what she wanted.

Nick shut the closet door and started to leave but paused and turned back to glare at him. "I just need to know one thing—did she know you were coming back? Is that what happened?"

"Um…no. I had a climbing accident and kinda guilted her into letting me stay with her while I recovered."

Nick scoffed. "I'm sure she was more than happy to accommodate."

Arron's jaw tightened. He had no idea what the guy was implying, but he didn't like his tone or the way he was talking about Alisha. "I don't think she is, actually. I was just going to leave."

Just then, Alisha entered the apartment and sighed, glancing back and forth between the two of them. She held out a hand to Nick. "Key, please."

He removed the apartment key from his key ring and dropped it into her hand.

"Thank you. You can go," she said, gesturing to the door.

Unfortunately, Nick didn't seem to be done just yet. "I

can't believe that you threw away everything we had for this guy." He jabbed a thumb in Arron's direction.

Arron frowned, too intrigued by the meaning of the man's words to be fully insulted.

Alisha looked uncomfortable as she shifted from one foot to the other. "Seriously, Nick. Get out."

"I'm leaving." Nick turned to him. "You missed one hell of a birthday party, man."

Arron frowned. "Excuse me?"

"The surprise party she threw for me...on your birthday. June third, amiright?"

Arron blinked, and one look at Alisha's flushed, embarrassed expression confirmed the truth of Nick's words. She held the door wide open and motioned Nick out of the apartment. Then she closed the door and avoided Arron's gaze as she went to the kitchen. "Are you hungry? I can make something..."

"Is it true—what he just said? Did you mix up our birthdays?" he asked, wheeling the chair into the kitchen.

She looked away and waved a hand. "Simple, stupid mistake. Don't read anything into it."

He pushed his body out of the chair and hopped on his good leg toward her. "I'm going to read everything into it."

She sighed in exasperation. "It was nothing."

"It caused your breakup."

"Fine." She placed her hands on her hips and squared her shoulders. "Maybe I wasn't completely over you, and it...interfered with my relationship with Nick."

His heart raced and a new hope surged as he moved toward her. "I never completely got over you either. That ill-timed attempt at a kiss last night was something I've wanted for a very long time."

She swallowed hard. "You were the one who left, remember? You ended things by driving away. I was here all the time."

He sighed. "Langdon's death hit me hard. I couldn't grasp the fact that he was really gone. I thought if I got away, I wouldn't feel it as bad, you know."

She nodded. "Well, you went to all four corners of the earth. Couldn't possibly get much farther away than that."

"It didn't work. The pain of losing Langdon didn't fade…" He paused. "And neither did the pain of losing you." He took her hands in his and stared into her eyes.

"Then why didn't you come back?" Her cool facade dropped and he saw the hurt and disappointment and questioning in her expression. It killed him to see it, but it also reconfirmed what he'd been hoping—that things maybe weren't as over for her as she claimed.

It was time to confess the truth. It might be the only way to move forward with her, the only way to get a second chance. He released a slow, deep breath. "I did. About three weeks after I left." He paused. "You were already dating Nick."

Alisha's mouth dropped open and he felt the energy shift between them, as realization seemed to dawn on her that maybe all of this hadn't been completely his fault.

ALISHA FELT ILL. Her stomach twisted into a tight knot as she stared at the man she'd always longed for.

He'd come back and he'd thought she'd already moved on. Technically, she had. Nick had been a good friend at first, a shoulder to cry on, and then it had led to something more… Or at least she'd desperately tried to force it into being something more.

She had no idea what to say. No way to really explain what had happened. The reality was she had fallen quickly into Nick's arms, seeking comfort, desperate to replace Arron in her heart with someone else so that she wouldn't feel so damn hollow.

But how did she tell him that?

Instead, maybe she could show him how she felt. Moving toward him, she steadied him against the kitchen counter and wrapped her arms around his neck. Her entire body tingled with the familiar sensation of being pressed close to him. The scent of his woodsy cologne enveloped her and she realized how much she'd missed that smell. She swallowed hard and licked her lips as her gaze flitted back and forth between his eyes and full, deliciously tempting mouth. "So I'm thinking about kissing you. I'm going off a vibe... Stop me if I'm reading the signs wrong," she said, moving closer.

His one good arm wrapped around her body, drawing her closer. His breath against her skin was warm and his gaze burned with desire. "There won't be any argument on this end," he murmured against her mouth.

She stood on tiptoe and leaned her head back, closing the gap between their faces. Arron's head lowered toward hers and she closed her eyes as their mouths connected.

A deep, happy sigh of release escaped her as she clung to him tight, deepening the kiss that she'd been craving for so long. How she'd refused it the night before, she had no idea. She should definitely win some kind of medal for self-control. Right now, she had none. She wanted to kiss him and hold him and touch him and never let go.

Being in his arms felt like home. Cheryl was so right about her heart settling on his. There was no questioning whether the relationship was right. There was no need to second-guess or wonder if he felt the connection too.

He separated her lips with his tongue and held her closer,

as though he too was struggling with not being able to get enough. She could stand here kissing him all day...

Out of breath, he reluctantly pulled back, and the smile on his face made her heart soar. She'd missed that smile so much. Seeing the look of happiness on his face that mirrored the happiness in her heart had her almost floating. The weight of all those months of missing him and longing for him and denying her emotions drifted away in that incredible moment.

"That was quite a kiss," he said, holding her tight.

"We had a lot of time to make up for," she said.

And for now, she refused to think about how much time they had together before they once again found themselves at a crossroads with a decision to make.

CHAPTER SIX

Two weeks later

HIS SOUL HAD always craved adventure. Spontaneous, un-predictable, impulsive…all traits that he didn't even try to deny. But no matter how far he'd traveled the past year, how high an adrenaline rush he'd found or how breathtaking the scenery around him, he'd been unable to erase Alisha from his thoughts, from his heart. He'd missed her every day and he'd have traded it all for her.

Knowing she was with someone had made it easy to stay away. Now, how could he possibly leave, knowing that she'd never gotten over him either and the connection he'd felt to her a million miles away was real and strong, and she'd felt it too?

He'd wasted more than a year looking for something, anything, that made him feel as alive, as happy, as com-plete as being with her did, and he'd be damned if he lost it again. Lost her again.

The last two weeks had done more than just heal his body; they'd healed the deep wound in his chest that sorrow had created. His brother was gone and he'd always honor his memory, but Arron was being offered another shot at love and he'd be a fool to let anything stand in the way.

Picking up his cell phone, he dialed the familiar local number and smiled when a female voice answered.

"Hello. Thank you for calling SnowTrek Tours. How may I help you?"

"Hey, Cass, it's Arron."

"I was hoping I'd get a call from you," she said, sounding genuinely happy to hear his voice.

"Yeah, well, I heard you might be looking for a free-climb guide." Cassie had never partnered with anyone else, telling him that the job would always be his if and when he ever wanted it again. Her trust in him and Langdon to ensure the safety of her clients had meant a lot to them, and he didn't take it for granted now.

"As soon as those bones of yours heal, the job's all yours," she said. "And, Arron—welcome home."

He breathed a sigh of relief. Not in a long time had he felt like he was in the right place. But Wild River *was* home and it was time to start putting down roots.

ALISHA TOOK A final deep breath, then hit Print on the staff room computer. She stood, gathered the letter from the printer and headed down the hall to the hospital CEO's office.

This was the right decision. She didn't question it for a second. Her footsteps felt light as she made her way down the hall.

The last two weeks had been everything she'd always wanted. Being with Arron was the future she'd do anything for. No matter what that looked like. They'd agreed to take things one day, one recovered bone at a time. And to not talk about what happened next or where things were headed.

They both knew they wanted to be together. And they both trusted that this time they'd figure it out.

This was the right decision.

Knocking once on the open office door, she entered as Grant looked up from his desk. "Hey, how's my favorite nurse named Alisha?" he said.

She laughed at the old, familiar joke he used on everyone. "Be careful. One day you'll hire a duplicate name and that joke will backfire."

He laughed. "Good point." He gestured toward the chair across from him and she sat. "What can I do for you?"

She slid the letter across his desk. "I'm requesting a leave of absence." It even felt right saying it. She'd thought it would be harder to take time off, to take this leap of faith, but it wasn't, and she saw it as a good sign. No matter what happened, this was the right decision for her life right now.

"Oh…" Grant didn't seem bothered, just surprised. No doubt he was, since she hadn't even taken a sick day in four years.

"Is everything okay?" he asked. "Healthwise? You're good?"

She nodded. Healthwise, she was better than ever. Being blissfully in love and spending every available moment wrapped in the arms of a man she was crazy about did wonders for the psyche. "I feel perfect." She paused. "I just thought maybe I'd do some traveling. See the world." Her excitement rose in her chest at the thought of something she should have done sixteen months ago.

But there was no room for regrets. Only new adventures awaiting.

"That's wonderful," he said, sitting back in his chair. "Where are you headed?"

"I don't know," she said with a small smile as she stood to leave. Wherever the wind and a certain tattooed, blond-haired man decided to take her.

HER NEW TRAVEL pack on her back, Alisha opened her apartment door later that evening. Her heart raced in anticipation of seeing Arron and telling him the news. Since making the decision, she'd gotten more and more excited about what lay ahead. Being with him was what she wanted, and it no longer mattered if that was here in Wild River or halfway across the world.

The sight that met her inside her apartment was one she'd never have expected in a million years. Tea lights flickering all over the room, the table set for two with wine and flowers, and the sound of soft, romantic music playing made her mouth drop.

"Welcome home," Arron said, appearing in the kitchen. He wore a pair of new, form-fitting jeans and a black Henley that hugged his body in a way that had her mind on things that didn't involve any clothing at all. But he'd obviously gone to some effort to make a nice evening, so she'd be patient.

"You cooked?"

"Close. It's takeout."

She laughed. "Even better." She set the backpack down against the wall. Her news could wait. "What's the occasion?"

Arron took her hands in his and led her to the couch. He sat beside her and stared into her eyes. "I have something I want to tell you."

Her heart beat so loudly she thought it might explode. This was it. The moment where he told her he planned on leaving soon. He was healed enough…

"I've decided that you're right," he said.

She was? About what?

"I mean, I always knew you were right," he said with a grin. "But I'm finally brave enough to commit to this…

us…life here in Wild River. A solid, stable life. No more living in a van and coasting from one odd job to another."

Her mouth gaped. He what?

"This is what I want. Being with you. I tried to ignore the feeling of emptiness in my gut for so long, but it never went away. Knowing you were happy with someone else was the only thing keeping me from coming back," he said, emotion evident in his voice. "But now I'm here and you're here and I don't want to mess this up again. I don't want to lose this." He gripped her hands tight in his and she returned the reassuring squeeze.

He was saying everything she'd always longed to hear. He was giving her what she'd always wanted. But now she knew that it didn't matter as long as they were together. "Arron…"

"Wait. I'm not done," he said. He took a deep breath. "I've applied for my old partnership with SnowTrek Tours again and Cassie's accepted. I can start leading free-climb tours as soon as I'm capable."

Her chest ached. That had to have been a hard call for him—going back to the career he'd shared with his brother. And he was doing it for her. For them. "Arron…that's incredible. Really, it is, and I'm…speechless about all of this."

He pulled her closer. "I love you, Alisha. Being with you is what matters. It's what I want and I'm willing to do whatever it takes to make this work."

Her breath caught in her chest. He loved her. He'd actually said the words this time, not a variation of them, and she knew he meant them. She loved him too…

She laughed through tears of happiness burning in her eyes as she picked up the backpack. "I was coming home with news of my own. I put in for a leave of absence at the hospital. I was going to tell you tonight that I'm ready to leave this solid, stable life behind and go with you to the far corners of the world."

He looked surprised and slightly overwhelmed. "You were willing to do that? For me?"

"Yes! I love *you*, Arron. I always have. You are a part of me, so ingrained…and I don't want to be without you. So, if that's here or anywhere else, I'm ready."

He pulled her into his chest and held her tight. She breathed in the scent of him, savoring this moment that couldn't possibly get any better. "I can't believe you were willing to do that," he whispered into her hair.

She glanced up at him. "So, what do we do?"

He took a deep breath. "Well…you did buy a new backpack… It would be a shame not to use it."

"I'm listening…" More than that, her heart was open to any and all possibilities.

"You've put in your time-off request already and I don't have a start date at SnowTrek…"

"Right. Technically, neither of us is tied to Wild River for the next little while…"

"So why don't we travel the world for a few months—" he took her face between his hands and kissed her gently "—then come back here and continue making a life together?"

She nodded. "I like the sound of that a lot."

"Then it's a plan," he said. He kissed her long and deep, full of passion and love. A kiss that held the promise of a future she'd thought they'd lost.

She hugged him tight, her heart at ease, knowing she wouldn't have to let him go.

Not now. Not ever.

* * * * *

HARLEQUIN
SPECIAL EDITION

Different worlds collide in Sera Taíno's debut novel.

IT'S HARD TO REMAIN ENEMIES
WHEN YOU'VE BROKEN BREAD TOGETHER.

Val Navarro's first mistake—going out dancing after a bad breakup when the chef should be focused on her family business. Her second mistake? Thinking the handsome, sensitive stranger she meets could be more than a rebound—until she discovers he's Philip Wagner of Wagner Developments. His father's company could shut down her Puerto Rican restaurant and unravel her tight-knit neighborhood. When Philip takes over negotiations, Val wants to believe he has good intentions. But is following her heart a recipe for disaster?

**From Harlequin Special Edition: Believe in love.
Overcome obstacles. Find happiness.**

Harlequin.com

HSEST46301MAX